Jerry's game had begun. Holly could tell she was in her apartment, and as soon as the door closed behind them, Jerry slipped her blindfold off. But it didn't make much difference, there wasn't a speck of light.

When they found the bed, Jerry indicated he wanted a kiss, and Holly kissed him again and again, drawing herself closer so that there was barely any space between them. She sighed when he caressed her breast and she felt her nipples harden for him. The pulse between her legs sprang to life when he rubbed himself against her. He was on his knees now, with her legs wrapped around his waist. The sex was wonderful; her whole body shuddered. This is what love should be like, Holly thought. Stretching luxuriously, she felt Jerry stirring beside her. Reaching over him, she switched on the lamp—and froze.

The dark-haired man lying naked in bed with her was a complete stranger. . . .

SUSPICION OF INNOCENCE

by Barbara Parker

This riveting, high-tension legal thriller written by a former prosecutor draws you into hot and dangerous Miami, where Gail Connor is suddenly caught in the closing jaws of the legal system and is about to discover the other side of the law. . . .

Available now from **SIGNET**

Pretty

Maids

in a Row

Marilyn Campbell

AN ONYX BOOK

ONYX
Published by the Penguin Group
Penguin Books USA Inc., 375 Hudson Street,
New York, New York 10014, U.S.A.
Penguin Books Ltd, 27 Wrights Lane,
London W8 5TZ, England
Penguin Books Australia Ltd, Ringwood,
Victoria, Australia
Penguin Books Canada Ltd, 10 Alcorn Avenue,
Toronto, Ontario, Canada M4V 3B2
Penguin Books (N.Z.) Ltd, 182–190 Wairau Road,
Auckland 10, New Zealand

Penguin Books Ltd, Registered Offices:
Harmondsworth, Middlesex, England

First published by Onyx, an imprint of Dutton Signet, a division of
Penguin Books USA Inc. First published in a hardcover edition by
Villard Books, a division of Random House, Inc.

First Onyx Printing, January, 1995
10 9 8 7 6 5 4 3 2 1

 REGISTERED TRADEMARK—MARCA REGISTRADA

Printed in the United States of America

PUBLISHER'S NOTE
This is a work of fiction. Names, characters, places, and incidents either
are the product of the author's imagination or are used fictitiously, and
any resemblance to actual persons, living or dead, events, or locales is
entirely coincidental.

BOOKS ARE AVAILABLE AT QUANTITY DISCOUNTS WHEN USED TO PRO-
MOTE PRODUCTS OR SERVICES. FOR INFORMATION PLEASE WRITE TO PRE-
MIUM MARKETING DIVISION, PENGUIN BOOKS USA INC., 375 HUDSON
STREET, NEW YORK, NEW YORK 10014.

To my brother and father, the original David and Harry. I love you both.

A special thank-you to Elizabeth Cavanaugh, agent extraordinaire, for believing in me and this book from the beginning.

1

Mizz Wallace, did you, or did you not, *willingly* take Senator Ziegler's penis into your mouth on more than one occasion?"

Holly Kaufman gaped at the elderly man on her television screen. The camera zoomed in for a close-up of Cheryl Wallace, a somewhat attractive, big-boned brunette who could not quite conceal her outrage as she replied. "Senator Manson, I am not on trial here—"

"Perhaps not, but neither is Senator Ziegler. I'm sure you are aware that by coming forward at this hearing with your strong accusations against the good senator, you have placed *your* morals under public scrutiny as well." The camera left Cheryl Wallace to pan each face of the all-male committee.

"I might remind you," Senator Manson continued in a superior voice, "that we are judging the fitness of our distinguished colleague for a cabinet post, and any aspersions cast on that fitness must be thoroughly examined. Now, please answer the question."

While Miss Wallace leaned toward her attorney, a bespectacled woman about the same age as she, the camera focused on a dark-haired man sitting with his lawyers, apart from the Senate committee. Holly's chest tightened with remembered panic as she recognized Tim Ziegler. His intent, concerned expression altered to one of relief the moment Cheryl Wallace began her response.

"Timothy Ziegler and I had been intimate . . . on more than one occasion . . . prior to the events detailed earlier. I already admitted that. I see no reason to get more explicit."

"Aah, but you found it necessary to be exceedingly explicit when you related your side of the story. Nevertheless, I believe your evasiveness speaks for itself. *Mizz* Wallace, there are many people in this great country of ours that consider oral sex a sin; it is, in fact, a *crime* in certain states. Your willing performance of such an act constituted lewd and lascivious behavior on your part. That, combined with your history of alcohol and drug use—"

"Objection!"

Holly switched off the videotape with her remote control, but her gaze remained on the screen for long seconds after it filled with gray static. She thought she had put the nightmare firmly behind her. Yet, in a matter of minutes, it had lurched back into her mind as if it had been last night rather than fourteen years ago—one year prior to the incident Cheryl Wallace was testifying about.

When she had learned that the hearing was to begin that day while she was at work, she had programmed her video cassette recorder so that she could at least scan some of the highlights when she had time. As an environmental lobbyist living in Washington, D. C., Holly had to stay informed of the gossip as well as the facts of current affairs, even when it was personally distasteful.

No one had expected any problems with the President's selection for the next secretary of housing and urban development. Although only thirty-five years old, Pennsylvania State Senator Timothy Ziegler had already gained the support of some powerful liberals by vocally supporting several bills that would make more housing available to lower-income families. He was a devoted husband and father and a regular churchgoer. He was practically perfect.

Except for that time in college that had been forgotten by everyone but the small group of those directly involved.

Because Cheryl Wallace could never forget what Tim Ziegler had done to her, she had decided to dredge up the past rather than see him placed in such an important position.

And because Holly Kaufman was not quite ready to dwell on how Tim Ziegler had damaged her own life, she rewound the tape to listen to Cheryl Wallace's account once more.

"It was thirteen years ago, and I had just turned eighteen," Cheryl Wallace began in a quiet, somewhat shaky voice. "I was a freshman at Dominion University in New York, and Tim was a senior. We met at a party. We had been dating about a month before the, uh, incident."

"Pardon me for interrupting," Senator Manson said politely. "But there are certain facts I believe should be brought to light before you recount your entire story. Approximately how many times did you go out on dates before the *alleged* incident?"

"Five, maybe six."

"Would you say these were casual, friendly dates, or did you become . . . intimate?"

Cheryl paused for advice from her attorney. "Intimate."

The senator raised an eyebrow at her. "On which date did you and Senator Ziegler consummate your relationship?"

She glanced at her attorney, then murmured, "I don't remember."

"Oh? Perhaps if you think a little harder you'll recall that it was the night of the party when the two of you first met. Of course, I understand there was a lot of drinking at that party, and some drugs were available. Is it possible that you were too intoxicated to remember what happened that night?"

Taking a deep breath, she replied, "A lot of kids, away from home for the first time, get a little wild."

"I see. Were you a virgin the first time you and the senator had sexual intercourse?"

"I don't see—" Her attorney touched her hand and she started again. "No, but he was only the second one—"

"Of course, of course," Manson cut in, but his expression clearly indicated he didn't believe that for a minute. "Please continue."

It was obvious that his effort to unsettle Cheryl had worked, and her attorney turned the table microphone toward herself. "In all fairness to Miss Wallace, what she is about to relate to this distinguished committee is extremely upsetting. We would appreciate the courtesy of your allowing her to finish her statement before any further questions are asked." Senator Manson nodded, and the attorney turned the mike back over to her client.

What little composure Cheryl had begun with was completely gone. Her nervousness manifested itself in a quaking voice and trembling hands, but she was determined to say her piece.

"One night, after we had been dating about a month, we went to a party. There wasn't much going on, so we had a few drinks, then went back to his fraternity house. Most of the brothers were there, working their way through a keg of beer. We sat around with them for a while before Tim took me up to his room. I had a hard time getting up the stairs and told Tim I just wanted to lie down for a while, but he talked me into smoking a joint he had been saving for a special occasion.

"Although I really wanted to sleep, he was determined to have sex. I remember him pulling my clothes off and entering my body without my consent or participation, but I was too intoxicated to put up a fight. I'm not certain exactly when I passed out, but something made me wake up again. At first I thought it was Tim on top of me, but then I heard his voice beside me. I turned my head and saw him sitting there, holding my hand. The room was filled with his fraternity brothers. Besides the one, uh, having intercourse with me, there were eight others, some with nothing on, some with just their pants open and their . . . privates exposed. They were . . . fondling themselves . . . getting ready."

Her voice cracked and she swallowed hard several times before being able to continue. "I told them no. I didn't want that. It was as if they didn't hear me at all. I tried to push the one on top of me away, but I couldn't seem to coordinate my mind and my body. I was crying and begging for Tim to stop them, but he only squeezed my hand tighter and said . . ."

She paused, closed her eyes, and took another steadying breath. When she reopened her eyes, they glistened with unshed tears, but the expression in them was pure hate as she glared directly at Senator

Ziegler. "He said, 'Just lie still, honey. It will be over in a minute.' I had no way of knowing how long they had been at me before I awoke, but *it* actually went on for another hour that I was aware of. They finally gave up when three of them tried to take me at once, and I vomited on the one trying to use my mouth. Then they let me get up and dress, and Tim drove me back to my dorm."

No one uttered a sound for several seconds, then one of the junior senators said, "Miss Wallace, what you described was such a hideous offense against you, I can't help but wonder why it took you thirteen years to report it."

The camera switched back to her just in time to catch her rolling her eyes in disbelief at his naïveté. "Surely, sir, you must realize that it is extremely difficult for a young woman to report a rape, especially when she'd been drinking and willingly went to the boy's bedroom.

"In spite of that, however, I did attempt to report it to the local police the next day, after I recovered a little. But they insisted it was strictly a college matter and would have to be handled by the authorities there. Campus security took a report, but I got the impression it went directly into the trash when I left the office. I was repeatedly told: 'Boys will be boys.' I did try to obtain a copy of that report before this hearing and was told they didn't keep the records that long.

"Instead of any of my attackers being punished, I was required to attend weekly sessions with the school counsellor—another man by the way. After the first humiliating session, I didn't return, and no one cared, as long as I didn't do or say anything that could ultimately hurt the school's reputation or their precious football team. You see, they were having a winning season, and, although Tim Ziegler was only second string, one of my rapists was Dominion's star quarterback and another went on to the pros." Offering up a piece of paper, she added, "I have the entire list of men's names—"

"Objection!" Ziegler's attorneys both shouted at once as Cheryl's attorney quickly covered her microphone with her hand and urgently whispered something to her client.

Holly let the tape continue running, but her mind had slipped off track the moment Cheryl stated that one of the rapists was the star quarterback. She knew, without seeing the list, what that man's name was, a name she thought she had purged from her memory. As Tim Ziegler had been Cheryl Wallace's guide into hell, Jerry Frampton had been Holly's. What he and Tim had done to her was a far cry from the brutal obscenity perpetrated on Cheryl a year later, but it had been no less devastating to her.

In one night, Holly had been transformed from an innocent young girl with romantic dreams to a bitter woman who would never again feel comfortable with a man.

Holly had to give Cheryl a lot of credit for being brave enough to report the crime back then—something Holly hadn't had the guts to do. Coming forward at this time, though, exposing herself on national television to denigrate a man who was admired by both his colleagues and the media—*that* went right past courage to self-destructive masochism.

Although she'd never met Cheryl, the newspapers had supplied some background on her. She was an award-winning poetess who had inherited the large sum of money that allowed her to concentrate on her writing. The money also granted her the freedom to be as reclusive as she wished to be.

But money wasn't going to spare her from the ordeal she had set herself up for. It was clear from this first day of the hearing, that the committee had already judged Cheryl Wallace and was planning to drag her through the mud for attempting to sully the good senator's name.

There was no way in hell Holly would put herself in that position.

Yet, she couldn't simply dismiss what she'd heard either. Fourteen years ago, when Cheryl would have been a senior in high school, Holly had left Dominion and never returned. She had never known for certain that other young women had suffered as she had, but she had received a letter once that hinted at it.

Some perverse quirk had made her keep that letter, though she never had any intention of doing anything about it. With Cheryl's tale still replaying itself in her head, Holly found herself going to the spare bedroom of her apartment where she kept her personal filing cabinet. The letter had been sent to her, in care of her parents, about six years ago. It was from a psychologist named April MacLeash and contained only one sentence:

If the names below stir any memories, it may be to your advantage to contact me. There were fifteen men's names below that sentence, some of which she may have recognized years ago; now, however, only two jumped out at her—those of Jerry Frampton and Timothy Ziegler.

"Calm down, Billy," Tim Ziegler told his fraternity brother over the phone. "Everything's going to be all right."

"All right?" Billy O'Day repeated, raising his voice. "That bitch practically called me a rapist on national television. It won't be too hard for my wife's lawyer to figure out which Dominion football player turned pro back then. She's already trying to take me for more than I'll ever earn in my life, and with my contract up for renewal at the end of this season, the last thing I need is a fucking scandal."

"Listen, I'm not going to discuss this with you over a hotel phone line. The odds are probably a million to one against your airhead wife watching a political telecast in the middle of the afternoon. You'll see, a week from now it will all be yesterday's news."

"Yeah, but what about today's news?" Billy asked, though most of the concern had left his voice.

"Did you watch it? The hearing got thirty seconds of coverage. They'd be fools to play up her insinuations without proof. My attorneys have assured me that she won't mention the other men involved again. Just relax, and we'll get together the next time you play the Redskins."

As soon as Billy hung up, Tim placed another call and was relieved when Jerry Frampton picked up his private line on the second ring.

"Speak to me," the infamous men's magazine publisher said, confident that his caller could only be one of a handful of people.

"Billy just called. He's worried."

"So? That asshole was born worried. How are you holding up?"

"Fine. It's going just like we figured, except for that bit about the list of names. But when I finish testifying about her, no one will care who the other men were."

"You know what my theory's been for some time.

As long as she stayed away from us, I didn't care what she did to anyone else, but I warned you, it could come around eventually. Some bitches just never let go. And you thought I was being paranoid."

"Maybe I'm ready to convert. The fact that Wallace would come out of hiding after all these years could be a sign that she's raising the stakes in the game."

"Agreed. And if my theory's right, Wallace isn't acting alone. Yet for some reason, she's not mentioning any other women. My guess is, whoever her friends are, they might have even more to lose than we do."

Tim snorted. "Whoever the hell *they* are!"

With a dry laugh, Jerry said, "It's a shame none of us kept our dance cards, but at least we're fairly sure of one name besides hers. Maybe it's enough. Got any ideas?"

"We could take a page from Wallace's book and have her investigated. An exposé about how she's been systematically seeking revenge against innocent men for years would be a nice follow-up to the hearing."

"Leak it to the press? But what if more comes out than you want? It could backfire."

"Mark my words, Jer, if the information leaked is from a reliable source, a decent reporter will check into it, but if the tip is very vague and nobody's willing to talk, there's no story. It's obvious that no one on either side is anxious for the whole truth to come out. At the first hint of a reporter being on to what she's been up to, I'm betting Wallace will crawl back in her hole and take her friends with her. I'm going to come away from this looking like the victim with her as my attacker. Besides, anything uncovered after this will only be another nail in her coffin, and I'll have the appointment secured already. Unfortunately, Billy could be ruined."

"Hey, better him than me," Jerry said with another dry laugh, then turned serious. "Those broads have to be taught a lesson. Do you want me to take care of it?"

"No," Tim said quickly. There was no telling what the repercussions would be if Jerry took care of this matter his way. "I know just the man for the job."

After hours of self-analysis followed by nightmares of being chased by demons, Holly awoke having come to one conclusion. It was past time for her to face those demons.

Cheryl's method of dealing with her nemesis was too extreme, and too public, for Holly. All Holly really wanted was to find a way to live a more normal life than she had been doing—a life in which she felt comfortable in her own skin. A life in which her inability to recover from an event of fourteen years ago could no longer hurt the ones she loved.

She had put her parents through hell back then, and though she'd apologized and they'd forgiven her, she'd never explained the cause. That omission had left a small but permanent scar on an otherwise close relationship, but she couldn't seem to repair it.

As difficult as that was to bear, the guilt was even worse with Philip Sinkiewicz, the man who had pulled her out of the depths of depression by giving her a new career, friendship, and unconditional love. A *normal* woman would have been able to give him the love he deserved in return. He was still her best friend and, technically, her employer, but she had failed at being his lover. She would change that if she could.

The cryptic letter from Dr. April MacLeash was

the only clue she had to a solution. Determined to make a change in her life and without any better alternative in mind, she placed a call to the psychologist.

She was a bit surprised that the office number in Wilmington, Delaware, was still correct, but when the receptionist informed her that the doctor was staying in Washington, D.C., for a few days, her surprise turned to curiosity. Could Dr. MacLeash's visit to the capital have some connection with the hearing? Holly left her name and both her office and home numbers, with the message that it was in reference to Ziegler.

April MacLeash returned the call within fifteen minutes and got right to the point. "I don't think we should discuss anything specific over the phone. Suffice it to say, your name was given to me quite a long time ago as someone who may have suffered a trauma at the hands of one or more of the individuals listed in my letter. A number of us discovered we shared similar experiences and formed a very unique therapy group.

"Because we're scattered over the country now, we only have semiannual meetings, but due to the current situation, several of us are in Washington this week. There's no cost to join our group or attend sessions, and, if you'd like to meet with us while we're here, there wouldn't be any obligation on your part to become a regular member. I assure you, it won't hurt to talk with us, and it might do you a lot of good, whatever your personal history is."

Holly was not one for joining groups—she had never even joined a sorority in college—nor did she normally make spontaneous decisions, but after the miserable night she had had, she was willing to try anything, including the outside help she had always avoided. "I've never talked about it with anyone. I'm not sure I can now."

"That's okay. You wouldn't have to talk at all this time if it makes you too uncomfortable. Just listening to the others might benefit you. The important thing is for you to realize that you're not alone and whatever happened was not your fault. The extent of your participation in our group after that is solely up to you."

"All right. I'll try," Holly said before giving herself time to equivocate.

"Good. We're meeting in the executive suite of the Kessler Hotel at noon tomorrow. There will be a buffet lunch served in the room. I look forward to seeing you then."

"Yes. Same here," Holly replied, but her voice belied the words. What had she gotten herself into?

David Wells sat in the luxurious lobby of the Kessler Hotel, pretending to read the newspaper he was holding up in front of him. It wasn't a very original ploy, but it was one that usually worked. The phone call he'd received Monday night from Senator Ziegler had convinced him to drop everything else he was working on and focus on what he'd been told. Although he was not one of the throng of reporters assigned to cover the Senate hearing, he had been keeping abreast of the proceedings. Since he wasn't reporting it, he could afford a bit of bias.

He had met the senator while investigating the top-heavy administrative staff of the Department of Housing and Urban Development. Ziegler was one of the few people he had dealt with who had come out crystal clean. The exposé David wrote for *The Washington Times* resulted in the resignation of the then secretary and the subsequent appointment of Senator Ziegler to that post.

David liked Tim, as a politician and as a man, and on the basis of the latest polls, more than half the country believed he was being unjustly accused by Cheryl Wallace.

It had been a long time, but David's own experience with being falsely accused was still a raw wound. When he was sixteen, he'd lost his job at a grocery store when the owner's jealous son blamed him for a shortage in the cash register—right after the boy had "loaned" David the same amount of cash that was missing, as a "favor." With the money in his pocket and the son's word against his, David hadn't stood a chance of being believed.

Firing David had meant nothing to the grocer, but it had devastated David, not only because he'd been framed, but the income had been helping to support his four brothers and sisters. Getting another job where he could work as many hours had been almost impossible, especially after the grocer spread word of the theft to other merchants in the neighborhood.

He couldn't change his own past, but perhaps he could help the senator with his present dilemma.

Altruistic motive aside, if what Tim Ziegler had implied was true, it would make one hell of a story!

When Ziegler had testified to the Senate committee the previous day he had spoken quietly, and with considerable embarrassment, about the wild fraternity parties he'd once participated in. He was obviously guilt-ridden over the youthful overindulgence, but he could look back with a clear conscience knowing that he had never hurt anyone, and the girls at those parties were there willingly. Cheryl was one of the regular attendees who was game for anything in the name of fun.

Privately, Tim had related to David his belief that Cheryl had never been quite right mentally. He knew she'd spent some time in an institution, but didn't have details. He also claimed that he wasn't the first target of Cheryl's unfounded hostility.

Some years ago, one of his fraternity brothers had been spied on by a private investigator. Because of the evidence of sexual misconduct collected by the investigator, the brother's wife sued him for divorce. He lost his family and most of his possessions, and through it all, he swore he'd been framed. Supposedly, the investigator had been hired by Cheryl Wallace. Tim didn't have the investigator's name or address, but he promised to look into it if David was interested.

Tim's story became truly intriguing however, when he implied that a second woman might be helping Cheryl with her revenge schemes. At the last fraternity reunion, it was discovered that two of the brothers had lost control of their businesses to the Donner Corporation, and a third man had been abruptly terminated from a high-paying executive position immediately after that same corporation bought the company he was employed by. An article in *Forbes* magazine about Donner gave Tim a bit more fuel for his suspicions.

He believed it was an incredible coincidence that the present owner of the Donner Corporation, Erica Donner, had attended Dominion University the same year as Wallace, long before she had met and married the wealthy George Donner. Tim couldn't recall ever meeting her, however.

David had heard enough to agree to meet with Tim after the hearing was over to get names, dates, and any other pertinent details. What he hadn't told Tim was that there was another coincidence right over his head.

Erica Donner had arrived in D.C. on Monday and was currently occupying the penthouse suite of the Kessler Hotel—just a few floors above where Tim was staying. Since her company owned the hotel, she could simply say she was on an inspection tour, as the staff had been told, but the fact that the hearings had begun the day of her arrival, combined with Ziegler's input, made David feel certain that he was on to something.

David credited his successful journalistic career to a combination of good luck and personal charm. He knew part of that charm was that he was a boyishly handsome, thirty-three-year-old bachelor, whose curly brown hair always looked mussed and whose bright blue eyes revealed a lighthearted nature. He loved women and instinctively knew how to please them. Though he often took advantage of them, he never lied to them and always made sure they had fun while they were with him whether it was business or personal.

In this case, it had been both. He occasionally dated Suzanne, one of the front-desk clerks at the Kessler, as he did women in other hotels around town. He never promised them anything more than a good time—he had been immunized as a child against ever getting seriously involved with the so-called gentler sex—and never did more than hint at the kind of information he could use if they were willing to pass it along.

They were always willing.

Suzanne had called him Monday afternoon to let him know what interesting people had checked in. Erica Donner was one of them. And David had served a romantic dinner to Suzanne in his apartment last night.

The first call David made Tuesday morning was to Valerie Glick, the best research assistant *The Washington Times* had ever hired. She was not only bright and ambitious, she had a sixth sense about ferreting out the most trivial data. David's charm had never impressed Valerie; she was happily married and immune to flirtation. What she liked about him was the way he respected her and admired her intelligence, never taking her efforts for granted. Thus, when he asked for "a little background" on Erica Donner, particularly what schools she had attended and when, an in-depth bio and folder of press clippings appeared on his desk a few hours later.

From the photos of Mrs. Donner, David was certain he'd recognize her. A woman of medium height and build, she wore her jet-black hair pulled back in a severe bun, which accented her widow's peak, dark, slightly almond-shaped eyes, and prominent cheekbones. Her Oriental looks were countered by a Memphis, Tennessee, accent that had coated many an unappetizing deal with molasses.

A few years younger than David, Erica Donner was already regarded as a phenomenon in the world of mergers and acquisitions. Rather than scaling the corporate ladder to the top, she had taken a faster route—she married the boss first and proved herself afterward. George Donner had been called a wizard on Wall Street before he had her on his team. Together, they had regularly caused tremors through vulnerable companies.

After George Donner's death, she took control of the company in spite of the scandal that erupted. It was made public that George was Erica's third husband to die under questionable circumstances, and she was instantly dubbed the Black Widow. Because of her ruthless business practices in the years that followed, the nickname stuck.

But the information that most interested David was the confirmation that she had attended Dominion University as Tim Ziegler had claimed.

Considering how few facts he had, David figured his first step should be a direct surprise attack, via a routine interview. An unexpected accusation, carefully phrased as a question, usually caused a guilty party to react. Even a flinch would be sufficient for David to decide if there was a story worth investigating.

As Cheryl Wallace was refusing to speak to any reporters during the hearing, David aimed his curiosity at Donner.

That afternoon, he left his name and office number with her secretary in San Diego, California, then left several messages with the hotel operator. Though he'd explained he only needed a few minutes of Mrs. Donner's time regarding her company's most recent acquisition, she made no reply.

After talking to Suzanne last night, he decided to hang out in the hotel lobby in hopes that the elusive businesswoman would make an appearance. If she never left her room, he figured he could try bribing a waiter to let him borrow a uniform and go to her suite the next time she ordered room service. Whatever trick he had to pull, he was now determined to get an interview with Mrs. Donner.

The bank of elevators across from David had been in constant use all morning, but he was only concentrating on the one that served as an express to the top floor. No one had come down from the penthouse, but he had watched three thirtyish women in business attire go up between ten and eleven. One was a petite blonde with a confident, athletic stride—a lawyer or other professional type, David guessed. Another was her direct opposite, with mousy brown coloring, beige clothes, and wire-rimmed glasses—a file clerk if he ever saw one.

The last had to be law enforcement of some kind from the way she scanned the lobby when she first entered and kept her back to the wall while she waited for the elevator. Of course, the bulge of a shoulder holster under her poorly fitted navy-blue jacket helped David's guess considerably. She might have been decent-looking, but her auburn hair was cropped too short for such a tall, broad-shouldered woman, and her lack of makeup and masculine way of moving detracted from whatever attributes she had.

David's imagination was already busy trying to put these three visitors into a scene with Erica Donner, when another woman entered the hotel lobby. She was vaguely familiar, though he couldn't place her. Then again, it could just be that she embodied everything he lusted after in a woman.

Her light-blond, chin-length hair was crimped in a current style and framed a flawless face. He couldn't see her eye color, but her full, rose-tinted lips were almost the exact shade of her simple, tailored dress.

Expert that he was, he noted that the cut and length of the dress were meant to hide a lush figure and long, shapely legs—two female characteristics he found irresistible. If he weren't working. . . .

Before he completed the thought, she had approached the express elevator and pressed the "up" button.

She was nervous. Though he'd been focusing on

her spectacular looks, he had also seen the way she slowed down as she neared her destination and, once there, shook her head and straightened her shoulders, as if she had to talk herself into going on.

Holly almost turned back. She could no longer remember why she had agreed to come here. She had managed this long without discussing her personal problems with anyone. Why should she begin now, with a group of strangers?

Yet, when the elevator doors opened, her feet took her inside. Her finger touched the only thing that resembled a button, a little red square on the wall with a credit card-sized slot beneath it.

"Hello?" asked a detached female voice a few seconds later.

Holly looked around the mahogany-paneled enclosure with its polished brass rails and saw a duplicate set of doors behind her, but no visible speaker. "Um, I have an appointment in the penthouse suite with Doctor MacLeash. I'm Holly Kaufman."

"I'll bring you right up."

The doors closed and the elevator began a rapid ascent the next instant. When it stopped, the doors opened and Holly stepped into a large living room, beautifully appointed with Italian and French antiques and rich brocades. A grand piano adorned one side of the room, where floor-to-ceiling windows offered a magnificent view of the capital.

An attractive woman a few inches shorter than Holly, with blond-on-blond frosted hair cut in a pixie style, stood to the side of the elevator. Offering her hand, she introduced herself with a warm smile. "Holly Kaufman? Welcome. I'm April MacLeash."

Holly surreptitiously wiped her damp palm on the

side of her skirt and forced a return smile as she briefly shook hands. "How do you do, Doctor."

"No formality here. I'm just April. Come on in and meet my friends."

Three other women were seated in a conversation area on the opposite side of the room from the piano. As Holly and April approached, they stopped talking and turned toward the new arrival.

"This is Holly Kaufman," April said with her pleasant smile firmly in place. The women remained seated as they were identified. "This is Erica Donner, today's hostess. Erica's company owns the majority of the stock in this hotel, so they usually give us special treatment."

Erica's mouth softened into a semismile, but her dark, slightly slanted eyes glittered with a permanent hardness that couldn't be disguised by a professional makeup artist.

"And this is Bobbi Renquist. The Internal Revenue Service is her employer."

Holly had an easier time smiling at Bobbi, whose timidity seemed to equal her own. If she hadn't been told Bobbi's profession, she might have guessed the extremely plain woman with the bifocal glasses was a librarian.

As Holly's gaze moved to the last woman, it caught on the weapon strapped to her shoulder.

"Our armed member is Rachel, also known as Special Agent Greenley of the Federal Bureau of Investigation. We've convinced her to remove her jacket, but she swears she feels naked without the gun, so I hope it doesn't make you nervous."

"Oh, no," Holly said quickly. "It just surprised me." Rachel toasted her with a Manhattan glass, half full of an amber-colored liquid, then drained it before setting it down again on the coffee table. As

April directed her to a seat, Holly was somewhat relieved to notice that the others had all been drinking coffee or tea.

Rachel's voice sounded perfectly sober though as she said, "Actually, I'm not the only armed member. Agent Renquist carries a cute little toy in her purse, the way a *real* lady who's licensed should." When Bobbi didn't rise to the bait, Rachel changed topics. "We were discussing the Ziegler hearing, Holly. I say we should just cut the bastard's balls off and be done with it. What do you think?"

April frowned, Bobbi blushed, and Erica rolled her eyes. Holly wondered if this was some sort of test and opted for the truth. "I think what I've seen on television the last two days was the most disgusting display of male power I have ever witnessed."

"Bravo!" Rachel said and toasted her again. "I especially liked the part when Ziegler made it sound like Cheryl regularly consented to gang-bangs when she was intoxicated."

Shaking her head, Holly admitted, "The worst part of it is, although I have no doubt it happened exactly like Cheryl said, he came off much more believably than she did."

"The fact that he performs in front of the public for a living and she's practically a hermit should have been taken into account in advance," Rachel said. "Slight miscalculation there, wouldn't you agree, Doctor?"

Holly noted the way April's cheeks flushed at Rachel's snide words, but she made no retort.

Without realizing her glass was empty, Rachel tipped it to her mouth, then stared at it suspiciously when no liquid poured forth. "You don't mind if I help myself, do you, Erica?"

As Rachel headed for the bar, April said gently. "Rachel, why don't you have a cup of coffee instead? Lunch will be served in a few minutes."

Rachel laughed as she splashed whiskey into her glass. "You know better than to try mothering me, April. I need alcohol, not caffeine."

"But you were doing so well," April continued in a nonpressuring voice. "It's been months—"

"Eight months and two weeks to be exact. Since the last bastard got—" She glanced at Holly and changed whatever she had been about to say. "Since the last time I got shitfaced. The only thing between me and Tim Ziegler's balls right now is this." She held up the refilled glass. "And as long as you panty-waists are still voting against violence, I'm going to stay drunk."

With eyes closed, Rachel savored a long swallow, then turned her attention to Holly. "You're our special guest today. Would you care to tell us what brings you here?"

Holly's uncertainty was obvious, and Rachel spoke again before she could answer.

"I've got a better idea. I'll go first. The good doctor always tells us talking about our problems with others who can empathize is the best medicine for what ails us." She came out from behind the bar, but rather than sitting back down, she paced as she prepared to relate her personal nightmare.

"You heard Cheryl's accusation against Ziegler and his buddies. Well, there's a little more to the bedtime story that she didn't tell to spare the rest of us. Like Cheryl, the four of us were freshman at Dominion, but only Bobbi and I knew each other at first. I'm sure you remember the fratemity Ziegler belonged to was mainly for jocks, but their competitive spirit took on a new dimension that year.

"They made up a game in which each brother had a 'dance card' with one hundred lines on it. Every time they could prove they *danced* with a different girl they wrote her name on the card. A freshman was worth a double entry, so we received the most aggressive attention. Once her name was on three cards, a girl was said to be a member of the Little Sister Society, and the boys made such a membership sound very elite. Understand, there were some girls who joined the society knowingly, but too often that wasn't the case. What happened to Cheryl was no isolated incident."

Holly turned in her seat to follow Rachel's progress around the room. Part of her was hanging on every word; the other part wanted to run before she heard more than she had bargained for.

"Each of the fifteen brothers competing in the dance contest put one dollar in a glass jar in the fraternity game room for every line he filled in. The one who filled up his dance card first won the jar. Rumor had it that the King Stud walked off with over a thousand dollars."

"Dear God," Holly whispered, and before she thought better of it, she asked, "What was the winner's name?"

Rachel took another swallow of her drink, then said, "Jerry Frampton."

2

"Holly?" April said softly. "Are you all right? You've gotten very pale."

A musical chime sounded and Rachel went to the intercom on the wall by the elevator. A moment later, she returned to the group and announced, "Lunch is on its way up now, so I'll be considerate of our guest's delicate sensibilities and save my story until after she's eaten."

Rachel's consideration came too late for Holly. Her stomach was already twisted into such a tight knot that all she could eat of the elegantly served luncheon was the lobster bisque and a slice of sourdough bread. As soon as the others had progressed to their brandy snifters of chocolate hazelnut mousse and cappuccino, Rachel picked up the thread of her account where she had left off.

"The one thing both Cheryl and Tim have agreed on so far is that a lot of young people get a little wild when they go off to college. I knew quite a few girls who did the kind of nonstop partying that Cheryl did. Unfortunately for them, they let their hair down in a year when that was all the encouragement the boys needed to take advantage of their disoriented condition."

Rachel absently stroked the grip of her gun as she continued. "I was different. Getting drunk or stoned held no fascination for me . . . in spite of the evidence before you," she added with a crooked grin. "I was at school to study, not blow off steam, but one night, a friend talked me into going to a fraternity party. You can guess which fraternity. As usual, I turned down offers of beer or drugs, although there was enough marijuana smoke in the game room to give anyone a buzz." She took a sip of the coffee April had poured for her, then made a face as she set the cup back on its saucer.

"The music was ear-splitting, and I was embarrassed by what some of the couples were doing right in front of everyone else. I was about to leave when a boy I knew from one of my classes asked me to dance. His name was Billy O'Day, and I had always thought he was kind of nice for a big, empty-headed jock. After a few dances, he yelled in my ear that he wanted to talk and motioned for me to follow him upstairs, away from the stereo speakers. It never occurred to me to be wary.

"He led me to his room, but I still didn't worry. Billy was a gentleman."

Rachel's gaze was fixed on the cup in front of her, but Holly was certain she was seeing something else entirely. No one else spoke, so Holly remained quiet as well, and waited until Rachel was ready to finish her account.

"Three of his brothers were waiting for us there. My mistake was that I fought them. They hadn't expected that, and it made them mad. I've always been tall and strong, and I had taken some judo classes. They managed to rip my clothes off, but I got in a few good licks while they were doing it. Unfortunately, so did they. The harder I fought, the rougher they got. I don't remember being raped, because they knocked me unconscious first.

"I came to in the college infirmary eight hours later. A nurse told me that sometime during the night, I had been dumped in front of the door, naked and bloody. Written across my stomach were the Greek letters of another fraternity and a happy face. I had stopped hemorrhaging, but I had sustained internal injuries and was warned to take it easy because of the concussion. The only thing that wouldn't heal was the membrane one of the bastards had broken when he took my virginity."

Holly's shock held her immobilized. She had had her virginity stolen as well, but at least she knew the name of the thief.

"The nurse was sympathetic and called the police for me. They gave her the same runaround Cheryl got."

"But you had visible injuries," Holly protested.

Rachel snorted. "Sure, but how did I get them? It was the precious football players' words against mine. No one at the party heard any screams, and no one remembered seeing me go upstairs with Billy. When it got around campus that I was trying to file assault charges, my fellow students harassed me until I gave it up. You see, I was there on scholarship and couldn't afford the luxury of transferring to another school or taking a year off until my attackers graduated."

Holly always knew how fortunate she had been to have that option. She steeled herself to ask, "Will you tell me who the others were?"

"Of course. One thing you'll discover is that our

fearless leader doesn't permit any secrets. Do you, April?"

April's expression was a mixture of concern and mild rebuke. "No one in this group is ever forced or coerced to tell more than they need to."

"Aah, but there's the rub. You always manage to convince us that we need to bare our souls . . . for our own good." She stopped and massaged her temples. "Sorry. My mouth seems to be on overdrive today." Rising, her body swayed for a second before she found her equilibrium. "If you'll excuse me, I need to wash my hands."

As soon as she had walked into the bedroom and closed the door, Erica Donner sighed aloud. "*Gawd!* If I'd known she was back to this again, I would never have told her we were meetin'."

Her melodious Southern accent was a surprise to Holly's ears.

"That's not fair," Bobbi said in a confident, husky voice that was just as wrong for her image. She removed her wire-rimmed glasses and leaned forward. "We've all had to deal with addictions of some sort. What about you, Holly? Any problems with alcohol or drugs?"

Holly was caught off guard by the swift change in Bobbi's demeanor. She shook her head. "No, I've never liked the feeling of being out of control."

Bobbi's soft gaze became a narrow-eyed stare that seemed to pin Holly in place for her inspection. "What about food? Or sex?"

The question disturbed her as much as Bobbi's aggressive attitude. "Food. For a while . . . it wasn't like I was truly bulimic, but . . ." She couldn't finish.

"Relax, Holly," April said softly. "You don't have to share until you're ready."

Bobbi replaced her glasses and leaned back into the cushioned chair, resuming her timid pose, but Holly had already gotten a glimpse of the real woman beneath the disguise. She took a deep breath to recover her own usual façade of calm. "That must be very effective in getting dishonest taxpayers to come clean."

All three of the women laughed aloud.

"Very astute, Holly," Erica said. "Bobbi is the chameleon of our group. Like Superman, she can slip into a phonebooth in her bookkeeper persona and pop out seconds later as whoever she chooses to be. Bobbi never suffered any addictions in the usual sense. She just developed a few personality problems."

Bobbi folded her arms and frowned at Erica. Her tone was now higher-pitched and defensive. "If we're going to tell Holly all our little secrets, I think the Black Widow should go next. How many husbands have you killed off now—seven? Eight?"

Erica arched one perfect eyebrow, then shrugged indifferently. "The police and insurance files say I'm innocent of any wrongdoin', and those are the only opinions that matter." She looked at Holly and said coolly, "I was married three times since college. The first was an addict who *accidentally* got hold of a bad batch of heroine, the second committed a very messy suicide in our bathroom rather than face bankruptcy, but the third, George Donner, I was truly sorry about. He was the first man I had ever known who could keep up with me mentally and physically. I almost miss him at times."

Holly suddenly remembered reading about the millionaire businessman's accidental death during a mountain-climbing vacation with his much younger wife. She hadn't connected Erica's name with the incident until Bobbi called her the Black Widow.

"At any rate," Erica continued, "your question to Rachel was never answered. The names of her other assailants were Kenneth Viello, Ike Brown, and Jerry Frampton." She smirked at Holly. "I hope y'all don't play much poker, because your expression is a dead giveaway. Obviously, Jerry Frampton was responsible for whatever happened to you, but don't let it make you feel special. As Rachel said, he was King Stud, so he had every one of our names on his dance card. He just acquired them in different ways. Just so you understand, we all have one or more names overlappin' on our personal hit lists."

David glanced at his watch, then returned his attention to the express elevator. A brief conversation with Suzanne had confirmed that there was a luncheon for five being served in Mrs. Donner's suite, but the names of her guests were unknown.

David couldn't help but wonder if the odd gathering had something to do with the information Tim Ziegler had given him. His reporter's nose told him it did. Even without the incentive of perhaps meeting that last blonde, his curiosity demanded he find out who the four women were, what connection they had with Erica Donner, and whether that connection extended to Cheryl Wallace.

He tossed out his plan to use the room-service waiter routine, and decided to go for a sneak attack through one of her guests. He could always return to the hotel later for another try at Donner. All he had to do was pick a woman and follow her. He smiled to himself; there wasn't much deliberation as to which one he would choose.

* * *

"Hit lists?" Holly asked, looking from one woman to another. She noticed how April stopped Erica from answering with nothing more than a slight twitch of her index finger, then spoke for all of them.

"Before we explain that expression, I'd like you to hear about the rest of our experiences and how we got together."

Bobbi's assault was similar to Cheryl's in that she had been extremely inebriated and had knowingly had sex with one of the boys before the others joined them. Though she was a friend of Rachel's and knew about what had happened to her, the fraternity brother she had been dating wasn't involved in Rachel's attack, so Bobbi hadn't thought anything like that could happen to her.

Bobbi had the unique distinction, however, of having been raped by all fifteen of the brothers involved in the dance contest.

Erica's case was more like Rachel's. She had gone to a fraternity party with other girls and was singled out by one of the brothers. She had only had two beers when he suggested they go upstairs. The alcohol had been just enough to blur her usual good sense, but it hadn't been nearly enough to keep her from realizing she had walked into a trap the minute they entered his room and he locked the door.

Two of the four boys who greeted them were Billy O'Day and Jerry Frampton. Like Rachel, she had struggled and screamed, to no avail. Unlike Rachel, she could see there was no hope of escaping what they had planned for her. She had avoided serious injury by lying perfectly still until they wore themselves out.

"You've heard the worst," April said. "Compared to the others, my story sounds like a fairy tale, but nevertheless, I was inducted into the Little Sister Society without my knowledge. Some people would call me promiscuous because I had sexual relations with quite a few boys in my teens. But I only had one partner at a time, always thought I was in love, and considered myself going steady with him before getting intimate. If someone else interested me, I broke up with the one I had been with before going on to the next one.

"So, I didn't think anything was peculiar when, after Tim Ziegler and I had dated a while, he lost interest. At the same time, Adam Frankowicz, another one of his brothers, started flirting with me. Rather than moaning over a broken heart, I moved on. I felt a little funny when it happened again, mainly because the timing and circumstances were so much like the first change of partners.

"Both Tim and Adam had romanced me until I agreed to have sex. The next date was spent making love in their rooms, then within a few days, they each drifted away. Jerry Frampton was the one that followed Adam, but he lacked the patience the other two had had. On our first date, he took me to his room and pressured me until I gave in. Immediately after he was done, he went to his closet and opened the louvred door. Standing inside was Adam. He had been watching . . . and masturbating. Jerry encouraged him to use me to finish himself off, but Adam was so embarrassed at being unexpectedly exposed that he lost his erection.

"Jerry thoroughly enjoyed himself as he told me how he had watched Tim and me, then Adam and me, and since each fornication had been properly witnessed, I was now officially a member of the Little Sister Society. I remember how stunned he was that I wasn't delighted with that news."

Holly had been so caught up in their stories, she had forgotten about Rachel until she came out of the bedroom and headed straight for the bar. All eyes watched her pour an inch of vodka into a tall glass, then fill it with Bloody Mary mix and an extra dash of Tabasco. "Did someone die while I was out?" she asked in a hoarse voice as she carried her drink back to the seat she had vacated earlier.

April visibly gathered her patience before speaking. "We've filled Holly in on our personal experiences, and I was about to tell her how we got together."

"Oh, please, Doctor, let me," Rachel begged with a slight slur. "You never give yourself enough credit when you tell this part. See, Holly, April was the one who figured out what had been going on and managed to steal one of the boys' dance cards. She contacted each girl on the card, even tracking down some of those that had left school. She managed to get thirty-five of them to meet to compare notes and talk. Some of them knew of others who had been taken advantage of, and eventually the Little Sister Society boasted over fifty members. We thought it was appropriate to retain the name. By spreading the word around campus, handing out flyers, and posting notices in the public restrooms, we put an end to the fraternity's reign of terror."

Erica added, "April was one of those fortunate people who knew what she wanted to be when she grew up and had a natural talent for her goal. The first point we all agreed on was that goin' to the police or college administration was a complete waste of time. The only thing that had accomplished was more humiliation for the victims and only an occasional verbal reprimand for the naughty boys. Some of the girls were helped just by bein' able to talk to someone else about what they'd gone through and how they felt. And then there were those of us who wanted revenge."

Rachel retrieved control of the narration the moment Erica paused for effect. "April weeded out the ones who just needed a hug and some encouraging words to get on with their lives. The rest of us, those who wanted blood, formed the inner circle of the society. Over the years, a number of the women in that circle dropped out, some because they had seen their personal attackers get punished and that was enough for them, others because their careers or families took precedence over their need for revenge. The four of us, Cheryl, and two others who couldn't make it, are still active."

Holly had the feeling she should have the whole picture by now, but it was still eluding her. "I'm certainly not a psychologist, and I can understand how it might help to talk about a bad experience, but is it really beneficial to keep rehashing it after all these years?"

Rachel laughed aloud. "Well, what do you know! Another blonde with a brain."

"You're right, Holly," April said. "Talking about it only goes so far. We all needed much more. Since the law wasn't interested in punishing any of the fifteen, we decided it was up to us. By our junior year of college, most of the men were gone, but we had a plan. I had already chosen my career, and under the circumstances, it made sense for me to continue along that line, if for no other reason than to keep our members on an even keel.

"Each of the others went into careers that would ultimately grant them certain privileges and powers. Cheryl's money was her contribution. With it, we were able to hire detectives to keep tabs on the fifteen men while we finished our schooling.

"From time to time another victim's name would surface, as yours did, and we would send off the form letter you received. Some responded immediately, others never did. As I mentioned to you, if you decide to join our group, the extent of your participation is up to you."

Holly nodded her understanding though she still didn't know exactly what April was leading up to.

"The goal of the Little Sister Society is simple— retribution. Our primary rule for exacting revenge is that the punishment should be of equal magnitude to the crime. In other words, we attempt to degrade, humiliate, and rape the target."

Rachel cut in. "Unfortunately, her usage of the verb 'rape' is in the figurative rather than the literal sense. I still think castration would be a lot more efficient."

With barely a glance at Rachel, April continued. "Since none of the women were permanently disfigured physically, mutilation would be considered excessive.

"The second fundamental rule is that every act we perform must be completely within the law. If our group or its goal ever became public, no one could be legally prosecuted. To insure that, one of our absent members, Samantha Kingsley, serves as our legal counsel and clears every one of our decisions before any action is performed. Rachel holds a law degree as well, but her network of information through the FBI is much more valuable.

"I'm sure you can guess how an IRS agent could benefit our group," April said, smiling at Bobbi. "And Erica is our resident genius in the business world. Erica, perhaps you'd like to tell Holly about our last success."

Erica's smile reached her eyes this time. "Did y'all know Kenneth Viello?"

Holly shook her head. "Actually, I didn't recognize that many names on the list."

"It doesn't matter," Erica said with a wave of her hand. "Viello had a construction company in Mobile, Alabama. He'd built it up from a one-man home-repair service to a general contractor corporation employin' hundreds of people. The construction business had a few bad years, and his company went from bein' very profitable to barely meetin' the payroll. He was certain things would improve eventually; he just needed enough capital to hang on until they did.

"That's where my company came in with a deal he couldn't resist. Explainin' that we were lookin' for a short-term investment for a cash surplus, we agreed to put capital into the business in exchange for a temporary fifty-one percent ownership and the right to put our employees in certain key positions . . . to insure an efficient turnaround. Once the business was back on profitable ground, Viello had the right to buy back our percentage at a reasonable price.

"As had happened before with other men, he assumed my bein, a woman would make it easy for him to maintain control of our business relationship. Once my own executives were in place, they followed my instructions for downgradin' the company. Within a year, not only was there no profit bein' made, there was no business left to salvage and no cash to start fresh. And Donner Corporation received a tax benefit for the losses sustained.

"It never seemed to occur to Viello that the lovely Mrs. Donner had purposefully set out to steal his company or ruin him financially. He actually apologized for my losin' my investment. There was never a chance that he'd make the connection with the Little Sister Society because I hadn't been on his dance card. Cheryl, Bobbi, and Rachel had."

Setting her empty glass on the table, Rachel said, "I've always wanted to send the men condolence cards from the society when we finished with them. It would be rather satisfying to let them know who got them and why. But April convinced everyone that the risk of exposure wasn't worth the extra satisfaction—at least until the last man receives his just deserts."

Holly gave herself a moment to see how she felt about what these women had done—and, apparently, were still doing. In a way, they were no better than the vigilantes in the Old West, taking the law into their own hands and meting out justice as they saw fit. But law and justice had failed them all and the men deserved punishment.

Considering the brutal beating and rapes the last man had participated in, he had gotten off rather easily by only being financially ruined. The truth was, rather than disapproval of the women's methods or sympathy for the men, Holly was feeling a very unchristianlike sense of righteousness. She found herself unable to stifle a smile. "How many of the fifteen have you managed to get to?"

Erica held up three French-manicured fingers and said, "Three by corporate takeovers. Two were sentenced to prison time through Rachel's efforts. Bobbi's gotten four for tax evasion and two others were publicly humiliated, careers destroyed, marriages broken, that sort of thing. In most cases, the initial evidence was provided by one of the many different detectives Cheryl hired."

Again Rachel cut in. "My personal favorite was Ike Brown. After graduation, he became a pilot and started his own charter service based in San Antonio. The detective reports showed that he made a lot of trips in and out of Mexico and had purchased a number of large-ticket items with cash. I did a little additional investigating on my own and came up with enough evidence to suggest that he was running drugs.

"It would have felt good to make the arrest personally, but he might have recognized me since I had given him such a hard time after my assault. I had to turn over the information I'd gathered to the agents in Texas, and they closed in on him."

"My leads usually begin with a detective's report as well," Bobbi added somewhat shyly. "You'd be suprised how many people have a regular job for which they report their income, but also have some sort of side business that they keep hidden. Normally the deceit would never be discovered. However, between the detectives and Rachel and my information networks, there is nothing about a man's life that can remain a secret."

Rachel snorted. "One thing you can count on is once a scumbag, always a scumbag. Every one of those fifteen frat boys were bound to stray from the straight and narrow as adults. All we had to do was wait for it to happen and be ready for them."

April nodded and said, "The main reason I've insisted we keep our motives secret is to avoid being discovered too soon. If the targets communicated with each other, they might try to stop us any way they could—not that we're doing anything criminal, as I said before, but our actions might not be construed as entirely ethical. There could be repercussions. Also, to keep the risk of being discovered to a minimum, we've concentrated on the lesser-known men up until recently."

Holly could see the logic in what April was saying, but it contradicted the present situation. "Having kept a low profile all these years, why did Cheryl decide to testify against Ziegler?"

"The society was never able to come up with a suitable punishment for him. Basically, he's been as clean as his political campaigns make him out to be. The only thing negative that's ever been uncovered is that his wife has a serious problem with depression—attempted suicide some years back. But we have no reason to hurt her. Stopping him from getting the cabinet appointment was the best revenge we had come up with, and Cheryl was the only one of the inner circle who did not have a career or marriage that could be damaged by going public."

April guessed Holly's next question. "Yes, some of us are married. My husband and I were married while I was a senior. He was a professor at Dominion and was aware of some of the incidents involving the fraternity, but not what the women were doing about it. Cheryl's husband is somewhat younger than she is and supported her decision to testify."

Rachel gave a nasty laugh. "Considering the allowance she gives that boy-toy of hers, he *better* support her decisions."

April shot Rachel another frown as she continued. "Samantha, the attorney, is not only married, but the reason she's not here is because she just gave birth to their second child. Our seventh member, Paula Marconi, is also married with two children. Paula's our computer wizard. The system hasn't been made that can keep her out. Both of them told their husbands about the rapes, but not what they've done to get even."

April picked up a thick, expandable folder that had been leaning against her chair, pulled a sheet of paper out, and passed it to Holly. "You can keep this."

Holly scanned the paper, which bore the fifteen names she had first seen years ago, but now, all had lines drawn through them except four: Adam Frankowicz, Jerry Frampton, William O'Day, and Timothy Ziegler.

April gave Holly a moment, then said, "Hopefully, Tim Ziegler will be scratched soon. Adam Frankowicz has been working for an oil company in Saudi Arabia for the last several years, so he's been out of our reach, but the latest report says he's being transferred back to New York soon. Bobbi's been compiling a file on him for years. It was just a matter of being patient. If you know anything about professional football, you know William O'Day is extremely popular. His celebrity status has kept him safe from any aggressive investigation till now."

April removed a large envelope from the folder and set it in the center of the table. Holly could easily read the name JERRY FRAMPTON on the neatly typed label.

"Was Erica right, Holly? Did Jerry Frampton hurt you too?"

Holly met April's understanding gaze and nodded. "Yes. Jerry and . . . and Tim Ziegler, but it was Jerry that—" The words she would have said choked her and she tried others. "It was the year before . . . before what happened to all of you. They were juniors and I was a sophomore. Jerry had hired me to tutor him." Again she found it impossible to say more. "I'm sorry. I really am. I thought—After you were all so open with me—But I can't."

"It's all right, Holly," April said. "Nobody's pushing you. If you change your mind, anytime, just call me. In the meantime, why don't you take that envelope home with you and go through it when you feel up to it. We're almost ready to close in on Frampton, but there's one step left. If you'd like to pull the last string, that would be rather appropriate, since you seem to be one of his first victims."

Erica gave Holly one of her half smiles. "There is nothin' quite so healin' as bein' an integral part of the retribution process. I highly recommend it."

"But he abused all of you—"

"Yes," April interrupted. "And each of us had a hand in putting his file together. You don't *have* to do anything. Just take a look at what we've come up with. Then call me if you want to be involved in bringing King Stud down to peasant level. But keep in mind, as long as your attackers go unpunished, you'll always feel like a victim. Once you take action against them, they'll no longer have any power over you."

They talked a little more about how the rapes had affected their lives and how they were still trying to cope with the leftover anxieties and fears. Repeatedly, Holly heard how talking about what had happened was the first step. She understood what they were saying and empathized with them completely, yet in her mind, these women were strangers. If she were ever to open up to anyone, she felt it should be her parents or Philip first.

"By the way," Erica said after they'd bid each other farewell. "There's a reporter in the lobby who's been tryin' to get an interview with me. Y'all may want to steer clear of any goodlookin' man wantin' to speak to you on your way out."

David had to force himself to sit still when the express elevator doors opened. He watched the same four women exit that he had seen go in, but no Mrs. Donner. Abiding by his earlier decision, he prepared to follow one of them and try to get a few questions answered.

Like a wolf sniffing out a wounded doe, he immediately noticed how the tall redhead's walk was not as steady as it had been earlier. With some reluctance, he gave up the pleasure of trailing the sexy blonde for easier quarry. All four moved across the lobby and headed out the front doors as if someone was chasing them, and within seconds, David was.

He couldn't believe his luck when the redhead decided to walk instead of ride. Perhaps she thought some exercise beneath the August sun would sweat some of the booze out of her system. As she headed down the sidewalk, he quickly made note of the call number of the taxi cab the mouse got into, then took off before he lost sight of the redhead.

She hadn't had that much of a headstart, but she managed to stay ahead of him for the next couple of blocks. It was almost as if she knew she was being followed and performed a few maneuvers through the crowd that might have thrown off a less determined hunter. He hadn't seen so much dodging and weaving since Muhammad Ali was Cassius Clay. At the intersections, she didn't wait for the proper signal before dashing across the street. David had no choice but to challenge the traffic right behind her.

The mystery of how someone who appeared so tipsy could move skillfully enough to throw off the average tail was solved a block later when she hustled into the building that housed the FBI. David reached the female guard posted at the entrance doors seconds behind her, but she was already out of sight. His charm couldn't wheedle the redhead's name out of the guard, but he had seen Red flash her indentification card as she flew by. The fact that she was instantly recognized combined with her carrying a concealed weapon told him she was probably an agent.

Bobbi's head had started pounding even before the group went their separate ways. She knew what the warning sign meant and, during the short cab ride to the IRS building, she practiced the control techniques April had taught her, but the need to submit was much too strong.

I can handle this, Roberta, Bobbi insisted.

No, you can't, a stronger voice replied in Bobbi's head. *But I can. Go to sleep, Bobbi.*

Again Bobbi concentrated on maintaining her identity and forcing Roberta into the background. Because of April's help, Bobbi understood about Roberta from a psychological standpoint, but neither comprehension nor control techniques were enough to keep Roberta subdued when she truly wanted out.

As a shy child, Bobbi had invented Roberta to blame for any wrong she was accused of, in an attempt to avoid a beating. In later years, when she was most frightened, she often fantasized about being a strong, aggressive girl like Roberta. Unlike Bobbi, Roberta was brave enough to fight back and always had the perfect comeback to an insult. Roberta wasn't afraid of anything or anybody—and the more dangerous something was, the more it appealed to her.

Sometime during her gang rape, Roberta had become as real as Bobbi had ever been.

Bobbi sat at her desk and strained her eyes to focus on the numbers on the form before her. Finally, she removed her glasses and put them in her purse.

There. That's much better, Roberta thought. She never understood how Bobbi could stand wearing those annoying bifocals. Contact lenses were so much nicer, but, as usual, Bobbi had left those at home.

Within minutes, Roberta had told one of Bobbi's coworkers that she was feeling ill and was outside hailing another taxi.

Roberta didn't know how or why, or even care, but when she was in charge, Bobbi slept, unaware of what Roberta was doing. When Bobbi was in control however, Roberta remainded alert in the shadows. On the way to their apartment, she considered everything discussed over lunch.

She despised the way Bobbi had just sat there instead of supporting Rachel's opinions. Tim Ziegler *should* be castrated. Or at least brought down a few notches. Next to cutting his balls off, what she really wanted to do was step forward and add her accusations to Cheryl's but she had promised Bobbi not to do that.

Suddenly an idea came to her and immediately made itself at home in her mind. She might have agreed not to confront Ziegler publicly, but she had made no such promise about privately. It would take some planning, but she was going to pay him a visit before he left town, and Bobbi and her friends would never be the wiser.

3

Holly felt some of her confidence return the moment she stepped into the old office building that housed Earth Guard on its fifth floor. When Philip first set up the nonprofit organization devoted to political lobbying for environmental concerns, he had told Holly it was only a temporary location, but they were still there thirteen years later, and that suited her just fine. She felt grounded there, knew where everything was, and what was expected of her. Changes were uncomfortable.

She paused outside the door of the Earth Guard offices to make sure her smile was cheerful enough to fool Evelyn, her eagle-eyed secretary and self-appointed surrogate mother. Evelyn was one of those women who had aged not only gracefully but beautifully, with attractively coiffed white hair and a dignified appearance that tended to demand instant respect from total strangers.

She had tried to retire last year, but within a month she was going crazy with boredom and Holly and Philip were being made miserable by a string of temporary secretaries. In the end, they had all agreed she was much too young to retire, and soon Evelyn was ensconced at her post again.

"Any calls?" Holly asked as she pushed open the door, intent on avoiding an interrogation about why her lunch appointment had run so long.

"Philip took care of all but these two," Evelyn replied, handing her the message slips. "One's from *Time* magazine and the other is a reporter for a newspaper in Madison, Wisconsin. Some complaint about the city's curbside recycling program. As usual, the boss left the press to you. How did your appointment go?" she asked before Holly could slip into her office.

Holly shrugged, recalling the explanation she had given. "They were a very *small* small interest group; nothing we could work with. On the way back I stopped in at that new dress shop you told me about." As expected, Evelyn's eyes lit up with hope. "I think I found a gown for Saturday night, but I can't make up my mind."

"Is it black and slinky?"

Holly laughed. "Yes. In fact, it was so slinky, I decided I'd better keep looking."

Evelyn clucked her tongue and rolled her eyes. "I swear, sometimes I think you act more matronly than I do. How about if I call the store right now and have them set it aside for you?"

"No," Holly replied quickly. "I mean, there's no need to call. I asked them to hold it until I can stop by again after work." She was certain the store must have something black and slinky that would meet with Evelyn's approval. She just had to remember where Evelyn had said the store was and go by there before going home. Nodding at the closed door to Philip's office, she asked, "Is someone with him?"

"The barracuda," Evelyn whispered behind her hand.

Holly knew she was referring to the woman from the Environmental Protection Agency who kept coming up with reasons to meet with Philip. She whispered back, "Who closed the door?"

Evelyn smiled. "I did."

Shaking her head, Holly went into her office. After years of failing to get Philip and Holly married to each other, Evelyn had started pushing both of them toward other eligible people. She simply couldn't accept the idea that the two of them might be content with the way things were.

Twenty minutes later, Holly had returned the two calls and moved all the papers on her desk around, but hadn't actually accomplished anything. There were several other calls she needed to make that afternoon, but each time she lifted the receiver, she realized her conversation with Evelyn had used up her reserve of false confidence.

Her mind kept drifting back to the folder in her briefcase, even though the office was not the place to look at it. *If* she decided to read the contents, it would have to be at home, in private, when there was no possibility of Evelyn or Philip walking in on her.

As if thinking his name conjured up the man, Philip's trim figure appeared in the doorway. Threading his fingers through his thinning ash-blond hair, he asked, "Have you got a minute?"

She forced a smile. "Considering how you probably spent the last hour, I can give you all the time you need. What excuse did she have this time?"

Philip's fair cheeks flushed as he sat down across the desk from her. "She wanted to know if we'd heard anything about a new incineration plant the

Japanese are developing. From what she said, it's supposed to be using laser technology rather than fire, so it would be completely smokeless. Sounds good in theory, but I hadn't heard that anyone had gone past the experimentation stage."

"Neither have I, but there's a stack of journals on my nightstand that I haven't gotten to read this month. Maybe it's been written up somewhere."

"If it has, her agency hasn't uncovered it. She asked me—as an independent lobbyist—to pose some questions to the Japanese consulate so that it wouldn't sound like the EPA was playing catch-up again. I promised to get back to her. So, how did *your* meeting go?"

She shrugged. "They talked, I listened, smiled, and politely put them off."

"What was it again? Otters?"

"Beavers," she corrected, recalling the fabricated reason she had given him before she left for lunch. "But it turned out to be two of them in a small creek on someone's private property."

Philip arched one light eyebrow. "And they talked about that for three hours?"

Holly thought it was probably her guilty conscience that made her hear the note of suspicion in his voice. "I also stopped in at a dress shop Evelyn recommended. Which reminds me, how long did it take your friend to switch from incinerators to Saturday night's benefit dinner?"

That got her a chuckle. "Is that a good guess or was Evelyn listening at the door and running in here with a report to make you jealous?"

"Now, Philip, you know Evelyn never *runs*. That would be unladylike. So, are we still on or should I step aside to make way for true love?"

He leaned forward and crooked a finger at her to

come within whispering range. "The only true love you're standing in the way of is ours."

"Philip . . ." she warned with a glance at the open door, then eased back in her chair.

"You know what Saturday is, don't you?"

Her glance at the calendar was unnecessary, but it gave her a valid excuse to look away from the solemn expression in his gray eyes.

"All I ask is that you consider it, Holly." He reached out his hand, but stopped short of touching hers until she met his gaze. As soon as she gave him a soft smile, he enclosed her hand in his and whispered, "I love you."

She raised his hand and brushed her cheek against his knuckles. "I'll consider it, but—"

Swiftly, he touched her lips to silence her. "No buts until Saturday night, and this time, I'll have an answer for every 'but' you can come up with." He rose with a closed-mouth grin that didn't quite reach his eyes and left her office before she could object further.

At least she hadn't had to tell another lie about where she had been for the last three hours.

Holly had hoped August 15 would pass this year without Philip realizing it. Of course, she had known that wasn't going to happen any more than he had let the last six "anniversaries" pass.

Though she had formally met Philip when she was in high school, she hadn't really gotten to know him or his wife, Cora, until she left Dominion and moved back to Butler, Pennsylvania.

The memory of that time still had the power to knot her stomach. Angry, hurt, and numb with shock, she had shown up at her parents' door with all her belongings in her car, and the simple statement that she would not be returning to college.

As the only survivor of three children, Holly had always been treated like a princess and, in return, had never given her parents a moment of difficulty. They had been willing to give her time to adjust to whatever had happened to her. They never insisted she tell them what had happened to drive her into the solitude of her bedroom, although they concluded a broken heart was involved. Instead, they stood by her, even when she inflicted on them her depression, crying bouts, and temper tantrums.

When months of patience failed, however, her father demanded she either return to school or go to work in the family's German-style restaurant. She chose to put on a waitress uniform.

Philip and Cora Sinkiewicz started out as customers of the Kaufman Haus restaurant, but quickly graduated to being personal friends of Bernie and Vivian Kaufman. At that time, Holly had thought Philip was much younger than her father, but she realized later that Philip worked at that appearance.

Where Bernie's waistline showed the results of too much of his own good cooking, Philip maintained a slim physique perfectly proportioned to his medium height through diet and exercise. Where Bernie's hair was now more gray than brown, Philip's blond hair stayed the same shade year after year, with a little chemical assistance. Overall, Philip looked very good for a man who'd passed his fiftieth birthday.

It was Philip who had given Holly the final shove back into the real world one evening at the restaurant by drawing her into a conversation about his work. He had finally secured the funding he had been seeking to establish Earth Guard, and delighted in telling Holly his plans to help save the environment. For the first time in months, she had found herself really interested in something.

Philip had informed her that the fledgling lobbying organization would be needing all the help it could get from intelligent, young people, and that they would have a place for her if she would like to move to Washington, D.C. Within a week she had decided to take him up on his offer.

They spent a great deal of time together setting up Earth Guard. His zealousness about saving Earth's resources was contagious, and she was soon caught up in his interests as well as the fast-paced life of the capital. He encouraged her to develop her untapped talents and convinced her to finish college in order to gain every advantage in the competitive city. She chose Georgetown University, as it was in the D.C. area and allowed her to continue working with him.

It wasn't long before she sensed his feelings for her went beyond that of a close friend and employer, but he never acted upon his obvious desire. He was a man who took his wedding vows seriously, regardless of how difficult that marriage was for him—and Holly had been around him and Cora enough to know that they had a multitude of problems.

Even if he had not been married, however, Holly never wanted another man in her bed.

The change in their relationship began when Philip's wife was diagnosed with cancer of the brain. For two years he suffered along with her as she underwent surgery and treatments, unspeakable pain and forgetfulness. As his closest friend, Holly was always there for him and shared his every frustration.

When Cora finally died eight years ago, Holly

cared too much to deny him the comfort he sought in her arms. Setting aside her vow of celibacy, she spent the night with him, but learned that compassion and friendship were not sufficient motivation for physical lovemaking. Either that, or her ability to enjoy the experience had been forever crippled before it had had the chance to fully develop.

She had allowed Philip into her bed twice more after that, mainly because she felt he deserved a fair chance to arouse her passion. Unlike other men, his touch did not repulse her; she just felt nothing at all. To her surprise and relief, he didn't seem to mind when she turned down his gentle hints to continue the intimacy.

They settled into an easy companionship, except for each August 15, the anniversary of their first, and only, full night together. Saturday would mark the eighth time he asked her to marry him, and the eighth time she would decline.

Always respectful and attentive, he was devoted to her and no other woman, and she was clearly uninterested in any other man. He could never understand her refusal to formalize their relationship, but he knew better than to push more than once a year.

Holly repeatedly explained her need for independence and privacy, though she admitted he filled other needs for her. In him, she had a good friend, an escort when she needed one, and a man to act as a buffer between her and all others.

For a while, Holly had felt guilty about using Philip, but he convinced her that he would take whatever she could give him rather than nothing at all. He swore he was satisfied knowing he was the only man that received attention from her, limited as it was.

She had no problem stroking his ego; he was attractive for his age, intelligent, mature, focused, kind, generous, and faithful, characteristics that would surely cause any normal woman to fall madly in love with him. But Holly had never been able to say the words he wanted to hear. The phrase "I love you" had been stricken from her vocabulary fourteen years ago, and she couldn't bring it to her lips, regardless of how much it would please Philip. Besides, he deserved more from her than a lie.

Perhaps this time, when he asks why I won't marry him, I should tell him the truth.

Her mind replayed comments made by each of the women she'd met earlier. The consensus was that talking about one's problems was the first step to recovery. Holly had already decided that if she was going to tell anyone about that night it would have to be her parents first, then, depending on how that went, Philip next.

Part of the reason she had avoided speaking of it was that she wanted to block it out. The other part, however, was due to the fear that her parents would blame her for what happened, the way some people had at school.

Logically, of course, she had always known the blame belonged solely on the shoulders of Jerry Frampton and Tim Ziegler, and that her guilt was completely unfounded. But no amount of logic had done quite as much for her self-assurance as listening to the confidences of the women of the Little Sister Society that day and discovering that she wasn't the only one. She couldn't help but wonder how much further she could progress by following their advice.

Why, it could even make a difference in how she responded to Philip on Saturday.

For the second time that day, she made an impulsive phone call. As it was Tuesday afternoon, she knew exactly where she could find both her parents.

"Kaufman Haus," her mother's cheery voice answered after the second ring.

"I'd like to make reservations for three for midnight tonight."

"Holly? What's the matter? Why are you calling in the middle of the week?"

Holly laughed lightly. "Nothing's the matter, Mom. I swear. There's just something I wanted to talk to you and Pop about, and I figured the best time was after you close up on a slow night. Correction, slower night. Everyone knows Kaufman Haus doesn't have slow nights."

The old line made her mother laugh, but she quickly became serious again. "If it's really important, we could take the night off—"

"No, no. It'll be late by the time I get to the house anyway."

"Will you be staying?" Vivian asked hopefully.

"Only tonight. I'll have to get back here first thing in the morning."

"Oh, I see. At least give me a hint so that I know whether to worry or be excited."

"Neither one. I just need to explain something, that's all. I'll see you tonight."

It took several more reassurances before Holly could hang up and get Evelyn working on reservations. She figured it was a good omen when she was able to book a flight out of Dulles at nine, which left her plenty of time to pick up a change of clothes at her apartment and have dinner. Evelyn confirmed that a rental car was reserved for her at the Pittsburgh airport. Even with the one-hour drive to Butler added to the hour-long flight, she would still be home before her parents.

When Philip heard what she was up to, he offered to accompany her. "I haven't seen Bernie and Viv in months."

"I know, and I'm sure they'd be happy to see you, too, but this time I need to see them alone." His hurt expression prompted her to add, "But I could use a lift to the airport later, if you wouldn't mind. I'd rather not leave my car there overnight." Guilt made her continue. "In fact, why don't you follow me to my apartment while I pick up an overnight bag and then we can go to dinner." Her extra effort earned her a grateful smile.

David's network of informants was not limited to hotel employees. In a transient city of power like Washington, there was an abundance of people in seemingly unimportant positions who were privy to interesting tidbits, and David had spent years cultivating friendships with a great number of those people. The fact that most of them were women was just as intentional.

Once he was back at his desk in the paper's newsroom, he needed to make only one call to the dispatcher at the cab company to learn that the driver of the taxi he'd observed in front of the hotel dropped the mouse off at the Internal Revenue Service building. He had no idea why employees of two branches of government would be meeting with Erica Donner, but he bet his next paycheck there was a story behind it. Again, his nose told him it could have something to do with Tim Ziegler's call. What he needed were some names to attach to the faces.

He didn't have a contact inside the FBI but he had a companionable relationship with a city police officer. It seemed reasonable that the man would know at least one agent that might be able to identify Red. If memory served, the officer was a big football fan. An invitation to an upcoming game would probably net him a name and maybe a bit more. Without giving it any more thought, David left a message on the officer's home answering machine.

Identifying the other three women was going to be more of a challenge, but he determined to describe them to everyone he knew until he got some answers.

Before he began that, however, he needed to ask Valerie for another favor—a roster of the students enrolled in the freshman class at Dominion the year Cheryl Wallace and Erica Donner were there.

"Is that it?" Valerie asked with a laugh. "You sure you don't want the upperclassmen as well? I've already been asked to come up with the names of all of Senator Ziegler's fraternity brothers. Don't you want a copy of that too?"

"That would be terrific," David replied. "If it's not too much trouble." He wasn't surprised that another reporter was working on that angle. Cheryl Wallace's list of alleged attackers had caused a lot of speculation all over the country.

"Well, I'll tell you the same thing I told the other reporter. That was a long time ago, before everything was computerized, and although the university would have retained the records, they've probably been buried in some storage vault. It's not going to be easy getting the information."

"I realize that, but if anybody can do it, I know you can," David said with complete sincerity.

He made several more calls, then headed back to

the Kessler Hotel in hopes that Mrs. Donner might
be planning to go out to dinner.

Holly and Philip arrived at her apartment in
Georgetown with plenty of time to spare, but Holly
was too anxious to be on her way to sit and relax.
Philip poured himself a club soda while she went
into her bedroom to throw a few things in a bag.

Thirty minutes later, she started to walk into the
living room and froze in the doorway. Philip was
seated on the couch with his back to her—and was
closing the lid on her briefcase. "Philip? Were you
looking for something?"

"Yes. Or rather I was about to." He latched the
case and set it back down on the floor where she
had left it. Standing up and turning to her with a
sheepish grin, he said, "I didn't want to admit to
Evelyn that I misplaced the last report from the
House Ways and Means Committee. I had the sudden thought that it had somehow gotten mixed up
with your folders and ended up in your briefcase. I
apologize. Without thinking, I opened it to check. I
should never have done that without asking. I swear
I didn't rearrange a single sheet of paper."

He appeared to be appropriately embarrassed at
having been caught, but it left Holly feeling a little
uneasy. Certain he was telling the truth, however,
she could see no reason to make an issue of it. "Did
you find the report?"

He laughed. "No. As soon as I opened that porta-
ble office of yours and saw how much work you
have in there, I just closed it up again. If you get a
chance, I'd appreciate your taking a look for it,
though. Are you ready to go?"

She nodded and let him take the bag from her.
Though she hadn't planned on taking her briefcase

along, his reminder of how much work she had to do changed her mind. Grabbing the case and her purse, she flicked the lights off and closed the door behind her.

"I'll be damned! Harry Abbott taking a trip around the world." David Wells shook his head at the balding man he considered his mentor. Harry had talked about this trip as long as they had known each other, but David had always figured the old man's plans had about as much substance as his cigar smoke. Yet here they were, sitting in an airport restaurant, drinking a toast to his adventure. On the other hand, Harry had retired as sports editor for *The Washington Times* several months ago, and David had never expected him to do that either.

David had already put ten years into *The Washington Times*—as a paperboy—before he got a job on the inside working as an apprentice to Harry on the sports desk. Those years, plus his family's poverty level, helped him gain the Newsboy Scholarship, which covered his tuition at George Washington University, but his part-time job for the paper paid for the rest. In truth, Harry taught him far more than four years of journalism class ever did, and because of that, David would walk barefoot across a desert for the man.

"How long do you figure you'll be gone?" David asked.

"As long as it takes. I'm going to play golf in Scotland, Ping-Pong in China, and whatever it is they do in Tahiti, I'll do that too. I've already got a publisher interested in the book."

"The book?" David didn't bother to hide his surprise.

"Sure." Harry leaned forward and lowered his

voice as if sharing a major secret. "You didn't think I'd take off without knowing it would all be deductible later."

"I wondered what you were up to the last couple of months when you kept putting off getting together."

Harry shrugged and took another swallow of his beer. "To tell you the truth, I was feeling too sorry for myself to be sociable. I just had to give myself a kick in the ass. Retirement's not for me. What else is an old ex-sportswriter going to do but write a book about sports? At any rate, I've been following your stories. Nice job on the HUD article. What are you working on now?"

"Just finished up an article on the local homeless situation. It wasn't too hard. All I had to do was go back and hang around the neighborhood I grew up in. Something else got my nose twitching today."

"Not going to sit on your laurels, huh?"

"Hey, you know what you told me years ago: 'Lots of people are satisfied being first string, but the one the fans remember is the quarterback.'"

Harry relit his cigar. "I never had any doubt you'd make it, kid. I pegged you the day you walked into the newsroom—smart, sassy, and hungry as hell. I figure by the time I get back, you'll be putting a dent in that list of yours, now that you're such a hotshot *investigative* reporter."

David laughed. His wish list of possessions he would have once he became *somebody* varied slightly from year to year, but a 1964 Corvette Stringray always remained number one. "Well, that's possible, now that Jill's got her doctorate."

"Hmmph." Harry refrained from repeating his opinion of how David's kid sister had made a career of going to college. Of the five children abandoned by their mother, David had turned out to be the one they all looked to for advice—or a handout. Jill's long-term education had kept her dependent on him for both moral and financial support longer than any of the others. David's family devotion was not a subject open to criticism, however, not even to Harry. The kid really deserved his success—and self-indulgence. "So, what got you going today?"

David gave him a brief account of Tim. Ziegler's call and his stakeout in the hotel, and described the women, being particularly explicit when it came to the taller blonde.

Harry blew a smoke ring over David's head. His protégé would never change. It was just a wonder his hormones hadn't gotten him into some serious mess over the years. At least he never let a woman interfere with his career. "Seeing as how you've had a close encounter with every D-cup blonde in Washington, she must have been a tourist." He waved to the waitress to get them another round.

"I don't think so. My nose says they were there for business and she had the stamp of a capital woman on her. I've just missed meeting her somehow."

"Maybe she's one of that rare breed, a happily married woman."

David shook his head. "No ring. I—" His thought was aborted as he caught sight of a couple entering the restaurant. "I'll be damned! It's *her*."

Harry turned and tracked David's gaze to a gorgeous blonde carrying a leather briefcase and a much older man, toting a small, brown tweed suitcase. As the man sat down at a table near the entrance, she headed for the restrooms beyond Harry and David's table.

As she passed him, David noted that her light-blue blouse was real silk and her black jeans had been washed just enough to hug her rounded hips without being too tight. She never made visual contact with him, but he couldn't help but notice that her eyes were almost the same shade of blue as his own. He let out the breath he had unconsciously held as she had glided toward him. Damn, she was gorgeous!

Harry blew a thick cloud of smoke at David to get his attention. "Aren't you getting a little old for the game?"

"You're the one to talk, old man. As I recall, you're the one who said, 'Why buy a ticket to the game when you can climb the fence?' "

Harry's lips formed a smirk around the stogie. Although he removed it to speak, the words still exited from the corner of his mouth. "What'd you do, write down everything I said for the last decade?"

"I didn't have to with you spouting Harryisms all the time."

"Harryisms? Well, now. I kinda like that. Maybe I can use that in my book. In the meantime, I'd like to add one more to your collection. There comes a time in every man's life when he's too old to climb the fence. Then it's sort of nice to be holding a season ticket."

David pretended to choke on his coffee. "What's this, Har? Is the confirmed bachelor hoping to find a little woman on his world tour?"

"Nah. It's too late for me. But it's not for you. I just wanted to let you know that since I retired, sometimes it gets a little lonely around my apartment."

"More likely, having to spend entire days in that place has gotten you thinking about how nice it would be to have someone empty your overflowing ashtrays, pick up the years of accumulated newspapers and magazines, and find a clean pair of socks for you." Their conversation stopped again as the blonde returned to her table. David decided that the rear view was almost as interesting as the front.

As Harry gave him a rundown of his itinerary, half of David's mind stayed with the unknown lady across the room. Who was she? Why had she met with Erica Donner? Did she work for the government like the other two women, or was she from the business world, like Donner? The man carried the bag, but was he or she leaving town, or both? To where? Why?

Questions were as enticing to David as a glimpse of a beautiful woman, but getting the answers was more exciting than any woman had ever turned out to be.

When he saw the waitress hand the man the bill, he excused himself from Harry and hurried over to the couple's table.

With barely a glance at the woman he dipped his head toward the older man. "Joe? Joe Thomas?"

The man looked up from signing the charge slip. "No. I'm sorry. You've mistaken me for someone else."

"You look so familiar. I'm David Wells, reporter for *The Washington Times*. Perhaps we've met—"

"No. I'm quite certain." He tore off his copy of the form and rose. "If you'll excuse us?" He nodded to the woman, and she gracefully departed with him.

David prided himself on noticing the little things. The average person would have introduced himself in return. This man had no intention of revealing who he, or his companion, was. Yes, he had seen the way the man's gaze briefly darted to the woman in a clearly proprietary reflex that couldn't be mistaken as fatherly.

Returning to Harry, David laughed to himself. Apparently other men had used the same method to try to wangle an introduction to the lovely lady, and the gentleman had seen through it. That was okay. The signature on the charge slip, a rather distinctive name, gave him something to go on.

Even without the question of the blonde's connection to Erica Donner, the very secretiveness of Philip Sinkiewicz spurred him to discover who they were. That, and the fact that when the woman stood up next to him, she unconsciously ran her palms down her thighs to smooth her jeans and took a deep, chest-raising breath that nearly took his own away.

He realized there was one other thing that had intrigued him about the woman. Even when he was speaking to her companion, she never looked up at him. David could not remember any woman being so completely uninterested in what he looked like.

All in all, the two of them might as well have waved a red flag in his face.

4

Despite the long night ahead of her, Holly turned down the cup of coffee offered by the flight attendant. Her nerves were already ragged. Undoubtedly, it was due to everything she had heard that day and the confession she was about to make to her parents, but Philip had added to her tension.

He hadn't said any more about it, yet she had the distinct impression he doubted her story about her lunch meeting. And he obviously felt left out when she didn't explain why she was going home so abruptly and didn't want him to go along as he normally would. She supposed his concern was understandable, considering the fact that she couldn't remember ever hiding anything from him before— with the exception of her one secret. She would have to straighten a lot of things out with him when she returned.

Like his jealous reaction to that newspaper person. She had seen the bold way the man stared at her when she walked past him, but she carefully avoided meeting his gaze, as she always did with men. And it wasn't her fault he used the old mistaken identity line to get a closer look. Rather than say what he was really upset about, Philip had suggested she dress less conspicuously when traveling. He was always protective of her, but he had never before made her feel—

She shook her head to stop that line of thought. One problem at a time. Philip had been disturbed with her and it had nothing to do with her outfit.

Could it have been more than the long lunch meeting or visit to her parents? Could he have seen the file April had given her? Surely if he had noticed it, he would have questioned her.

She set the briefcase on her lap and opened it. On top, exactly as she had left it, was the alphabetical list of the fraternity brothers. The four names without the lines drawn through them seemed to jump off the page. Philip had to have seen it. And right beneath that was the file. One glance would have been enough to tell him that these things had nothing to do with Earth Guard.

Could he have been so intent upon locating his missing report that he hadn't paid any attention to anything else, or had he not been completely honest when he said he had opened the case, changed his mind, and closed it again without looking through it?

Even if she told him the whole story, she wouldn't want him to know the men's names. There was always the possibility that he would run into one of them and feel obliged to say something. In fact, with Ziegler in Washington, the odds of that happening increased. She couldn't imagine how a confrontation would accomplish anything but embarrassment all around.

She scanned the list of names again, wondering which might sound familiar to Philip, and decided it was highly unlikely that he would know any of those already scratched off. She wasn't certain if she had ever met them herself, though as they were all Jerry's fraternity brothers, she probably had. She also doubted that Philip would know Adam Frankowicz, but the last three names would be recognizable to a great many people.

Moving aside the list, she stared at the name on the folder, debating whether she really wanted to open it and read what was inside. The letters swam together, but the name had been indelibly etched in her mind fourteen years ago. For the first time since then she allowed herself to remember it all. . . .

"Jerry Frampton. *Mrs*. Jerry Frampton. Holly Frampton." Holly smiled at her mirrored image. Yes, she definitely liked the sound of that. And after tonight, she could shout it to the world if she wanted to. She would have preferred to have seen a reflection weighing thirty pounds less and wearing contact lenses instead of thick-lensed glasses, but Jerry had told her she was beautiful so often, she was beginning to believe it.

Holly's mother had convinced her long ago that God gave her a special gift that could only be given away one time, and that she should be absolutely certain the recipient was deserving of the honor. She had also told her daughter that gift should only be given in exchange for a wedding ring. Because of her determination to choose well, Holly was probably one of the few twenty-year-old virgins left on Dominion's sprawling campus.

Tonight that was going to change.

A month ago, when Dominion's star quarterback had approached her about tutoring him in three of his required subjects, she had turned him down flat. He had heard how she had helped two of the basketball players pass math, but *she* had heard about his reputation as a walking sex organ.

A lot of girls might have jumped at the opportunity to spend time with the most popular guy in school. He was tall, wellbuilt, and handsome as a movie star with his sun-bleached hair and sparkling smile, but Holly had no intention of letting him try to add her to his list of conquests.

But then the football coach had practically begged her for the sake of the school. If Frampton didn't pass those courses, he had said, he would soon be in the bleachers during the game instead of on the field. He swore he would warn the young man to behave himself if she would take the job.

She wasn't sure whether the coach had actually spoken to Jerry or if all the terrible things she had heard about him were only malicious gossip spread by a brokenhearted ex-girlfriend—as Jerry kept insisting. Whichever it was, he behaved like a perfect gentleman during their tutoring sessions and really worked very hard to improve his grades. By their third lesson together, Holly knew all her worries about protecting her virtue from Jerry were groundless.

As she changed her earrings for the third time, she mentally replayed the moment their relationship had changed. During their fifth session, Jerry had finally grasped the concept of an algebra equation they had been working on for some time. She recalled how his hazel eyes lit up with delight as he pulled her face toward his and kissed her mouth with a loud smack.

She had tried to hide her surprise, tried to pretend it meant nothing to have his lips come in contact with hers, and tried to ignore her heart crashing agamst her rib cage. She quit trying to do any of those things when his hands slid from her cheeks to her shoulders, and he kissed her again . . . for real.

Her entire previous experience consisted of parental pecks or shy kisses from suitors in her own social and intellectual class. During the weeks that followed her first passionate kiss with Jerry, Holly spent as much time learning the nuances of necking as she did teaching him math, literature, and philosophy. But she always stopped him before he got too carried away.

She was now glad the girl who had planned to share her small apartment this semester had changed her mind. At first it had made her quite nervous to be there alone with Jerry, but he repeatedly proved that she could trust him.

Because of Jerry's curfew and the fact that he spent every hour outside of the classroom with her, she knew he was telling the truth when he said he wasn't seeing any other girls. She had discovered he thought better on his feet, so English lit. was covered as they walked around campus, holding hands, talking and laughing. She noticed the way other students looked at them when they passed, and she guessed what they were saying, but Jerry always told her his opinion was the only one that counted.

She finally believed him when they were in the library one day. While their heads were bent together over a question of philosophy, some of his fraternity brothers stopped to say hi, just as he rubbed his nose against hers. Jerry didn't pull away from her or act ashamed to be caught nuzzling a nerd, as she had thought he might. He introduced her to them respectfully, adding a compliment about her intelligence and helpfulness. By the end of that

day, everyone knew she was "Jerry's girl," and
started treating her like she was one of the in crowd
instead of just a sophomore with a high IQ.

Holly picked up the cute little stuffed dog he had
given her a week ago and kissed its nose. He was
always bringing her something—a flower, a chocolate kiss, or a poem that had made him think of
her. The puppy was her favorite, though, because
of what it represented.

When Jerry had handed it to her, it had a pink
ribbon around its neck with a small card attached.
It read, *I love Holly, and so does the big guy next to
me.* That was the night they progressed to making
out in a prone position with Jerry's hips pressed
against her own. He left no doubt that he wanted
more than kisses and touching her breasts through
her clothes.

She was not so foolish as to let his sincere pleading alter her good sense. Saying he loved her more
than any girl he'd ever known, wanted her so bad
he ached, needed her *desperately,* were not the
words she waited to hear, even though she believed
that when he said them, he meant them.

Two nights ago he finally spoke of the future,
their future, and what it would be like if they were
married and didn't have to part because it was time
to say good night. He still had a year and a half
before graduation. It seemed like such a long time
away. He pushed a little harder after that discussion, and Holly had let him unhook her bra and
fondle her bare breasts beneath her sweater, mainly
to let him know it had made a difference to hear
him make a commitment to her, but again, she
stopped him from going further.

He had raised his voice to her for the first time,
questioning how true her love really was, and com-

plaining that she couldn't feel the same way as he did, or she would want to share the ultimate experience with him. She realized just how angry he had been when he had gone to last night's fraternity party without her. But he had called this morning and apologized, and asked to take her to a movie to make up.

His talk of marriage, and how very far away graduation was, helped make up her mind. She would give up her plans to finish college; she had never really decided what she wanted to do anyway. Tonight she would tell him about her money—the fund that would enable their dream to come to fruition right away.

For the first time, something positive would come out of the tragic deaths of her brother and sister. Their parents had bought life insurance endowment policies on each child at birth with the intention of using the proceeds for college. When death benefits were paid instead, the money was placed in a trust fund for Holly.

She was really quite wealthy and could support Jerry until he graduated and got picked up by a professional team. There would be time enough in the future, after their babies were out of diapers, for her to finish her education if she wished to.

She was not going to send him away again with a telltale bulge in his jeans.

Holly heard his knock at her door and made one last appearance check in the mirror. The fact that Jerry saw through the exterior to the woman inside proved how special he was.

For someone who had said they were going to make up, Jerry seemed awfully quiet. Holly figured he was probably still a little embarrassed about some of the things he had said to her the other night and decided it would be best not to talk about it at all. Instead, when they got back to her apartment, she would show him that he had been wrong about the depth of her love.

Needing an injection of courage, when they stopped by the fraternity house after the movie, Holly indulged in several glasses of wine, something she'd never done before. On the way to her apartment, Jerry was slightly more talkative, but his conversation centered on the team's chances of winning the championship that season. With her head buzzing from the wine and preoccupied with building up her nerve, Holly barely heard what he was saying anyway.

At her apartment door, she put her key into the lock and was about to turn it when he stopped her.

"Wait a minute," Jerry said, as he brought her hand up to his lips for a quick kiss on her fingertips. "There's something I heard about in psych class that I want to try. You'll have to really trust me for this to work. Can you do that?"

She laughed at how serious he looked. "Of course I trust you, you know that." He let out a breath he must have been holding until she answered. It made her stomach flutter to know she had the power to make him nervous.

"Good. The theory is that if someone loses one of his senses, like his eyesight, his other senses become more acute, or at least the person learns to tune in on them better. You know, like how a blind person seems to hear little things you or I might not notice."

"Yes, I know what you mean." Holly angled her head a little, waiting to find out what he had in mind, and wondering why they couldn't go inside for this conversation.

"Well, there's a, um, what was that word? Oh yeah, he's a pa-ra-psy-chologist. Anyway, this guy believes that if our ability to communicate with our usual senses was eliminated, we would learn to use mental telepathy."

"Hmmm. I don't know about that."

"C'mon. Try it with me. It'll be fun. Who knows, you and I have gotten real close. Maybe we could read each other's minds if we did what that guy said. Unless you're afraid of the dark."

Holly stifled a laugh. It suddenly occurred to her that this was probably an elaborate ruse to sneak past her defenses, including the traditional challenge to her courage. What Jerry didn't know was that the joke would be on him, since she was already bent on surrender.

"Okay, but there's something important I wanted to talk to you about."

"You could have *talked* to me for the past hour," Jerry grumbled. "Sorry. I didn't mean it that way. It's just that I have this, uh, paper due and . . . well, if you don't want to help—"

"You don't need to pout, honey. We can play your game and we'll talk afterward."

"No. I mean, not tonight. We'll talk tomorrow. Once we start, neither of us is allowed to use our voices or turn on a light for the rest of the evening. No talking, no humming, nothing." He pulled out a white handkerchief and shook it loose of its folds. "I'm going to blindfold you until we get inside. I figure we can use your bedroom since there aren't any windows in there, and then I'll take the blindfold off. Ready?"

Holly nodded her head and smothered another laugh. Did he honestly believe she would fall for such a harebrained excuse to get into her bedroom and throw her off balance? He was just lucky his plans went along with her own. Later she would tell him he hadn't fooled her for a minute, but for now she'd let him think he was terribly clever.

He removed her glasses and handed them to her. Without her glasses the world became a murky place, but she was accustomed to dealing with that shortcoming. The instant he secured the makeshift blindfold around her head, however, a surge of panic welled up inside of her.

She felt the keys being tugged from her clenched fist and had to force herself to relax. The lock clicked back into its chamber. A slight puff of air blew into her face, notifying her that Jerry had pushed the door open. This experiment could prove to be interesting after all, she thought. Jerry grasped her hand to guide her.

"Oh, wait," Holly said, thinking of the bottle of wine in the fridge that would help them both relax. His fingers pressed lightly on her lips, reminding her not to speak aloud. Forget the wine.

The game had begun.

It was her apartment; she should have been able to maneuver around the few pieces of furniture without difficulty. Instead, she found herself taking shuffling steps and clutching Jerry's hand tighter than necessary, as he led her into her bedroom and closed the door behind her.

As promised, he slipped the blindfold off with his free hand. It made no difference whatsoever. Her eyes were open, but there wasn't a single speck of light.

Remembering her glasses, she pulled Jerry further into the room, until her knee nudged the bed. Feeling her way along its edge, she was able to locate her nightstand and place her glasses in their assigned position. Only once before had she failed to be so careful, and the result was an inch-by-inch, two-hour search of the apartment. Some lessons were learned the hard way.

A slight pressure on her shoulder suggested she sit on the bed. The mattress bounced again as Jerry settled next to her. Lifting the hand he was still holding, he pried her fingers loose one by one, then shook her wrist until she let those fingers dangle. Holly giggled softly. She had not even realized how tense she was. A deep slow breath helped, but his comforting touch unwound her the rest of the way.

Jerry's fingertips found her face and slowly traced each of her features. When he outlined her lips and paused there, Holly understood he wanted a kiss. This game was more familiar and she flicked her tongue out to lick his fingers. His response was two taps on her nose. *Behave?*

From her nose he moved to the center of her forehead and tapped again. Apparently he wanted to try the experiment in earnest.

Holly concentrated on the one thing she had been thinking of all day. Perhaps he could read her thoughts, because his fingers grazed her scalp, then trickled through her long hair to the ends. She heard him inhale slowly and guessed he was smelling her hair by the way the strands moved along her cheek.

Her own fingers followed the trail of her hair to where it ended at his nose, and she drew a picture of his face with gentle hands. The tiny stubble on his jawline revealed his beard had begun to sprout. It struck Holly that, although Jerry's intentions may not have been completely honorable to begin with, this experience of seeing without sight was one she would always remember.

He sat very still for her loving exploration. His breathing was so shallow, she could barely hear it. He seemed to be waiting for her to decide which direction this game would take. So she did. Keeping her thumb on his mouth for guidance, Holly leaned forward until her mouth contacted his. Her kiss was sweet and he responded in kind. In the past Jerry had always been the aggressor, making all the first moves. Could she take the lead, tonight of all nights?

Holly kissed him again as she closed the small space between them. Her hands moved to the back of his neck and pulled him closer. He parted his lips and teeth when her tongue asked for a deeper kiss. Yet still he remained passive.

Her stomach contracted when she realized he wanted even more from her before he would act. Perhaps the experiment was working, because she was sure she knew what he wanted her to do.

She moved her hand to his shoulder and traveled down his arm to capture his hand. Slowly, trembling inside with uncertainty, she brought his hand to her breast, and held it there, until he kneaded the flesh on his own. Relaxing his fingers a moment later, he rotated his palm over the tip with a restrained patience he had never before exhibited. Holly sighed as she felt her nipple harden for him. His sound of masculine approval melted into her mouth, and the pulse between her legs sprang to life.

This much she had permitted before. She needed to show him he did not have to stop this time. Her hand shook slightly as she searched for the buttons on his shirt, clumsily opening them from collar to belt buckle.

Jerry removed his hand from her breast and lay back on the bed, as if to say, *Do with me as you will.* She pushed the shirt aside and discovered the thick mat of springy hair on his chest. She had never seen him shirtless and was pleasantly surprised by what her touch learned. Hard muscles reacted to her unskilled movements. She had not known a man's nipples were as sensitive as a woman's, but his flinch and the tightened nubs quickly educated her and made her smile confidently in the dark.

Holly suddenly understood why Jerry had planned the game. In the darkness she could do things she would never dare if she could see him watching her. Her cheeks warmed just imagining it, but she was greedy to know more of his secrets. Her nerve was bolstered when his sharp intake of breath followed her stroking of his flat stomach. She moved her hand lower, and lower still.

Through the thickness of material and zipper she found the part of him that she would soon welcome into her body. She straightened and shaped him beneath his slacks, and felt the muscle grow in length and breadth. She firmly shut out the knowledge that this would be an instrument of pain before the pleasure.

After a moment he moved her hand away, gave it a reassuring squeeze, and got up off the bed. The rasping sound of a zipper being lowered echoed through the room, formally sealing her fate. Other sounds inspired her imagination. In her mind Holly saw him removing his shirt, slipping off his shoes, and discarding his trousers and underwear. She supposed she should do the same, but could not bring herself to be so nonchalant about it.

Jerry's hand brushed her arm, then, grasping her elbow, he helped her rise. She felt the heat radiating from his body as he brought her close for another passionate kiss. His male scent would have warned her of his fierce arousal even if his sex had not been pressed against her stomach.

He proved quite adept at undressing her in spite of the lack of light, and in no time he was lowering her nude body onto the bed. His hands kneaded her generous curves as his mouth loved one breast, then the other. The pounding heartbeat in her lower body grew stronger, and she felt the dampness of desire accumulate.

She almost felt relieved when he moved his heavier weight onto her, pressing her into the mattress. His breath was coming in short, erratic puffs in between urgent kisses on her mouth and neck. Holly had planned to savor her last virginal minutes, to memorize each wonderful sensation, but his actions suddenly became hurried, almost desperate, and she was so swept up in his passion that she didn't dwell on her innocence.

When he spread her thighs with his and the tip of his shaft nudged at her opening, she instinctively bent her knees up along his hips. She could not prevent her soft gasp or the tension that invaded her muscles, but her own lubrication made his progression velvety smooth—until he struck her natural barrier.

He stopped. Rigidly holding himself on his elbows above her, Holly absorbed the fact that he was struggling for control. He hadn't known she was a virgin!

She could feel him pulling out and clenched her unpracticed vaginal muscles. It was not the game that kept her silent now. She did not want to have to say this aloud. Her hands ran down his back and grasped his buttocks, holding him in place. She pressed wet kisses on the shoulder above her face and arched her back in an effort to make him continue despite his discovery.

A moment later he pushed forward, breaking through her membrane in one determined thrust. Holly relaxed as soon as she realized the pain was slight and quickly diminishing. The novelty of having him inside her was worth the temporary discomfort. But he didn't seem to notice her tension or subsequent acceptance. Plunging to her depths was all he had on his mind. A few jerky movements, and he collapsed on top of her with a muffled groan.

That was it? All the love songs and whispers in the girls' room were about *that?* Holly's body was achingly unsatisfied. She knew there had to be more to this business of making love. Perhaps she needed more experience to reach the mysterious climax as fast as she was supposed to. Or perhaps—Jerry lifted himself up on his elbows and took a deep breath. He was still engorged and throbbing inside her, and she didn't know if she wanted him to go or stay. Taking her finger in his hand he used it to draw a cross over his heart. He was promising something.

"What—" Quickly his hand covered her mouth. He still wanted to play the quiet game.

He had her make another cross and rubbed himself against her sensitized flesh. He was promising it would get better.

And it did. Before he began again, he repositioned himself so that he was on his knees with her legs wrapped around his waist, and his fingers performed the service she required. A soft cry escaped her throat as her whole body shuddered its relief.

She heard his muffled chuckle of masculine triumph and thought it was over. But his hands and body began to stroke her inside and out, and waves of pleasure lapped at her again. This time, she knew what her body strived for and had no trouble grasping her climax when it approached.

A short while later, when he wordlessly showed her how to use her hands and mouth to make him ready for her again, she was anxious to learn everything he had to teach her.

This was what it should be like; this closeness, this shared passion was worth any sacrifice she had to make to be with Jerry forever, from this moment on.

Holly couldn't actually remember falling asleep, but her internal alarm told her it was morning. God, she was sore, but at the same time, she felt marvelous. She was certain no other woman had ever had such a unique introduction to sex. They would probably still smile about it on their fiftieth wedding anniversary. That thought made her want to make love to him all over again.

Stretching luxuriously, she felt Jerry stir beside her. As she did first thing every morning, she reached for her glasses and switched on the lamp.

Holly turned back to wake her future husband with a kiss, and froze.

The dark-haired man lying naked in her bed was a complete stranger.

5

Excuse me. Miss? Are you all right? You'll have to stow your briefcase under the seat for landing."

Holly blinked at the flight attendant hovering over her and the world came back into focus. Her insides were quivering and her upper lip was damp with perspiration. She should never have allowed herself to fall asleep.

When she had first gone home from Dominion, she constantly escaped into sleep. For a while it worked to keep her from thinking. Then the nightmare had come, and she stopped sleeping altogether.

It had been several years since the dream had last haunted her, but she should have known that recalling the details might bring it back. Occasionally the stranger turned out to be an animal of some sort, or even a grotesque monster. Once or twice, he had the face of someone she had seen on television before she went to sleep.

Most often, however, she saw Tim Ziegler, exactly as he had looked that morning in her bed.

As the plane taxied down the runway at the Greater Pittsburgh International Airport, Holly hoped that April was right—that this visit would be a step toward eliminating the nightmare permanently.

She fought off the feeling that automatically came over her every time she returned to the old house. Tonight, she couldn't allow her personality to regress back to that of the shy, overweight girl with glasses she used to be. Tonight, she needed all the maturity and confidence the years had given her to apologize and explain why she had been so hateful fourteen years ago.

Back then, the sheer helplessness of her situation had had her searching for someone she could safely strike out at. Her parents' fear of losing her made them the perfect target. Somehow, in the aftermath of trauma, Holly had decided they were at fault. She had determined that their overprotectiveness had kept her naive enough to believe in Cinderella stories and fall for Jerry Frampton's lies. Knowing the truth of why they were so protective of her made her behavior toward them that much more cruel.

Bernie and Viv Kaufman had originally been blessed with three holiday babies. Their son arrived on Lincoln's birthday, so he was named Abraham Lincoln Kaufman, better known as Linc. Four years later Holly was born on Christmas Eve, and two years after that, a week after Easter, Viv delivered Bunny.

Bunny was ten when her life was stolen. She and her father had been walking her new puppy when she accidentally dropped the leash. The little dog dashed into the street and Bunny took off after it— right into the path of an oncoming car. Before Bernie even knew what his baby's fate was, he caught the puppy and broke its neck.

Holly remembered the awful funeral, her mother crying continuously for months, and the subsequent move to a different neighborhood where they wouldn't have to look at the street day after day where the accident had happened.

While their parents grieved, Linc grew up. By the time Bernie and Viv remembered they had two other children, Linc had enlisted in the marines and was sent to Vietnam. One month before the war officially ended, Linc was killed by a lone sniper.

Bernie had never fully forgiven himself for failing to prevent Bunny's accident, and then he blamed himself for Linc's enlisting the way he did. Instead of withdrawing into grief once more, though, he focused all his love and attention on the one child he had left—Holly. And she had thrown that love back in his face rather than trust him to be supportive.

Her parents were already waiting for her when she pulled the rental car into their driveway. No sooner did the headlights shine into the living room window than the front door opened and they hurried out to greet their little girl. Holly always wondered how two people with their excessive girth managed to have so much energy. Other than their blond heads turning silver, the years had barely taken a toll on them.

Viv gave Holly the thirty seconds it took to exchange hugs before demanding, "Okay, what is it?"

Holly smiled and kissed her mother's plump cheek. "You know, I think this is the first time in years you didn't greet me with food in your hand."

"She left it in the oven to keep warm," Bernie assured her with a laugh as they walked arm and arm into the house. "There's sauerbraten and noodles and some apple strudel for dessert."

Knowing she would have to eat a several-course meal regardless of the hour, Holly had purposely eaten only a salad with Philip.

"You look like you're dieting again, honey," Viv lightly scolded. "You know how unhealthy that is."

"I'm not dieting, Mom. In fact I've gained a few pounds since you last saw me."

Her mother moved away to scrutinize Holly's figure, then shook her head. "Come. Sit. You'll talk in between bites."

"If you don't mind, I think I'd rather say what I came for first. It isn't exactly conducive to digestion."

Although Viv reluctantly agreed to postpone putting food on the kitchen table, they still sat around it, the way they usually did for a family discussion.

Now that the time had come, Holly wasn't sure how to begin, but her father helped.

"Everyone at the restaurant today was talking about our Senator Ziegler and that woman. We don't have time to watch television, but when I heard the two of them went to Dominion, around the same time as you, well, it got me thinking. Did you know them?"

"No," Holly said, having previously decided naming names would be a bad idea, considering her father's hot temper. "But the hearing is what made me realize I should have told you about what happened to me there years ago." She took a deep breath and found her courage. "Before I came home, I had a boyfriend . . . or rather I thought I did."

Viv interrupted. "We figured he must have broken your heart, and, since you hadn't had much experience dating, it sent you into a tailspin."

Nodding, Bernie added, "You had called us about him. Said you were in love. Was it Ziegler? No. I'd have remembered that."

Holly held up her hand. "The name isn't important anymore. What—"

"Jim," Bernie guessed. "John? That doesn't sound right either."

"Jerry," Viv supplied quietly. "I remember she said his name was Jerry, and he was a football player. Tell us what happened, honey."

Holly glanced from one to the other and saw nothing but pure love and compassion ready to be offered, no matter what she had to say. In that moment, the nightmare began to unravel. She told them of her deep feelings for the young man, without confirming her mother's recollections about his identity, and of the plans she had had for their future. When she described the game and her morning discovery, they were as shocked as she had been at the time.

"*What?* How the hell did *that* happen?" Bernie exclaimed, his short fuse instantly igniting.

"It was a fraternity prank," Holly replied, unable to hide the bewilderment the truth still made her feel. "It seems that my beloved told his fraternity brothers that I wouldn't come across for anything short of a diamond ring, and one of them bet him that he could change my mind with one kiss. The whole group took part in coming up with a way to trick me into giving the challenger a fair advantage, then bets were placed on the outcome."

She couldn't meet her parents' eyes, as she said, "I had had a few drinks, and I guess I was a little disoriented. I didn't notice the difference in the dark. When I first woke up the next morning, I had no idea who was in my bed, but then I remembered having met him at the fraternity. I kept thinking I was still asleep and having a nightmare. But then my dear boyfriend was banging on the door and shouting obscenities. I was too numb to think clearly. I let him in.

"He went completely berserk when he realized what had happened, but it was *me* he was furious with, not his so-called brother. He hit me and knocked me down. He called me ugly names and said I owed him while he tore off my robe. I tried pleading with him, then with his friend."

Holly closed her eyes and swallowed hard several times before she could continue. "I had the insane notion that, even though we were virtually strangers, our night together might have meant something and he'd help me. Instead, he was getting aroused watching. When his buddy had a little trouble getting his pants open and holding me down at the same time, he gave him a hand."

"Dear God," Viv whispered. "Did they—"

"Yes. Both of them. I know they hurt me . . . because of the blood . . . but I didn't feel a thing. I couldn't."

Bernie's fist slammed the table top. "*Bastards!* Son-of-a-bitching bastards." He got up, stormed across the room, and pounded the wall. "I'll kill them. I'll cut their fucking nuts off!" His face was crimson as he strode back and looked down at Holly. "You give me their names. I'll take care of them."

"No, Pop," she countered as she rose. "I knew that's how you'd react, but I didn't come here for that. I came for your forgiveness."

"Forgiveness?" Viv asked and got up to join them. "I could never forgive them, whoever they are."

"Not the men, Mom. Me. I ran home to hide, but rather than explain, I treated the two of you like dirt."

Viv embraced Holly and squeezed her tight. "Oh,

honey, we always knew there had to be a good reason, but never in a million years would we have imagined anything so horrible."

Bernie enveloped the both of them in his big arms, and for a moment they were all silent. Then Viv sniffled and Holly felt her mother's chest tremble as she tried not to cry aloud.

Suddenly the anguish broke through Holly's wall of stoicism and the tears that had not come forth at the time trickled down her cheeks.

Minutes passed before they could all dry their eyes and sit back down at the table. Then her father said the kindest words he could.

"I understand why it took you so long to talk about this. Time doesn't always lessen the horror, or the need for revenge. I am completely serious now, baby. If you want me to punish them for you, I'd take a great amount of pleasure in it."

Holly shook her head. "Doing anything now could backfire—on *all* of us. I didn't have the nerve to report the rape that morning like I should have. I would have had to admit how stupid and vulnerable I was to begin with. The whole situation seemed too unbelievable for words. I guess I was in a state of shock afterward, but somehow I managed to get cleaned up and went to class, as if nothing unusual had happened.

"By that afternoon, half the campus was gossiping about the bet, and how the two guys had settled it by sharing me in a wild ménage à trois. Even one of my professors believed what was being said and made a pass at me. Reporting it after that would have sounded like I was only trying to save my damaged reputation. Instead, I crawled home to the two of you."

They talked well into the night, and eventually

Holly had to have "a little something" to eat before they could all retire.

She didn't know if it was the power of April's suggestion or if the confession really had made a difference, but when she boarded the plane the next morning to return to Washington, she felt considerably lighter in spirit.

Since discovering that she was not alone and sharing her story with loved ones had both helped so much, she felt compelled to consider the comment Erica had made about retribution being part of the healing process. Her father had implied the same thing, but she didn't want him involved.

With that in mind, she took the Jerry Frampton file out of her briefase and opened it. Inside were a number of reports issued over the last ten years from various private investigative agencies, a few computer printouts, and several sheets of typed notes with the initials "R.G." or "B.R." on the bottom.

During the next hour she learned more about Jerry Frampton than she knew about her own father, but only a portion of the information was relevant to her.

Jerry Frampton graduated from Dominion twelve years ago. As a first-round draft choice of the prior season's champion football team, he received an exorbitant bonus and was to be paid one of the highest salaries offered that year. In the third game of the season the ligaments in his right shoulder were torn so badly that even after two operations and a year of recuperation, he was unable to regain the strength in his valuable throwing arm. By the next year he permanently retired from the game.

This much would have been well publicized at the time, but Holly had purposely avoided reading the sports section of the newspaper and closed her ears to any conversation in which his name might have been mentioned.

The year after his formal retirement, Frampton set up a small publishing company in Fort Lauderdale, apparently using the money he had earned in football. Six months later the first issue of *Jock*, a men's magazine devoted primarily to sports articles and photographs of nude women in ludicrous poses, was printed. Within the next five years, circulation of *Jock* skyrocketed until it was competing with *Playboy* on the newsstands.

Holly was aware of what career he had gone into after football, but since that wasn't a magazine she ever needed to look at, she was able to ignore its existence as she did its owner's.

The reports and notes in the file written during the years of his climb up the publishing ladder indicated his handsome face and charisma attracted a kaleidoscopic array of female companions; his showmanship and questionable morals attracted the press.

Despite continuous rumors of lewd behavior, he had never been charged with any offense. He was only made more interesting by the tales of private parties where cocaine was served from a punch bowl and where group sex was said to include at least one animal. Even if every one of the Little Sisters came forward and told their story, it would probably only enhance the wicked reputation that served him so well.

The IRS reports supplied by Bobbi Renquist contained similar information. He was a sleazy character, and undoubtedly guilty of something, yet nothing definite could be turned up against him. Holly's eyes widened at the figure that represented

Frampton's estimated net worth. Her first thought was of how much Earth Guard could accomplish with only a fraction of that amount.

Her second thought was how satisfying it would be to see Jerry Frampton lose it all.

It was the last report by Rachel Greenley that offered some hope of that event coming to pass. A new detective hired by Cheryl had snapped a candid photo of Jerry Frampton in the midst of a heated argument with an ex-con named Mick D'Angelo. The picture was taken on the grounds of Frampton's well-guarded private estate in Boca Raton, Florida. Rachel had used the FBI's resources to confirm and elaborate upon the information the detective uncovered.

After Frampton's football injury, he shared a room in a Miami, Florida, hospital with D'Angelo, a man with a long list of misdemeanors on his official police record. On several occasions afterward, Frampton was observed dining with D'Angelo in the Hon Choi restaurant on Miami's South Beach. The owner, Tommy Li Chen, said that Frampton was a close friend of D'Angelo's, a regular at the establishment.

About the same time that the first issue of *Jock* came out, D'Angelo was arrested on several counts of child abuse and possessing and selling child pornography. One hour after an extremely high bail was set, it was posted by Jerry Frampton. When the case went to court, D'Angelo had the best attorney that dirty money could buy. Charges of child abuse were dropped owing to the withdrawal of the testimony of the minor involved, and D'Angelo ultimately served only one year in prison.

Holly could see how a connection between Jerry Frampton and Mick D'Angelo could be detrimental, but she hadn't an inkling of how she could assist in his downfall, as April had suggested she might. Nevertheless, the idea intrigued her. A full schedule awaited her at the office, but she promised herself at least to call April and find time to listen to what she had to say.

David Wells was batting a thousand that morning. First he had received a call from his police friend with the information he'd requested. Red's name was Rachel Greenley, and a coworker at the FBI disclosed that she was a top agent whose special domain was serial murders. She was also a loner and an alcoholic.

Interesting data, but it didn't give a clue as to why she would be meeting with Donner.

After setting a date to take the officer to a Redskins game, David visited the newspaper's graveyard files to see why the name Philip Sinkiewicz had rung a bell. An hour later, he knew the public facts about the man who had founded Earth Guard, and his lovely associate, Holly Kaufman. Although the lobby represented many environmental concerns, Holly's efforts focused primarily on ridding the planet of garbage.

For the private information, he turned to Christine Crowley, the paper's society columnist and D.C.'s favorite gossip. She was a woman past middle age, whose less than perfect features looked only slightly better with makeup and a fancy silver hairdo—but people didn't court her because of her appearance. Christine knew everything about everybody in the capital, including tidbits that couldn't be printed in her column.

"There's not much to tell," she told him without hesitation. "They've been considered a couple for

years, since his wife's death, and the word is he was
a friend of her family's long before she went to work
for him. Mind you, I said *considered* a couple. As
far as I know, there have never been any weekend
rendezvous in the country, no public kisses, and no
cohabitation. If they're lovers, they're fanatically private about it."

"Good."

"Hold on there, Romeo. Do I detect the rum-
blings of male hormones? Let me save you some
time and energy. Some powerful men have tried to
storm that pretty fortress and wound up slinking
away without winning so much as a smile from her.
From all reports, Philip Sinkiewicz is the only man
with whom she conducts more than business and,
as I said, no one can confirm exactly how much
more that actually is."

David smiled as he felt himself automatically rising to a new challenge. "Then there's no problem,
because my interest in her is strictly business. She
knows something that I don't, and I want to find
out what that is."

Christine smirked at him. "Right. I'll pretend to
believe you're not interested in doing anything with
her but talking, if you'll promise to keep me posted."

"Will do," David said with a wink and returned
to his desk. Now that he knew who the blonde was,
where she worked, and what she was interested in,
it was a simple matter to call her secretary and make
an appointment to interview Ms. Kaufman for an
article on recycling. After that, he could let nature
take its course.

Much to his surprise, Earth Guard's secretary
pitched him his first strike. After he asked for the
interview, she put him on hold to check the calendar. It took so long, David instictively knew that the

woman was discussing him with her boss, and that the lady was leery of what he really wanted. His assumption was proved accurate when the secretary informed him that Ms. Kaufman's schedule was full for the next week, but that he could get any information he needed for his article from Mr. Sinkiewicz. Insisting that he preferred to speak to the woman who was considered an expert on the subject got him nowhere with the stiffly polite secretary.

He got the message. Ms. Kaufman was not available. And if she refused to talk to him—as a reporter—about her favorite project, she certainly wasn't going to readily confide in him about why she met with those other women at the hotel.

David acknowledged that standard approaches weren't going to work this time. What he needed was a side door to slip through. He called Christine and asked if she knew of any social functions that Holly Kaufman would be expected to attend.

"As a matter of fact, there's a major benefit Saturday night. Plenty of politicians and industrialists; lots of guilt combined with an excess of money. There's no way she or Sinkiewicz would miss that kind of opportunity to schmooz."

David knew he couldn't afford to miss such an opportunity either. "What would it take to get seated at her table?"

"Invitations are available to anyone willing to part with the minimum thousand-dollar donation, but I think I could arrange to have that waived for a member of the press. As to the seating, I might have to twist an arm or two."

"Name your price."

Laughing, Christine said, "I just want to be there when the princess of garbage puts you out with the rest of the trash."

"Oh, ye of little faith. You've got a deal."

Christine told him when and where to pick her up. "By the way, it's black tie, and I expect a corsage!"

Holly had hoped to get out of the office without having to give Philip any explanation of her evening's plans. Originally, she had intended to have him come to her apartment for a romantic candlelight dinner, but her brief conversation with April that afternoon had forced her to alter the plan. The only time the psychologist could give her was this evening, since she had to leave town tomorrow, and she didn't want to discuss the matter over the phone.

Considering the odd looks Philip had been giving her all day, she should have known he wouldn't be that easy to avoid. The second after she closed the clasp on her briefcase, he appeared in her doorway with an optimistic grin.

"Ready to go? I know we didn't make plans to go out tonight, but if you'd like, we could try that Thai restaurant that just opened."

"I'm sorry, I can't." She got as close to the truth as she could. "A friend of mine from college called me this afternoon. She's in town for the night and I promised to meet her for dinner."

His smiled faltered. "I always enjoy meeting your friends. I'd be glad to treat both of you."

She stood up to leave, but he remained in her path. His eyes held the same pleading expression she had noticed yesterday when she told him she was going home to see her parents. "That's sweet, but it wouldn't be fair. We'd bore you to tears with all our girl-talk. But I do have something I want to discuss with you . . . in private. Could I come by your house later?"

"Of course," he said, stepping aside for her to pass, but his smile hadn't returned.

Hoping to allay his concern, she kissed his cheek and promised, "I won't be too late." She felt him staring at her as she walked away and reassured herself that the plans she had for this evening would soon restore his faith in her.

As soon as she and April were settled in the restaurant Holly had suggested, April asked, "Did you hear the closing statements of the Senate hearing today?"

"No, I didn't have a minute to spare."

April sighed. "It wasn't good. They've torn Cheryl apart like the proverbial pack of hungry wolves. She got confused a few times and reacted emotionally more often than logically—not that I can blame her." She shook her head as she straightened her silverware into precise parallel lines. "I shouldn't have let her do this. She doesn't have the strength."

Holly felt the woman's sadness as if it was palpable. "I got the impression Cheryl volunteered."

"Yes, but I could have stopped her. I should have guessed how that committee might react. It's my responsibility to know things like that."

The waitress came to take their order before Holly could think of anything consoling to say. By the time she left them alone again, April seemed to have shed her self-doubt.

"So tell me, Holly, what did you think of our research on Frampton?"

"I was impressed with the quality and quantity," she replied formally. "It was very . . . thorough."

"And?"

Holly met April's steady gaze. "And disgusting."

"And?"

Holly hesitated a second, then admitted, "And I'm intrigued by what you said about retribution."

April's soft smile was a reward for honesty. "Very good."

"I don't see how I could help, though. It looks to me like this would fall under Rachel's area."

April nodded. "It could, but she's having some trouble at work, and calling attention to herself by investigating something with so little to go on could make matters worse. I had a different approach in mind, one that you might be equipped to handle better than the rest of us."

"I'm willing to hear what you have in mind," Holly answered cautiously.

Delivery of their drinks and salads delayed April's explanation a moment, during which Holly's curiosity increased.

"No law enforcement agency has the time or manpower to follow up on information as sketchy as ours. Nor do we want to involve a private detective whose only interest in the case would be monetary payment. If he was unscrupulous, he could be bribed to bury the evidence. Even if he was law-abiding, he might reveal who hired him, which could put us in a difficult position. There are simply too many risks. What we need is someone who would look under every rock to get to the truth. Someone who would rather discover a shocking secret than a bag of gold."

Holly leaned forward. "You're talking about a reporter, aren't you?"

April gave her another approving smile. "Right. A hungry, aggressive investigative reporter who would snap up our bait and go fishing on his own if he smelled a possible exposé about a celebrity."

"I can see how that would work, but where would I fit in?"

"If I'm not mistaken, as a lobbyist, you've had to deal with the press on a regular basis."

Holly smiled. "Reporters provide our best and cheapest advertising. Dealing with them is an absolute necessity."

"That's what I thought," April said with a wink. "My idea is this. You could choose a reporter who would meet all the requirements I mentioned and anonymously pass the file on to that person. The ideal scenario would be for you to select someone you're already friendly with or could get close to, so that you can encourage them to take the lead, then follow their progress through to the end. It would almost be like doing the investigation yourself. I believe you'd find it very satisfying."

Holly realized she was about to make another impulsive decision, but it didn't worry her as it normally would. In fact, it felt rather good to be taking action without fretting over it for days first. "All right. I'll see what I can do."

"Wonderful. You won't be sorry. I don't know if you're familiar with him, but Erica gave me the name of a *Washington Times* reporter who's been very persistent about getting an interview with her."

"A *Washington Times* reporter?" Holly asked warily. "By any chance, is his name David Wells?"

April nodded. "Yes. That's the man. Do you know him?"

"No, not really." Holly's brows narrowed in thought as she recalled the scene at the airport. "He called my office today for an interview, but Evelyn—our secretary—had the feeling there was more to it. She has a little test she uses when she's not sure if a man is truly interested in Earth Guard or just trying to get to me. I know that sounds a bit egotistical, but I've had a few problems with men. It seems the more men I turn away, the more of them approach me."

April laughed. "I'm not discounting your feminine appeal, but it does sound as though you've become a bit of a challenge to the collective male ego."

Holly shrugged. "I wonder how many of them would still be challenged if I hadn't lost a ton of weight since college or traded my thick glasses for contacts."

"If the changes make you feel better about yourself, that's all that matters. A poor self-image is one of the common problems a woman faces after rape. You must constantly remind yourself that you're a beautiful person. *They* were the ugly ones."

Holly gave her a small smile. She had read that in a book about abused women a long time ago. That book was as close to professional help as she had ever gotten.

After a thoughtful pause, April said, "Unless you have someone better in mind, this David Wells could be the right man for the job with Frampton. You should check out his reputation first, but if he's honest and hungry, he might work out very well. If you're right about his attraction to you, half your mission would be accomplished."

Holly frowned and inched back in her seat. "I don't know."

"I'm not suggesting you have an affair with the man. Just don't push him away so fast. Since he came to you first, he'd have no reason to suspect you of using him. Yet by becoming *acquaintances*, you could easily follow his progress after you anonymously pass him the file."

April made it sound so simple, Holly couldn't

come up with any serious objection and agreed to ask around about him the next day.

"Now, I hope you don't mind my saying this, but I get the impression you feel more comfortable with me today than you did yesterday. I am a psychologist, Holly, but I'd also like to be your friend. If you want to talk, I'll listen. If you want my help, just ask."

April's way of offering without pushing allowed Holly the freedom to maintain her privacy. But the doctor's kind smile and compassionate expression made Holly want to confide in her. After opening up to her parents, she found talking to April extremely easy.

Over dinner she told her new friend of the experience that changed her life. A few subtle questions from April had her relating her resulting problems since then.

Holly was terrified of the dark.

Someone touching her unexpectedly caused her an unnatural fright.

She had no desire to have sex and couldn't sleep unless she was alone in her bedroom with the door locked and a light on.

"As to your sleeping difficulty, I'll be glad to write you a prescription for something. There are times when a crutch is totally acceptable. It doesn't mean you're a weak person, just sensible enough to know when you need help."

"Thank you, but I'd rather not start with drugs, even for a good reason. My mother has had some problems with tranquilizers in the past, and I heard that kind of dependency can be hereditary."

Holly then told April about her relationship with Philip and how understanding he was about her idiosyncracies.

"I'd say an explanation from you is long overdue," April advised. "But be very careful not to name names or let him know what you're doing about Frampton. You may not think he's like your father because he doesn't display a bad temper, but it still sounds like he's very protective of you. Keep that in mind when you talk to him. And be aware that he might not be so understanding if you suddenly strike up a friendship with Wells or some other male reporter."

Holly promised to call April every Friday to update her or just chat.

"I have one last bit of professional advice," April said before they parted. "If you decide to use Wells, you might consider him practice for coming to terms with other men. You definitely could use a little more exposure to the opposite sex than just Philip and your father."

April's warnings about Philip stayed with Holly as she drove to his house in Georgetown. She had been considering telling him everything, including what the Little Sister Society was up to, but she knew April was right. Philip could not be told the whole truth, for his own good.

Philip greeted her at his front door as if he hadn't seen her in years. He crushed her to him in an embrace so tight she could barely breathe.

She resisted as mildly as possible. "Philip *please*. What will your neighbors think?"

"They'll think I'm a very lucky man," he said, relaxing his hold, then pushing the door closed behind her. "Wine or tea?"

"A very small glass of white wine would be fine," Holly said as she took her usual place on the couch.

A few minutes later he returned with two glasses and sat down next to her. His eyes never left her as they both took a drink and set their glasses on the coffee table. "How was dinner?"

"Very nice. I'm sorry—"

"Tch-tch. There's no need for an apology. I shouldn't have tried to muscle my way in on you."

Holly took his hands in hers. "Philip, I know you think I've been . . . behaving strangely—"

"It's all right, darling. I understand."

Holly shook her head. "No. I need to explain."

He squeezed her hands. "First, I have a confession to make that might save you any explanation. Please don't be angry with me. I was worried, so I called Bernie."

Holly's chin lifted defiantly. "You called my father?"

Philip shrugged and lowered his eyes. "I love you, Holly. I thought something was wrong and you were keeping it from me. I only wanted to find a way to help."

"He told you what I talked to them about?"

"Yes. And I'm absolutely sick about it."

Holly didn't care for the fact that Philip had gone behind her back for information or that her father would betray her confidence. Her voice was tight with displeasure as she spoke. "I was planning to explain everything tonight."

"Don't you think you should have explained years ago?" he admonished testily. "All this time, I thought I was an inadequate lover."

Guilt diluted her annoyance.

"Oh, Philip, no. I never wanted you to think that. I told you I was the problem, not you."

He stroked her cheek and softened his voice. "I know, but I always wondered if you were just trying to spare my feelings."

Holly leaned toward him and lightly touched her lips to his. "Please forgive me."

He gave her a brief kiss in return. "You know I'd forgive you anything. If you want to talk about it, we can."

"Actually, I'm a little relieved that I don't have to repeat it again."

"Who were they?" he asked abruptly.

Holly blinked at the harsh tone of his voice, then shook her head. "I'd rather not say. It isn't important anymore."

Philip frowned, but let it drop. "This also explains why you've changed the subject every time the Ziegler hearing came up this week."

Holly prevented herself from visibly reacting and cautiously asked, "Why do you say that?"

"The similarities are rather obvious—like you, Cheryl Wallace was a young co-ed brutally raped because of a man she trusted, he and his friends went unpunished while she suffered more abuse and held the secret inside for more than a decade. The fact that her assault also occurred at Dominion must be upsetting to you as well. Unfortunately, it looks like Ziegler is still going to go unpunished."

"Then you believe Cheryl Wallace's story?"

"Absolutely. But I'm not on the Senate committee."

"Too bad. She really could have used a friend like you on her side. But at least I have you on mine. Thank you for believeing in me . . . and her." Her arms circled his neck and she gave him a more sensual kiss. She knew that years of anticipating her rejection kept him from immediately responding.

"I had more planned for this evening than just talking. I had wanted to start with a romantic dinner, but my friend's schedule fixed that. And now that you and my father have eliminated the need for a lengthy explanation, the only part of the plan left is the seduction." She saw Philip's reaction in his eyes, yet he made no move toward her. "I've done a lot of soul searching recently and I believe I've come to terms with what happened. I'm hoping it will make a difference between us."

Philip swallowed hard. "It's been a very long time, Holly. I don't want to misunderstand what you're saying."

Holly lowered her eyes. "I'm— I'm asking you to make love to me— If you want to, that is."

Still prepared for rejection, Philip's kiss was hesitant, until her lips parted invitingly for him. His hands shook as they spanned her waist then eased up her back.

Holly ended the kiss and whispered, "Let's go into the bedroom."

She felt the old fear and ordered it away. This was Philip, she reminded herself. A wonderful, sweet man who deserved her love. She turned the light on next to the bed, then turned her back to him as they both began to undress.

The suggestion of what they were about to do had him partially ready. Watching her remove her skirt and blouse took him the rest of the way. He folded back the bedding and got under the sheet while she removed her hose and underpants from beneath her full slip.

She turned toward him, hoping he'd not ask for more.

Reading the uncertain look in her eyes, he patted the spot on the bed next to him. "It's all right, honey. You don't have to do any more than you're ready to." He reached toward the lamp, but she stopped him before he could turn it off.

"Please leave it on. You know I'm uncomfortable in the dark."

"I've never known why. Is that their fault, too?" he asked, easing her down next to him. She nodded. "I don't mind the light. It lets me see how beautiful you are."

Holly tried to relax as he kissed her. She ordered herself to enjoy the feel of his hands kneading her breasts and his male body pressing insistently against hers. But when his fingers slipped between her thighs, her muscles clenched tight before she could prevent it.

Even if he hadn't noticed her reaction, the tight, dry flesh he encountered would have alerted him to her unaroused state. "They're here, aren't they?" Philip said as he rolled onto his back.

She blinked at him, not comprehending his words or why he had stopped touching her.

"The bastards that raped you. They're here, in this bed with us. That's why you can't relax—why we can't have a normal relationship."

She raised herself on her elbow and turned his face to hers. "I *want* to do this, Philip. Don't you see? I want you to make me forget what they did."

He hugged her to him. "This isn't the way. I would do anything for you, honey, but I'd only hurt you if I went further. Your body doesn't want mine." He kissed her nose. "It is gratifying, however, to know that your mind is willing. Perhaps it's only a matter of time before the rest of you gets accustomed to the idea as well."

Holly's thoughts wandered to something April had told her. *As long as your attackers go unpunished, you'll always feel like a victim. Once you take action against them, they'll no longer have any power over you.* Philip could not wipe all the memories away any more than talking about her experience had. She had to try the one course left open to her. Retribution.

Philip took a deep, ragged breath, and renewed guilt washed over her for tempting him into the condition he was now in. She placed her hand on his lower stomach. "Just because my body isn't accommodating, doesn't mean you—"

He stopped her hand from touching him more intimately. "Until you can find pleasure in our being together, I would rather do without also." He waited until she relaxed in his arms. "Will you stay tonight?"

She immediately tensed again. "I can't. I have an early appointment and I didn't bring a change of clothes or a toothbrush, or—"

"You don't need an excuse. I understand. Just let me hold you for a while before you go."

Holly laid her head on his shoulder. "Sometimes I wonder why you put up with me."

Philip kissed the top of her head. "You're all I have, honey. I'd do anything for you."

6

For four days, the news had been filled with video clips from the Senate committee hearing, opinions from women's groups as well as the general citizenry, and speculation about the names of the other men Cheryl Wallace claimed participated in her gang rape.

The top story on the eleven o'clock news Thursday night was the confirmation of Timothy Ziegler's appointment to the position of secretary of housing and urban development.

The President, who was expected to attend the private celebration for Ziegler in the Kessler Hotel the next evening, issued a statement to the media. "The Senate committee members deemed Miss Wallace's testimony insufficiently supported by facts to negatively affect their decision."

Stricken with a case of flu, Mrs. Ziegler would not be able to fly in for the party, but she was relieved that the hearing had ended so satisfactorily for her husband. She had never doubted him for a minute.

Senator Ziegler's sterling reputation remained intact . . . publicly.

Privately, the truth was known, and those knowledgeable people had to find ways of coping with the unjust decision. Though the individual reactions ranged from resentment to fury, only one person determined to give Ziegler the party that he truly deserved.

That person counted on the probability that Ziegler would be feeling very self-assured by the decision, perhaps even a bit indestructible. Such a feeling could cause him to use poor judgment in the hours before his victory celebration. Because of the news, the time and place were easily chosen. Between six and seven o'clock, Ziegler would undoubtedly be in his hotel room getting ready for his big evening.

All that was needed to implement justice was already at hand or could be easily purchased before then.

It began with a phone call from the crowded lobby of the Kessler Hotel.

"Hello?"

"Is this the new HUD secretary, Timothy Ziegler?"

With a smile in his voice, he answered, "Why, yes, it is. Who's this?"

"Someone who knows more about your past than what came out in the hearing." Knowing how protective Ziegler had been about his wife's privacy during interviews throughout the hearing, the caller added, "If you hang up, the next call I make is to your wife." The gamble paid off. Ziegler stayed on the line.

"I can't imagine what you're referring to, but if you're looking to blackmail me about something, you must not be aware of my bank balance."

"I don't want your money, only a little conversation. Are you alone?"

Ziegler frowned at the woman impatiently waiting for him to get off the phone. She had arrived only a moment ago, but it wouldn't do for anyone to know she was there. "Yes, but I'm due downstairs soon. Can't this wait?"

"No, it can't, and it won't take that long. What's your room number?" Ziegler muttered directions and soon his caller was ascending one of the lobby elevators and walking down the empty hallway toward his suite. A beige canvas tote bag concealed a number of essentials, including latex gloves, which were donned just before the caller knocked.

As soon as Ziegler opened the door, his visitor pulled a gun out of the bag and motioned him back into the room.

Ziegler's gaze briefly darted to the closed bedroom door. Now he was glad she had insisted on waiting. Surely she would be curious enough to peek out, then call security.

Keeping a wary eye on the deadly weapon pointed at his chest, he said, "I thought you wanted to talk."

"I do. This will insure that you'll be attentive. And obedient. Go to the bar and pour yourself a glass of water, then back away." After he did as he was instructed, his visitor removed from the bag a plastic pill container partially filled with blue powder. The contents were then emptied into the water, and stirred with a swizzle stick. "Now, drink it."

"No, thank you. I don't indulge."

Although the senator tried to sound sarcastic, the perspiration dotting his forehead and upper lip revealed his fear. "It's only a truth inducer," the visitor lied. "It will make you more cooperative while we talk. I assure you it will be completely worn off in time for you to go to your party."

"I don't need a drug to tell you the truth. Ask me whatever you want."

The visitor's finger moved on the trigger of the gun. "You can drink it or you can die. Note how steady my hand is. I have no qualms about shooting you, and I'm absolutely certain I could get away from here before anyone would come to investigate."

Tim watched the finger slowly tighten on the trigger, pulling it back a fraction of an inch closer to the grip. His gaze darted to the eyes of his visitor and the raw hatred he saw there convinced him he was about to die. "All right. I'll drink it."

Only when he lifted the glass to his mouth and drained it did the visitor allow the trigger to ease back into a somewhat less threatening position.

Fear clouded Tim's thought processes as he tried to imagine what this was about. The visitor looked slightly familiar, though he couldn't think why. "What is it you want me to talk about?"

"I'll tell you in due time, but first I would suggest you choose a comfortable seat. The medication could make you a little dizzy."

Tim sat down, but the other remained standing with the gun pointed at him.

"We'll give the drug ten minutes. You may want to use the time to contemplate your sins."

When the allotted time passed, the visitor said, "Let's begin with something simple. Where did you go to college?"

Tim arched an eyebrow. "After the past week, most of the country knows the answer to that."

"Cut the sarcasm. Just answer the question. I assure you they'll get harder as we go along."

"Dominion University."

"Did you date Cheryl Wallace?"

Tim frowned, but answered in the affirmative. When asked if he had set her up to be raped, however, he denied it as vehemently as he had during the hearing and insisted she had been a willing participant.

As the sedative overdose flooded Ziegler's system, he was questioned about details of his relationship with Cheryl, but he stuck to his public story. When he was asked about other women he had dated, he continued to deny that he had ever forced himself on a woman. Even when his inquisitor grew furious and waved the gun in his face, he refused to admit he had ever abused a woman in any manner. He fought the effects of the drug as long as he could, but within half an hour, he began losing the battle.

When he was barely able to hold up his head and his words became so slurred they were unintelligible, he was told who his visitor was and why he was about to be punished.

Comprehension flickered in Ziegler's eyes, and he thought to call out to the woman in the bedroom, but he passed out before he could put a voice to the thought.

Ziegler's body was adjusted so that he was slouched down in the armchair with his legs stretched out in front of him. It took a little more effort to tug his slacks and briefs down his legs.

The visitor donned a vinyl rain poncho, and removed another item from the tote before realizing what had been forgotten. Luckily, a suitable tool was stored in the bar.

Using the ice tongs to raise the male flesh from Ziegler's body without risking any fingerprints, the visitor switched on the battery-operated carving knife. With the double serrated blades swaying back and forth, justice was swiftly delivered.

As Ziegler's life blood pumped from his body, the severed penis was stuffed into his mouth and a bloody testicle placed over each eye. In case that message wasn't clear enough, a white cardboard sign was propped on his chest. Black stick-on letters formed the words:

Just punishment for a rapist

At nine-fifteen P.M., Rachel Greenley received a phone call from her supervisor, Senior Agent Matt LaRue, informing her of a new assignment. She was to head up the team investigating the murder of Timothy Ziegler.

"Naturally, this is to remain confidential for the time being. I need you to meet me at the Kessler Hotel as soon as you can get here," Matt said. "And Rachel, I need you clearheaded."

"No problem, sir. I'm sober as the proverbial judge." Rachel hung up the phone before allowing herself to react. The incredible irony of it was too beautiful not to share. Before she left her apartment, she made two phone calls, but neither of her friends was where she was supposed to be.

Philip's call woke Holly Saturday morning long before her alarm went off. "Did you hear the news?" he asked instead of greeting her. A hoarse mumble was her answer. "Senator Ziegler was murdered last night."

"*What?*" Holly drew herself upright in bed.

"Someone killed the new HUD secretary, although details haven't been released yet. A secret service agent was first on the scene and apparently they were able to keep it under wraps most of the night. Can you imagine? While guests were celebrating his appointment downstairs, he was getting stiff up in his room."

"Philip! That's not funny."

"I know. It just struck me as an extreme case of poetic justice that right after his colleagues saw fit to reward him in spite of everything they'd heard, he's now in the hands of the one judge who knows the truth."

Holly rubbed her eyes, uncertain why Philip thought she needed to be awakened by such morbid news, or why he sounded so satisfied by it. "I'm still half asleep, Philip, but I'll turn on the news as soon as I get out of the shower."

"I thought perhaps you'd like me to take you out to breakfast."

"Thanks, but I'll have to pass. I have an appointment to get my hair done for the benefit dinner tonight."

"All right. I'll see you later then. Is six-thirty good for me to pick you up?"

"Fine." As Holly hung up, she thought it was odd of Philip to ask her out to breakfast when they would be going out that evening.

It wasn't until she was standing under the hot spray that the purpose of Philip's call truly sunk in. *Timothy Ziegler had been murdered!* One of the men featured in the nightmare that had disrupted her sleep last night was now dead and would soon be buried. Questions of how and why popped into her head, but Philip had said details hadn't been released.

So why had he called so early? Just to let her know that a man who had gotten away with a crime would no longer be freely walking the earth? Or was

it more than that? Could Philip have guessed the
connection between her and Ziegler? What if he *had*
looked at the list of names in her briefcase the other
day, then talked to her father, and somehow pieced
it all together?

That was incredibly farfetched. If Philip had seen
Ziegler's name, he would have mentioned it by now,
and she hadn't given her parents any names. Besides
that, Bernie was a strong supporter of his state senator. He had even spent some time talking to Ziegler
at a rally once. No, there was no way Philip could
have concluded that she had any personal interest
in Ziegler's fate, other than empathizing with
Cheryl Wallace.

As soon as she had the thought, she realized that
had to be it. The other night Philip had mentioned
the similarities between Cheryl's plight and her
own. He must have assumed she'd be pleased that
Tim Ziegler had received a sort of divine retribution.

Timothy Ziegler had been a loathsome slug, but
even in her deepest depression, Holly hadn't wished
him dead.

But someone had. Was it a robber? A person who
held a personal or political grudge against him?

The first face that appeared in her mind was
Cheryl Wallace's, followed by Bobbi Renquist's.
Though April had also been used by Tim, she didn't
seem nearly as hostile as the others, but since she
was the one who had formed the group and held it
together all these years, perhaps beneath her cool
exterior seethed the most hatred of all.

Erica Donner and Rachel Greenley had not been
on Tim's dance card, but they both radiated a chill-
ing contempt for men in general. Rachel had actually spoken of violence, and Erica seemed fully
capable of committing murder—as Bobbi had im-

plied—without so much as an increase in her pulse rate, if she had one at all. On top of that, the murder had occurred in Erica's hotel.

Then again, they all had sound reasons for their unusual personalities . . . as sound as the reasons for her own eccentricities. She had at least as strong a motive as any of them for hating Tim Ziegler, but she would never have killed him, so why should she suspect the other women?

Considering what she knew about Ziegler, it was unlikely that he was as clean-cut as the press made him out to be. Surely he'd made enemies in the past other than the Little Sister Society, and one of them had simply caught up to him.

Or it was a robbery gone bad, as she first guessed.

The news report Holly watched before she left her apartment revealed only that the senator had been killed in his hotel room prior to his celebration party, and that there was no sign of forced entry. It seemed very curious that the method of murder had been carefully withheld.

The media had been unable to reach Mrs. Ziegler for a statement.

Although Holly may have despised Ziegler, she couldn't help but care about his wife and children. Because of his public position and recent television exposure, they would not be granted the privacy normally afforded to the grieving.

When she returned to her apartment after her hair appointment and a stop at Evelyn's favorite clothing store, Holly received the second bewildering call of the day.

"Please come to room four-thirteen at your earliest convenience. I suggest you take the stairs to avoid bein' noticed."

Holly heard the phone disconnect before she fully

comprehended the politely phrased order. The Memphis accent identified the caller as Erica Donner. Thus, it would be logical that the room referred to was in the Kessler Hotel. But why the mystery? Or the urgency? The answer had to have something to do with Tim Ziegler's murder. Holly's curiosity was sufficiently aroused for her to drive into town.

As soon as she entered the hotel, she understood Erica's suggestion about the stairs. The lobby was packed with people—police, reporters, photographers, and onlookers. She couldn't have reached the bank of elevators without elbowing her way through the crowd.

She climbed the four flights of stairs so quickly, she had to pause to catch her breath upon exiting the stairwell. Because of the secretive way Erica had called her, Holly found herself making sure there were no other guests in the hallway before knocking on the door of Room 413. Erica admitted her immediately.

Sitting on the edge of the bed was a woman dressed in a tailored red suit and a red hat with a veil that partially hid her eyes and nose. As Holly waited for an introduction, the woman smiled seductively and crossed her legs.

"I see you're not wearing black either," the woman said in a husky voice.

Holly looked down at her own purple silk blouse and white skirt, but was thinking about where she'd heard that voice before.

"Pay Bobbi no mind," Erica said, sitting down in one chair and motioning for Holly to take the other.

"Bobbi?" Holly's surprise was evident. "I'm sorry. I didn't recognize you."

"It's Roberta actually, and that's quite all right. Nothing could bring me down today. In fact, this just might be the most *up* day I've had in thirteen years. Don't you think my wearing red is symbolic Holly?"

Holly had no idea what to think, but Erica spared her from saying as much.

"It was good of you to join us on such short notice. Y'all undoubtedly heard the news about Timothy Ziegler. Well, as fate would have it, Rachel has been assigned to head up the team of agents investigating the murder. She paid me a visit a while ago and asked me to pass some advice on to the two of you."

"Advice?" Holly grew more tense by the second.

Erica nodded. "Yes. She strongly recommended that each of us make sure we have an airtight alibi for last evenin' between the hours of six and eight, documented if at all possible."

Holly glanced at Bobbi, but she wasn't giving away any hints.

"April and Cheryl both left town before the murder took place, but Rachel said she'd be speakin' to each of them about this anyway. She insisted it was only a precaution. But take it from me, bein' at the center of a homicide investigation can be terribly disruptin' to one's schedule." For Holly's sake, she elaborated further. "If anyone was clever or nosy enough to discover our little secret, we would be prime suspects. You see, the manner in which he was . . . *executed* suggests the killer's motive.

"Our late friend Timothy Ziegler wasn't simply murdered, he was—Oh, my, there just isn't a delicate way to put this. He bled to death after he was castrated. No, that's not technically accurate, since castration is the removal of the testicles. Those *were* removed, mind you—but his, uh, shaft, was also sliced off and—stuck in his mouth, like a little cigar.

Of course, that information hasn't been released to the public as yet, and Rachel's going to do her best to keep it that way as long as possible."

Erica closed her eyes and gave a small shudder as a testimony to her delicate sensibilities, but Holly thought she looked like she was fighting the urge to snicker over the gruesome picture she described.

Bobbi, or rather Roberta, had no such ladylike restraints. She burst out laughing.

Remembering Philip's bad joke, Holly wondered if a case of black humor was spreading around her. "I don't mean to question Rachel's professional advice, but surely it would take a very strong man to do that to someone Ziegler's size. No one our size could feasibly overpower him." It crossed her mind that Rachel might accomplish it, however.

"Not normally," Erica explained. "But Rachel said the preliminary lab report showed his system contained enough Valium to knock out a horse. The only question was how it got into his body. He didn't have a prescription for it. But, like half the population in the country, all of us do."

"Not me," Holly denied, recalling April's generous offer to write her a prescription.

"Oh, that's right," Roberta said with a sneer. "You don't like being out of control. But I'll bet someone you know has a prescription that you could tap if you really wanted to."

Holly wanted to deny that as well, but the truth was she knew both Philip and her mother took Valium to help them sleep. "It doesn't matter. Not only am I incapable of butchering a man—no matter how much I hated him—I wasn't anywhere near the hotel last night."

Erica leaned forward. "Can you prove that?"

Holly opened her mouth to back up her claim of

innocence and was stunned to realize she couldn't prove a thing. She had left work at five and stayed home all evening. She couldn't remember seeing any other tenants when she arrived at the apartment building. There had been no phone calls or visitors, not even Philip. She had fallen asleep around eleven o'clock reading a magazine, been awakened by the nightmare, finally fallen back to sleep about four, and Philip had called at six.

All things considered, if someone chose to accuse her of committing a crime, she would have one hell of a time defending herself. A week ago, she had never even heard of the Little Sister Society. Now, a group of virtual strangers could connect her to a murder.

7
_____

By the time she returned to her apartment, Holly realized how ridiculous it was to worry over something so remote. No one had discovered the Little Sister Society in all the years they had been performing their secret operations, and there was no reason someone would learn about them now. There was as much chance of her being accused of robbing a convenience store Friday night as of killing Timothy Ziegler. The burden of proof was not on her, but the courts, and since she had been at home that night, no one could place her at the hotel. Case closed.

The more she pondered it, the more she was convinced that Rachel's drinking was the real problem. It was probably making her paranoid and she wanted to get everyone else as frightened as she was. If anything, *she* was the one who'd better have an alibi. Holly specifically recalled her saying she wanted to castrate Ziegler. Maybe that was what her *advice* to them was really about. Rachel wanted to scare everyone enough to make certain no one repeated what she had said.

Holly even began to wonder if the information Erica had passed on was accurate. There hadn't been a single hint of it in any news coverage she'd heard. More than likely, the whole description of the castration had only been a wishful delusion of Rachel's. And Erica and Bobbi seemed to be taking too great a delight in the details for Holly's peace of mind.

If it had happened that way, though, she could see how Cheryl could instantly become a suspect on the basis of motivation. For her sake, she hoped someone could verify that she'd left the city and stayed away.

As Holly got ready for the benefit dinner, she made up her mind to have nothing further to do with the three of them. Neither the uncomfortable meeting nor Ziegler's death changed her mind about going ahead with the Frampton matter, however. Thoughts of revenge had taken root in her mind and sprouted shoots of anticipation. She would simply limit her communication to April.

Holly made one last check in the full-length mirror. Hair and makeup, perfect; the black silk Japanese-style sheath showed off her figure without being the least bit revealing. Only the rightside slit from ankle to mid-thigh gave a teasing glimpse of black-stockinged flesh. Her lips and fingernails were a brazen shade of crimson, and the only jewelry she wore was the onecarat diamond stud earrings Philip had given her for her birthday several years ago.

Though she normally played down all her natural attributes, dressing up that night was a gift to Philip for his incredible patience. Everyone who was anyone would be at the benefit dinner, and they would all see Philip walk in with a desirable woman on his arm. Even if she couldn't give him the real thing, no one but the two of them would know that.

As she walked into the living room where he awaited her, his fawning reaction assured her she had achieved the proper balance of sensuality and remoteness.

David frowned at his image in the mirror. He hated having to wear a monkey suit, no matter how good he looked in it. Yet his instincts told him it would be worth it tonight. Somehow, before the evening was over, he would begin a connection with the aloof Ms. Kaufman.

Tim Ziegler's hints at a deeper story had taken on monumental proportions the moment David heard about his death. His first thought was that he wouldn't be able to get the names, dates, and other details Tim had promised. The second thought was that the senator may have died because of those details.

If he went with that supposition, it meant Cheryl Wallace or Erica Donner could have been involved in his murder. Which in turn brought up the possibility that the women who met with Donner could know something as well. Questions flitted around in his head like lightning bugs, but there were too many unknowns to guess at answers just yet.

His original plan to openly question Donner or one of the other women to see how they might react was too blatant under the new situation. More subtlety was called for, and subtlety took time. The most efficient route seemed to be to establish a relationship with one of the women and work the story from the inside. After he reached this conclusion, it had taken him two seconds to decide that Holly was his best choice, particularly since he hadn't

been able to get to Donner or Wallace, the FBI and
IRS agents would be too suspicious of his motives,
and he hadn't been able to come up with any identity for the other blonde.

Aside from the obvious, however, he sensed a certain feminine vulnerability in Holly that he was
rather good at homing in on. Following up on
Ziegler's lead could prove to be quite pleasurable,
in fact.

He simply had to remember that the woman
could be a murderess.

Holly and Philip's entrance into the hotel ball-
room where the dinner was being held was noticed
by more than a few people, and their progress
through the room was impeded by greetings and
brief conversations. Keeping her arm linked with
Philip's, Holly was more than satisfied with the
looks of female jealousy and male envy they
received.

However, as they approached their assigned
places at a round table for ten, her composure
slipped. Sitting directly opposite them was the reporter, David Wells. She had only seen him the one
time in the airport restaurant, but his handsome
face, too-blue eyes, and cocky grin were extremely
recognizable.

He and the other gentlemen at the table rose as
Philip held out a chair for her. Wells was appropriately dressed in a black tuxedo, but he struck her
as more the jeans-and-sweater type. Somehow she
knew it wouldn't matter what he was wearing or
what setting he was in; he would be relaxed and in
total control. She wondered if that control would
be shaken if he knew she'd been checking on him
and considering how to tie him to her.

"Hello, again," David said, making certain that his greeting was heard across the wide table and that it encompassed both Philip Sinkiewicz and Holly Kaufman. They each gave him the same kind of noncommittal half-smile that one would give to any total stranger sharing one's dinner table for several hours. He reminded them of their previous encounter. "I mistook you for someone else at the airport the other night. I'm David Wells, *Washington Times* reporter. You might be more familiar with my associate, Christine Crowley, D.C.'s loveliest busybody."

The older woman with the elaborately coiffed silver hair and twinkling eyes smiled at them both, then the others at the table introduced themselves. When Philip identified himself and Holly, David sounded genuinely surprised.

"*You're* Holly Kaufman? I wish I had known that the other day. I've been trying to get an appointment with you. You're one busy lady." Her answer was another meaningless smile. "I'm working on an article about the success of various recycling plans, and I've been told it wouldn't be complete without your input."

"What is it you'd like to know?"

He felt her silky voice reach beneath the table to stroke his lower abdomen, while her eyes met his in challenge. "I hardly think garbage is an appropriate dinner topic for mixed company. What do you say we meet for lunch Monday?" There was no way she could refuse in front of all these people.

"I'm sorry. The first opening I have is Tuesday at four. My office."

She had offered no explanation for not returning his call, then sidestepped his invitation without being impolite. So be it. "Great. I'll be there."

David had observed the way Sinkiewicz straightened in his seat at the mention of lunch. The man clearly suspected his real reason for wanting to meet with Holly, but this time, he could do nothing about it.

His traditional seduction techniques were unavoidably constrained that evening. Conversation was impossible during the before- and after-dinner speeches, and the table was just large enough to prohibit any personal comments. He quietly accused Christine of arranging the seating to increase the odds against his getting to first base with the lady.

On the few occasions her glance slid over his, he had the uncanny feeling it was *he* who was being seduced instead of the other way around. He threw her his best I-want-you-naked-beneath-me look. Nothing. Not even a blush of comprehension.

He settled for watching her—and Philip. The man reminded David of a big puppy dog panting around his mistress's feet hoping for a pat on the head. But he didn't get one. In fact, Holly rarely looked at him, and other than having her hand on his arm when they walked up to the table, there was no further physical contact between them. At one point he saw Philip almost touch her hand to get her attention, but at the last moment his fingers curled back into his palm. Interesting relationship. If it could be called that.

It was inevitable that someone would bring up the Ziegler murder. David only had to wait and watch.

"A friend of a friend, who knows someone at the FBI, said it was probably a woman," a congressman said.

"Maybe Cheryl Wallace decided to make sure he couldn't enjoy his victory," his wife added.

As the speculation continued, David noticed how

Holly lowered her gaze, and the way she slowly lowered her fork onto her half-full plate. She was very cool. If he hadn't been watching so closely, he might not have picked up any change in her at all. Either something she had eaten or the topic of conversation had clearly upset her. When the subject changed a moment later and her shoulders relaxed ever so slightly, he knew it had to be the latter. David's instincts told him she had a strong personal opinion on the matter of Timothy Ziegler, but had purposely squelched it. The way Sinkiewicz glanced at her with concern confirmed that impression.

When the band began to play, David thought his chance had come. She and Philip went out on the dance floor and he and Christine joined them. David smoothly managed to end the dance next to them, but when he suggested they exchange partners, they begged off and departed a few minutes later.

Christine had her laugh, but he wasn't discouraged. He had an appointment to try again in four days.

"Please, Philip, don't be like this. After the other night, I thought you understood."

"I understand why you can't enjoy sex. I understand why you have a fear of the dark. I even understand why you're turning down my proposal of marriage . . . *again*. But I do not understand why I can't stay the night. For Christ's sake, it isn't like it would be very often."

A heartbeat later, he regretted his words. "I'm sorry, honey. I didn't mean to push. I just love you so much and you look so delicious in that dress." She let him embrace her, but said nothing, so he told the truth. "It was that reporter tonight. I hate the way men like that look at you. It's degrading. But then, I don't know why I get so jealous of them. You never look back, do you?"

She smiled up at him and shook her head. "You have my undivided attention. If I could give you more, I would."

He asked for one more kiss at the door, then he was off, to his own empty house and a little blue pill to help him sleep.

Holly took a deep breath as she closed the door behind him. She had hoped her relationship with Philip would get easier now that she was dealing with her problem, but instead, the situation seemed to be growing more tense every day. It was a good thing she had followed April's advice and not confided everything to Philip. He would never understand what she was about to do with David Wells.

Checking out Wells's credentials had been a relatively simple matter of making a few discreet phone calls. He was hungry, aggressive, and scrupulous in his reporting. Personally, he had the morals of a tomcat, but with a decided preference for buxom blondes. When Holly had finished checking him out, she had no doubt he would be back for another try at her. All she had to do was wait for him to make his next move.

She knew she had been right when he showed up at the benefit. Although it could have been another coincidence, attending with Christine Crowley and being seated at the same table with her and Philip had all the earmarks of an arranged meeting. Putting off an appointment with him for one more day had been a reflex on her part, but if her intuition was on target, the more inaccessible she was, the more intrigued he would be. She would let him think his persistence had won her attention.

Assuming he would take the bait about Frampton, she had already determined that she wanted to stay close to him during his investigation. To do that, she would exercise every feminine wile she had ever heard of to keep him dangling.

Considering the fact that she had kept Philip dangling for years, she didn't think Wells could be that much more difficult. To her dismay, the way Philip had behaved tonight, it looked like she would have to exercise a few wiles on him as well.

Tuesday afternoon at exactly four o'clock, David Wells presented himself before Earth Guard's formidable secretary and flashed his most charming smile.

"Oh yes. I'm Evelyn. I spoke to you on the phone. I'm afraid Miss Kaufman is running about an hour behind today. She asked me to make you another appointment."

David raised one eyebrow at the woman who would have made an excellent sorority housemother and wondered if her job description included the ability to lie with a straight face. "No, thank you. I'll wait."

Evelyn was momentarily thrown off by his answer. "It might be more than an hour." She gave up trying to discourage him as she watched him select several pamphlets from her desk, then stretch out in a chair in the small lobby. Holly had not given her instructions about what to do if he didn't go away.

Now that she had gotten a good look at the man her boss had wanted to avoid, she decided not to send him away after all. He was adorable. From his head of unkempt brown curls, past his mischievous little-boy smile, down his lean, casually clad frame, to his sockless feet shod in worn loafers, everything about the man made her want to wrap him up and take him home. And if she had been thirty years younger, she would have. Unfortunately, Holly probably wouldn't even appreciate the snug fit of his slacks.

She knew she should warn Holly, but then her boss might choose to hide in her office all night to avoid the man. Holly really needed to spend more time with young men, and occasionally Evelyn had to consider Holly's personal needs over being a proper secretary. She decided to keep Mr. Wells's presence to herself.

At 5:05 P.M., Holly emerged from her office. As soon as she entered the reception area, Wells rose to his feet and she halted in her tracks with her mouth agape. "Oh, Mr. Wells. I hadn't expected you to still be here." She glared at Evelyn and received an innocent look in response. As her cheeks warmed uncomfortably, she vowed to put the meddling woman out to pasture.

With a deep breath, she reclaimed her composure. "Evelyn apparently misunderstood me. I meant for her to reschedule our appointment. I'm sorry you were kept waiting."

David grinned. "Evelyn gave me your message. It was my choice to wait anyway."

"Oh. I see. Well, I haven't had a chance to eat all day and I'm starved. If you'd like to join me, I suppose we can talk over dinner." Rather than wait for his acceptance, she walked to the office door and held it open.

It took him a few seconds to recover from this unexpected turn of events—long enough for her to leave and let the door close behind her. He had to hurry a bit to catch up to her at the elevator.

"Where to?" he asked once they reached the ground floor.

"The coffee shop around the corner. I only have time to grab a quick bite. I have another appointment."

He moved quickly to hold open one of the double doors for her. She exited at the same moment through the other door. Again he found himself several steps behind. For a moment he considered letting her go without him, but he had the feeling that was exactly what she was hoping for. He reminded himself that this wasn't just another blonde, this was a blonde with a secret that could lead to a major story. He wasn't about to give up until he figured out what that secret was.

In the coffee shop, he held out a chair for her. She sat down in another one. He attempted to order for her. She made her request directly to the waitress.

"I don't like to be patronized, Mr. Wells. I am perfectly capable of opening doors and seating myself, and any other male gestures of superiority you had in mind. You said you had some questions for me. I assure you I am also capable of making statements in between bites."

"Why do I get the feeling some of those bites are going to be out of my hide?"

"I'm certain I don't know. Perhaps you have a guilty conscience?"

He offered her a deep-dimpled grin. "Okay, you got me. I confess. I'm guilty as sin. But it's your fault."

Her stern expression barely altered. "I beg your pardon?"

"I said it's your fault. From the moment I saw you, all I could think about was stealing you away to a private island in the Pacific where I would ravish your sexy body for several weeks without interruption."

She stared at him. "That was probably the fastest, crudest, and least original pass I have ever received. I gather I was right in assuming that you aren't really doing an article on recycling."

"Wrong. I am completely legitimate. But first you're going to tell me why you're so hell-bent on freezing my ass."

"Because I know you. Or I should say your kind. When you speak of a woman, you describe her physical attributes or sexual talents, because you can't remember her name or what she told you she does for a living. You never have a doubt about how you and your date will end an evening, because, after all, what woman in her right mind would turn you down? Shall I go on?"

"Unnecessary, since you're wrong again. On the first count, I would be a lousy reporter if I didn't have an excellent memory for detail, every detail, including the names of my lady friends. As to your second accusation, I'll have you know there have been one or two occasions when I haven't been absolutely certain."

"How exciting for you."

"This evening, on the other hand, holds no surprises whatsoever." The waitress arrived with their order, and he waited for Holly to spoon some cottage cheese and melon into her mouth before explaining. "After we're finished eating, I'm going to interview you. Then I'm going to walk you to your car or your appointment—if indeed you have one, which I doubt." He was pleased to see a hint of pink color her cheekbones. Apparently a reaction could be forced out of her if he worked at it. Or was it being caught in a lie that fractured her cool? "And before I leave you alone, you're going to let me kiss you, just to prove you haven't the slightest interest in me as a man."

Her eyebrows raised a notch. "You are truly unbelievable."

"I've been told that once or twice before," he automatically replied with a teasing smile.

For the next half hour David conducted a serious, efficient interview, and Holly was suitably impressed with both his questions and his knowledge about the recycling bills already in effect and those currently on the House floor. At least he had done his homework.

"Now that I've convinced you of my sincerity, will you permit me to accompany you wherever you're headed without fear of ravagement?"

"I'm not afraid of you."

"Liar." He grasped her hand and turned it palm up in his. When she made a fist and tried to pull away, he held tighter. "Public scenes don't bother me, lady, but I'm betting you don't care for them. Open your hand." She frowned, but did as he asked. He ran a finger over her palm. "Damp."

"It's warm in here." Through gritted teeth, she added, "And my name is Holly, not lady."

"Oh, you're a lady all right. A very cool, smooth lady. I told you I notice little details. Let me tell you a few. You avoid looking me in the eye, even when you're insulting me, you lick your lips much too often, and you've been wiping your hands on your napkin every few minutes. You said you were starving, then you order cottage cheese and a glass of milk—the kind of bland food that would pamper an ulcer, or a very nervous stomach.

"If that's not enough, when I reached for your

hand just now, you looked like a deer caught in the headlights of a hunter's truck. You're not afraid of me, huh? Bull. You're scared shitless, and I want to know why."

Holly fought the panic gnawing away at her stomach lining. When had her nice orderly plan gone off track? She had no choice but to brave it out. Taking a deep breath, she tried again to reclaim her hand. After a long moment, he let her go. "I have to be on my way now." With an outward show of calm, she pulled several bills out of her wallet and tucked them under the saucer. "Earth Guard's expense tonight, Mr. Wells. Thank you for the opportunity to update your readers. Please call Evelyn if you have any more questions."

She realized he was right behind her as she exited the deli, but she ignored him. While she was determined to escape his company, he was equally intent on denying her that freedom.

"I told you I was escorting you. Of course, if you prefer to pretend I'm not here—" He cocked his head at her as if she had interrupted him with a question. "What's that? Oh yes, I wanted to be a reporter for as long as I can remember. I meet some very unusual people in my line of work. Take this lady environmentalist for instance—a real tough nut to crack. But once I got her talking about her pet project, she bubbled over like a glass of champagne.

"She's an incredibly beautiful woman with an intellect to match. The strange thing was, she seemed to be coming on to me and pulling away at the same time." He had to pick up his pace to stay with her as she entered a parking lot.

He closed in on her as she stopped beside a dark compact car and fumbled with her keys. Before she could insert one in the car door, his fingers closed over her shoulders. In one abrupt move he swiveled her around and pushed her back against the car door. Straddling her thighs with his own, his head lowered to within an inch of hers. He glared into her wide, terrified eyes and murmured, "I don't like to be played with, lady. I'm not a little boy, and I'm not your lapdog, Philip. For some reason, you wanted me chasing after you. Well, I caught you. Now, what do you want from me?"

Holly knew she was still standing only because the grip on her shoulders and the brace of his thighs were holding her up. What insanity had possessed her to imagine she was woman enough to deal with this man, to manipulate him for her own purposes? *Fool.* She forced a whisper through trembling lips. "Nothing. I don't want anything from you."

"Liar."

She felt his hot breath against her mouth and tried to slow her rapidly beating heart.

"Prove it. Prove you want nothing from me. Prove you're not the least bit interested."

Holly closed her eyes and prepared herself for his assault. He could take his kiss. When he discovered just how cool she really was, then he would have all the proof he needed.

She didn't expect the spark.

Certainly he felt it, too, for his sharp intake of breath sucked her own gasp into his mouth. When his lips brushed gently over hers, she almost sighed from the exquisite sensuality of it.

Dear God! She had forgotten what it felt like to be immersed in liquid heat. His tongue slid across her lower lip, then withdrew, only to return again with increased pressure.

Her mind went to war with her body. She should be fighting this intrusion. After all the years of existing in a passionless void, how could she respond so easily to a man she hardly knew? But she couldn't resist the melting sensation she had experienced only once before. Her fists clenched and unclenched against the steel of the car to keep from showing him just how strongly he affected her. Maybe she could enjoy it for another moment or two, then she would push him away.

Parting her mouth beneath his, she allowed him access. It was impossible to prevent the shiver of pleasure that ran through her when his tongue met hers, and he deepened the kiss. She had to stop him, but not just yet. It had been too long, and she was too starved for this sweet torture.

She felt his fingers release her one shoulder and skim down her arm. Taking her hand in his, he slowly dragged it up between his thighs. And pressed.

In her slightly dazed state it took her a second to realize that the flesh cupped in her hand was flaccid. His biting words completed her humiliation.

"Now who's not the least bit interested?"

8

Timothy Ziegler's murderer glared at the Friday morning newspaper. Unbelievable! Not even a single line of coverage. Why couldn't the body have been found by a hotel employee or other nongovernment person who would have gone screaming to the press? *That* was what was supposed to have happened. Instead, a secret service agent had been given a key to the senator's suite to check on him, ruining a perfectly good plan.

Even after death, another rapist was being protected!

Just as the murderer's biological father had been protected in spite of impregnating his victim. Rather than that man being held responsible for what he had done, it was his unwanted child who had been sentenced to years of hate and neglect—abuse for which there had seemed to be no way to seek adequate revenge.

Until now.

A cryptic, anonymous phone call or note to the media would undoubtedly stir up some attention and possibly force some details out of the FBI. But that was the sort of act a psychotic killer might perform—someone who really, subconsciously, wanted to be caught. The message had to be spread without personally going public, because this murderer had no intention of being caught.

There were three more names on the list. Surely the message would be made public with the next execution.

How convenient that Billy O'Day's itinerary was published in the sports section of every newspaper in the country.

9

Three days had passed since David had blown it with Holly Kaufman, and he was still kicking himself. He had acted like a cub reporter, letting his personal feelings interfere with a story. The recycling article had come out fine, but the other, the one he smelled, had slipped right through his fingers, and all because the lady got to him.

He had gone over the ninety minutes they'd spent together at least a dozen times. The conclusion wasn't very attractive. Like a teenage boy with his hormones in an uproar, he hadn't been willing to accept no for an answer. Was it because she was more seductive than every other woman he'd ever encountered, or because she was the first who seemed immune to his charm? Even though he had accused her of it, he was no longer certain she had been trying to seduce him. That left the latter reason.

He had used his sex appeal as an investigating tool for so long, he hadn't considered the fact that it would have the opposite effect on Ms. Kaufman, even though he had been well warned.

He should have acted strictly professionally during that first meeting. His plan to establish a relationship, befriend her, and gain her trust would have eventually earned him the answers he was seeking. But her obvious fear combined with her show of indifference had clouded his brain.

Instinctively, he knew a traditional apology would not be sufficient to wipe out the damage he'd done. Considering the dead ends he'd run up against with this story, he definitely needed another chance with Holly Kaufman.

Though he knew there was a connection between Donner and Wallace, he had yet to find a similar tie between them and Holly and Greenley. Valerie was still working on getting a roster of students enrolled at Dominion when Wallace and Donner were there.

A general background check through the investigative computer service the newspaper subscribed to showed the four of them were born in different states—Holly was a year older than the others—and had graduated from different colleges, and so far, there didn't seem to be any organization that they all belonged to. The fact that they seemed to have so little in common was the one element that would drive David until he uncovered the reason for their meeting. In the meantime, he still couldn't identify the other two women he had seen at the hotel, the mouse and the other blonde.

He had no choice but to find a way to make amends to Ms. Kaufman. Tim Ziegler's murder was incentive enough to convince him to bend a few of his personal rules about women if he had to.

Holly frowned at the calendar on her kitchen wall. Friday. She had promised April she would call every Friday, but what would she say?

That Timothy Ziegler's murder had frightened her

into not wanting to get further involved with the Little Sister Society? There was some truth to that, but she had already come to the conclusion that she could carry out the assignment given her without having to associate with the entire group of dysfunctional women.

That she had changed her mind about wanting retribution against Jerry Frampton? There was no truth to that at all. If anything, before her disastrous encounter with David Wells, she had begun to imagine how exciting it would be to track the reporter's investigation and how satisfying it would be if he uncovered something horribly detrimental that Frampton would then be suitably punished for. She had heard revenge is sweet, and she already had acquired a taste for it.

The real truth was, she had nothing substantial to report to April, as she had hoped to have by now, and she was embarrassed about that. Almost as embarrassed as she was over her miscalculation with David Wells.

Since April had suggested she use David as practice for dealing with other men, it wouldn't be out of the question to discuss with her what had happened. She would probably be very understanding and have some reassuring comments, but Holly wasn't yet accustomed to sharing her problems so easily.

No, she didn't want to call April until she had made a decision about a reporter. There was no question she had to eliminate Wells. As crude as he was, he had effectively demonstrated that she was no match for him. Her amateurish ploys to lure him to her had achieved nothing but a severe case of humiliation.

All in all it was a good thing he had seen through

her act. He made her feel something she had never expected to feel again, nor did she want to. Sexual desire had made her a helpless victim once before, and that was one time too many.

Of the other reporters she was considering, there were two that came close to matching Wells's qualifications and credentials—one was a happily married man and the other was a razor-tongued woman whom Holly had always avoided. She wouldn't be able to believably establish a relationship with either of them that would allow her to remain close throughout an investigation of Frampton. Wells would have been perfect, if he had not been so astute, so egotistical . . . so much more man than she was woman.

It appeared that her only choice would be to pass on the information she had to one of the two less perfect reporters, then hope a story appeared in the newspaper. It didn't sound nearly as satisfying as going along for the ride, but it seemed to be the only option left to her.

She interrupted her mental debate to watch the evening news. Timothy Ziegler's murder had taken a backseat to other stories within forty-eight hours. That night, the weather held the top spot. "The National Hurricane Center reports Brigitte's winds are now averaging one hundred forty miles per hour and building. Although it had been assumed that the storm would slow down as it passed over the Bahamas, the opposite has happened, leaving a path of destruction in its wake. At this time, it is estimated that Brigitte will hit Key West, Florida, by four A.M., but there is still the possibility it could veer off. Residents from Key West to Miami Beach have been issued evacuation instructions, and any women more than six months pregnant are urged to go to a hospital and remain there until the storm passes."

Holly listened as the reporter read off statistics from other hurricanes that had hit the East Coast of the United States in the last hundred years. South Florida had barely recovered from 1992's Andrew, which was ranked tenth in severity among all recorded hurricanes. The worst recorded storm of the century had landed in the Florida Keys in 1935, but it never received a name, and no other sizable storm had hit the islands since then.

Officials were gravely concerned over the fact that the population there had grown from approximately thirteen thousand to eighty thousand since that last hurricane, but evacuation routes remained limited. Small craft warnings had already gone out due to choppy seas and most airplanes had flown to more secure fields earlier in the day. The only safe passage remaining to the mainland was the Overseas Highway, a series of forty-two bridges that connected the individual islands.

Extensive efforts were being made to encourage the residents to head north immediately rather than wait for Brigitte to get any closer. Additional police had already been called out from nearby Dade County to help direct the evacuation and generally maintain order, but it was reported that traffic was already bumper to bumper and being further hampered by accidents on the bridges. A considerable number of Keys residents interviewed were planning to ride out the storm rather than risk being on the highway.

The one estimate Holly was listening for, she didn't hear. Of course, back in 1935, no one would have thought to record environmental statistics. The Florida Keys and surrounding waters housed a delicate ecosystem of plant and animal life, coral reefs, mangrove stands, and nesting grounds for shore birds. Man was not the only destroyer of Earth's resources; sometimes Mother Nature could be just as cruel to her own children. Either way, Earth Guard was standing by to offer assistance.

The eleven o'clock news brought a confirmation that the Keys were in severe and imminent danger. Brigitte was now a Category 5 hurricane, sustaining winds of 158 miles per hour with gusts up to 180. The eye stretched twenty-five miles in diameter and hurricane force winds spread approximately fifty miles away from it. Based on its current path, the eye was heading for the middle islands. Nothing from Key West to Key Largo was expected to be spared extensive damage.

Holly napped on the couch, waking from time to time to catch the latest news bulletin. At four-fifteen Saturday morning disaster struck.

After listening to the scant details available on the six-thirty A.M. news, Holly called Philip. He hadn't been feeling well when he left the office yesterday, but she knew he would want to hear about this.

His muffled answer let her know he had gotten worse during the night.

"You sound awful. Did you get any sleep?"

"A little. And I can't possibly sound as bad as I feel. Even my hair hurts. Have you heard the news this morning?"

"That's why I'm calling. I realize this is your bailiwick, but the way you're feeling, I don't think a field trip to the tropics would be a good idea."

"Damn. I hate to admit it, but I barely have the strength to make it to the bathroom let alone the airport. I suppose an inspection could wait a few days—"

"And miss getting pictures before the cleanup begins? I don't think so. I'll go."

"Since I agree with you, I won't argue. Call me when you get there."

"Yes, dear."

"Okay, so I worry. Be careful. I love you." His voice was barely audible, as if it took all his energy simply to speak.

"You just take care of yourself and get better. I'll be back in a couple of days."

David's editor woke him up with the kind of announcement every reporter loves to hear. He'd been assigned to cover the worst disaster in the history of the United States.

The earliest Holly could take off was a two o'clock flight to Miami out of Dulles with a forty-five-minute layover in Atlanta. She was normally as thrifty as possible with Earth Guard's funds, but coach class was booked solid, so she splurged for a first-class seat.

She couldn't help but think about the fact that she was practically flying into Jerry Frampton's backyard. If she were a stronger person, perhaps she could do a little investigating on her own. But she couldn't see herself seeking him out any more than she could imagine having a cozy chat with his pornographer friend, Mick D'Angelo. Then again, maybe she could just ask a few questions at that Chinese restaurant on Miami Beach that was mentioned in the last report.

On her way to the airport, she made a trip by the office to pick up some reference material on the

Florida Keys and used the waiting time to refresh her memory about its natural resources.

As soon as she was settled in her window seat on the plane, she went back to perusing one of the books. A man's voice behind her broke into her concentration. It couldn't be!

"I'm a real white-knuckle flyer, Jennifer. You can bring me a double bourbon as soon as you're allowed to serve it. And if you could sit on my lap during takeoff, it would calm my nerves considerably."

An insincere feminine chuckle reached Holly's ears. "As much as that sounds like fun, I'm afraid it's against regulations, Mr. Wells."

The pounding in her ears prevented Holly from hearing any more of the flirtation. His velvety-smooth voice brought her humiliation back in a rush. It was difficult enough to forget how he had made a fool of her, without having to see him so soon after their last encounter. How could fate have played such a trick on her?

Reminding herself that she had been as much at fault as he erased the anger, but reinforced her acute embarrassment. Perhaps, if she was lucky, he was only going as far as Atlanta. Surely she could stay hidden in her seat for the next hour. The restrooms were in the rear of the cabin. There would be no reason for him to see who was seated in front of him.

When they touched down in Atlanta, she remained seated until she was certain everyone had deplaned. Then she stood, stepped into the aisle to stretch her legs, and . . . groaned. It would be rather ridiculous to pretend she didn't recognize him or see him slouched there, looking like death warmed over, especially since he was staring right at her.

She nodded at him and headed for the exit before he had a chance to make whatever glib comment was surely on the tip of his tongue.

As soon as she reboarded the plane, she grew wary. The man who had been seated next to her was now in the aisle seat previously occupied by David Wells and vice-versa. She walked to Wells's side and stated, "You're in the wrong seat." His mischievous grin was annoyingly in place. She noted the drink in his hand and the empty miniature of vodka on the tray in front of him. She thought he'd already overindulged on the way to Atlanta, but apparently he had completely recovered and was starting over.

"Actually, I'm not. I explained to the gentleman that I needed to interview you for my paper, and he was glad to oblige."

"If you think for one minute—"

"Uh-uh. Hold it right there. This is strictly business. Did you read my column about the recycling bills in yesterday's paper?"

"Yes. It was very good."

"Thank you. Are you headed for the Keys?"

"Yes."

"Same here. I was hoping you would give me the benefit of your expertise on the environmental impact of a hurricane. That is, if you can stop huffing and puffing."

"I am not—" How could she deny it when he was watching her chest rise and fall much too rapidly. "Are you going to let me sit down, or am I supposed to stand the rest of the way?"

He raised his gaze to her face. "Oh, you wanted me to stand up? But I thought you hated such overt masculine gestures. I figured you could just climb over me, maybe hike your skirt up a mite—"

"Mr. Wells!"

"Sorry, I can't seem to help myself."

She sighed, and he stood up and moved aside just enough for her to squeeze by.

As soon as they had both fastened their seatbelts, she offered him the book she had skimmed on the first leg of the flight.

"I can't read on a plane, or in any moving vehicle for that matter. If you don't mind, I'd appreceiate your filling me in verbally. Actually, it would help a lot if you would start talking now and just keep talking until we're in the air."

"What?" Then she saw him grip the arms of the seat and his whole body went stiff. She hadn't even realized the plane had started to back away from the terminal, but he had. So he really was a white-knuckle flyer. After the way he'd treated her when he sensed she was nervous around him, she should repay him in kind. But as she saw the color drain from his face, human decency won out, and she began to tell him about the coral reefs in the Straits of Florida, and how they could be damaged by a storm of the magnitude of Brigitte.

The airplane started its ascent and David closed his eyes. He concentrated on Holly's voice and the information she was relaying about the high winds and rough waters. He listened to her explain about the sea creatures whose survival depends on the living reefs.

"We know from Hurricane Andrew that damage to the reefs can go to depths over a hundred feet. There were cases of sunken ships being ripped apart or moved great distances, and the coral that had been growing on them was totally destroyed in the process. The elkhorn coral and sea fans are at the greatest risk because they're so fragile. But even the sturdier species like the brain coral will die if they're smothered in shifting sands."

Holly kept talking even though she couldn't tell if he was listening. A fine sheen of perspiration coated his upper lip and he hadn't moved a muscle in a full minute.

When the plane leveled off in the sky, she watched his breathing regulate and his fingers relax; finally, he opened his eyes.

"Thanks. That was very nice."

"You're welcome. Now, do I have to say it all over again?"

He smiled his little-boy smile. "I told you I have an excellent memory. Besides, there's something about being terrified that intensifies everything else that happens at the same time. Have you ever noticed that?"

She caught the heat of his gaze and blushed before she could control her thoughts. Turning her head away, she made a pretense of examining the clouds. So much for being nice. It was somewhat comforting, however, to know there was something she was more confident about than he was. His irrational fear of flying made him a little less frightening to her. But only a little.

David motioned for the flight attendant and asked for another drink. Even for him, he thought, that last shot was pretty low. She had just witnessed him at his weakest moment, and didn't take advantage of it, yet he had gone right for the jugular. What was it about Holly Kaufman that brought out his worst behavior?

It was more than simply having his male ego bruised. Seeing her again had him coming up with new answers. He despised liars, and, although he couldn't put his finger on it, there was something basically dishonest about her. The possibility that it had something to do with Ziegler took a backseat to his personal response to her. She had made him react in anger. He didn't like that. She had made him want to crawl inside of her and stay there forever. He was scared to death of that.

Upon reflection, he did know what one of her lies was. On the surface she appeared to be a sophisticated woman of the world. That was the lie. One kiss had informed him she was as innocent as a girl. Christine had told him Holly had nothing to do with any man but Philip, and he had witnessed that peculiar relationship first hand. When he had accused her of being scared of him, he hadn't considered the possibility that it was simply because he was a man. This lady hadn't been playing "hard-to-get" as he had first suspected; she *really* didn't want to be caught.

And now, at his first opportunity to make amends, he had stuck another needle into her thin skin. Perhaps, subconsciously, he wanted her to dislike him, or at least be leery of him, because for the last three days, he had had one hell of a time staying away from her—and not just because of the story. He didn't like that either.

He tossed back his drink and put his mind on the assignment ahead of him. "What arrangements do you have to get to the Keys?"

She studied his expression for a moment and decided he was back to business again. Safe territory. How did he turn it on and off like that? "My travel agent reserved a rental car for pickup at the Miami airport."

"Really? I understood all the phone and power lines in South Florida were down."

"Parts of Miami were back on-line within a few

hours. The utility companies were more prepared than they had been for Hurricane Andrew."

"Where are you staying?"

"A hotel in South Miami. It's some distance from the heart of the disaster, but my agent couldn't get anything closer. At any rate, I plan to charter a helicopter to view the area."

"I'm surprised you could get a room at all today. Besides people seeking shelter, I assume reporters from every major television station and newspaper in the world are on their way there by now. Not to mention government reps, insurance adjustors, and every unemployed carpenter and roofer in the southeastern United States."

She nodded her agreement with his assessment. "I've suspected my agent is a miracle worker on occasion. Are you going to be covering the disaster in general or do you have a specific angle?"

"Basically, I'll be on the lookout for the kind of government snafus that went on during the first week after Andrew, such as inadequate relief efforts and rescue missions, though the hope is they learned their lessons well on that one. Listening to you talk about the effects on the environment makes me think that would be a good secondary story. It would make a nice follow-up to my recycling article. I'd need to learn a lot more about it, though. Of course, I'll be happy to quote you as often as you'd like."

"It's a shame Philip couldn't be here. He's really much more knowledgeable about specific ecosystems than I am. As you know, I keep pretty busy working on waste management."

"Well, just for the record, I'm glad he's not. I can't imagine his voice talking me through a takeoff." He stopped himself from paying her the compliment he was really thinking. Stick to business.

They had been in the air a short while when David interrupted their discussion to order drinks for both of them.

"I don't want anything alcoholic," Holly said quickly.

"Good. I'll drink yours, too. In less than one hour, this plane is going to land again and I intend to be as close to unconscious as possible."

"I don't think getting drunk is a very sensible solution. Why don't I just talk to you again?"

"Because I'm twice as bad going down. Do you have any idea how many plane crashes happen during landing?" He downed both drinks without taking a breath, then motioned for the flight attendant to bring two more.

"Have you ever tried taking one of those workshops for your, uh, problem?"

"No. There's nothing anybody can tell me that will convince me this is a sane way to travel. I've read all about the theory of flight, aerodynamics, and so on. It doesn't make any difference. Nothing this big and heavy should be suspended in midair—particularly with me in it."

"Then why do you do it if it's so hard for you?"

He shifted in his seat to face her. "I accept the fact that I have the fear, but I refuse to let that fear stop me from living or from getting what I want out of life. But you know all about fighting fear, don't you?"

She met his gaze, because he sounded perfectly serious, not hurtful or teasing. "Yes, I do."

"Of course, if you really want to help, I can think of something you could do to distract me."

She started to agree when he wiggled his eyebrows at her. "You're disgusting. You know that? How can you speak so intelligently one minute and be so . . . so . . ."

"Earthy? I always liked that word. C'mon, lady, I was teasing." He tried to take her hand, but she yanked it away. "You don't like that, do you?"

"*Lady* was a dog in a Disney cartoon. My name is Holly."

"I'm not talking about your name. You don't like to be teased. In fact, I can't imagine you laughing. Do you ever smile, *Holly*?"

"Of course I smile." She pulled her lips back in a wide, toothy grin, then frowned at him again. She couldn't handle him sober; how much worse did he get when he was drunk?

In a much too sudden movement, his hand came toward her face. She jerked back so quickly her head banged against the window.

"Whoa," he said in surprise. There was that flash of panic in her eyes that he had seen before. He withdrew his hand and watched her slowly lower her eyelids. When she raised them again, she was back in control. "What's your problem?"

"You."

"Naw, that's too easy. You know my greatest fear. It's only fair you tell me yours."

She took a slow breath. Maybe if she told him part of it, he would back off. "I have . . . a little difficulty when someone . . . touches me unexpectedly. It's no big deal."

David studied her, while she studied her fingernails. What caused such a hang-up? Childhood abuse? Rape? Certainly nothing insignificant. Chalk up one more reason to progress carefully with her.

"Okay. So, if I wanted to brush your hair off your

cheek—like I was about to—how would I do that without scaring the hell out of you?"

"You could try asking first."

"Ask permission to touch you? Hmmm. Do you always make Philip ask first?"

She narrowed her eyes at him before turning back to the window.

"None of my business, huh? You're right. It's that terrible earthy side again. Jus' refuses to stay submerged." He snickered, then grew very quiet for a minute. "Mos' women kinda like it, ya know. Why couldn't you be like all the res'?"

Holly slowly turned toward him, not certain what he meant by that comment. His eyes were closed. Hopefully he had passed out.

David considered the idea of asking permission completely ludicrous. Through experience, he had developed his own theory about women. To succeed with one, all a man had to do was home in on her primary desire to be given precisely what she wanted without asking her or waiting for her to voice a specific request. Obviously, it required a delicate balance and a great deal of finesse, and David believed his exceptional intuition had helped him master the subtleties of the game.

So where was that intuition when it came to Holly?

"Holly?" His lashes fluttered open. With a bit of effort he focused on her eyes, verified that she was listening, then lowered his eyelids again. "May I have your permission to hold your hand? Jus' while we land. Please?" He held out his hand, palm up, above her lap.

She looked skeptically at him and his hand. She definitely didn't trust his innocent-little-boy routine. There was no question about his being frightened,

nor that he was quite drunk. But if she held his
hand, would he appreciate it, or find a way to humiliate her again? Would he even remember when he
sobered up? Finally, she placed her palm on his and
let him thread his fingers through hers.

As they waited for their descent to begin, Holly
realized she was losing most of her fear of David.
He was a very astute man and a good listener when
he wanted to be. She simply had to ignore the corny
come-on lines that seemed to thoughtlessly slip out
of his mouth every so often.

He had demonstrated quite dramatically that he
didn't find her irresistible. But he *did* seem to like
her a little and respect her intelligence. And he *had*
trusted her enough to let her see his weakness. Was
it enough to form a friendship?

Perhaps the error in her original plan to establish
a relationship with him had been the basic approach. He had an unlimted choice of beautiful
blondes in Washington who could play at flirtation
much more skillfully than she. Maybe the man
would appreciate a friend. Or a mother.

David Wells had the extraordinary ability to bring
out her caretaker instincts. Ridiculous. She didn't
feel that way around Philip. But then Philip was a
mature man, not an adolescent in a grown-up's disguise. She guessed David's boyishness made up part
of the charm she had heard about, but hadn't quite
discovered for herself.

By the time the plane touched down on the runway, Holly's fingers were completely numb.

The landing had been smooth, but that hadn't
helped David nearly as much as the comfort he received from Holly's hand. He could have sworn he
felt her calm strength flowing right into his arm
where it was pressed to hers.

When the plane came to a complete stop, David opened his eyes, took a deep breath, then released her hand. "Thanks. That helped a lot."

"Think nothing of it." Impulsively she raised her hand in front of her, crooking the fingers into an arthritic pose. "I hardly ever used my left hand anyway." Then she smiled. A genuine smile.

The softness that possessed her features stunned him so that it took him a heartbeat to realize she had made a joke—*and* smiled. The next moment he laughed out loud. It made his head hurt like hell, but it felt good everywhere else.

Holly hadn't thought it was *that* funny, but when he couldn't seem to stop, somehow she contracted his silliness and ended up laughing along with him.

Those same caretaker instincts had her agreeing to keep him company at the coffee shop until he sobered up. He insisted it wouldn't take long, since most of the alcohol had been countered by the adrenaline surge he'd gotten while the plane was descending. He hadn't eaten anything on the plane, but he more than made up for that omission in the coffee shop. Along with his meal, he swallowed a handful of aspirins and downed at least a quart of coffee. It was a routine he'd been through countless times before.

In return for her patience, he accompanied her to the rental car counter to make sure she got off all right.

She didn't. Her reservation for a car had come in over the computer as soon as the power was restored, but there weren't any rentals available. People hadn't returned cars due in, and hordes of visitors who couldn't get flights out of the area had rented anything with wheels. Holly's turn for an anxiety attack came as she went from agency to agency and received the same information.

"No luck, huh?"

She spun around at the sound of David's voice. She had actually forgotten he was there. "It's times like this that I wish I could just say, *Beam me up, Scotty.*"

"I'm doin' the best I can, Cap'n," David responded in a brogue so awful she couldn't help but laugh. Again.

He readjusted the bag hung over his shoulder then took hold of the extended handle on her rolling suitcase. "C'mon," he commanded and started to walk off when he realized she hadn't moved, not even to pick up her tote bag. "What are you waiting for?"

"Better question: What are you doing with my suitcase?"

"I thought I'd take it for a little ride. Want to stay here or come with it?"

"*You* were able to rent a car?" she asked as she caught up to him.

"Sort of. I have a very smart editor whose hunch paid off. In case Brigitte hit, he made arrangements yesterday to have a twenty-six-foot Winnebago motor home standing by for his reporter. It's totally self-sufficient. Has a generator in case there's no power available, and a fully stocked kitchen. And at least one bed," he added with a wink.

"Mr. Wells!"

"Uh-uh. Caught you jumping to earthy conclusions, Mizz Kaufman. I only meant that you could stretch out while I drive you to your hotel. You look like you haven't slept in a while."

His perception was accurate and disconcerting, and she hated the fact that he could make her blush so easily, but his offer was too good to pass up. Besides, there was that theory of hers about becoming his friend. "Deal."

"Deal?" He leaned toward her ear and half-whis-

pered, "Lucky for me you didn't ask what your payment would be."

April snatched the receiver off her kitchen wall
the moment the phone rang. "Hello?"

"It's me."

April frowned. She had been hoping for a call
from Holly Kaufman, not Rachel. "I hope this call
doesn't signify bad news."

"I suppose that depends on your outlook on life.
We need to talk. I'm calling from the number I gave
you while you were here. How long before you can
call me back the way I explained?" Rachel imagined
April taking a slow, calming breath to prepare herself not to overreact while she figured out how long
it would take to get to a public pay phone.

"Fifteen minutes."

Rachel hung up without saying goodbye and, as
soon as April called back, she launched directly into
her report.

"The fingerprint tracing is finally finished from
the Ziegler case. The lab techs and their assistants
really had to work on this one. You can imagine
how many different fingerprints might be found in
a hotel room—even with the maid service, they
don't wipe off every surface. There were prints from
former guests, people who had visited the victim
during his stay, and hotel employees, and every print
had to be tracked down.

"On top of all that though, the doorknobs had
been wiped clean of all prints, including the victim's, which implies that it might have been done
at the last minute, and that presents a very interesting problem."

"Why do you say that?"

"Ice tongs were left by the body that were definitely used during the castration. They weren't wiped clean, yet there were no prints on them. That means the cutter wore gloves, probably surgical latex, so there'd be no reason to wipe door handles. Are you following me?"

"I'm afraid so, but I'd better hear it all."

"One deduction might be that somebody else— possibly a witness to the murder—wiped the door handles on the way out, after Ziegler was killed. But since that was all that was wiped, either that person was sure he or she hadn't touched anything else or was in one hell of a hurry."

"I see," April said slowly. "The prints that were picked up, were they all identified?"

"All except one set." Rachel purposely paused for several seconds. "But those aren't on file anywhere. We do know one thing, though. Because of the surfaces they were found on, it's fairly certain that whoever the prints belong to was in the bathroom sometime after the maid had cleaned that afternoon. Also, there was one more piece of evidence that points to the theory that there was a woman in Ziegler's room sometime before he died." This time Rachel could actually hear April inhaling.

"Oh?"

"Yes. A used tampon had been wrapped in tissue and dropped in the trashcan. A blood sample means DNA testing and positive proof that the woman was there shortly before he was killed—*if* she's ever found."

"Couldn't you do something about that?"

Rachel laughed. "You mean like make the tampon disappear? No. Too many people know about it."

"What about Cheryl?"

"All taken care of. I filled out the report showing I questioned her and have witnesses to the fact that she checked out of her hotel that afternoon, immediately drove out of the city and was at her home in Connecticut at the time of the murder. All nice and tidy. Did you speak to her husband?"

"Yes," April replied. "Just like we discussed. He should be sunning himself on the Riviera about now."

"Good. As to the rest of us, we should be in good shape. Except for Holly Kaufman. Erica said she talked to her and wasn't sure if she had a reasonable alibi for that night. I've got to tell you, April, I'm a little worried. We don't know her or how she thinks. There couldn't have been a worse time to bring a new person into the group. This whole situation is liable to get her nervous enough to talk to someone about what she's learned."

"I don't think she'd do that," April said instantly. "She may get a little nervous, even suspicious, but not enough to expose herself to public scrutiny. Especially if there's a problem with her alibi. Don't help her with that just yet. Besides, I think she's been well tempted by the idea of being involved in Frampton's retribution."

"I hope you're right, but I think I'll have a talk with her to make sure."

"I'd rather you didn't, Rachel. I've already started forming a bond with her. She trusts me."

"Doesn't everyone?" Rachel retorted sarcastically.

"She's due to check in with me on her progress. In fact, I thought you were her calling. If I don't hear from her by Monday, I'll call her. Just leave Holly Kaufman to me," April said firmly. "Haven't I always taken care of our group?"

Rachel hesitated just long enough for April to get the message. "So far, Doctor. So far."

10

Another hour crept by while David and Holly took a cab to where the motor home was parked and David received operating instructions and a map of the area. Additional bottled water had been stocked due to contamination of the regular supply further south.

The first film footage of the affected area had just been broadcast over the television, and David and Holly were told that it didn't look like anything south of Key Largo was left standing. They were warned that although the expressway and turnpike had been cleared already, side roads were still covered by debris and fallen trees. Rescue workers were busy searching for bodies of those who had refused to evacuate, while the police had their hands full keeping the curiosity seekers out of the way and the looters under control.

While Holly and David had been in transit, the President had pronounced the Keys a disaster area and promised to send in the National Guard to render immediate assistance. At least the government had learned something from Hurricane Andrew.

As tired as she was, Holly was too keyed up to take advantage of the bed in the rear of the Winnebago. She wanted to see as much as possible before the sun set completely. She'd already seen broken tree limbs and palm fronds littering the ground around the airport, and as they headed south, more evidence of the storm was apparent in the neighborhoods beside the turnpike—roofs with missing shingles, furniture and other objects in swimming pools, broken windows. They were about fifty miles north of where the edge of the hurricane had hit, but they had been told that tornadoes had caused considerable damage in the outer regions.

David kept his eyes on the road, determined not to think about the bed behind him. He was absolutely exhausted, but it wasn't thoughts of sleep that were disturbing him. It was a mental picture of Holly, stretched out on the compact bed dressed only in her diamond earrings. He couldn't stop himself from imagining how close two people would have to be to share that bed for a night.

What he could not imagine was Holly allowing anyone to get that close to her. That lady had a barrier of granite around her. His wayward thoughts drifted to the night he had hammered a crack in that barrier. After what he'd done, though, she would be twice as defensive the next time.

The next time? Where the hell had that thought come from? Walking away from their first encounter had damn near killed him. Yet he knew he had to find a way past her defenses. What he needed was more time than it was going to take to drive her to her hotel. It was too bad she wasn't a different kind of woman—one who would easily accept his invitation to share his camper, and his bed, for the time they were both in Florida.

He shook his head to rattle his brain back to a saner topic: Florida, a place he had not previously visited. He wondered if the debilitating humidity and sweltering heat outside were normal or made worse by the hurricane. At least the motor home's air conditioner made driving comfortable. The clear blue sky and brilliant red-and-gold sunset seemed incongruous with the storm wreckage they were passing.

Traffic was moving slower than a person could walk. As a reporter, he wasn't surprised at the number of people wanting to get a closer look at a disaster, but he was irritated that they were preventing him from getting his job done.

It was nine o'clock by the time they reached the hotel where Holly had reservations.

"Thank you very much for the ride, Mr. Wells. I really appreciate it."

David grinned. "It was my pleasure. Listen, you were right about this being a good distance from the disaster. You're welcome to come with me the rest of the way."

"Thanks, but I doubt if I could get a room for the night anywhere else."

"You could stay with me." He saw Holly's disapproval and added, "I'd be a perfect gentleman, I swear."

Holly was certain his definition of best behavior and hers would differ greatly. "Thank you again, but I don't think so."

David shrugged. "Suit yourself."

As she climbed out of the camper, he did as well. "I can manage my bags myself," Holly assured him.

"I'm sure you can, but a gentleman always sees a lady safely to her door."

Holly thought he was being a little silly, until she

reached the front desk and learned that her reservation had been given away when she didn't show up by six P.M. and hadn't called to let them know she'd be late.

"But I'm sure my travel agent would have guaranteed it for late arrival with my credit card," Holly protested.

They were very apologetic, but there was nothing they could do for her. There were no vacancies anywhere that they knew of.

She was considering camping in the hotel lobby when David once again picked up her suitcase and headed for the exit. "Let's go," was all he said.

As he pulled the camper out of the parking lot, Holly pointed across the street to another hotel. "I could try that one. Maybe they have something."

David shook his head. "You heard the clerk. The motels and hotels are full. The campgrounds probably are, too. Fortunately, we don't need anything but a parking space."

"*We?*"

He shook his head at her. "Be reasonable, lady. I'm dead on my ass. I'm not going to drive around for another couple of hours in the dark in a strange area when we've been told it's a waste of time. You can try to find a place for yourself tomorrow. For tonight, you can sleep with me."

"David!"

He clutched his chest and gasped for breath. "Oh my God! She called me by my first name. Was it good for you too, darling?"

"Stop it. I'm serious. We hardly know each other. Quarters this small would be cramped for an old married couple."

"Look, I am so tired, I can't even think of a snappy comeback to that great opening you just gave me. It's getting late. All I want is a few hours' sleep, and you don't have any options —unless you want to go wandering around in the dark with the looters." A shudder gave her fear away. "Okay then, I'll take the bed, since it's the only mattress long enough for me. You can have the bunk above us. You'll be perfectly safe up there, I swear."

"Why? Are you afraid of heights, too?"

"Ouch. No, I'm not. But I'm afraid of falling on my head, and that's a very narrow, short shelf. Not at all conducive to fun and games, even if I was up to it. Okay?"

What choice did she have? She sighed; it seemed she was doing that a lot around him.

Another hour in bumper-to-bumper traffic got them only halfway to Key Largo. Needing another injection of caffeine, he pulled the motor home into a rest area. He excused himself and slipped into the tiny bathroom.

When he came out, he opened one of the cabinets and removed a jar of instant coffee. "Would you like something to drink? Coffee, tea, soup? If it mixes with water we've got it. Or there's cold sodas in the fridge."

She poked her head around the edge of the big captain's chair. "Tea would be nice. Need help?"

He laughed and shook his head. "This is strictly a one-person kitchen." From another cabinet he removed two mugs, filled them with water, and stuck them in the microwave oven.

"Don't tell me you're one of those liberated males who knows the difference between a pot and a pan. I would hate to have to alter my biased opinion of you."

That earned her one of his teasing winks. "Nope. Strictly a macho-man through and through. Besides, if I learned how to cook, a whole string of restaurants would go out of business. What about you? Like to play with food?" He placed the two steaming mugs on the ledge below the dashboard, then climbed into the driver's seat.

"I'm one of those modern women who believe the microwave was the greatest invention of the twentieth century."

"Well, hell! And here I was about to suggest you could repay me for my hospitality with a few days of cooking."

"Fat chance!" she said, laughing. "Once I left my parents' restaurant, I swore I'd never work with food again." A stray memory of the day her father had ordered her out of her bedroom and off to work took away her smile.

David took a sip of his coffee as he watched Holly deal with some inner conflict. His natural ability to read people by their expressions and body language gave him an advantage in his career and personal life. It was also natural for him to use that talent to analyze an adversary. And Holly was definitely an adversary.

Every time she started to relax around him, he said something that got her uptight again. This time however, it was her own words that had caused the mood swing.

"Where was their restaurant?" he asked, more to get the dialogue flowing again than out of real curiosity.

"They still have it, in a northern suburb of Pittsburgh, Pennsylvania."

"Oh? Is that where you grew up?"

"For the most part."

"Any brothers, sisters, childhood pets you'd like to tell me about?"

She glanced at him and took a drink of tea. His voice had a strange edge to it, as if he was interviewing her, rather than having a friendly, getting-to-know-you chat. It was probably only because he was a reporter, but it made her uncomfortable. "Haven't you heard enough of my voice for one day? Why don't you tell me about yourself instead."

He considered her reluctance to give personal information proof that she had something to hide. Of course, he'd already uncovered the basic statistics about her, through the newspaper's computer service, but he had thought if he could get her talking about her background, she would say something that would give away her connection to Erica Donner. Perhaps if he opened up to her first, she'd relinquish a few tidbits about herself in return. "What would you like to know?"

"Whatever you'd like—Let me rephrase that. Whatever you can tell without bringing up your intimate encounters with the opposite sex."

"Well, hell. That wipes out half my life story!" He gave her another wink that could have meant he was joking or it was the complete truth. "Okay, let's see. I grew up in a relatively seedy area of Washington, D.C., along with four brothers and sisters. Nancy and Patty are older, Gary and Jill, younger. That made me the middle child, but I was the smartest and bestlooking, so I never suffered for it."

He ignored her groan. "With my old man, that made six of us in a two-bedroom, one-bath apartment. You can't imagine how strange it seemed when I moved out and had a bathroom all to myself. Every once in a while I still expect somebody to bang on the door when I'm taking a shower."

Holly angled her head at him. "What about your mother?"

David shrugged. If she had a heart at all, this next truth would win him a few points. "She took off right after she dropped number five in seven years. We never heard from her again." Bingo. Her heart was in her eyes.

"How awful."

He raised his brows in surprise. "Not really. We learned to make do. Sometimes I think we had a closer-knit family because we had to help each other. Dad did the best he could, under the circumstances. His job in the factory never earned enough to take care of five kids, but we managed with welfare, and as soon as I was old enough, I got a job as a paperboy for *The Washington Times.*

"It didn't get really tough until Dad was laid off when I was in tenth grade. I skipped the rest of that school year to take a full-time job working for the neighborhood grocer, besides keeping up my paper route. The other kids earned a little money too, but I wouldn't let any of them quit school."

Holly frowned. "What do you mean, *you* wouldn't let them. What about your father?"

Again David shrugged. "I don't know. It just sort of happened. One day, he was in charge of the family, and the next day, I was. Like I said, he did his best, and eventually he found another job, and I went back to school."

"How did you manage college?"

His grin revealed his pride. "Fortunately, schoolwork came easily to me. Between being a paperboy most of my youth and maintaining a straight 'A' average through high school, I won the Newsboy Scholarship. Since I couldn't afford room and board, I chose George Washington University, not far from where we lived. You'll never guess what I majored in."

"Girls?"

"Smart-ass. Look, the traffic's finally let up a little. Why don't you use the bathroom while we're still parked? It takes a little improvising to get around in there anyway, but I bet it's damn near impossible when we're moving."

Holly felt the blush coming and tried to get out of her seat before he could see it. His arm instantly formed a barricade across the space in front of her.

"Do you always embarrass so easily?"

She sighed loudly and glared at his hand. "No. I don't."

He raised his arm and smiled at her back as she moved away. It didn't make sense, but the realization that he could so easily fracture her composure, and she knew it, made him feel rather cocky.

He had hoped his sad but true tale would put another crack in the lady's barrier, and it looked like he'd accomplished that much. But it had also served the purpose of reminding him of his vows where women were concerned. Vows that Holly could make him forget for a few hours if he let her.

Women had their functions, and he used them whenever the opportunity arose. But developing feelings for them, forming relationships, even friendships, were completely out of the question. No woman would ever have the chance to do to him what his mother had done to his old man. No woman would ever leave him with a broken heart and a brood of children. He'd take what they had to offer and go on to the next one when they got too possessive.

As soon as she was buckled back into her seat, he eased the big motor home onto the turnpike again.

Holly thought they had been making some progress toward friendship, but now she wasn't so sure.

Something had changed in the minutes she had been away, and she wanted to quickly recapture whatever ground had been lost. "Are you and your family still close?"

He seemed surprised that she wanted to know more about him, but he replied without hesitation. "Not in real miles. We're spread all over the country now. . . . but inside"—he paused to tap his temple—"that won't ever change.

"There was this one time, a fancy-dress high school dance. My two older sisters were certain they would die if they couldn't attend. Dad and I pooled our money. I had a pretty big paper route by then. We only had enough for one dress. Now you know, most girls would have fought tooth and nail to be the one to get a new dress. Not my two. Nancy wore the dress for the first half of the dance, then turned it over to Patty for the second half. That way they both had a night to remember. The only problem was, Patty was about four inches shorter and ten pounds heavier than Nancy, so we got a dress size in between. It didn't fit either one of them perfectly, but the rest of us convinced them they both looked like movie stars. Luckily, everyone at the dance was too preoccupied with their own appearance to notice the switch, or at least they had the decency not to mention it."

He related a few more family stories and moved on to anecdotes about Harry Abbott, the sportswriter who had taken him under his wing, until he had her laughing along with him. When she accused him of making them up, the tales became even more outrageous.

When was the last time she had laughed so much? *Jerry.* The answer sobered her slightly, but she didn't let the realization ruin the fun she was having.

There *were* similarities between the two: They were both extremely handsome, self-centered men who went through women faster than toilet tissue, they both teased mercilessly and made her laugh, and they could both kiss like the devil. Only this one couldn't take her to hell, because she no longer had childish fantasies about falling in love.

There were also great differences. Where Jerry cared about no one but himself, David obviously loved his family and his friend, Harry. Jerry never had to work to get what he wanted. David had known hard times and had struggled to overcome the odds without feeling sorry for himself. Where Jerry had carried out an elaborate farce for his own pleasure, David had been blunt about his intentions and brutally honest about his subsequent disinterest.

And thank heaven for that fact. The way she had responded to his kiss was not only mindless, but dangerous. She would never be able to keep him at arm's length as she did Philip. With David, her own passion could be her undoing . . . again. Yes, it was definitely a good thing he wasn't interested in that sort of relationship with her.

As a friend, she would be free to notice the way his smile showed off perfect, white teeth, or that his hair hadn't been trimmed in some time. If he caught her staring he wouldn't be driven by a primitive need to pull her against his hard body and—

"Hey! Here I thought you were enthralled by my stories and all the time you were off in another world."

She tried to look indignant. "I heard every word you said. You're very funny."

"So? Answer my last question."

Once again heat flushed her cheeks, but this time it was too dark for him to see it. "All right. Maybe I drifted a little." Suddenly she noticed the line of traffic had come to a complete stop. "Where are we?"

"The last exit, Florida City. According to the map, from here, U.S. One runs all the way down to Key West."

The tollbooth worker took the money from David and asked, "Where're you headed?"

"As far as we can go," David replied.

"I'm afraid that won't be but about twenty-nine miles. Then you'll reach the roadblock. Curfew went into effect at eight o'clock and all traffic into the Keys is being turned back until sunrise tomorrow."

"But I'm a reporter sent to cover the story."

"The police aren't making any exceptions."

"The roads are that dangerous?"

The man laughed. "It's hard to say what's the most dangerous, trees across the roads, downed power lines, the looters, or the displaced snakes and gators. Regardless, you'll have to wait till tomorrow. But I can tell you one thing right now—there's nothing left to see."

Holly tapped David's arm. "Ask him if there's a motel near here."

David motioned for her to be patient. "Is there a campground anywhere near here?"

The man gave him simple directions to one close by, but added, "The power hasn't been restored in this area yet, and the water's not safe to drink, so be careful. Oh, and you may as well be prepared for a pretty steep price—*if* they have any spaces available. Everything around here filled up hours ago."

As they pulled away from the tollbooth, Holly said, "You didn't ask him about a motel." David didn't bother to answer her with words. His eyes showed that he had no more patience for that discussion.

The campsites on the grounds the man had directed them to were all rented, but for a mere $100 they were given permission to park on the property without any hookups. They could use the facilities, however. Just don't drink the water, and be sure to use lots of insect repellent. The mosquitos were worse than usual after a storm.

David paid the owner and drove to a vacant space of grass barely large enough to fit the motor home. He got the generator going a few minutes later, then went to "visit the facilities."

While he was gone, Holly inventoried the contents of the refrigerator and cabinets. It had been quite a while since she'd eaten, but she didn't want to be fussing with things if he wanted to go right to sleep. By the time David returned, Holly had set out cold cuts, bread, and condiments on the counter and was making a sandwich.

"That guy wasn't kidding about the mosquitos. I just met a couple in the men's room that were big enough to shake hands with. I hope that's for me," he said, grinning at the sandwich.

She handed it to him on a paper plate. "Only because you asked so politely," she returned, and proceeded to make another for herself. "I owe you a proper thank-you," she said when she joined him at the little table.

"I'd prefer an improper one."

"I'm serious."

"You're always serious."

She grimaced. "Now I forgot what I was going to say."

"Thank you, David, for—"

"Oh. Yes. For not leaving me stranded. I'm not much good at winging it. I . . . tend to work better in an organized, wellplanned situation. Anyway, I appreciate your letting me stay here with you."

His eyes twinkled mischievously. "We still haven't talked about your payment, have we?"

"Don't you ever think of anything else?"

"Don't you? I didn't say a single lascivious word. Admit it, lady. You're earthy, too."

"And you're incorrigible."

"I know, but I've thought of a payment that won't cost you much at all."

She refused to be baited again.

"You have to get on that bed with me."

She stopped in midchew for a split second, then continued eating. She was not going to give him the satisfaction of seeing her blush again.

"And watch a movie."

Her eyebrows lifted a notch. The smug expression on his face warned her she hadn't heard all of it.

"If I lay down now, without unwinding, I wouldn't be able to fall asleep, no matter how tired I am. The television and VCR are built into the wall at the foot of the bed, and there's a whole library of movies in the headboard. Oh, and one more thing, I get to pick the movie."

Totally exasperated with his game, she threw her hands in the air. "All right. Spit it out. What triple-X-rated film are you going to make me suffer through?"

His smile was so big, it crinkled the corners of his eyes. "How about *Star Trek IV*? Earthy enough for you?"

He'd done it to her again. "The one with the whales? It's my favorite."

"Somehow I knew you'd say that."

"You have the most beautiful breasts, baby. I could spend all night loving them."

Rachel whimpered as her nipples reacted to the flattery and expert suckling. A sharp spear of pleasure cut through her. She opened her eyes so that she could see the talented hands molding her flesh into two mounds and watch the tongue circling and teasing each peak. If she didn't climax soon, she would surely die. "Please," she begged. "Finish it."

Erica knew precisely what words to say and what actions to perform to bring Rachel to a point of desperate, near-mindless need. She liked to be kept hanging on the edge, wet and wanting, and so aroused that nothing mattered but the intense pulsing between her legs. When Erica was in a particularly spiteful mood, like now, she could drag it out for hours, until she was administering more torture than pleasure.

It infuriated her that Rachel could tug on her strings and make her jump as if she was no more than a marionette. Yet what else could she do? She'd made one mistake years ago, and it looked like she would go on paying for it for the rest of her life.

Or Rachel's.

That thought caused her to deliver a much harder bite than she meant to, but Rachel was beyond noticing any pain. While Erica's hands and mouth automatically eased downward over Rachel's large, muscular body, she mentally replayed the events that had put her in the position of having to dance to Rachel's tune.

She had known from the moment they were introduced that Rachel was sexually attracted to her, though the other woman hadn't seemed to understand it herself. The sheer perverseness of it titillated Erica's ego enough that she allowed Rachel to think they were friends, when in reality she simply found humor in the way Rachel adored her and found excuses to make physical contact.

Because of the Little Sister Society, they maintained their peculiar friendship and continued to see each other several times a year even after Erica transferred out to Berkeley to finish college.

Shortly after graduation, Erica met and married her first husband, a young man with a weakness for drugs, whose only redeeming quality was his sexual prowess, and even that vanished almost overnight. She got a job in marketing while Rachel spent her time in law school, then went on to become an FBI agent.

It wasn't long before Erica tired of supporting her husband and his heroin habit with her hard-earned money. She wanted to be free of him, but was determined to make him repay her. Unfortunately for him, the only thing he had of value was a life insurance policy.

Rachel supplied her with the means to implement her payback plan during one of their get-togethers. She was a rookie agent by that time and had bragged about being involved in a major drug bust where a quantity of poisoned heroin had been confiscated. The lethal drug had been turning up all over the country, leaving a trail of bodies behind. That night, Erica talked Rachel into going skinny-dipping with her—for fun. She teased her and tempted her and promised that they could have a lot more fun . . . if Rachel could get hold of some of that special heroin for her.

Rachel complied the next day, and Erica made her first payment on her debt that night.

Always having been a quick study, Erica did what came naturally and discovered that what Rachel wanted most of all was to be treated like a beautiful, desirable woman, despite her big body, masculine appearance, and employment in an aggressive career.

Rachel never said a word about Erica's first husband's sudden demise, until after number two succumbed to severe depression and committed suicide in their bathroom. According to the police report, he'd taken an overdose of a narcotic that had been prescribed by his psychiatrist, climbed into the bathtub, then neatly sliced his wrists and ankles with a razor blade. Only Rachel surmised that the man may have had a little assistance getting into the tub.

Erica had been trying to break it off gently with Rachel, but when Rachel's plea that they get together one more time had a hint of a threat in it, Erica paid her a visit.

It hadn't taken much urging on Rachel's part for Erica to get very drunk that night. The next day, she didn't recall everything they talked about, but Rachel reminded her. With a little prodding, Erica had described how she had sent both husbands to meet their maker, and to this day, Rachel never let her forget that she had made that confession to an officer of the law. Though Erica was of a mind to extend Rachel's torture, time did not permit such diversion. She brought Rachel to a grand finale, then cuddled and caressed her until the spasms of pleasure subsided.

"Do you really have to go so soon?" Rachel asked a bit petulantly.

Erica laughed and nipped her ear. "So soon? I really didn't have time to make this little detour at all. But you begged so prettily, I couldn't resist. I've got a morning appointment in my West Coast office. A captain of industry can't just abandon her ship— no matter how enjoyable the distraction."

She had instructed her pilot to stand by at the airport for a quick departure. She knew just how much time was required to calm Rachel for a few weeks. And under the circumstances, it was more necessary than usual that Rachel be kept level-headed. Fortunately, she could sleep on the way home. Her private jet was equipped with a comfortable bed because of the number of cross-country trips she was required to make.

Rachel smiled and stretched her sated body as the slender, dark-haired beauty rose from the bed. Not having to go anywhere herself, she gave in to the luxury of simply lying there, watching Erica get back into her public persona.

It began with her slipping on the sheer beige bra and panties that made her look like she was still nude. When Rachel was with Erica, she felt pretty, feminine, *petite*. Like she should be the one wearing the sexy lingerie. But somehow, she never got the nerve to buy herself anything like that.

"Anything new on the Ziegler murder?" Erica asked as she brushed her hair back into its normally severe style.

Rachel had been thinking of how that hair felt unbound, draped across her thighs. The question abruptly reminded her of how easily her hot lover could turn cold. A moment ago, she had been feeling beautiful and sexy, sprawled out on the satin sheets. Now she felt exposed. As usual, however, she said nothing as she got up and put on her robe.

She told her the same facts she had related to April. "The media has been put off with the explanation that it could be a serial-style killing, and we don't want to encourage any copycats by releasing details. Other than that there's nothing the investigative team can really sink our teeth into." Rachel snickered. "And you *know* how badly I want to catch the murderer of such a *good* man."

Erica's eyes sparkled back at her as she clucked her tongue. "Such a terrible tragedy." She set her suitcases on the foot of the bed and opened them to pack. "Have we got anything new on our other friends?"

Rachel propped herself up on a pile of pillows. "It looks like Holly Kaufman will try to handle the Frampton file, so we'll see how she does before going any further. I told April my concerns about Kaufman, but she's convinced we won't have any problems from her. I'm going to keep an eye on her anyway, though.

"Bobbi's all set to move in on Frankowicz the minute he steps foot back on U.S. soil. That should be next month."

"And O'Day?" Erica's voice could have cut glass. He was the one she and Rachel wanted the most, the one that had gotten as much pleasure from using his fists as his penis.

Rachel shook her head. "His wife is going to take him for everything he's got. But according to the sports pages, his new contract will fill his bank account back up in no time. I swear, the guardian angel of the big and stupid must be working overtime."

"Well, then," Erica said, smiling slyly. "Perhaps

we need to arrange something *special* to see that Mr. O'Day receives his just rewards."

As Erica finished packing, they exchanged a few ideas.

"Oh, shit," Erica muttered and hurried to the side of the bed, where she pulled an automatic pistol out from under the mattress.

Rachel nodded her approval as Erica efficiently unloaded and dismantled the weapon and placed the sections in separate suitcases. The law still permitted civilians to transport weapons on airplanes as long as a few simple rules were followed. It had taken Rachel a while to convince Erica to carry a gun when she traveled, but once she got used to handling it, the weapon became one of her regular accessory items.

"All set," Erica declared as she locked the cases. "Now promise me you'll try to stay straight while I'm gone." Drunk, Rachel was unpredictable, dangerous . . . talked too much.

"Don't worry. I haven't had a drop since Ziegler was sent to hell. But if I get to feeling edgy, I'll call you."

With a wink and a thumbs-up sign, Erica picked up the phone and dialed the bell captain. "Would y'all please send a bellhop up to the penthouse?"

Hearing Erica put on her sweet Southern accent so easily had Rachel laughing.

Erica snaked her arms around Rachel's neck, and gave her a slow, wet kiss, then smiled. "You keep my secrets, darlin', and yours will always be safe with me."

There were times when Rachel despised that knowing little smile of hers.

For the first half hour of the film, Holly had sat stiffly on the edge of the bed, her arms crossed protectively over her stomach. Poised for flight, she was prepared to scurry away at the first suspicious movement on David's part.

Her peripheral vision had taken in his reclined body, legs stretched out with ankles crossed, hands behind his head supported by several pillows. When she finally convinced herself that his full attention was on the movie, she had relaxed enough to scoot back to the pile of pillows he had arranged for her use.

David willed himself to follow the dialogue between Spock and Captain Kirk, and ignore the nervous woman next to him. He analyzed that his inability to concentrate stemmed from the fact that the last woman with whom he had shared a bed and remained fully clothed was his kid sister. *This* was unnatural.

It was also uncomfortable for a reason that had nothing to do with sex. From vast experience, he knew when a woman was filled with nervous anticipation. Holly's case of nerves seemed to originate in fear. He reminded himself of his conclusion that that was exactly how he wanted her to feel. His instincts told him she was dangerous for him, that she might have the power to get under his skin. And yet he didn't care for being cast in the role of villain either.

Besides, he had yet to find a smooth way to introduce the name Erica Donner into their conversations. He was fully aware of the fact that she had turned his interviewing techniques back on him. She now knew his life story and he had had a wonderful time spilling his guts to her. He, on the other hand, hadn't gained one new tidbit about her.

By the time the credits were rolling, he decided a slight alteration in their relationship was absolutely necessary to get through the next few days. He intended to insist that she stay there with him, if only to get some questions answered.

As she started to inch off the bed, he made up his mind about what had to be done. "Wait a minute." She stopped, but the wariness in her eyes told him it was hard for her not to run. "This isn't going to work, you know."

"I'm sorry. I'll find a place in the morning."

"That's not what I mean. You know you won't find anything better than this, nor should you waste a day looking when you should be working. No, I'm talking about this tension between us. I'll admit I had no intention of mentioning it, let alone apologizing, but it's obvious we can't share this space with you scared to death I'm going to jump on you every minute."

"I'm not—"

"Yes, you are. I figured you deserved the big, bad wolf treatment the other night. You got me pissed and my reaction was—"

"Childish? Beastly?"

"Not one of my better moments. I think we could be friends, if you could forget our rough start."

Friends? Her smile spread slowly over her features. *He* was suggesting they be friends. She couldn't have planned it more perfectly. Holding out her hand, she said, "Friends."

He clasped her hand and moved closer. "No more jumping if I touch you? I'm afraid I'm a habitual toucher."

She grimaced. "I can't promise, but I'll try to anticipate it."

"And I'll try to move slowly enough for you to see it coming. One more thing. I only know one way to erase your memory of that . . . incident. I'll even ask permission." His gaze settled on her mouth. "May I?" She parted her lips in answer. Continuing to hold her hand, he leaned forward and touched his lips to hers.

Lightly. Tenderly. Briefly.

And with an impact more devastating than any blatant open mouthed kiss could ever be.

"You see?" He whispered the words against her mouth. "I can be nice. There's nothing to be afraid of."

She raised her lashes and met his gaze. They both knew just how wrong he was.

11

The sun peeking in through the sides of the curtains worked as well as an alarm clock for Holly. She was surprised that she had gotten a few hours sleep in spite of the fact that the excessive humidity made her sticky and she was still wearing the same clothes as yesterday. Not to mention that there had been a man not twenty feet away from her all night. Leaving on the small light over the stove had helped somewhat, but she had not actually *slept* in the same room with anyone in fourteen years. The one and only night she had stayed with Philip, she hadn't closed her eyes.

Sometime during the night, Holly had talked herself into believing David's caress had been a friendly gesture, even brotherly. To be on the safe side, however, she'd make sure it didn't happen again.

For his part, David had determined that the insistent throbbing of his sex was due to almost two weeks of celibacy rather than a physical contact that could hardly be called a kiss. He had firmly shut out the irrational voice that reminded him that he had not bedded a woman since first seeing Holly in the hotel lobby.

The whirring sound of the microwave roused David, but he feigned sleep a little longer. The more he thought about the two kisses they had shared, the more certain he was that he had been wrong to think that seduction was not the right tool to extract information from Holly. Her being an innocent only meant he had to proceed more slowly than usual, but the end result would be the same. She would soon be happy to tell him anything he wanted to know, including whether or not any of her friends was a murderess.

He suddenly realized that somewhere along the way, he had eliminated the possibility that *she* could be a killer. Her reaction to being touched was his biggest clue. She'd been a victim once and had never fully recovered, of that he was certain. He couldn't imagine her becoming aggressive enough to kill, even in self-defense. His conclusion was that she could not have murdered Tim Ziegler ... personally.

But his nose still told him she knew something about it that she was keeping to herself. The task he'd assigned himself was to get her to share that secret. He would begin by showing her how much he respected her privacy.

Since the generator-run window air conditioner was in the center of the camper, he had left the vinyl accordion door open throughout the night. With his lower half discreetly covered by the sheet, he rose and pulled shut the divider before donning his slacks.

Holly's modesty was getting the best of her. She needed to use the bathroom, but hated the thought of traipsing outside to the public—probably filthy— facilities, even more than she dreaded using the one inside.

"Good morning," David offered with a cheerful grin when he emerged from his sleeping area. He had a roll of clothing in one hand. "I'm going to take advantage of that undrinkable water to shower and shave, but I would recommend you make do with what we have here. There's no telling who or what is lurking in and around the women's area. I'll just fill the water tank up again later."

She wondered if he was psychic or just very considerate. Her eyes expressed her gratitude as clearly as her shy "Thank you."

Holly was bathed, dressed, and on her second cup of coffee by the time David returned. She had begun to wonder if he had gone off to survey the area without telling her, when he appeared wearing a bigger smile than when he'd left.

"I've got great news," he said, pouring himself a mug of coffee. "I went by the management office to ask a few questions and got more than I expected. The manager agreed to rent me his son's moped for a couple of days."

"This is a good thing?"

He smirked at her. "It would be rather foolish to try driving this monster on roads that haven't been cleared yet."

"But have you ever driven a moped before?" she asked, continuing to sound skeptical.

"It's a bicycle with a motor. How hard can it be?"

She raised her eyes to the ceiling.

"Well, of course, you don't have to come along. I'm sure you'll find other transportation eventually."

She realized she was about to sigh again and stopped herself. "I would very much appreciate your being my chauffeur through the disaster area, on one condition. I pay for half of the rental cost, on the bike and the campsite."

David raised an eyebrow. "Does that mean you've given up the idea of finding a motel room?"

She shrugged and tried not to blush. "If you'll let me share expenses, I'd be most grateful for the use of the bunk for another night."

He toasted her with his coffee mug. "I assure you, it will be my pleasure."

An hour later, Holly had her arms wrapped around David's waist from behind and was praying for salvation as he learned the feel of the moped. But as they sputtered their way onto Key Largo, she forgot all about her own safety.

A few of the newer hotels and condominium buildings still had concrete shells to mark their existence. No roofs, windows, or signs had remained intact, however. In several instances, walls of homes had collapsed completely and the furnishings had been strewn over parking lots, swimming pools, and the beach.

She was stunned to see so many people wandering through the wreckage, some searching for things, others just looking dazed. David barely avoided running into a toilet perched in the middle of the lane. The small, two-wheeled vehicle allowed them to skirt fallen trees, broken glass, and sizable sections of concrete walls.

David stopped from time to time so they could each take pictures and dictate notes into their tape recorders. He interviewed the first police officer he saw. The man had been on duty for thirty hours, in spite of learning that his own home had been leveled. He just kept repeating how glad he was that he had forced his wife and kids to go north.

"Any idea how the evacuation went?" David asked.

"It could have been worse I suppose. Andrew

taught a lot of people a lesson, you know, sort of prepared them for this one, so they got moving at the first hint that Brigitte was headed this way. But there were still a lot of people who just refused to leave. I heard a couple of the older bridges further south collapsed with full loads of cars on them. They'll be searching for bodies for weeks."

"Any numbers yet?" David prodded in a concerned tone.

The officer shook his head. "It'll be a while before anything's substantiated, but I heard it could be in the thousands." A shoving match in a driveway across the road caught his attention and, warning David to be careful, he took off.

They passed a fishing boat lodged in a palm tree that had been split in half, and a sailboat skewered on a concrete dock piling. Twisted automobiles had been hurled into houses as well as the ocean. Where an expensive home used to stand, a crowd had gathered to see the nurse shark that had landed in the swimming pool.

David was able to continue driving south as far as Islamorada, but the bridge between Upper and Lower Matecumbe keys was gone. There weren't even pilings sticking out of the murky water to show where it had once stood. Very few people had ventured this far, and there was no sign of any police or cleanup crews.

Holly asked David to stop so she could walk along the beach and get a closer look at the shore. "I thought that's what I saw," she said with a frown, then began taking pictures. "This was a large mangrove stand. It looks like someone just came along with a giant buzzsaw and mowed them down. It's probably like this the whole way up and down the coast."

David shaded his eyes as he tried to see what she was talking about. "So?"

She lowered her camera and met his gaze. "The mangroves are vital to coastal ecology. The fallen mangrove leaves feed hundreds of species of fish, which become food for larger fish and birds. Without the mangroves, the food chain is disrupted and many of the animals may leave to find a new breeding area, if they survive at all."

Shifting slightly, she captured David's profile in her sight. He was staring out at the water as if looking for an explanation for all the destruction they had witnessed. Her finger twitched on the button before she realized she wanted a picture of him just like that.

They returned to Key Largo and tracked down every person in a position of any authority they could find. Sea and air rescues were being organized for the lower islands. A considerable amount of friendly conversation earned David and Holly their choice of hitching a ride in an observation helicopter or a boat the next morning. Considering the choppy sea and the twelve-hour duration of the boat trip, they opted for the bird's-eye view. David swore helicopters didn't bother him the way jets did, but Holly thought he still looked a bit squeamish.

By late afternoon they returned to the mainland and found two working pay phones. Holly's phone calls to Evelyn and Philip only took a few minutes each, but David was dictating a lengthy article to his paper, so she made one more.

"Hi, Mom. Sorry I didn't phone first thing this morning, but I have a good reason. Guess where I'm calling you from."

"Unless it's Pittsburgh International Airport, I don't care."

Holly heard the hint of depression and instantly tensed. "What's wrong?" She heard her mother's sigh and realized it was the same sound she had been making a lot lately. "What's Pop done now?"

"I always try to be understanding, you know that. But every time there's a crisis, he acts like he's the only person in this house that's upset by it."

Holly knew her mother was referring to the deaths of her brother and sister. Although her mother had been devastated by the losses and suffered severe bouts of depression to this day, her father's anger had consumed all his thoughts, blinding him to his wife's needs. Holly deduced that she had now brought more trouble down on them with her confession rather than clearing the air. "I didn't tell you about what happened to get either of you upset—"

"I know that, baby, but he's completely irrational when it comes to protecting what's his. Right now, it's like a fresh wound and all he can think about is finding a way to get even. I'm sure he'll get over it sooner or later, but it might help if you came home for a whole weekend soon."

"I'll try, I promise." She told her mother where she was and what she had seen that day, but she had the feeling her words went unheard.

"Problem?" David asked behind her.

She forced a bright smile. "Not at all. But this heat is killing me. It must be over a hundred degrees out here. And I'm starving. Remind me to pack a lunch tomorrow."

"Yeah. You'd think Brigitte would have had the decency to leave at least one McDonald's standing."

They headed back to the motor home, only to find the interior more stifling than the outdoors. After turning on the a.c. unit, they both opted for cold showers in the public facilities with the mosquitos while the camper cooled down.

Clean and somewhat more comfortable, they combined their culinary talents to boil some spaghetti and heat up some bottled sauce. When David opened a bottle of blush wine, she accepted a glass without hesitation. It had been one hell of a day.

Their conversation flowed more easily over dinner, as if they had known each other much longer than a few days. Holly was again amazed at the very different extremes David had to his personality and wondered if he saw her the same way. At least it appeared that her plan for them to become friends was moving along just fine. She decided right then that, as soon as she returned to Washington, she would forward the notes on Jerry Frampton to him.

Remembering her idea of doing some investigating on her own, she now firmly discarded it. Not only did her staying with David make it difficult, her decision meant it was no longer necessary for her to attempt something she had no experience with.

Without discussing it, she cleared the small table and started washing dishes. He automatically picked up a towel to dry.

"So what do you think about accenting the environmental impact of the hurricane?" she asked.

"I think it'll work. Of course, I have to verify some of the information you gave me."

"Of all the nerve. Are you insinuating you can't take my word for it?"

He started to stammer out an explanation of his cautious method of reporting when he caught the glint in her eye. She was actually teasing *him*. In a flash, he twirled the damp dishtowel into a weapon and delivered a sting to her backside. "That was for leading me to believe you had no sense of humor. But just to prove I don't hold a grudge, you can pick the movie tonight."

In spite of the fact that she knew better than to climb on that bed again, she did. Scanning the labels on the tapes, she chose a nice, family comedy: *Overboard.* They both laughed over the silly plot, and both held their breath when Kurt Russell and Goldie Hawn ended up making love. Holly scolded herself for not remembering just how steamy that scene was.

The moment the first credit appeared she said good night, but her escape was halted when David's arm shot out in front of her.

"Hold it," he said as his fingers closed over her shoulders and forced her to twist toward him. "This still isn't working, is it?"

"I don't know what you're talking about." She purposely kept her eyes averted. "Let me go, David. I didn't give you permission for this."

Her gaze darted back to him a moment before his mouth pressed against hers. She tipped her head back and turned aside, as her fists pressed against his chest.

He kept his grip on her shoulders as he murmured into her ear. "Just one real kiss, lady love. One without anger, without pretended indifference. Then I'll let you run away. You know you want to taste that kiss as much as I do."

"I do not."

"Liar."

His lips grazed her cheek and sought her mouth again. Instead of the pressure she expected, he brushed his mouth back and forth, teasing until she began to move to the lazy rhythm. She could not stop herself from closing her eyes to savor the exquisite sensation. Only then did he take the real kiss he had spoken of. As his mouth slanted over hers, his hands eased her backward until she was lying beside him.

It was the first kiss again, and more, because this time he was caught up in the same maelstrom of wonder as she. When his tongue entered the play, she was already open and waiting to meet him.

Twice he broke the kiss and returned with a feeling of disbelief. *It wasn't supposed to be this good.*

She was warm, wrapped in a cocoon of luxurious velvet. Why did this man have to be the one to reawaken her desire? He had drawn one knee up and over her thighs, and she felt his male body hardening and tensing all along her own. What happened after their first kiss came back to her in a flash, and she pulled her head away.

"I thought you weren't interested, Mr. Wells."

"I'm not."

"Liar." She slid her hand down his shirt to his belt buckle, but he grabbed her wrist and pinned her arm down on the bed beside her.

"If you start that, you'd better be ready to finish it. Are you?"

She blinked in an effort to reorient herself. For the moment her mind was fully occupied with the need to catch her breath. It took another moment to realize what she had almost done.

He saw the confusion in her eyes and gave her a break. Gentling his hold, he placed a light kiss on her parted lips. "Easy, lady love. I was just doing my damnedest to live up to my promise not to take anything more than a kiss. Gentlemen always keep their promises, you know." He grinned down at her and she relaxed in his embrace. "I have a confession to make," he whispered, stroking her hair.

"Do I want to hear it?"

"I hope so. The evening I saw you at the airport, I didn't really recognize Philip. I was trying to find out who you were."

"Surprise, surprise," she said with a dry laugh.

"Because I had seen you before and was intrigued as hell." He made her wait a few seconds for the rest. "About two weeks ago. In the lobby of the Kessler Hotel. You walked by and I felt like I'd been hit by one of *Star Trek*'s tractor beams. It was all I could do not to follow you into the elevator." He felt her breathing change and purposely lightened his tone. "It's too bad I didn't know you then. You could have saved me a lot of time trying to get an interview with your friend."

She felt the color draining from her face and sat up slowly. "My friend?"

He nodded. "Yeah. Erica Donner. That *was* who you went up to the penthouse to see, wasn't it?"

"Oh. Yes, of course. I remember."

He sat up, but was careful not to crowd. She looked like she was preparing to fly away any second. "She's a real piece of work. Can't say as I understand you two being friends."

"We, uh, haven't seen each other in years. Since college," she added, unable to instantly think of anything more believable than a partial truth.

His mind automatically called up the facts that Holly had graduated from Georgetown and Donner from Berkeley. But Donner had once attended Dominion as well. "Really? Where was that?"

Her pupils dilated a mere fraction, enough to give her fear away. "Georgetown."

He narrowed his eyes in thought. Could Donner have attended Georgetown and it never showed up in her bio? He didn't think so. Holly was lying about that. He knew it as well as he knew his own name. He also knew that whatever her connection was with Erica Donner had Holly scared to death. But it wasn't time to challenge her yet. If he pushed for the truth now, he could be sacrificing the chance to get bigger truths later.

Being reminded that she was a liar who could be involved in something deadly helped him control his desire enough to let her leave his company, and made him more determined than ever to uncover her secrets.

April forced herself to wait until Sunday evening before taking action. She had called Holly's apartment Saturday afternoon and evening, then two more times on Sunday, but there was no answer, not even a machine. Finally, she placed a call to Bobbi.

"Hello?"

The strong tone of the voice put April on alert. "Roberta?"

"Yes. How are you, April?"

"I'm fine, but I need to speak to Bobbi."

"I'm sorry. That's not possible right now."

It was difficult to deal with the Roberta personality face to face; over the phone was nearly impossible. April strengthened her own voice to one of supreme authority. "How long has Bobbi been away?"

"About a week, maybe a little more."

April deduced that the personality change probably occurred after their group meeting. "What have you done, Roberta?"

She paused long enough for April's tension to mount. "Nothing."

"You and I both know that's probably not true.

Otherwise, Bobbi would be back. What did you tell her employer?"

The voice lost a good deal of its confidence. "She has a bad case of strep throat. She couldn't call in for herself."

"Listen to me, Roberta, you and I will have a long talk about this the next time we get together, but Bobbi has to come back now. She needs to report to work, and I need her to do an important favor for all of us."

"I could do it," Roberta countered a bit testily.

"Bobbi is better suited for this," April stated firmly. "Now let me talk to her." There was another momentary pause on the line, during which April could almost visualize the transfer of control.

"Hello?"

"Bobbi, it's April. Are you all right?"

Bobbi took a deep breath. "Yes. I'm just a little tired."

"What's the last thing you remember?"

"I, uh, I'm not sure. We were all meeting at the hotel, and I went back to my office and . . . I'm sorry, April. She was too strong this time."

"It's all right, Bobbi. We'll talk about it some more the next time we're together. The important thing is that you're back, and I want you to work very hard on staying in control. Okay?" When Bobbi didn't answer right away, April used her most sympathetic voice to say, "There's nothing to be ashamed of, Bobbi. You've made incredible progress, but I warned you that there would still be times when the pressure got too great. If it starts again, I want you to call me right away. Don't try to handle it yourself for a while."

"All right."

"Good girl." Knowing that Roberta never allowed

Bobbi to see or hear what was going on when she was in control, April brought her up to date about the Ziegler murder and Holly Kaufman's acceptance of the Frampton assignment.

"I would like you to give Holly a call at work tomorrow and suggest you get together for lunch. One of us needs to stay very close to her for the time being. I can't be there, and I think she'd be more apt to accept you as a friend than Rachel."

"Do you think she's going to cause problems?" Bobbi asked fearfully.

"No, no. Not at all. It's just a precaution because of the murder investigation."

"All right then. I'll keep an eye on her."

Holly had the old dream that night, only this time, instead of turning to find Tim Ziegler or a monster beside her, she saw David's face. At the point when she normally awoke covered in perspiration, he grinned at her and she nestled into his arms. Threads of the dream were still with her when the real David's travel alarm clock went off on the other side of the camper.

Friends! What an insane notion. What happened last night was proof that there was too much sexual attraction between them for a simple friendship. Twice he had shown that he could banish her common sense with nothing more than his kisses. Twice he had shown more control than she.

Last night she would have made love. . . . *No.* Philip made love. With David it would have been fornication—a clinical, unemotional, biological function. But she had been ready to do it, enthusiastically, until he spoke and jarred her back to reality. Did that make him a gentleman, or a cold, calculating machine who could turn off his passion rather than be harassed by a clinging woman the next morning?

Though she realized she couldn't handle him the way she did Philip, the fact remained that David wanted her. Even with as little experience as she had, she knew that part of his interest stemmed from her disinterest. She may not know the game as well as he, but if she could keep from giving in to him, she might be able to hold his attention long enough to watch him investigate Frampton. It was worth considering.

His comments about Erica Donner had shaken her, but on reflection, she realized they weren't un-called for, since he was the reporter Erica had told her about. She was certain her answer had been logical, almost truthful, and that there really wouldn't be any reason for him to question her further about that relationship in the future. She would just have to keep in mind what an excellent memory for details he had and never reveal more about herself than she absolutely had to.

She hated the fact that David was completely at ease when he came out from behind his partition fully dressed. Busying herself with the coffeemaker gave her an excuse to avoid meeting his eyes. Again he surprised her by acting the part of the gentleman.

"While the coffee's brewing, I'll take care of re-filling the water tank so you can shower later. Is fifteen minutes enough for you?"

She smiled, less shyly than she had yesterday. "Yes, thank you." Just before he walked out the door, she stopped him. "David? Could you do me another favor? I have a nine o'clock flight back to Washington tonight. Would you mind asking the manager if there's an airport shuttle that might pick me up here?"

His frown revealed that he hadn't realized she was leaving so soon, but he merely gave her a mock salute and left.

The rain that had not come with Hurricane Brigitte had arrived during the night to drench the savaged land and scattered belongings of the dispossessed. Although it had stopped by the time David and Holly were riding to the site where they were to board the helicopter, the intense humidity made Holly think they were enveloped in a giant steam bath.

The observation flight was slightly delayed, but it gave them a chance to speak with the other man and woman who would be sharing the ride. The woman was the local newspaper reporter David had met the day before who had told him about the flight. The man was a marine biologist with the state Department of Natural Resources. His presence was considered a stroke of luck, and the other three immediately took advantage of his knowledge.

Headphones allowed the conversation to continue after they were in the air. The islands looked as though they had been bombed by an enemy intent on total devastation. Key West had suffered damage similar to Key Largo in that some structures were still partially standing. However, the islands in between had been decimated.

The biologist pointed out that for another week or so, the water would be too murky to judge the damage to the reefs, but it was expected to be massive. They passed over a sunken ship in shallow water, and he explained how it had undoubtedly been pushed there by one of the tidal surges during the storm. It could be dragged back into deeper water again, but it would be years before its previous function as an artificial reef would be restored.

Holly was disappointed that she could not get any clear indication of reef damage and that the cloudy day was going to limit the quality of the pictures she was taking.

Unfortunately, the weather reports sounded as though this was the way it was going to be for the rest of the week, so it would make no sense to extend her stay. It would be more efficient to go home and update Philip. Together, they would put pressure on the government to act quickly and attend to the needs of the environment as well as the people.

Concentrating on the biologist's monologue and the scene on the ground occupied her thoughts until David distracted her. He didn't speak to her, or touch her; she could *feel* him watching her, daring her to look at him. She ordered herself not to let him see that she picked up his unspoken message, but her eyes betrayed her.

Turning her head toward him, she was suddenly caught in a visual snare that no gentleman would have cast in public. He should not have been looking at her that way, as if he was remembering the way she moved beneath his hands. It was possibly the most erotic moment she had ever experienced. She dragged her gaze away from his, but the effort caused a shiver to streak through her that was more telling than any verbal admission would have been.

David smiled to himself as he noted the hot flush on her cheekbones. It was gratifying to know that she hadn't been able to banish the memory of last night's kisses any better than he had. He hadn't been able to sleep all night, and her indifferent attitude that morning had him searching for a bit of reassurance. Now he was certain her imminent departure would not prevent him from establishing the bond he wanted. He would just pick up where they left off once he was back in the capital.

Then he would keep after her until he knew every last secret she had.

Around midday, a steady downpour forced them to give up. The heated glance they had exchanged in the helicopter seemed to have sparked a chain reaction of looks and accidental touches that made it difficult for them to keep their minds on their work. The necessity of their bodies' positioning on the moped now seemed more intimate than it had before, but the rain required David to give his full attention to the road ahead of him.

By the time they returned to the motor home, they were drenched to the skin and chilled, despite the warm temperature. David hustled Holly inside the camper and straight into the small shower stall.

"Why are we squished inside the bathroom?" Holly asked, laughing as he closed the plastic accordion door on them.

"Saving the carpet—and getting us warm." He shifted so that he could turn on the shower behind him.

"David! My shoes—"

"—are already soaked. Now get undressed while there's still some hot water."

"I am not taking my clothes off with you in here. In fact, there isn't enough room for two people to breathe let alone perform the contortions it would take to undress." He proved her wrong by kicking off his shoes, then pulling his shirt over his head. The shirt landed on top of the shoes with a wet plop as his fingers undid the button on his slacks. Her eyes widened as she realized he was quite serious, but she was determined not to give him the pleasure of seeing her run from him.

"What's the matter, lady, haven't you ever seen a male striptease before?"

She couldn't make herself return his easy laughter any more than she could tell him the truth—that she had never watched a man undress, that in her few previous encounters, she had been in the dark or had averted her eyes.

He was lean, but solid, with a smattering of wet brown hair on his chest that arrowed down into his pants. She continued to stare as he tugged the clinging material down his hips and maneuvered in the narrow space to shed the remainder of his clothing. Looking at his body made her want to know if it felt as firm as it appeared. Only when he straightened, allowing her to see the full effect her staring had on him, did she manage to turn away.

A second later he spun her back around and used his body to pin her against the fiberglass wall. "Too late for games, lady. I came in here with a practical purpose in mind, but the way you were looking at me wasn't at all practical." His lips brushed over hers. "Time for show and tell."

She frowned at him, finding it impossible to think with him so close. Her hands came up to push him away, but contact with the slick muscled flesh of his shoulders made her fingers crave for more.

"Show and tell, lady-love. I went first. Now it's your turn. Tell me you want me."

She moved her head from side to side. "I don't."

His hand slipped between their bodies and captured her breast. "Liar," he whispered, pinching her taut nipple. "If you won't tell me, I guess you'll have to show me." His mouth took possession of hers before she could deny him again.

Instead of the seductive tenderness he had lured her with before, his new weapon was raw hunger. It drew her into him, making her taste his need, demanding she appease it. And, God help her, she wanted to, for the same hunger was searing her insides.

In a frenzy of arms and legs, pulling and tugging in the cramped quarters, her clothes joined his on the shower floor. Desperate gnawing kisses and groping hands made words unnecessary. Yet, with her arms and legs wrapped around him, and his shaft rubbing urgently against her sensitized flesh, he spoke.

"Say it. Tell me you want me, and you can have me."

The arrogant bastard was not going to win this one. "Go to hell."

"Fine. But you're coming with me." His body penetrated hers in one hard, fast, upward thrust.

She cried out, unable to hide the relief she felt to have the teasing end. Anchoring her nails in his back and her heels in his thighs, she rode the violent waves he created, unaware of anything but the sensations spiraling through her. There was no right or wrong, goals or reasoning.

Only pleasure.

The explosion of her climax and the shimmering aftershocks held her immobilized until he separated their bodies and set her back onto her feet.

Some time ago the water had stopped flowing, but only now did he turn off the faucets and open the door to let the steam escape. Holly remained where she was, feeling strangely detached as he took a towel off the rack and dried them both off. When he tugged on her hand and led her out of the bathroom, the liquid warmth began to evaporate, but not enough to stop her from following him. At the foot of the bed he let go of her hand to pull down the spread.

"What are you doing?" she asked even as he eased her onto the bed beside him.

"Now, Holly, I know you're stubborn, but you're not stupid."

"What's that supposed to mean?" She tried to sound indignant, but didn't quite make it as she watched his finger circle the outside of her breast then spiral closer and closer to the tip. Involuntarily, she arched into his palm and he chuckled.

"I mean, you can't possibly think that was it. *That* was fucking—not what I wanted to do with you at all. But you just had to be stubborn about it and, well, you know I have a bit of a temper. However, I'm not going to let your stubbornness or my temper rob us both of a memorable experience. Now we're going to make love."

She narrowed her eyes suspiciously. No, he couldn't possibly know she had been mentally comparing him to Philip earlier.

"The manager said he'd personally drive you to the airport at six-thirty." His hand moved down to shape her hip and stroke her thigh. "Hmm. Four hours. I'll have to cut out a few of my special interrogation techniques, but I should still be able to manage it."

"*Now* what are you talking about?" She swatted at the hand creeping up her inner thigh.

"Before you leave, I want three things from you. One, you're going to admit you want me. In fact, you're going to beg me to satisfy you." His tongue stroked the curve of her ear. "Again."

"Never," she stated confidently, in spite of the ripple that passed through her stomach.

As if he had sensed her physical response, he traced an abstract design over her abdomen. "Two, you're going to tell me what you wanted from me to begin with."

She stiffened. "That's ridiculous. I told you be fore, I didn't want anything from you. Somehow your overblown ego caused you to jump to a very wrong conclusion about me."

"Maybe. We'll see. But that brings us to three. The last time we parted, we were furious with each other. I have no doubt you never intended to speak to me again." He smiled at the admission in her eyes. "This time, when you walk away, you won't be able to forget you ever met me. You won't be able to forget one"—he gave her a soft kiss on the forehead—"single" —on the tip of her nose—"minute." His lips caressed hers with infinite tenderness, over and over until she turned into his arms and gave herself up to whatever he had in mind.

Good lord. Had she really thought Philip made love to her? The phrase, as she had interpreted it, had no correlation to what she and David shared for the remainder of the afternoon. He made love to her fingers, her toes, the sensitive skin behind her knees. He aroused her with erotic whisperings and promises, then proved the actual deeds more exciting still. Each time she felt as though she could go no higher, he carried her beyond. He made her sigh and moan, laugh and groan, and sigh again.

Where Philip was grateful to worship at the passive shrine of her body, David demanded her full participation, made suggestions that became orders if she hesitated or showed reluctance, then teased her when her innocence showed through.

She had never made love in the daytime. She had never made love with a mature, virile male animal, when she could see that every inch she touched was one hundred percent solid, delicious man. At the ripe old age of thirty-four, Holly could honestly say, she had never made love.

At six-thirty, while David lay sound asleep, she left the motor home. She had successfully managed to withhold the first two things he had wanted, but she knew he had scored an overwhelming victory with the third.

There was no turning back now.

She would be David Wells's mistress, and he would be her instrument of revenge.

12

You've got till the count of five to clear out."

The cub reporter's mouth dropped open. "I'm right in the middle of a paragraph, Mr. Wells. The boss said I could use this desk while you were gone."

"So, now I'm back, and that's my desk you've buried with shit." He frowned at the overflowing ashtray, crumpled fastfood wrappers, and half a stationery store. "One."

The young man hesitated long enough to determine that *Mr. Wells* was sincere about removing him, and started gathering up his garbage.

The five-count passed numerous times before the desk looked somewhat like it did before David had left five days ago. "You forgot this," David said as the squatter was making his exit. He picked up a plain white envelope.

"Oh, no. That came for you yesterday." He took off before Mr. Wells could ask his name.

David turned the envelope over and saw his name typed in capital letters in the center. He used the envelope to brush the crumbs and ashes off his chair and desk before sitting down. He straightened the desk pad, lined up his calendar, pencil cup, and memo pad, then adjusted the computer monitor a fraction of an inch. Good. It was *his* again. It had been a long climb to having things of his own, like a desk and a chair, and the hunger hadn't dissipated yet. He had a toehold, but he still needed to do a lot of fancy footwork to secure himself a place at the top of the hill.

With his teak-handled letter opener, he neatly sliced through the top edge of the envelope. Inside were several typed pages and photographs, but no indication as to who had sent it.

One sheet of paper contained a brief synopsis of the meteoric rise to success of Jerry Frampton, publisher of *Jock* magazine. A copy of a clipping from what was probably a sensationalist tabloid was attached to that. It gave some facts about his life and the magazine, and emphasized the rumors of his wild lifestyle. It looked like it had been cut and pasted, as if a few lines had been eliminated between the parts about where he was born and how he put together the first issue of *Jock*.

The next photocopied sheets resembled reports prepared by professional investigators or law enforcement personnel, though any identifying marks had been blocked out. David scanned the data that gave evidence of a connection between Jerry Frampton and convicted pornographer Mick D'Angelo. It was backed up with D'Angelo's criminal record and a copy of a form signed by Frampton when he once posted bail for D'Angelo.

The photographs had all been taken very recently, on the same day and at the same time, according to the digital imprint across the bottom. Frampton and D'Angelo were obviously involved in a heated discussion, and a cover note stated that the pictures were taken at Frampton's private estate in Boca Raton, Florida.

The final sheet contained two typed paragraphs. The first suggested that Frampton still had his fingers in D'Angelo's very dirty business. The other was an assurance to Wells that no other reporter had been given this information, but the reason for singling him out as the recipient had been omitted.

He reread the pages with a critical eye. What could the sender hope to gain? His first guess would be that he wanted to see Jerry Frampton hung out to dry. A disgruntled employee? A jilted lover? By giving the information specifically to a reporter as reputable as himself, that person would be aware that he would check out the facts before maligning someone's character, particularly a well-known someone.

What if it was true? What if Jerry Frampton had a little help from the dark side in setting up his magazine? What if he was still involved in child pornography on the side? What if he, David Wells, was the investigative reporter to expose him?

The "what if's" balanced out his hesitancy to automatically accept the evidence before him. He already had more projects going than he could juggle, however. He'd have to give this some thought before he took any action. He put everything back in the envelope and slipped it into his desk drawer.

Turning on his computer, he switched mental gears to his summary article on his tour of the disaster area. His hands hovered over the keyboard for a fraction of a second before attacking. Halfway through, he reached for his phone, lifted the receiver, and replaced it again. He needed to verify a fact. All it would take was a call to Valerie, but it would also be a good excuse to call Holly. With a disgusted shake of his head, he picked up the receiver again, punched the interoffice code for research, and was put on hold.

He wasn't going to call Holly just yet, because more than anything else he wanted to hear her voice. That in itself was a bad sign. One of his personal rules was never to call a woman from the office or when he was out of town on business. In his mind that implied that he was thinking about her when he should be working, that there was a depth of affection he didn't feel.

He tried to always play it straight with women. He made sure they knew the only commitment they would hear from him was his commitment to remain a free-wheeling, unfaithful bachelor. For some reason he never understood but thoroughly enjoyed, that knowledge rarely turned a woman away.

As part of an investigation, however, Holly wasn't protected by his personal rules.

The sense of freedom he had expected to feel Monday night after Holly left hadn't come. During the next two days alone in the camper, he had thought about calling her to make sure she had returned safely and to firm up the bond they'd begun. The more often the thought occurred, the more determined he became not to call her until he got back. At any rate, it would be infinitely better for his plan if she started to worry whether he would get in touch with her again.

It would be even better if she called him first.

"Research. Sorry to keep you holding."

"Hey, Valerie. Did you miss me?" he asked with a smile in his voice.

"Oh, were you away?" she replied in the same tone.

"I guess you've been busy."

"Swamped. My husband is threatening to sue the paper if I don't start getting home before midnight."

"Well, as much as I hate to add to your troubles, I need a few statistics for my hurricane wrapup."

"That's an easy one. I pulled together a whole folder of facts right after Brigitte hit. Come on down and take a look at it."

David was at Valerie's desk within a few minutes.

"Have fun," she said, handing him the thick folder. "I can't let you take it away, but you can copy whatever you need on my machine."

He found what he needed, and while making the copies, he duplicated a sheet of paper he'd brought with him—the tabloid write-up on Frampton. Returning the file to her desk, he showed the paper to her. "It looks like something was cut out and it might be important to a piece I'm working on. Could you track the original article down for me?"

She smiled. "The computer should have a listing of all articles printed about him. But it may take me a while to get to this. I have a long list of top priority questions to work through first."

"No problem. It's on my back burner for the moment. Still no progress with the Dominion rosters?"

Valerie shook her head. "Sorry. With all my calls, I've gotten chummy with a lady in the registrar's office and she said that the FBI has ordered all the old files temporarily sealed."

David let out a whistle. "That's a little telling, wouldn't you say?"

She gave him a shrug. "I just do research, not analysis."

David grinned and started to walk away when an idea occurred. "You can't get the whole rosters, but do you think you could verify if a specific person attended Dominion the same year as Erica Donner?"

"I can try. Like I said, that lady and I are best buddies now."

"The names are Rachel Greenley and Holly Kaufman. They might have been freshmen or sophomores. I need you to put this one on your top priority list."

Valerie smirked at him and he blew her a kiss on his way out the door.

Satisfied that he was doing something toward the story that he was still certain was hiding just around the corner, he got back to his article on the hurricane.

Why had Holly left without a word or note of goodbye?

He cut off his train of thought. Images from their last afternoon together were not conducive to productivity, and he had to get this piece finished in less than two hours.

Would she ever think to give him a call? Of course not. She was more stubborn than anyone he had ever known. Why couldn't she just have admitted that she wanted him the same way he wanted her? Why did she have to leave him feeling like the big, bad wolf all the time? Why did she have to turn out to be such an innocent?

He still had the outfit she'd left on the floor of the shower stall, but he could have a runner return her things to her office for him—when he had a free moment to take care of that detail.

The fact that he couldn't keep her out of his head was a sign that discovering her secrets could be seriously hazardous to his mental health. He might be better off putting the whole story idea aside until he came up with another way to investigate it. Of course, if he found out she was lying about where she went to college, then he'd have an excuse to confront her without desire getting in the way.

That excuse was taken away when Valerie called him back that afternoon. Rachel Greenley was definitely a freshman at Dominion the same year as Donner, but Holly Kaufman was not registered at all.

On the one hand David was disappointed that he still didn't have the full picture. On the other hand, he had one puzzle piece more than he had yesterday, and enough to convince him to keep digging. The only thing to do was follow through on his original plan to seduce Holly into telling him her secrets. His nose told him it was a risk he was going to have to take.

It was too bad Harry had chosen this time to take off around the world. The old guy would have known just the right thing to say to keep him on track.

The next morning he took a walk by the front of her building, timed to what he assumed should have been her arrival. It would have been an accidental meeting, where neither had to be the one to give in.

When she didn't show, he went up to her office and visited with Evelyn. He quickly discovered that she was anxious for Holly to "form new friendships, particularly with nice young men." Hinting at a possible romance in the wings, he convinced the normally protective secretary to let him wait in her boss's office as a surprise.

Once ensconced there, his natural curiosity took control of his better judgment. At first he only leafed through the files on her desk, but the more time passed without her appearing, the more daring he became. Her desk drawers were neat and tidy, no excess clutter, nothing out of control, nothing that could be construed as purely personal.

Until he opened the bottom left-hand drawer, removed a lined pad, and saw his face. He hadn't realized she had taken his picture that day on the beach. Not only had she taken one, she had kept it . . . hidden.

Holly rushed breathlessly through the lobby and into the elevator. Why did her car pick today to go on strike? A full day of paperwork and phone calls awaited, and Philip was tied up at the Senate. She spoke to Evelyn as she breezed by, knowing from previous experience the woman would follow her into her office for instructions. "Good morning. My car battery died. Were there any calls? I think you'd better—"

Her voice, and the rest of her body, came to an abrupt halt in the doorway to her office. David was leaning back in the chair behind her desk with his feet propped up. She turned back to ask Evelyn how he got there, but the woman had wisely disappeared.

"I'd better do what?" he asked in the tone of voice that let her know it didn't matter what she answered, he'd have a wisecrack ready.

"Get your shoes off my desk." He didn't. He just sat there, or rather, reclined there, watching her with those eyes that said all sorts of things he shouldn't, the sort of things she didn't want to think about this morning. "How did you get in here?"

"Evelyn has a romantic soul."

Her eyes widened apprehensively. "You didn't—"

"No, I didn't. But it was worth seeing you blush to let you think I did."

She shook her head and sighed. "You're impossible."

"Hmmm." He rubbed his chin thoughtfully as he drew himself to his feet. "Let's see, so far you've described me as an inconsiderate womanizer, told me I'm crude, I'm incorrigible, and now I'm impossible. Not much to feed my overblown ego, is it?"

"What do you do, tape-record our conversations?"

He tapped his temple. "The memory I told you about."

She set her briefcase beside her desk. When he moved out of the way and headed toward the door without touching her, she relaxed a little. Instead of walking out the door, however, he closed it.

With a calm she didn't feel, she sat down at her desk and opened a file. "Please reopen that door, then walk through it. I have a lot to do today, and exchanging witticisms with you is not on my agenda."

"Would you rather exchange kisses?" He sauntered around her desk, then perched on the corner next to her. "Hmmm?"

She wished she could answer as casually as he had asked the question, but since she couldn't, she simply ignored him.

"Still trying to convince me you're not interested, lady?"

"I'm not."

"Then why'd you keep this?" He pulled open the bottom drawer where he had tossed the photo when he heard her voice in the hall. Her gasp told him what she refused to admit. "I've got better ones at home, but you'll have to ask real nice." She groaned, but still didn't lift her eyes from her file. He took a breath, then asked her the question he swore he wouldn't. "Why did you leave without saying goodbye?"

His words were softened by a sincerity that

sounded alien coming from him. It was enough to make her look up and give an answer. "I thought you needed the sleep."

He slid off the desk and swiveled her chair toward him. Grasping both arms, he leaned forward so that she was caged by his body. "Try again."

Tilting her head back, her gaze moved from his eyes to his mouth and back up. This was no time to be thinking about his mouth. "I thought we both said goodbye very eloquently."

His head dipped down until his nose rubbed hers. "I like the fact that you can't say something like that without blushing. But it's still not the truth. Try again."

With him this close, it was impossible not to think about his mouth, and his hands, and every other body part he had. "I didn't want to say goodbye. I wanted to stay. If I had awakened you, I wouldn't have gone, and I had to."

"Much better," he whispered against her mouth. "For that the pretty lady wins the prize." He ran his tongue over her lips and waited. When he did it again, she extended her tongue to caress his with the same leisure. He caught hers between his teeth and sucked as his mouth pressed forward. With a great deal of effort he stopped his hands from proceeding to the next stage, and broke the kiss instead. "Meet me for lunch today."

She took a deep breath and cleared her fuzzy brain. "I can't. I'm really backed up."

Moving his mouth to her ear, he whispered, "I have a bag of your clothes in my car. Do you remember why you left them behind? I want you to think about what happened the last time you wore them. Now, if you don't promise to meet me, I'll kiss you senseless, then take you right here on your desk." To prove his point, he dove into an eating kiss that had her clinging to the front of his shirt. He backed away an inch to murmur, "The correct answer is 'Yes David.' Say it."

Raising her eyelashes, she offered him a reminder of how she looked the afternoon they had made love. "Yes, David."

They figured out a time and place that was most convenient for them both. He gave her one quick kiss, started to leave, and returned for two more before he left for good.

Holly heard him whistling as he departed and allowed herself a satisfied smile. Yesterday she had begun to worry that he wouldn't recontact her. Now she was certain everything was going to work out just fine. The pleasure she had discovered in his arms was an unexpected bonus to her plan, and harmless enough as long as she remembered it was only temporary.

She made a point to be precisely five minutes late to lunch —late enough for him to wonder if she would come as commanded, but not so late that he would be annoyed. Her scheme did not take into account that he would not be there when she arrived. He had made reservations however, and the hostess seated her immediately.

After five more minutes passed, she ordered lunch. When he arrived, he would see that she had not sat waiting docilely for him to make an appearance. He finally showed up at the same time as her meal. Barely sparing him a glance, she started on her chef's salad.

"Sorry I'm late." Without looking at a menu, he asked the waitress to bring him a lunch steak, medium rare, fries, and coffee. "It couldn't be helped," he told Holly as he watched her fork a tomato and place it in her mouth. "I'm glad you didn't wait to order." He winced when he saw how hard she stabbed an artichoke heart. "All right. I confess. I was in the middle of an article and I lost track of time. I figured in the time it would take me to call, I could be here."

She rewarded his honesty with a smile. "You know, I bet with a little practice, we could get pretty good at this truth business."

He returned her smile and added a wink. "But why is it that I have to pry it out of you, and all you have to do is ignore me?"

"Probably has something to do with your basic insecurities as a man."

"If I am so insecure, what am I doing having lunch with a woman known throughout the city for her ability to render a man impotent with no more than a look of disgust?"

Her smile remained in place. "The average, intelligent man stays away when he is told point blank that the woman is not interested. What does that make you?"

His laugh made several people turn in their direction. "A sucker for a challenge, I guess." He reached across the table and covered her hand with his. "I missed you, Holly."

She tensed from the unexpected touch, but relaxed the next instant. "I think I missed you, too."

"You think?" It was the first time he could recall admitting that he missed a woman, and her response was hardly flattering.

"Well, since you seem to like the truth, I'm not entirely sure. The jury's still out."

"Fair enough. Could I try influencing the outcome by taking you to the symphony tomorrow night?"

Her first thought was that she would have to

come up with a good excuse for not seeing Philip. "Why don't we try getting through an amicable lunch first?"

For the next hour he filled her in on what had happened in the Keys after she'd gone, and she admitted she'd been impressed with his articles in the paper. Her answers to his questions about federal aid for the environment would go into another piece he was working on.

He had paid the check, and they were lingering over a second cup of coffee, when he changed the subject. "I need an unbiased opinion on something."

"Is it a topic appropriate for discussion in a public place? Wait, let me rephrase that. Would *I* discuss it in a public place?"

"You are such a suspicious lady. It's just a lead that's been dropped in my lap, and I can't decide what to do about it. You've got a good, analytical mind. I thought you might be able to talk it out with me."

She couldn't believe he was going to make it this easy for her. Her expression turned serious and she leaned forward on her elbows. "I've tracked down my share of leads over the years. Sometimes they pan out, sometimes they don't. But I would think you'd be accustomed to ferreting out stories from no more than a lead."

"Oh, yeah. Don't get me wrong. That's how my biggest story originated. But this is different. It's not local, and it's too flimsy to get backing from my editor to go chasing after it on the paper's time. That means I'd have to cover my expenses as well as taking time off. Besides that, he gave me something else to follow up on since I've been back."

Holly twisted her mouth as if she was considering his dilemma. She hadn't thought of the possibility that money would be a problem for him, and it was too late to rectify that. It took all her self-control to give the kind of answer she would if she were not personally interested. "Then pass it on to somebody else, or forget it completely."

"That's where the problem comes in. I rely on my instincts, and they're telling me there might be a hell of a story here."

"Would the end justify the means, like prize-winning stuff?"

He gave her a sly grin. "Possibly."

"Maybe if you tell me about the lead I could be more helpful. I swear it wouldn't go any further." He only hesitated a moment before relating to her the information he had received about Jerry Frampton and Mick D'Angelo. She asked the expected questions about where he thought it might have come from, then offered, "It sounds like it could be a dynamite exposé if it's based on fact. Tell me this, would any innocent people be hurt by your checking it out?"

With a shrug, he said, "I could do some preliminary verification without anyone being the wiser. However, if it's true, there are already innocents being hurt."

"If you don't follow it up, can you ignore that possibility? The David Wells I've gotten to know wouldn't be able to."

He narrowed his eyebrows in thought. "Now that you said it aloud, I realize that point has been nagging at me along with my instincts."

"Then it's a matter of how and when. Could you handle the story your editor wants, then take some time off?"

"Actually, he's so satisfied with the coverage on the hurricane, I doubt if he'd gripe too loudly."

"Next problem—money for expenses. I can't help you solve that one."

"I really shouldn't have included that as a factor. I've had to live on a starvation budget for so long, I'm afraid I place spending money in the same category with having blood drawn."

"It sounds to me like you've made a decision. You mentioned a lead in Miami. Will you be going back down there soon?"

He laughed and leaned closer. "If I wasn't so secure about my manhood, I'd think you were anxious to see me gone again."

"Perhaps you'd like me to help you pack." His wounded look was as false as her disinterest.

Since she had taken a cab there, she let him drive her back to the office. He stopped in front of the building, but before she could get out of his car, he pulled her close for a soul-wrenching kiss.

"David! You can't keep doing that to me."

"Why not? It feels good, and I know you like it."

"Because . . ." She heard several horns blaring behind them. "We're stopping traffic, that's why."

"Always thinking of others. How very ladylike. Okay. I'll pick you up at six tomorrow; dinner first, some place extravagant to show that I do part with my money from time to time, then the symphony. Wear that sexy, black number you wore at the fundraiser. I want to act out a fantasy I've had about you and that dress."

She sighed loudly and pushed open the car door. "You are truly . . . *impossible!*"

As she ducked out, he called, "You'd better dust off your thesaurus, lady. You need some new adjectives!"

Holly could remember her father saying "The best defense is a good offense." He may have been referring to football, his favorite spectator sport, but she had often used the strategy when she was unsure of her opponent. Hopefully it would work on Philip. Because he accepted her need for independence, they rarely saw each other more than once over a weekend, so if she went out with him that night, she would be free to go to the symphony with David on Saturday.

As soon as she picked up her messages from Evelyn, she went into Philip's office. Guilt prompted her to sound more enthusiastic than she felt. "Would you like to come with me to a movie tonight? The new Mel Gibson one sounds good."

Philip beamed up at her, clearly pleased with the suggestion. "Only if you'll feed me first. I'm easy, but I'm not cheap."

Holly wondered if he realized how many times he had said that over the years, and how many times she had smiled at the tired old line. Funny, it had never really bothered her before. "Good. Tonight will be my treat. I'll even pick you up and do the driving." *That way, I can drop you at your house and go home alone.*

Philip was delighted with her unusual assertiveness and moved on to discuss a report he was working on.

When Holly had returned to her office on Tuesday, there had been phone messages from Dr. MacLeash, Bobbi Renquist, and Rachel Greenley. She guessed April was checking on her, since she hadn't made the promised call Friday night. She had no idea what the other two wanted, nor had she changed her mind about avoiding contact with them.

Since Evelyn had told everyone that her boss was in Florida because of Hurricane Brigitte and it wasn't known when she would be back, Holly had decided to put off calling April until she was certain David had received the envelope on Frampton. She realized the overachiever in her wanted to prove herself to her new friend.

As soon as she got home, she placed the call and caught April just as she arrived home. After the necessary apologies from Holly and assurances from April that it was no problem, Holly was ready to report.

"Holly, I hope you'll understand if I'm not able to respond as freely as I'd like over the phone."

Holly understood and heard an unspoken suggestion that she be careful about what she said as well. She supposed it was wise under the circumstances. "Yes, of course. I'm pleased to say that I've spent quite a bit of time with the man we discussed, and he's going to follow through on the information."

"Does he know how he came by it?"

"No."

"Good. And will you be able to keep apprised of his activities?"

Holly hesitated a second. "I think so. He's not . . . the kind of man I'm accustomed to dealing with, but I'm fairly sure a tie has been established." She could almost see April smiling her approval.

"That's fine. Remember the advice I gave you, Holly. Think of him as practice. It's not important if you make mistakes, because you're not looking for a permanent relationship with him. If you take off the pressure of being perfect, you'll find it's not so difficult to be with a man."

"I'm trying, but—"

"It's *not* important," April repeated. "Do you enjoy his company?"

Holly was tempted to lie rather than hear herself say it aloud. "Yes. Very much."

"Then take the pressure off and have fun for a change. You've accomplished the fundamental part of your assignment. The rest, keeping track of his activities, would be a bonus."

"But I *really* want that part of it, now that I've begun."

"So you do understand how we all feel? I'm very relieved to hear that. Listen, I hate to cut you short, but I must feed my poor husband. You know what would be very nice? If you would come up here for a visit next weekend. I'd love to get to know you better."

"I'd like that, too," Holly replied instantly. She felt good after each talk with April and wouldn't mind deepening the friendship. Holly remembered promising her mother to spend a weekend with them. "I'll see how my schedule looks and let you know."

That evening was like so many others she and Philip had shared, a blend of friendship and business, but Holly sensed an undercurrent of tension and sought to relieve it by having a cup of coffee with him at his house after the movie. It was the sign Philip must have been waiting for.

"I hope you don't mind my bringing this up, honey, but I've noticed a change in you in the last two weeks."

Holly's years of concealing her emotions helped her to show nothing but mild curiosity. "Oh?"

He shrugged. "Ever since you spoke to your parents about what happened to you in college, you seem a little . . . I don't know . . . stronger might be the best word. It frightened me at first. I thought you were . . . well, it's not important now. I read a book about rape victims and one of the recommendations for recovery is talking about it."

"Yes, that was the advice a friend gave me. I think it helped."

"But the book also stated sometimes that's not

enough. One of the recurrent problems of the victim is the fear that the attacker will find her again. As long as he's free, she feels threatened."

She had heard that before, too, but he continued before she could say so.

"There's something I should have told you when we first talked about it, but you seemed adamant about wanting to keep the identity of your rapists a secret, so I let you think it was."

Holly didn't bother to hide her bewilderment.

Philip cautiously patted her hand. "It's all right. Your secret's safe with me. You see, after you talked to your parents, your mother pulled out what she called your memory box. Although you'd left Dominion, they'd sent you the yearbook and she had put it away, in case you ever wanted to look at it. Did you know she'd kept every card and letter you ever sent them? Well, in several letters, right before you quit school, you wrote about your new boyfriend, Jerry Frampton, and his fraternity brothers.

"It was a simple matter to look up the fraternity in the yearbook and find out who those brothers were. Frampton was obviously the boyfriend who hurt you. Your reaction to the Ziegler hearing and the way you freeze every time his name is mentioned suggests Ziegler was the other one. Was he?"

Holly's mind was spinning. Philip had guessed all along! She could deny it, but she would have to name one of the other brothers to be convincing. At least with Ziegler gone, Philip wouldn't be able to confront him. Finally, she simply nodded her head.

Philip gave her another sympathetic pat on the hand. "The point that I'm trying to make is that I want you to know that it's perfectly normal if you're feeling relieved that Ziegler is dead. You don't have to hide it from me."

Holly shook her head in protest. "No matter what he did, I couldn't be happy he's dead."

"Of course you're not *happy*. Only a wicked person would be happy, and I know there's not an ounce of wickedness in your whole beautiful body. I was only trying to understand the change I've noticed. You must realize it started around the time of the murder."

Holly considered the timing he referred to and all the things that had recently taken place in her life. She still didn't think it would be wise to tell him about the Little Sister Society, or their goals, and she certainly couldn't confide in him about David. Instead, she let him believe what he wanted. There didn't seem to be any harm in it.

"Any plans this weekend?" he asked as she was leaving.

As casually as possible, she lied. "I think I'll pamper myself a little. Get a manicure, read a good book, sleep a lot."

"Call if you want company," he said, knowing she wouldn't, but desperately hoping she might.

"I will," she promised, giving him a friendly hug. As his arms loosely circled her waist, she thought he felt rather frail and realized she was comparing him to another man—a younger, stronger, more sexual man. On impulse, she pressed her lips to Philip's, hoping to find the spark of passion that had failed to surface in all their years together, wishing that he could be the one whose kiss had the power to take her to heaven.

Philip inhaled deeply when she ended the kiss. "Are you sure you want to go home?"

Her smile was neutralized by the sadness in her eyes. "Yes, I'm sure."

13

Good morning, Pop. What's cookin'?"

"If you hadn't called within the next ten minutes, it was going to be your bottom."

"Sorry I'm late. I slept in. You okay? Mom?"

"Mom's also sleeping in this morning, but we're fine. And we'll soon be even better. I'm going to take her on a little vacation next weekend, maybe up into the Poconos."

Holly thought he sounded lighthearted—not at all disturbed as her mother had described him. "What about the restaurant?"

"Got it covered. Anyway, Mom needs a break. She's been . . . a little down lately."

"Oh, no . . ."

"It's okay, baby. I think she just needs a change of scene. The doctor recommended that rather than a new prescription so I'm willing to try."

She considered asking about what her mother had said about him being preoccupied with thoughts of revenge, but figured it might cause problems between them.

"Then I guess Mom's invitation for me to come home for a weekend is postponed?"

"Since when do you need an invitation to come home? Why not make it the next weekend? And bring Philip. We could have a marathon pinochle game."

Holly forced herself to sound pleased with the idea, but she was already thinking up excuses to avoid a weekend that would include her parents' not-so-subtle hints that she should marry Philip and have babies while they still could. She didn't think she could laugh it off under the present circumstances.

"I've got to run, Pop. Why don't you give me a call when you return from your little getaway, and I'll let you know then how the following weekend is shaping up."

"Sounds good to me, sweetie."

"Take care of Mom. I love you both."

At ten minutes before six on Saturday evening, the lobby security guard buzzed Holly's apartment. "There's a David Wells here to see you, Miss Kaufman."

"Tell him I'm not quite ready, Pete. Make him wait until six o'clock, then let him up."

She was ready and waiting, but it wouldn't do to let him know that. As she had guessed, it hadn't been necessary to give him her address.

At exactly 6:01, there was a knock at her door. She opened it, certain she was in control of all her faculties. The sight of him, handsomely clad in his black tuxedo, holding a single pink rose, rearranged the circuits in her brain. She told herself he probably chose the symphony because he knows how great he looks in a tux. She took the rose, sniffed it, then walked to the kitchen. He didn't need to be invited in.

"I'm partial to pink roses. Did you research me?"

He came up behind her and kissed the bare curve

of her neck as she filled a bud vase with water. He smiled when he felt her shiver of response instead of the usual flinch away from his unexpected touch. "Didn't need to. It's how I think of you—beautifully delicate, yet complicated, with lots of layers, like a rose, but also innocent—pink."

Turning, she smiled up at him. "Why, Mr. Wells, you should consider a career in writing. You definitely have a way with words."

He stepped back and scanned her from head to toe. The dark-blue beaded sheath she wore fit as if it had been designed for her—except for the scooped neckline: More of her appeared to be out of it than in. A thin diamond choker complemented her stud earrings, and he promised himself he would see her wearing nothing but the diamonds before the evening was over. "I may have made a slight miscalculation about the innocence, though. That dress doesn't promote innocent thoughts. It's very . . . alluring."

"Thank you. I've had it for ages." *Ever since this afternoon.*

"Why didn't you wear the one you wore at the benefit dinner, like I asked you to yesterday?"

She touched his cheek as she moved around his side carrying the vase. "Probably because you *told* me to. Now, had you asked . . ."

"Like a good little boy? Sorry, lady. You can't turn a big, bad wolf into a good little boy. Only witches can do that." He followed her back into the living room, where she set the vase down on a table and picked up a small silver purse that matched her shoes.

With a perfectly sincere expression, she said, "Perhaps I forgot to mention, my mother's name was Esmeralda. But don't worry. I hardly ever practice the old ways any more. Shall we go?"

He rolled his eyes to the ceiling, wondering if she hadn't already worked some sort of spell on him. How in the world was he going to keep his hands off her for the next five hours?

As it turned out, he didn't, but not in the way he had been imagining. During dinner he opened his hand on the table and she placed her palm on his. As they spoke of inconsequential things, their fingers intertwined, slipped apart, and came together again. He fed her a bit of buttered bread, and she licked his thumb. She pushed a wayward lock of hair out of his eyes, and he kissed her wrist.

Although he had been to the symphony with women before, he couldn't remember actually enjoying the music. It was just one of those places sophisticated men took classy ladies to impress them. But Holly loved the music, so *he* loved the music.

And they held hands. No playing footsie or running fingers up and down thighs until they could finally escape the necessary preliminary rounds and get on to the main event. They held hands and let the music of Brahms and Mozart stimulate their souls. He had never experienced anything quite so sensual.

For the first time in his adult life, he accepted a woman's invitation to "come in for a nightcap," and actually sat down to have one. He found he really wanted to continue talking to Holly. But when the brandy in their snifters was drained, his mind, and body, were ready for what came more naturally to him.

She could not recall ever having such a perfect evening. As much as she would have preferred to dislike David and remain unaffected by his charm, it was impossible. Throughout the evening he behaved like the suave gentleman he appeared to be. In spite of a restaurant and concert hall full of beautiful women, he only had eyes for her.

He had suppressed his innate sexuality beneath a civilized veneer, and her reaction to that was somewhat shocking. She realized she had come to enjoy his innuendos and the constant teasing that kept her in a state of expectancy. All evening his touches and caresses were attentive without being aggressive. She should have been pleased with that. Instead she was wondering how long he was going to make her wait for another of his kisses. God help her, she was dying for him to make love to her again.

As if admitting it to herself was the key, her waiting was ended. He took her glass and set it on the table, then helped her rise from the couch. Only one word was needed, and he spoke it. "Where?"

She led him to her bedroom.

Unlike the first time, they savored each moment of their undressing. Their kisses were a physical reflection of the tenderness that had been building between them all evening. And when they moved to the bed it was with a mutual desire to please and be pleased. "Holly, as much as I'd like to continue this without further discussion, there's something we neglected the last time. I'm normally very careful, but I wasn't exactly prepared for what happened between us."

She tilted her head at him. "Are you admitting that David Wells, Super-Stud Extraordinaire, lost his cool?"

He nipped her earlobe. "And whose fault was that? Don't answer. The point is, we're both mature,

responsible adults, and should have known better.
It's a little late, but I want you to know I have
always used protection when I, um, have been with
other women, so—"

"So, I won't catch anything? Neither will you, if
that's what you're worried about. I'm perfectly
healthy."

"Actually, it never occurred to me that you
weren't. I mean, you're not known to— What I'm
not doing a very good job of saying is, could you
have gotten pregnant?"

Her eyebrows shot up. "Pregnant?" She laughed
and couldn't help but tease him for a change. "Gee,
David, would you make an honest woman of me if
I was?"

He blinked a few times and his gaze darted away
from hers.

When she saw the drastic change in his expression, she let him off the hook. "I'm only kidding.
Relax. I have no interest in getting married. If I
wanted that, it would have happened years ago. As
far as my getting pregnant goes, I'm on the pill. The
only way I'd ever leave birth control up to a man is
if he was the one that could end up paying the
penalty."

His relief was obvious. "I was pretty sure that's
what you'd say, but I wanted to get it out of the
way." The most foolish notion had wormed its way
into his thoughts since yesterday. In his rehearsal
of this scene, she was going to confess that she
hadn't had a sexual relationship with a man in years,
that she had been as unprepared for their encounter
as he had been. Of course she wouldn't be pregnant,
but they would discuss what measures would be
taken in the future. If she was on the pill, then
. . . He felt his erection dwindling and banished the

mental picture of her in Philip's arms. He pulled her against him and began once more.

He wanted to put his mark on her in a way that was unfamiliar to him. Their loving was alternately gentle and fierce, and he demanded everything she could give and more.

David had no idea why it bothered him so much to think of Holly with another man. After all, he was hardly a celibate. The difference seemed to be that he couldn't remember which woman had been the last one before Holly. She was the only one he had been thinking of lately.

For that night he chose to forget the fact that he had an ulterior motive for establishing a bond with her. He only wanted to gather as much of this sweetness as he could before it turned sour, as he knew it would once he uncovered her secrets.

Perhaps she really was part witch.

Holly sensed that an important change had occurred in their relationship. As before, he drove her wild with desire, then satisfied her to an extent she hadn't known existed, but he seemed to be more emotionally involved this time. She wanted to believe it meant she had put a dent in his arrogance, that he was beginning to care for her a little.

He had to want to keep her by his side for a while; he had to want her more than the parade of women before her. Perhaps she should be unavailable the next time he asked her out. But how could she put him off, knowing how wonderful he made her feel?

After he was satisfied a second time, he curled himself around her spoon fashion and went still.

"David?"

"Mmmm?"

"I'd like to go to sleep now."

"So, turn off the light."

"No, I mean, alone."

He raised himself up on an elbow to look at her. "I beg your pardon?"

"Aren't you going to leave?"

"No."

"But I never let, I mean, um—"

"I'm staying, lady-love. Turn off the light and go to sleep."

"I always leave it on."

"Fine." He fell asleep with two thoughts—she was not used to sleeping with Philip, and she had a vulnerable spot in her psyche. She was afraid of the dark.

He'd have to remember that.

She had been certain she wouldn't even close her eyes, not with him literally wrapped around her. She fell sound asleep, though, only to be awakened again hours later by the most delicious dream turned reality.

They were still on their sides with him behind her, but the hand that had been covering her breast was now stroking between her legs. Even in her sleep he had aroused her to the brink of explosion. When she moved against his hand, he slipped inside her without the slightest effort. They rocked together slowly, and came together quietly, and fell back to sleep, still together.

In the morning, she was hardly surprised to discover that he had come prepared with a change of clothes in his car. They went to the zoo and imitated the monkeys, ate cotton candy, and talked about everything and nothing. David insisted it was the only way to balance out an evening of fancy clothes and the symphony.

For dinner he took her to a sports bar, where he

and Harry often watched the game of the week together on a big-screen TV. Instead of flatly informing him of her lack of interest in such a pastime, she was flattered that he wanted to share a favorite spot with her.

They arrived during halftime of an exhibition football game and ordered steak sandwiches and draft beers while a film clip of bloopers was running. As they were eating, the two commentators discussed the teams that would be playing each other in the season's opening games next Sunday. One player's name caught Holly's attention—a name she hadn't known three weeks ago, but which now held meaning.

"A lot of people were surprised to hear that Billy O'Day signed on for another season," the announcer was saying. "I figured, at thirty-four, he'd be ready to retire."

"Yep, time for the old man to join us up here in the booth," the ex-quarterback quipped in reply.

"It looks like Coach Hubbard plans to make the most of it, too. Billy's in the starting lineup next week in Philadelphia."

"Holly?"

She jerked her gaze back to David. "I'm sorry. What were you saying?"

With a laugh, he said, "I thought you said you didn't follow football. I would swear the look on your face was one of rapt attention."

"Oh, I, uh—" Holly swallowed her nervousness with a sip of beer. "I just thought how terrible it must be to be considered over the hill at thirty-four."

He nodded his agreement. "Yeah, but O'Day's had a good long run and been paid plenty over the years. He won't suffer. Hell, I wouldn't mind being able to retire a millionaire next year."

"Hah! You wouldn't last a month before you'd be back to work."

He raised an eyebrow at her. "Think you know me so well already, huh?" Her answer was a slow, confident smile. "Then what am I thinking right now?"

She stared into his eyes, but the sensual message she received made her lower her lashes shyly.

"I guess that one was too easy." His tone was light, but inside a heaviness invaded his thoughts. Second-guessing a man was one of the lines women cast when they went fishing for a mate. It was one of many clues David had trained himself to beware of. Holly may have said she wasn't interested in marriage, but other women had said that also. He had wanted to form a bond with her, to gain her confidence, and he thought he was beginning to make progress, but what might it end up costing him personally?

Holly had no idea what had happened, but David's mood changed during the third quarter of the game, and she had the distinct impression it had nothing to do with the action on the big screen.

When they returned to her apartment, he kissed her quickly and left without following her inside. Though she was confused by his abrupt departure and the absence of any request to see her again, Holly had been hoping he wouldn't insist on staying.

Hearing William O'Day's name had been a sharp reminder of why she was with David Wells and it had nothing to do with great sex.

14

Someone else had been watching the same broadcast as David and Holly and was delighted to hear that Billy O'Day would be in the starting lineup next Sunday in Philadelphia.

Philadelphia was an ideal location—near enough to come and go by car, no travel reservations that could turn into evidence.

Discovering what hotel O'Day was staying in would only take a few phone calls. Assuming the old rule still stood about retiring early and alone the night before a game, the same plan that went so smoothly with Ziegler should work again, only this time there would be no Secret Service agents to prevent the message from being made public.

The first execution had been dedicated to rape victims in general, with one particular person in mind. Perhaps this one should be devoted to Stella.

Of course, it would have to be done privately. One couldn't publicly dedicate a murder to one's own mother without being implicated. But the thought would be there.

Images flashed of the woman who had insisted

her child call her by her first name rather than anything vaguely maternal, a woman who preferred the company of a bottle to that of her baby. The baby was a teenager before discovering the reason its mother couldn't tolerate the sight of it, but understanding hadn't erased the hurt.

Stella had been only a teenager herself when she gave birth. Her parents had tried to get the baby's father to do the right thing, but he had friends who swore they had all enjoyed Stella's generous favors around the same time. The picture they painted shamed her and her family—not enough for them to go against their religion and help her get an abortion, just enough for them to banish her from their home.

Stella hadn't been raped in the physical sense, but what her boyfriend had done was even worse—he had raped her soul and stripped her of the future she had deserved.

It was the baby's further misfortune that it bore a distinct resemblance to the father.

When the child had grown to adulthood, it had searched for the father, only to learn that he had died a few years before.

Perhaps, instead of thinking of the mother, Billy O'Day's execution would be carried out in the memory of the father. The man who had escaped both his duty and his punishment.

15

Monday morning Holly was still bewildered by David's withdrawal, but she had plenty of work on her desk to occupy her mind. Unfortunately, it wasn't quite complex enough to keep her from being distracted by thoughts of him. If it wasn't his image creeping into her thoughts, it was some small thing he had done, not to mention the secret tingles that stole through her body at the thought of his kiss, or his touch, or even the way he grinned at her.

If that wasn't disruptive enough, both Bobbi Renquist and Rachel Greenley called her. Bobbi asked if she'd like to meet for lunch. Rachel asked if she'd like to go out to dinner. They had each said any day, any time, to get better acquainted. Holly put them both off with the explanation that she was backlogged from her Florida trip, and promised to call them as soon as she had more time. Right after Hell froze over, she added to herself.

When she finally felt as though she was getting her mind back on her work, Philip appeared in her doorway with a deep frown on his face.

"Didn't your appointment with Senator Iverson go well?" she asked.

"Where were you all weekend?"

Holly blinked up at him. She took a slow breath and tried to ignore her guilty conscience. "Hello to you, too. I was in and out shopping, walking."

"I must have called half a dozen times. If you would quit being so stubborn about answering machines, I might have been able to leave a message. Sunday, too?"

Guilt was rapidly being replaced by discomfort. "The weather was so nice yesterday, I went to the zoo."

He stood rigidly on the other side of her desk, his hands fisted in his pockets. "The zoo? Why didn't you call? I would have gone with you."

She didn't like the way he was questioning her, but she reminded herself that she had never given him reason to question her whereabouts before. She was always exactly where he expected her to be. Forcing herself to soften her voice, she shrugged and said, "It was an impulse. Did you need me for something?"

The creases in his forehead deepened as he shook his head negatively, then nodded. "Yes. I had a question . . . but I worked it out." Turning to leave, he paused with his back to her and asked, "Are we still on for tonight?"

"Of course. We've gone out to dinner every Monday night for years. Why would you even ask?"

Because you were out Saturday night after you told me you wanted to stay home and relax alone. "Never mind," he said, walking away. He didn't really want to know.

David caught himself smiling . . . again. This time, however, the cause was quite rational. His editor had questioned him until he revealed the true reason he wanted time off. Fortunately, he agreed with David that the lead about Frampton might be the basis for a really hot story and was allowing him to check it out on the paper's time and money. David had a few items to finish up, then he would begin.

He quashed the urge to call Holly and let her know. At least he could keep from breaking his telephone rule. It was one of the few he hadn't broken with her. In Florida, he had lost control and practically raped her that first time—and without precautions. Then this weekend he broke several more of his rules for dealing with women.

Never spend the night. He had rationalized that with the logic that *technically* they had already spent two nights together in Florida. The truth was he had never before wanted to stay with a woman after he was satisfied.

If she had been the least bit encouraging last night he would not have been able to walk away without having her again. But she hadn't, and he had, breaking another rule. He could almost hear Harry telling him, "Let me give you some advice, kid. Never pass up a free meal or free sex. You might have to do without tomorrow." Unfortunately, Harry's advice didn't hold up against David's need to prove to himself that he *could* walk away from Holly.

It had to be the novelty of her resisting him that made her so fascinating. She never made the initial move; never touched or kissed him first. Though she burned hot as hell once he started her fire.

She had balked about him spending Saturday night and looked relieved when he didn't go for more than a friendly peck before leaving her last evening. Her surface indifference would be a blow to his ego, if he wasn't so damn certain she loved every minute they spent together. His real problem was that he had no experience with women who didn't chase after him. Holly was an enigma, and he knew he wouldn't shake her out of his system until he had her figured out. He also knew they were nowhere near the point where she was ready to spill all her secrets to him.

All he had to do was break through that stubborn resistance of hers. Once he made her admit she was crazy about him, couldn't stop thinking about him, wanted him with her every minute of the day—then he would be able to put his own feelings back onto a more familiar track and get back to working on her connection with Donner.

Not calling Holly to share his news was hardly sensible. After all, she would be interested in hearing that he was going to be looking into the lead they'd discussed; would probably even be pleased for him. But somehow that small gesture of familiarity had come to symbolize his control over their entire relationship. If he phoned her once, there would be no reason not to call her about other, less important things, and sooner or later, he'd be calling just to say hello. Eventually she would be *expecting* his calls, and before he knew it, she'd be bitching at him when he forgot. The best thing was never to initiate telephone communication at all.

On Wednesday, he decided he'd given her enough time to wonder if she would see him again. With Evelyn's cooperation, he was once more seated behind Holly's desk when she arrived.

"Go away, David," she said as soon as she saw him. After the weekend they had shared, she had at least expected a phone call from him. By this morning she had worked herself up to being angry over his lack of attention, but she couldn't reveal that without giving away that she cared one way or the other. "I don't have time for any nonsense this morning."

"I woke up with this insatiable craving to have a hot-blooded blonde snuggle on my lap. Care to oblige?" He pushed the chair back from the desk and patted his thighs.

Keeping her distance from him, she crossed her arms in front of her and ignored her body's instantaneous response to seeing him. "I have a meeting in a half hour that I need to prepare for. I'm afraid my schedule doesn't allow for snuggling today. In the future, try calling for an appointment first."

"If I called first, you'd only have Evelyn say you're too busy, then I wouldn't get to watch you pretend you're not happy to see me." He stood up and walked slowly toward her. Her heart picked up its pace, but she stood her ground. Shaking his head at her, he unclasped her arms and placed them on his waist. His fingers threaded into her hair, immobilizing her head. "One of these days, lady, you're going to do precisely what I want without my having to seduce you into it."

She took a deep breath that caused her breasts to brush against his shirt, then smiled ever so slightly. "Never." His lips parted, drawing her attention, but before he could begin his seduction, she heard Philip's voice in the reception area and immediately pulled away. By the time Philip entered her office, she was behind her desk.

"Good morning," he said brightly. Then his gaze fell on David and his smile slipped. "Sorry, Holly. I didn't know you had an appointment." He nodded to David, but pointedly did not offer his hand. "Walsh, isn't it?"

"Wells. David Wells," he replied, not giving any

better than he got. "I'll only take a few more min-utes of Holly's time. I'm doing a follow-up on Hurri-cane Brigitte, and I needed to go over something she told me while we were there."

Philip's shoulders straightened. *We?* He looked to Holly for an explanation, but she was glaring at Wells.

David grinned with exaggerated innocence. "You mean she didn't tell you about our cooperative ven-ture? It's really a very funny story. Ask her to relate it when she has more time."

Philip noted Holly's flushed cheeks. "Holly? Do you need my assistance?" His voice remained level, thoroughly disguising the turmoil inside him.

She made herself meet his eyes and give him a reassuring smile. "No. It's all right. I'll give Mr. Wells what he needs, then I'll be right with you."

As soon as Philip left, David closed the door with a soft click, then leered at her. "Just how are you going to give Mr. Wells what he needs? On the desk? Or maybe up against the wall, for old times' sake."

"Shut up!" she hissed through clenched teeth. "How *dare* you do that to me?"

He raised one eyebrow. "How was I supposed to know it was a secret?" He turned his back on her and studied a picture on the wall.

"That was the most infantile display of male ego I have ever witnessed. If you had any decency, you would understand that I don't want to hurt him."

He whirled around on her. "Oh, no? There were a number of people in Florida who knew we were sharing that motor home. Add to that how many people saw us at dinner, the symphony, the zoo, and the bar. How long did you figure it would be before your pet lapdog heard about us? If I'd known you wanted to be discreet, believe me, I could have arranged it."

"Oh, I'm sure you could. I heard cuckolding husbands is one of your specialties."

His expression hardened as he stared down his nose at her. "The last I heard, you weren't married. At least I don't pretend to be faithful to one person while I'm screwing my ass off with another one."

She bolted from her chair and closed the distance between them. "No. You'll just screw your ass off with any woman that stands still long enough."

He grabbed her upper arms and yanked her hard against him. "Like this? You're standing still. Since I'm nothing but a walking prick, I should just take what I want right now and the hell with you." His mouth crushed hers with brutal intent, demanding she submit to his greater strength, insisting she accept his will over hers. He paid no heed to her frightened whimper as his fingers tangled in her hair and tugged until she opened her mouth for his deeper assault.

But, moments later, he couldn't ignore her lack of response or the dampness on her cheek.

Though he could not release her, he gentled the kiss and stroked her face with trembling hands, wordlessly begging forgiveness. He made love to her mouth until she was moving against him on her own. Ending the kiss, he continued to hold her in a possessive embrace with her head pressed to his chest. "I guess I wasn't very nice."

"No." She sniffed. "But neither was I."

"Are you going to tell Philip you're seeing me?"

"Yes. He doesn't deserve to hear it from someone else."

"I've never been jealous before. I don't like it."

She tilted her head back and looked at him with a surprised expression.

David smiled at her. "After what I just pulled with Philip, I'd rather confess than have you think I'm a complete asshole. Ever since you told me you're on the pill, I've had these visions of the two of you. . . . I know I have no right to ask about your relations with other men, and I should drop this while I'm ahead, but like I said, this is new to me."

Holly felt a flurry of pure feminine satisfaction at his discomfort. "You can ask, if you're willing to answer the same question for me."

David narrowed his eyes and wondered if she had any idea what this was going to cost him. He rationalized that telling her the truth wasn't the same as making future promises, and it would encourage her to return the honesty that he suddenly, irrationally, needed. "I haven't been with anyone else since the first time I saw you."

Another flurry tickled her lower abdomen. She was tempted to keep him hanging, but her experience with his temper discouraged that notion. "I take the pill because I have horrible, irregular periods without it. Philip and I are close friends. We work together and often socialize together . . . but I go to bed alone." She didn't count the unsuccessful attempt she'd made a few weeks ago.

He was shocked to realize even the idea of her sharing a restaurant table with Philip upset him, especially when he remembered the intimate dinner she had had with him on Saturday. Holly's intercom buzzed in time to prevent him from making more of a fool of himself. While she spoke to Evelyn, he pulled out his handkerchief and wiped the smudged makeup from under her eyes and the lipstick from his mouth.

She hung up and clucked her tongue. "My appointment's waiting in Philip's office and I'm not ready. As illuminating as the past half hour has been, please believe me when I say, I don't *ever* want to start another day this way. Now, please go away."

Instead of obeying, he pulled her back into his arms. "I want three things first."

She groaned loudly. "What?"

"A kiss." She touched her lips to his for a split second. "Hmmm. I should have been more specific. Next, come away for the weekend with me, to an incredible place I know up in the mountains." When she hesitated, he added, "My editor gave me the time off to follow up that story we talked about. I've done some checking, and I'll be leaving town on Monday. I don't know how long I'll be gone. Say yes."

The trip to her parents was off and she could easily postpone the weekend with April. "All right," she said, as pleased about spending the weekend with him as with his announcement that he would be following up on the Frampton information.

"And third, admit you're crazy about me."

After item number two, she was ready to grant him a concession. "Well . . . I don't dislike you anymore." She pulled his head down for a real kiss, then said sternly, "But I want you out of here before I change my mind."

Touching up her makeup didn't take away the sensation that his lips were still on hers, nor did gathering up the papers needed for her meeting banish him from her thoughts. His confession of jealousy and admission that he wasn't seeing other women elated her, while a separate realization of her own brought her down again.

For a short time there she had been truly furious with him, hurt by him, had said hateful things to try to get back at him, then enjoyed making up more than anything else they had done together. In effect, she had been reacting as if they had a *real* relationship.

A real relationship didn't fit in with her plans. All her efforts would be wasted if she lost sight of the true reason she was spending time with him.

And all her hard-earned independence would be forfeited if she opened her heart to someone like David Wells.

If only she could remember that longer than two seconds after he kissed her.

For the next hour, Holly struggled to maintain her professional composure on the outside while juggling a myriad of emotions on the inside. In spite of all her years of practice, guarding herself against men and their attempts to attract her attention, David continually undermined her equilibrium as if she were a complete novice. Thoughts of the up-coming weekend kept breaking through her best attempts to concentrate on the business at hand.

If that wasn't bad enough, Philip's scowl was so severe, he was making their guest nervous. Each time Holly glanced at him, she could see a mixture of accusation and pain in his eyes. She had promised David she would tell Philip about them, but that was while David had her in his arms—a clear case of duress. Looking at Philip, her longtime friend and mentor, she realized she couldn't fulfill that promise, at least not in the way David intended.

There was no question she would have to make some explanations. They would just have to be tempered to cause Philip as little concern as possible. After all, Philip was the one who had always been there for her, the one who would still be there long after David tired of her.

By the time the meeting wound down, Holly came to a conclusion. She would have to tell Philip about the Little Sister Society and why she was spending time with David.

The moment Evelyn left at the end of the day, Philip came into Holly's office, clearly prepared for a confrontation. "How could you do this to me?"

"I know I should have explained sooner, but I really didn't want to involve you."

Philip's expression was one of pure disbelief. "Good Lord, Holly! How could I not be involved if you're seeing another man?"

"It's not what you think. Let me—"

"Not what I think? I don't need to think. I saw it. Written all over both your faces this morning." His own face flushed with anger.

"Please—"

"I *love* you," he interrupted as he paced off the few steps in front of her desk. "You've never said you loved me, but I accepted that, as long as I was the only man in your life. It might not be so bad if I was losing you to a better man. David Wells isn't good enough to . . . to . . . wipe your shoes on!"

"I am trying to explain—"

"I asked a few people about him this afternoon," he continued as if she hadn't spoken. "He's known more for his stud capabilities than his journalistic fervor. I also heard he has a particular preference for buxom, blue-eyed blondes. You're nothing more than another matched trophy to him, and you don't have enough experience to realize it. I can't imagine what kind of act he put on to win your attention. Knowing from *personal* experience that you haven't the slightest interest in sex, he must have some other talent no one else is aware of. What did he do, Holly?" Suddenly he sat down on the chair across from her, his shoulders slumping with dejection. In a voice barely above a whisper, he asked, "What was it that I *didn't* do?"

She saw the moisture in his eyes and felt his grief. She owed him so much, and everything he said about David was true. Hearing it aloud helped her stand by her earlier decision not to tell Philip the whole truth.

She moved to the chair next to him and covered his hand with hers. "David Wells means nothing to me. This is all my fault for not explaining everything right from the beginning." She meant to be brief, but once she began telling him about the Little Sister Society, she found herself describing each of the women and their personal experiences.

When he asked, she only hesitated a moment before giving him the names of the men. Somehow she convinced herself that the more honest she was about this, the less guilty she would feel over lying about David. The odd part was, Philip didn't seem surprised by anything she revealed, almost as though he had heard it all before. He just sat there nodding as she spoke. She wondered if he could be in shock.

"And so, the only reason I have spent any time at all with David Wells is to make sure he follows up on the lead about Jerry Frampton. The fact that we were both in Florida at the same time was a coincidence caused by nature. You must have seen the articles he's done on the environmental impact of the hurricane."

Philip shrugged. "I did, but until he threw it in my face, I wasn't letting myself consider how he had gotten his information."

"I was wrong not to let you know we had spent some time together down there, but I was afraid—"

"That I'd react exactly like I did," Philip completed with an embarrassed smile.

"I'm sorry."

He shook his head. "No. *I'm* sorry. I should have known I could trust you." He lifted her hand to his mouth for a kiss.

She felt her stomach turn to lead and reminded herself this was for the best. Everything would work out fine in the end. But for now, she had one more lie to tell. "By the way, one of the women asked me to visit her this weekend, and I decided to take her up on it."

"Oh? Which one?"

"April."

"The psychologist?"

"Yes. Maybe I'll come back Sunday night with a whole new outlook on life."

Holly's attitude actually began changing Friday as she and David were driving up into Maryland's Blue Ridge Mountains. Up to that point, she had purposely stopped herself from initiating any action between them, be it communication or lovemaking, in order to keep him coming after her. Once he did, of course, she found it impossible not to respond to him.

After the volatile scene in her office, she had no doubt he was captivated, at least momentarily. The problem was, he continued to withhold one nicety that could no longer go unnoticed. He had never once called her on the telephone. Oh, he always had an excuse for not calling, but Holly had finally realized he had a quirk about it.

He was about to embark on a trip of unknown

length, the details of which had become vitally important to her. How could she get a vicarious thrill out of his investigation, if he didn't call her while he was on the trail? Their relationship had not progressed to the point where she could logically ask to accompany him on a business trip. His antipathy toward Ma Bell was an annoying factor she hadn't counted on.

Thus she set out to make his weekend so memorable that he couldn't possibly put her out of his mind while he was gone. If she was attentive enough, entertaining enough, *good* enough, perhaps he wouldn't be able to resist giving her a call or two. Then it would be natural for her to question how his investigation was going.

She decided to follow April's advice and take the pressure off. Surprisingly, once she removed the restrictions she had placed on herself, she didn't have to consciously think about how to act. It felt right to reach over and stroke his neck while he was driving, or lean over and whisper something outrageous in his ear while they were having dinner in the public dining room, or suggest that they order the rest of their meals from room service. Making love in the woods where he had taken her on a hike had been his idea, but she didn't let her normal inhibitions stop her from enjoying it to the fullest.

Everything about their stay in the romantic hideaway was as memorable as she had hoped it would be . . . until Sunday afternoon.

David had made arrangements for a late checkout, so they still had the whole day to spend any way they wanted. He was willing to miss the football game, but she assured him that she wanted to watch it with him. When the time came, he turned on the television and settled on the big bed with her cuddled in his arms.

After the usual run of commercial announcements, a serious-faced commentator came on-screen.

"As the first game of the season is about to begin here in Philadelphia, rather than the usual festive atmosphere, the mood is somber. In case you just tuned in, we have tragic news to share. Billy O'Day was brutally murdered in his hotel room last night. The police—"

"No," Holly uttered, abruptly sitting upright. "That can't be."

"Holly—"

"Sh-shh," she said, waving him to be quiet so that she could hear what was being said on the TV.

". . . FBI involvement in the case. Although exact details have not been released, it has been revealed that certain gruesome aspects bear a distinct similarity to the recent murder of Pennsylvania Senator Timothy Ziegler. The possibility of a serial killer stalking public figures is being considered. In the meantime, although Billy O'Day will not be on the field today, his teammates and all his fans will be thinking about him."

David eased Holly back beside him. "My God, you're ice-cold." He studied her face. "And you're white as a ghost." He suddenly remembered how intently she had listened to the comments about O'Day when they had been in the sports bar last week. "Holly, did you know him?"

"I . . . no . . . I . . ." Her mind scrambled to form a logical answer. The implication of what she just heard was so mind-boggling her only thought was of self-preservation. She needed time alone to think this through. Taking a slow, deep breath, she pulled herself together. "I'm sorry. I don't know what came over me. It probably had something to do with that conversation we had last Sunday about him having to retire at such an early age."

He wanted to believe her. He really did. But she was such a poor liar. Despite all the progress they'd made that weekend, she was still not confiding anything truly personal. He could try forcing it out of her, play it tough and threatening, but he knew instinctively that would only push her away from him completely, and as much as he hated to admit it, he wasn't yet ready to let her go.

No, this one he was going to have to figure out another way. He mentally added the name Billy O'Day to his list of people Holly had a connection with. He would do a little investigating about that man's background right after he got back from his trip to Florida.

They both made an effort to restore the former mood of the weekend, and they both pretended not to notice that it didn't quite work.

With David leaving for Miami early the next morning, there was no question of his staying at Holly's apartment that night. She barely managed to keep thoughts of O'Day, Ziegler, and the Little Sister Society submerged until David left her alone.

The two murders couldn't possibly be coincidental, and yet she couldn't see herself walking into the FBI and suggesting that one of the women she had met was a deranged killer. How could she say anything to anyone without revealing how she had come to that conclusion? She'd practically be handing herself over as a suspect, and as Erica had made her realize, she had no alibi for the night Ziegler was murdered.

A faint knock interrupted her analysis. Assuming

it was David, returning for some reason, she opened the door . . . then wished she hadn't. The visitor was Bobbi Renquist, in her drab, IRS agent persona.

Looking meek and a little frightened, Bobbi asked, "May I come in please?"

Holly considered the possibility that this woman could be a murderess, but Bobbi stepped inside before Holly could think of how to turn her away. "It's very late," she said, rather than what she was thinking.

"I know. I've been waiting for you to come home all evening."

Holly cocked her head at her. "Why— Wait a minute. How did you get up here without the guard calling me?" She felt her fingers growing cold again.

Bobbi's brown-eyed gaze skittered away as she spoke. "I showed the guard my ID and he let me pass."

"Oh, that's great. So now he'll think I'm being investigated by the IRS."

"Better that than the FBI."

Holly crossed her arms protectively. "What do you mean?"

Bobbi sighed. "Please. Can we sit down? I'm here as a friend, I swear."

Holly motioned her toward the couch and sat stiffly on a chair opposite her.

"Where were you last night?" Bobbi asked quietly.

"I was in Maryland all weekend, with a friend."

"Good. I was certain it couldn't be you."

Holly knew exactly what she meant, but asked anyway. "I couldn't be what?"

Bobbi narrowed her eyes in confusion. "Why, the killer of course. Surely you heard the news about Billy O'Day."

"I heard, but I haven't decided what to do about it yet."

Bobbi gasped. "Dear God. You can't be thinking of actually *doing* something about it. You mustn't. We could all end up being investigated. Things could come out that have nothing to do with the murders. I—I could lose my job."

"Two men have been murdered. I can't just pretend that I don't know they had something in common."

"Yes, you can," Bobbi said, nervousness making her voice crack. "Rachel is on the case. She'll handle everything without any of us being implicated. All she wants us to do is make sure we have alibis, just in case the worst happens and someone makes the connection. That was one of the reasons I came to see you. But since you were with a friend, you're covered."

"And everyone else?" Holly asked warily.

Bobbi picked at something on her skirt and answered without looking up. "Rachel said everyone else is taken care of."

"But you're not so sure, are you?" Holly ventured. "Do you think Rachel killed them?"

Bobbi's head snapped up. "Rachel? Heavens no. She and I have been friends since high school. She would never do anything to jeopardize the rest of us, no matter what she says when she's . . . not feeling well."

Holly had to find out what the woman thought. "Then who?"

Bobbi frowned. "I shouldn't say it. Rachel said she didn't do it, and I should believe her, but it's just that she's so blinded by her."

Holly waited, sensing that Bobbi wanted to share her opinion, despite her hesitancy.

"I think it's that bitch. If she could kill her own husbands, Ziegler and O'Day would be nothing to her."

"Erica?"

"Of course, Erica. She's mean and vicious and has no conscience. For some reason, Rachel is too infatuated to see her for what she really is."

Holly's brain was frantically assimilating all the different hints Bobbi was dropping. "You mean Rachel and Erica . . ."

Bobbi nodded. "Please don't think badly of Rachel. We each have different ways of coping with what happened to us. Rachel happens to prefer the company of women to men. But Erica, that's a different story. She doesn't have feelings for either sex. She just does whatever will most benefit Erica."

"Are you suggesting that Erica not only killed her husbands, but also Ziegler and O'Day, and Rachel would protect her?"

"Rachel would do *anything* for Erica."

"Even murder?"

"No!" Bobbi exclaimed. "Rachel couldn't kill someone any more than you or I, or Cheryl or April, for that matter. Except in the line of duty, of course. No. It can't be anyone but Erica."

Methinks thou dost protest too much, Holly thought. "Why are you telling me this?"

Bobbi got up from the couch and walked across the room. For a moment, she just stood there, with her back to Holly, then she removed her glasses, straightened her spine, and turned slowly around.

Holly had encountered Bobbi's other personality before, but seeing the change occur before her eyes was much more disturbing. It was not only the glasses and posture that had changed, Bobbi's whole demeanor became strong and aggressive.

"To warn you," she answered in a deeper, clearer voice than she'd been using before. "You're new. I was afraid you might feel obligated to report what you know, and you can't possibly understand all the repercussions that would have on the rest of us. Besides that, I think you should consider the risk you'd be taking. If Erica thought you were going to talk to someone other than Rachel, she might stop you from talking to anyone ever again."

Holly was stunned at her own naïveté. It hadn't even occurred to her that the murderer or murderess, whoever it was, could turn on her.

Roberta laughed lightly. "Finally got the picture, huh? Just keep what you know to yourself and no harm will come to you. You haven't told anyone else about us, have you?"

Holly thought about her confession to Philip the other day, and how much her parents knew, but there was no reason to put them at risk as well. "No. I haven't told anyone. But now that you mention it, there *are* other people who know about Ziegler, O'Day, and most of the other men, too. Besides the rest of the Little Sister Society and any people they may have told, Cheryl Wallace waved a list of names on national television. Who knows where that list ended up?"

Roberta laughed again. "Very good, Holly. You just came to the same conclusion that the FBI team of investigators arrived at . . . with Rachel's guidance. O'Day was drugged and his genitals were removed, exactly like with Ziegler. Also, just like the first time, a message was left behind with the words, 'Just Punishment for a Rapist.' Since Cheryl was the only person known to have a relevant motive and her alibis are airtight, the general consensus is that the perpetrator is a militant feminist who's gone off the deep end. Since none of us publicly fall into that category, there's no reason for anyone to look our way. So you see, there's no need for you to do anything about this matter yourself. No need at all."

Holly might have been more receptive if the woman offering her such assurance had been the same one that had walked in her door fifteen minutes ago, but this one, her alter ego, gave her the creeps.

"I understand you've already passed the Frampton information on to a reporter. Rachel and I are very concerned about you, Holly. The last thing we need right now is some nosy reporter in the middle of this mess. You can't do anything to stop him at this point, but we strongly suggest you forget the idea of staying in contact with him."

Holly nodded, though she had no intention of taking suggestions, no matter how strong, from either Bobbi or Rachel.

Roberta walked toward the door, then faced Holly with an expression that was as threatening as her words. "Remember what I said. No talking to anyone about us, or I guarantee you, you'll regret it."

Holly locked the door as soon as she ushered Bobbi out. Her head was pounding and her stomach burned with acid. What should she do?

The safest course of action would be to follow Bobbi's orders. Let Rachel handle it. Don't talk to anyone.

What had Bobbi meant by saying that she'd regret it? What could she do to her if she told anyone about what Ziegler and O'Day had in common, or that there was a group of women systematically seeking revenge against the list of men? The answer came easily enough. If Bobbi was a cold-blooded butcher, she would kill Holly as well.

But what if she wasn't? What if none of the women had done anything more than what they had told her about originally? After all, none of the other men on the list had ever been physically hurt. That fact, more than any others, seemed to point to the killer being an outsider. The murderer could turn out to be a total stranger and going to the authorities would call attention to herself and the other women unnecessarily.

However, that still didn't explain why Bobbi would threaten her. If none of the women were responsible for the murders, why the threat? It seemed much too extreme just to maintain their privacy. The more she considered possibilities, the more frightened and bewildered she became.

Her thoughts abruptly turned to David. What if Jerry Frampton was next on the killer's list? Could David be walking into a deadly situation unknowingly? She should have told him everything as soon as she heard about O'Day, but her brain hadn't been working fast enough to overrule her natural tendency to keep her problems to herself.

Curling up on her couch, she let herself think about David. Her scheme had clearly backfired. She may have captivated him, but he had ensnared her just as securely. She genuinely cared about him. No, that was too mild. She was crazy about him, thought about him constantly ... couldn't get enough of him. Though she knew nothing permanent could come of it, that didn't stop her from acknowledging the fact that she had fallen in love with him.

She should have confessed everything that afternoon. Making the decision to rectify her mistake immediately, she looked in the phone book for his name. He had never offered her his home number,

and she had never asked for it. When she didn't
find it, she dialed information, but his number was
unlisted. Stomach acid started churning again as
she realized that since she didn't know where he
lived, she couldn't go to see him before he left in
the morning. She didn't even know what airline he
would be flying out on.

The only thing she could do was call his paper
first thing in the morning and leave a message for
him to contact her as soon as possible. She couldn't
count on him calling her, but she was fairly sure he
would keep in touch with his editor.

Holly tried to get some rest, but concern for
David, as much as Bobbi's upsetting visit, kept her
awake.

By the time she reached her office in the morning, she knew she had to seek someone else's advice,
and Philip was the most logical person, since she
had already confided in him.

His reaction took her by surprise.

"Bobbi was absolutely right," he firmly pronounced. "You mustn't talk to anyone else—especially not the authorities. And considering the fact
that Bobbi did threaten you, I'd avoid the women
in that group from now on. You could be putting
yourself in serious danger, to say nothing about the
fact that you could also be implicating a lot of innocent people who could be hurt by any action you
take at this point."

He rose from his chair and came around his desk
to where she was standing, too nervous to sit. When
he spoke again, his voice was hushed, almost secretive. "I'm sure it didn't occur to you, but those
women are not the only ones that could become
suspects. If you reveal what you know, sooner or
later, the investigation would turn to the loved ones

who might have acted against the men on behalf of the victims."

"What do you mean?"

"Just for a minute, pretend you're an FBI agent, and you don't know me personally. Couldn't it be possible that *I* committed those murders to get revenge for you?"

"Philip, *really*—"

"Now, think about it. Everyone knows I'm totally devoted to you. I've often said I'd do anything for you. The first murder occurred shortly after you joined the Little Sister Society. Add the fact that I have no alibi for the times of either murder. It just so happens, I was home alone."

She made a face at him. "That's ridiculous. You know Billy O'Day didn't do anything to me."

He shrugged. "Can we prove that? Or better yet, couldn't someone suggest that I might purposely choose him to make it look like the murders had nothing to do with you?"

"I still don't think—"

"Then consider something else. Your father was completely irrational when I first spoke to him about you. He made threats. If the bureau started checking on your parents, what do you think they'd come up with?"

"But he was in Butler, Pennsylvania, and the murders occurred in Washington and Philadelphia."

"Not far enough to eliminate him as a suspect."

"Philip, please tell me you don't really believe that Pop—"

He touched his fingers to her lips. "Of course not. I was only making a point. But I think you should know, I called your parents the evening Ziegler was killed, mainly to see how Bernie had taken the news of Ziegler's appointment. They weren't at their house or the restaurant. I didn't think much of it at the time, but now . . ." He shook his head. "Who knows what someone else would think? Please promise me, you won't try to do anything about this on your own."

She remembered that her parents had gone away this past weekend as well. Where had her father said? The Poconos. Perhaps an hour's drive from Philadelphia. She shook her head and wondered how she could even think of such a thing.

Considering all the complications Philip had brought up made her more confused than she already was, but she reluctantly gave him her promise not to do anything that would put herself or her loved ones at risk. To herself she amended, *until I can reach David.*

David would never advise her to do nothing. She didn't have the nerve to act on her own, but surely he would offer support and advise her of the wisest course to take. She only hoped she hadn't waited too long to turn to him for help.

16

Jerry Frampton reread the article on the front page of his morning newspaper. It said a lot about Billy O'Day's career, but very little about how he died. The little it did say, however, combined with what he knew was enough to make him suspicious.

He had thought it was terribly ironic that Tim was killed right after he was vindicated by the Senate committee and got the appointment he'd wanted so badly. It hadn't occurred to Jerry that Cheryl Wallace could have anything to do with that murder. He figured, after the embarrassment of the hearing, she would have no choice but to crawl back into her hole and never come out again.

But now, with O'Day being what the news called "butchered in a manner similar to the murder of Senator Ziegler," Jerry was not so sure about Wallace's forfeit of the game. It could be that she had decided to change the rules.

Considering the time between his conversation with Tim and Tim's murder, he assumed Tim never had the chance to contact a reporter as they'd discussed. Otherwise, the news would be full of suppositions about the women somehow being involved in the two men's deaths.

Was he next on the list? For his own protection, he thought it might be best if he stepped forward and told the whole story himself.

Then again, the public was so fickle, he couldn't predict how they'd react to learning that Ziegler *had* set Wallace up to be raped and that he'd been one of the men who'd used her, as well as others. Advertising in *Jock* or even actual sales of the magazine, could be affected. Nor could he predict how the senators would respond to having their poor judgment exposed—his magazine could suddenly be labeled pornography and pulled off the general newsstands.

For the time being, he decided to keep what he knew to himself, but to beef up security around his estate. No one could kill him if they couldn't get to him.

Bleary-eyed but surfacing, David scanned the interior of the airport coffee shop and wondered how long he had been vegetating there in his alcoholic fog. He popped three more aspirins into his mouth, swallowing them with a huge gulp of black coffee. He judged the state of his intoxication by how many seconds passed before he realized the scalding liquid had burned his tongue. The flight to Miami had been piloted by a character out of a Stephen King novel. He didn't care how long it took—when it was time to return to D.C., he was taking the train.

It took one hour and two more cups of coffee to clear his head enough to leave the airport. Guessing in advance what his condition would be, he had made arrangements to pick up a rental car at his hotel, which was only a short cab ride from the airport.

As a reporter, he probably would have had little trouble getting an interview with Jerry Frampton, but the man was not going to hand himself up just because someone had taken a picture of him with an ex-convict. David knew he needed more than that, and Mick D'Angelo was the source that could provide it. As was his way, David didn't have a specific plan. He would just follow his nose and see where it took him.

By late afternoon he was refreshed and ready to check out his first lead: the Hon Choi restaurant on Miami's South Beach. Tommy Li Chen, the proprietor for twenty-three years, was not only in, but very available for an interview by a reporter. When he realized the questions did not involve the quality of his cuisine, however, he shed a considerable amount of his Oriental charm.

"I tell you same thing I tell other man. Jerry Frampton, big shot now. No come here long time. But I remember and tell people big shot eat here sometimes. They come back again to see. No harm. Good for business."

"Wait a minute. You said another man was asking about Frampton?"

"Yes. Private investigator, he say."

That would make sense. Someone had unearthed the facts that had been passed to him. The question was, why? "What about Mick D'Angelo? I understand they used to meet here."

"Yes. Some years ago. Mr. D'Angelo still come in once in while." Li Chen glanced furtively around him before speaking. "He different kind of big shot in Miami. Bad kind."

"Did you tell the other man who was here anything about D'Angelo?"

"Same thing I tell you. He good buddy of big shot Frampton. I hear him bragging to lady friend last time he here."

"Any idea how I could find D'Angelo?"

Li Chen's straight eyebrows arched slightly. "Better you ask girls on Seventy-ninth Street. They not charge much to talk to handsome boy like you." He gave David a wink, then excused himself to supervise the dinner preparations.

David spent most of the night cruising the street Li Chen suggested. Although he would have willingly parted with some cash in exchange for information, the only expense he had thus far was for the overpriced drinks in the various pickup joints he stopped in. Most of the women he met denied knowing Mick D'Angelo, but one suggested he try a few places on Biscayne Boulevard, another area known for its abundance of flesh for sale.

Part of the next day he spent sleeping and reading the local newspapers. A few more details had been revealed about the O'Day and Ziegler murders, but not enough to encourage any copycat killings. And not enough to make any guesses as to what they had in common besides being famous.

David couldn't forget how Holly had reacted to the news of O'Day's murder, or how she had focused on the piece about O'Day the week before. It reminded him of her reaction at the fund-raiser when someone brought up the Ziegler murder. He had gotten the impression then that it was something more than an objection to the topic as unsuitable dinner conversation. Now that he knew her better, he would bet there was more to it—something more personal.

He was certain she was lying about not knowing O'Day. Had she known Ziegler also? He doubted if murder in general made her that squeamish. Obviously, he was going to have to wait to get back before the answers could be unearthed, but he still had a strong feeling her connection to Donner was an important key. If only he could figure out what all the cast of characters had in common!

The feelers he sent out about Mick D'Angelo paid off that evening. While chewing on a juicy rib in a restaurant on Biscayne, a fairly attractive redhead sat down at his table. Her teased, shoulder-length hair, makeup, and attire were flashy without being obscene—just the right amount of blatant sexuality to operate successfully in the restaurant's busy cocktail lounge. From where he sat, he had seen her approach two different men at the bar, one of whom slid his hand over her buttocks while she negotiated with him. David acknowledged her with a nod as his teeth tugged a piece of meat off the bone.

"Buy me a drink?" Her eyes traced his face and dallied over his mouth and hands in a provocative manner. David motioned to a waitress and waited for the redhead to speak.

"My name's Cinnamon. I can't help but wonder what such a gorgeous man is doing all alone."

"Maybe I was looking for someone to keep me company." David dropped the picked bone onto his plate, tore open the wet-wipe, and meticulously cleaned each finger. His gaze traveled from her eyes, to her mouth, to the pointed nipples beneath her thin sweater.

She watched each movement, as practiced as her own, and let out a husky laugh. "Not bad. But tell me this, which one of us is workin' this table?"

He returned her easy smile. "I guess that all depends on who wants what from whom."

She leaned forward, retaining the expression and body language of her profession, but her voice altered from suggestive to serious. "I heard you've been lookin' for Mick D'Angelo. Word is you're heat of some kind."

"I'm not. But I'll pay for information about him. Are you selling?"

"Come with me, and find out."

David's life lessons had been learned on the streets of a lower-class neighborhood. He automatically weighed his chances of getting what he wanted against the possibility of getting mugged.

Cinnamon reacted predictably to his hesitation. "Listen, I can't just sit here and bullshit with you. Either we leave here with you looking like you're about to get laid, or I'm movin' on."

He let his instincts make the decision. Without answering, he rose, pulled out his wallet, and placed several bills next to his plate.

Once outside, she suggested they take his car. Following her succinct directions for about fifteen minutes, David found himself in an almost vacant parking lot of a shopping mall.

"Nice location you've got here, Cinnamon. I assume you don't normally conduct business until all the kiddies have been taken home."

"Don't be an asshole. If you want to do somethin' besides talk, we can go to my place. But I'd bet a night's wages you ain't never paid for it in your life."

Holly's face flickered in his mind. "There's paying, and there's *paying*."

She gave him another knowing smile. "No kiddin'. Okay, as of fifteen minutes ago, you went on my clock. It's a hundred an hour. Why don't you start by tellin' me who and what you are and why you're looking for Mick."

Something told him to play it completely straight with her. "I'm David Wells, a reporter for *The Washington Times*. I'm doing a story on an acquaintance of D'Angelo's and I was hoping he could give me a little insight."

"Lots of luck. The only time his acquaintances make the news is when they get arrested, and even then, they're usually too small-time for anybody to cover their story."

"That's not what I heard. In fact, the one I'm interested in is quite well known—Jerry Frampton, publisher of *Jock* magazine."

She frowned in concentration. "Now that you mention it, I did hear somethin' a while back about him, but it's old gossip. I couldn't help you there, and I'm not sure anybody else would either. But if you want a story on D'Angelo, I've got one so hot it could singe you just knowin' about it."

"Go on."

"You gotta promise to forget where you heard it. I mean, if I wanted to risk gettin' killed for openin' my mouth, I'd of gone to the police."

"I don't reveal my sources, but if you're that worried about it, why tell me?"

Cinnamon studied her decoratively painted nails a moment before answering. "Because it's driving me crazy to keep it inside. And Nikki Farris was my friend."

"Was?"

"Yeah, was . . . as in no longer is. She was beaten to death and left in a garbage Dumpster about a year ago. Word is she was tortured some, too, but that didn't make the local papers. They said there were no clues. What the hell do the police care if some hooker gets herself killed anyway? They figure it's one of the hazards of the trade."

"I gather you think Mick D'Angelo had something to do with your friend's murder."

"I don't just think. The night she was killed, she had a job with him. He was gonna make her a star. See, she really wanted to be an actress. I know, you've heard that one before. Well, in Nikki's case, she wanted it bad enough to do porn flicks. That's Mick's main business. I'm not talking about X-rated stuff you can rent at your local video store. He doesn't touch anything that legitimate. His specialty is kinky porn—the kind you have to know somebody to get hold of, and it costs big bucks to even get a peek at it."

"Children?"

"And animals, torture, you name it. Besides Nikki wantin' to call herself an actress, she had a coke habit that hookin' alone couldn't pay for. The kind of stuff Mick produces pays well enough for some girls to go along with all kinds of shit. Nikki told me about one film they made where they faked a virgin sacrifice on a stone slab, phony blood and all. Another time she showed up at my apartment with a black eye and a swollen lip. She said one of the actors had gotten carried away with his role, and she hadn't ducked fast enough. I'm positive her death was a result of one of those films."

"You mean she might have been accidentally killed?"

"Maybe not so accidentally. Maybe D'Angelo did a real snuff film—not a mock-up."

David felt his pulse race with anticipation. This wasn't what he had set out to find, but it could be even better. "Have you heard of anything like that being for sale? I don't know that much about it, but

I would assume it would be worth a small fortune if the owner wanted to part with it. Although I can't imagine anybody being stupid enough to hold on to a video of an actual murder."

"Mick's greed is a lot bigger than his brain. The grapevine says he's got a very special product—an original tape, with a price tag that he could retire on."

"Shit." David uttered the one syllable while his mind raced over the possibilities. There was no question as to whether he would follow it up, only how to proceed. "Could you help establish me as a buyer?"

"Not directly, but you've already made it known around town that you're lookin' for Mick. You just haven't asked the right question to the right person. Tomorrow night go to the Peacock Lounge near the University of Miami. One of Mick's scouts hangs out there solicitin' talent from the co-eds. If you bring up Mick's name to one of the bartenders there, his scout'll find you. You can figure how to play it after that. Don't pretend to be anybody but who you are, though. Mick's probably already heard about you and checked your background by now."

"You think he'd buy the idea of a Washington reporter looking to agent a lucrative deal for a rather perverted politician?"

"Honey, I'd believe anything you told me when you bat those eyelashes of yours. Just don't be surprised if the scout propositions you as part of the deal."

"One more thing. Do you have a picture of Nikki Farris? If there is a film, and I do get to view it, I need to know who I'm looking for."

She took him by her apartment and gave him a

photo of her and Nikki. Before leaving, he counted out one hundred dollars for her time.

"There's a little time left on the clock." She wet her lips and moved closer. "I'd hate to think you didn't get your money's worth."

He chucked her under the chin and grinned. "Aah, but then I couldn't say I'd never paid for it, could I?"

She shrugged her shoulders and headed for the door with her dignity intact. "It's your loss, honey. Okay, take me back to the restaurant. There's still plenty of good workin' hours left tonight."

The ability to improvise in almost any situation was one of the characteristics that made David such a good investigative reporter. He admitted to himself that he had no idea what he was doing—he had never put in any time on the crime desk—but it felt right, and he never fought those feelings when they came to him.

Since it would be a waste of time to go to the Peacock Lounge before dark, he decided to use the daylight hours on Wednesday to do some research before getting any further involved.

About a year back he had met a Miami reporter at a press conference. He had given the guy some guidance on protocol, shared a few war stories over drinks, then later fixed him up with a friend of a friend. The friend was known to be very kind to lonely visitors. David doubted that the reporter would have forgotten either his companion or him. He was right.

By the time he and the reporter parted company, David had copies of the newspaper accounts of Nikki's murder, the police homicide report, Mick D'Angelo's criminal record, and a confirmation that Jerry Frampton had once posted bail for him. Of course David had to promise to keep his friend apprised of his investigation.

A few hours later, David elbowed his way up to the bar in the Peacock Lounge. As Cinnamon had predicted, a question about D'Angelo soon brought a man to David's side.

"Hey, sport. Hear you've been asking about a friend of mine. Mick doesn't come in here, but I might be seeing him later. I could give him a message."

David paused to give the man the once-over. He looked more like an accountant than a scout for a pornographer—very slight, at least sixty years old, with a gray crewcut and thick, horn-rimmed glasses. Only his tight-lipped mumbling and furtive glances hinted at his true line of work. David knew better than to appear too anxious. "I represent someone from Washington, D.C., someone who's familiar with Mr. D'Angelo's . . . products."

"I handle most of his business transactions around here. If you can be a little more specific about the category of the product your client is seeking, I'll see what I can do."

David shook his head no. "Sorry. I heard this particular product was available only through D'Angelo himself. I understand it's quite unique—the type of thing that might make an excellent gift to a foreign dignitary whose tastes are a bit . . . different. I'm willing to pay the fare to get a look at it."

The scout studied him for several seconds before coming to a positive conclusion. "I'll pass on your request. It may take a day or so. Where can he reach you if he's interested?"

David extracted his business card from his wallet, wrote the name of the hotel and his room number on the back, and handed it to the man.

With nothing more to accomplish and looking forward to a full night's sleep for a change, David returned to his hotel. Sleep eluded him, however. He told himself it was the thrill of the chase that was keeping him awake. That, and trying to figure out where he would come up with an unknown quantity of cash to get a look at a movie that could turn out to be worthless.

He glared at the tent his erection was making in his sheet. Since when did working on a story do that to him? If anything, the excitement of a great lead usually had quite an opposite effect.

Usually. As in, before Holly. How many times had those words come to mind in the last month when he found himself behaving peculiarly? He wasn't literally keeping count, but off the top of his head he would say a thousand was probably close.

For three days, he'd been fighting to keep her out of his thoughts. Obviously, his body wasn't paying the least bit of attention to his brain.

By the end of last weekend, he should have been ready to move on to fresh game. She had finally dropped all pretenses of indifference and had even initiated their lovemaking several times. He had also extracted her admission that she enjoyed everything they did together. Still, the little voice in his head nagged, there was something he was missing, something she withheld that kept taking him back to his first impression that she wanted more from him than stud service. And when she'd had the chance to confide in him and tell him why O'Day's name affected her, she'd lied.

She had asked if he would call while he was away. No begging or whining, as another woman might have. She only asked once, in a conversational tone that implied that it didn't really matter. But he knew

she wanted that phone call, and he knew she sensed
that such a call would be an admission of sorts from
him. Calling her would be akin to giving in to her
power over him. His ability to hold out in this one
way had begun to feel like a lifeline to his carefree
bachelor days.

As much as he hated to recognize what was happening to him, it was beginning to look like the
mindless appendage between his legs had been
joined by his heart, and he felt his brain slowly
switching sides as well.

Damn, but he missed her. He missed her eyes,
her smile, her innocence, her passion. He missed
her incredible breasts and the way her body took
his in and continued to please him long after he
was spent. He missed their intellectual debates and
her biting sarcasm. He even missed her lies.

What a wretched state she had reduced him to
that he thought the sound of her voice fifteen hundred miles away would ease his agitation and let
him drift off to sleep.

Thoughts of how good it had felt to sleep next to
her instantly increased his state of arousal. He
grasped the source of his discomfort and closed his
eyes. No, not good enough. He wanted Holly.

Suddenly he thought of a way he could have her.
It required a phone call, but he would still be the
one in control. As he reached for the phone on the
nightstand, he noted the time: two-thirty. For what
he had in mind, the groggier she was, the better.

"Hello?"

The huskiness in her voice assured him she had
been sound asleep. "What are you wearing?"

"David?"

He could imagine her rubbing her eyes and pulling herself upright. "Don't get up. I want you just

how I picture you in my mind, stretched out on your bed, all warm and dreamy. What are you wearing?"

"My blue nightgown."

"The one you had on for about five minutes Friday night?"

"Yes, but David—"

"Take it off."

"What?"

"Take it off. Slowly. Slide it up your thighs, then lift your hips just enough to pull the gown up to your waist. You know what I mean. Do it the way I would if I were there. Are you doing it?"

"David, this is—"

"Either do what I say or I'm hanging up. I want you so bad right now, I hurt, but if you don't want to play with me—"

"Okay."

"I want you exposed to me, lady-love. No nightgown, no underwear, no sheets. Is that how you are now? Is your gown up around your waist?"

She didn't answer for a few seconds, but David was certain she was complying. "Did you make yourself ready for me, Holly?"

"Yes."

"Good. Now keep your eyes closed. I'm there with you. At the foot of your bed. You're going to have to spread your legs wider to make room for me. I can feel you resisting, Holly. Do you want me to hang up?"

He heard her sigh, and her whispered "No."

"All right then. I'm kneeling between your legs. Your hand is my hand now. I want to touch what I see, but you'll have to help me. Run my fingers up and down your thighs, outside, then in. Lightly. Barely graze your skin. Yes, that's it. You feel like expensive silk to me. Did you know that? I see you arching. You want me to touch you there, don't you?" He waited a heartbeat. "Say it."

"Yes."

"Brush my fingers over your curls. Easy. Don't sneak inside. It's not time for that yet. That's enough. I want to see the rest of you now. You can move the phone away from your ear long enough to pull the nightgown off completely." He paused, sure of her obedience. "Are you back?"

"Mm-hmm."

"You're absolutely beautiful, just like the last time I saw you. I'm going to need both hands from here on. Cradle the phone between your ear and the pillow. That's the way. You know how crazy I am about your breasts. Offer them up to me, love. Lift them and press them together so that I can bury my face in them both at once. *Yes.* You really are so perfect. I've got your right nipple between my teeth. Oh, God, you taste good. Squeeze it, Holly. Feel me there, sucking on your sweet tit. I'm kissing my way over to your left breast now, but I need you to touch me, too. Reach down and stroke me with your right hand. I'm glad you're not shy about touching me anymore. Do what you did on Sunday morning, love. Oh, that's good. Don't forget, I'm still loving your left breast. Are you with me, Holly? Do you feel my tongue licking you?"

She let out a small moan, and he tightened the fist around his shaft.

"Are you wet? Let my fingers find out for themselves. Slide them very slowly down over your stomach and through those pretty curls, right over that sensitive little bump of flesh. No, don't dally there. Go further. Slowly now, dip two fingers inside. I always use two fingers to get you ready for me. Do you ever think about that? I do. I think too much about you, and kissing your breasts, and slipping my fingers in and out of you while you rub yourself against my palm and purr in my ear. God, you're so tight . . . and hot. Tell me how hot you are."

"*David* . . ." Her voice was raw with need.

"You can have me, love. Your hand feels so good wrapped around me. I'm big and hard, and just about ready to burst, but you'll have to guide me. Press me against you, right where you want me. Now move me, up and down then in and out. That's it. Up and down. In and out. Don't stop. C'mon, stay with me, honey. A little faster now. Oh, God, you're good. I'm almost there. Come with me, *please*."

He could hear her breathing clearly now—short, broken gasps that harmonized with his own. "Say when." He clung to the edge of the cliff, waiting for her.

"*Now*."

He let go, knowing she was with him all the way.

Moments later, releasing his own ragged breath, he murmured, "G'night, Holly." And hung up before she could say a word.

The dreamy cloud of pleasure lifted from Holly's mind with the disconnecting click. It took a little longer for her body to catch up.

Damn him.

For three days she had fretted over how she could reach him. His editor swore he didn't know where David was staying in Miami, then took her messages twice, but she had the feeling he'd given the same speech before, many times to many women.

It would serve David right if he— She cut off the vindictive thought. This wasn't his fault. It was hers, for trying to play a game that was beyond her experience. If anything happened to him, she would never forgive herself.

So far she had heeded Bobbi's and Philip's advice—only because she wanted to talk to David before doing anything else. But it still didn't go down well. As soon as the sun came up, she called the one other person she felt comfortable talking to. She had called April on Friday before leaving for Maryland, just to let her know their plan was moving along.

With each conversation they had, Holly felt more comfortable about confiding in her. It had been a long time since she had had a best friend that she could talk to that way, and although April was free with her advice, Holly never felt as though she was being treated like a patient.

"April? It's Holly. I hope I didn't wake you."

"Oh no," April replied with a smile in her voice. "I'm an early riser. Is everything all right?"

"Yes. No. I'm not sure. Can I talk something out with you?" She heard April murmur to someone who must have been in the room with her.

"Actually, it would be a bit difficult for me at the moment. Could I call your office later today?"

Holly chewed on her lower lip as she imagined Evelyn or Philip overhearing her conversation. "I don't think that would be a good idea. It's about the two murders and—"

"This really is a bad time," April interrupted, enunciating her words with exaggeration. "I'll tell you what. Why don't you come up here this weekend for that long visit we talked about? It's only about a two-hour drive. You can come up on Saturday morning and stay overnight."

Holly hated having to put it off that much longer, but it was clear that April was reluctant to discuss the situation over the phone. She accepted April's invitation and wrote down the directions to her home in Newark, Delaware.

As soon as she hung up, her thoughts went to how she would explain her absence to Philip. She had lied to him about visiting April last weekend and now she would be going there legitimately. At least this time she wouldn't have to give him a phone number with transposed digits so that he couldn't possibly call to check on her. All she had to do was convince him that April wasn't like the other women in the group.

17

David had only been asleep a few hours when the call came. Mick D'Angelo was willing to meet him at the Peacock Lounge in two hours. At the appointed time, David strolled into the bar as if his heart wasn't racing with excitement.

He mentally dismissed the couple in a booth and the lone woman talking to the bartender. Only one other patron remained, and he was either a professional wrestler or Mick D'Angelo's muscle. The only hair on his big head was a thick, brown Fu Manchu moustache. Even his eyebrows had been shaved off. The fact that he was seated at a table in the far corner of the room did not hide his considerable size.

As soon as the hulk spotted David, he stood up and jerked his thumb toward the men's room. David realized he had underestimated the guy's height and weight—he was literally a giant. It occurred to him that the man wouldn't need a weapon to be frightening, but he probably carried one anyway. Something like a chainsaw perhaps.

In spite of the little voice screaming that this was

one of the stupidest things he had ever done, David followed the hulk into the restroom.

"Stwip to the skin."

David's head tilted back with a jolt. Hulk not only had a lisp, but a decidedly feminine pitch to his voice. And he was blocking the exit. "Hey man, I thought you were somebody else. I'll just go back out there and wait—"

"Aren't you David Wells? Word was you were a pwetty boy. Be cool. I pwefer tits with my piece of ass. I work for Mr. D'Angelo. You don't get to see him unless I guarantee you're not wired . . . anywhere."

David's mind ran through his options, which were severely limited by his desire to meet D'Angelo. He unbuttoned his shirt and removed it. Hulk took it from him, gave it a thorough inspection and hung it over the door to a stall. Next went his shoes, socks, and slacks. Feeling less certain about his need to see D'Angelo every minute, he tried to remain as nonchalant as one could while wearing nothing but bikini briefs in front of a giant fruitfly. A disgusted sneer from his tormentor got him to remove the last of his clothes.

"Arms over your head. Spread your legs."

David did as he was told and gave in to the urge to close his eyes as Hulk circled him. Three swipes of the man's big, calloused hand verified that David had nothing hidden in any crevice.

"Okay. Get dwessed and come back out. I'll get Mick."

David had his clothes back on a minute later. It took several minutes more to replenish his lungs with air. When he reentered the lounge, he saw Hulk standing beside the table he had vacated. Seated next to him was an overweight, middle-aged man with thinning black hair slicked straight back from his face and a bulbous nose that had experienced one fight too many.

"Mick D'Angelo," the man said, introducing himself with a friendly smile that didn't reach his eyes. He didn't rise or offer his hand, merely waved toward the chair on the other side of the small table.

"Your receptionist has cold hands, D'Angelo," David stated in a flat tone as he sat down. "A little extreme for a simple conversation."

D'Angelo shrugged. "I can't take chances. I already know you're a reporter, and a reputable one at that. I figure you could be looking for a hot story."

"I'm not."

"So you say. At any rate, now that I know you're not taping our little chat, I can say anything and it would be our word against yours. So, tell me what I can do for you."

"I represent someone who might be interested in buying one of your special films."

"This person's with the government?"

"Yes, but he wants it as a gift for a rather influential foreigner."

"Middle East?"

"I believe so, but I really don't want to know."

"That's okay. I have a fair idea. At least now I understand how you got my name. This isn't the first time a politician has come to me for a buy. When you carry a unique line of products, word gets around. Tell me, Mr. Wells, where do you fit into this goodwill operation?"

"The secretary, er, I mean, the government employee did me a big favor a few months back. Slipped me some highly confidential information. I thought I was repaying it in kind until your trained ape redefined the term 'close encounters.' "

D'Angelo allowed himself a horselaugh, then instantly got serious again. "I'm going to go with my gut on this and believe you. I can usually judge a man's honesty by looking in his eyes. You've got honest eyes, Mr. Wells. But if I've made a mistake this time, I guarantee you, you'll suffer ten times more than I will. You might consider what a *real* close encounter with Butch would be like."

He paused to make sure his threat had taken root. "Okay. I've got something for every taste. Depending on the subject matter, the tapes run from a hundred to a thousand dollars each. You want to see them first, that costs, too."

"Just to see what I'm buying?"

"Sometimes that's all a person wants is to see it once. Nothing's free. So, what's the man looking for?"

"Actually, I don't think what he wants would be in the price range you mentioned. He was under the impression you had an original movie . . . the kind someone would die for." He kept his eyes on D'Angelo's and saw the acknowledgement there.

"There is only one tape, no copies. It would suit my purposes for it to leave the country. But it's a big risk for me to even take it out of safekeeping. Viewing cost will be ten grand. Purchase price is one million."

David managed to keep from gaping only with the greatest effort. Instead, he nodded as if it was what he had expected to hear. "I have to see it first. The fee's no problem. I'll decide if it's worth the price tag after that. When and where?"

"I have a specially equipped screening room. I could have the tape available tonight. You stay by your phone in the hotel, and I'll call you with the directions when it's time. Cash only, nothing larger than hundreds. Come alone, and if you start getting any funny ideas about what a good story this would make, just think about Butch's cold hands."

By the time David returned to his hotel room, he was seriously questioning his sanity. He had never taken a risk this big for a story. His *life* was actually on the line. And where the hell was he going to get ten thousand dollars by tonight?

On the other hand, *if* he could get the money, and *if* he could get a look at the film, he would have the kind of story that could put his career over the top. Did the end justify the means?

You bet your ass!

His editor ran over the same ground when David called in, then came up with the same conclusion, but he refused to go along with David's plan to stick his neck out all alone. He told David to stand by while he made a few calls.

Two hours later, David had an appointment at the Miami headquarters of the FBI. Not knowing whether D'Angelo would have him followed, David walked partway, changed cabs once and direction twice. As soon as he gave his name to the guard, he was taken to an office where Senior Agent Quick and two of his underlings awaited him. All three were of medium height and weight, had medium-brown, regulation-cut hair, and wore navy-blue suits and ties, white shirts, and wing-tipped brogues. They made a point of having him sit before they would. It took considerable restraint for David not to voice any of the sarcastic quips that came to mind.

Living up to his name, Quick wasted no time on preliminaries. "Washington has confirmed your identity and the fact that you're looking into a story.

But I gather you weren't expecting this. Who put you on to D'Angelo?"

"How did you manage to get to him?" Number Two asked less casually.

"Why are you so certain it's a genuine snuff film, and not a good fake?" Number Three demanded.

The questions went on, with David answering as concisely as possible, except on the matter of his informant. He refused to divulge more than that some hooker in some bar had given him a lead. Before leaving the hotel room, he had trimmed the photo of Nikki Farris to cut Cinnamon out.

Finally convinced David had told them all he could, or would, at this point, Quick moved them to the next stage. "Normally, we would set it up so an agent could take your place for the buy."

"Fuck that." David let them absorb his refusal before explaining. "The strip search should give you some indication of how careful D'Angelo is being. There's no excuse in the world that would convince him to accept a substitute for me. He'd know something was up. And his orders were that I come alone, so you can forget assigning me a guide dog, too."

Quick gnawed on the end of his pencil, but he agreed with David. "We've been trying to get something substantial on D'Angelo for a long time. His file is overflowing with penny-ante shit, but this could be the break we've been waiting for to really nail him. Besides the snuff film, we'd like to get our hands on a variety of the other stuff he's peddling, especially kiddie-porn. That goes over with a jury better than some whore getting herself killed."

Quick turned to his two colleagues. "We're going to have to bring in Miami's homicide people on this one. The murder isn't our jurisdiction, just the pornography." He returned his attention to David with a frown. "The only thing I hate more than getting a civilian involved in a case is having a loose-lipped reporter underfoot."

David bristled. Everyone knew a newsman and a cop made poor bedfellows, but the guy didn't have to get insulting. "I have no intention of risking my neck only to bury the story. I'm a professional. I know just what I can and cannot report to keep from jeopardizing a case." Quick was clearly not convinced. David had two choices—drop the whole thing, or come up with a compromise. "I'll agree to giving you a preview of what I'm writing, then consider any revisions you suggest with an open mind."

Another few seconds passed before Quick gave in. "All right. I don't have any better idea. You'll have to be the front man."

Number Two stood up. "I'll put in an emergency request for the money and set up the equipment to trace any calls going into his hotel room. I'll stay with him while he waits."

"I don't think the trace will help much," Number Three put in. "More than likely the call will come from some public place other than where the screening room is. We'll have to come up with a different way to wire him for sound in case they strip him again. And a homing device, so we don't have to follow too closely after he gets the call. We have to figure somebody may be on the lookout for heat following him." He walked over and threaded his fingers through David's hair.

David jerked his head away. "What the hell?"

Number Three grinned. "It's perfect. A few snips underneath, two drops of super glue, and no one would ever guess he's got bugs in all those curls."

Another couple hours passed before David and

Reese—Number Two had eventually deigned to give his first name—returned to the hotel room to wait for the call.

It was determined that David would have to sit through the videos long enough to be positive about what he was seeing. Three taps on the bug in his hair would signal Agent Quick that the jackpot was waiting for him to come scoop it up. There were no guarantees about David's safety. The best they could offer was to arrest him along with D'Angelo. If he was good enough at acting shocked and scared, maybe D'Angelo wouldn't figure out who'd set him up too soon. David assured them that he understood the risks of what he was about to do.

At midnight, the call came in from D'Angelo himself. It took less than a minute for him to give David directions.

"Hold it," David said, responding to Reese's hand motions to extend the call. "Just so we don't have to go through this twice, I wonder if you could have another one or two of your products available."

"Such as?"

"I know someone who likes his, uh, entertainment, on the young side."

D'Angelo laughed. "No problem. We'll make that the appetizer before the main course. I'll wait for you until one. After that, I split."

Reese gave David a thumbs-up at the same time D'Angelo cut off. The conversation had been recorded and traced.

David reached the miniwarehouse in Hialeah, west of Miami, with fifteen minutes to spare. When he saw Butch standing outside one of the garage-type doors, he hoped the homing device glued to his scalp was still functioning. As soon as the hulking bodyguard was positive David had come alone, he directed him to park some distance away.

David was amazed that he was able to walk back without his knees giving out. Butch raised the door and waved David forward.

All David could see in the dark interior was a barrier of drywall with a very narrow door on one side. The giant opened it, motioned David through, then closed the garage door behind them. The next instant, a dim light came on from a lamp across the room where Mick D'Angelo was seated.

Directly ahead of David was a big-screen television, and opposite that was a double bed covered by a dingy-looking, rumpled sheet. A dripping air conditioner in the upper corner of the back wall was putting out more noise than cool air, but at least it was enough to keep the windowless room from being suffocating. Between the air conditioner and the sound-absorbent tiles covering the ceiling and walls, David figured almost anything could go on in there without anyone outside questioning it, particularly in the middle of the night when the place was deserted as it was now.

D'Angelo waited until David's attention returned to him. "You have the cash?"

David handed him the thick brown envelope and watched him leaf through the bills.

"I regret the necessity to inconvenience you once again, Mr. Wells, but due to the unusual quality of the film you're about to see, I'm not about to take any chances."

At first David didn't follow his meaning, then Butch stepped forward and held out his hand with a smirk on his face. David frowned, but unbuttoned his shirt. The sleazy room and having another pair of male eyes on him made the process that much more embarrassing, but he survived unscathed.

Butch confirmed David's cleanliness and went back outside, apparently to resume his guard duties. David thought about the agents and police that should be getting into position about now and hoped they saw the guard before he saw them.

On top of the television was a video recorder and a stack of cassettes. D'Angelo picked the one off the top. "If you decide to buy what you came here for, I'll throw this one in as a bonus. I think the acquaintance you mentioned will recognize that it's first quality, but you can check out a few others here if you aren't sure. Make yourself comfortable. And don't hesitate to . . . *relieve* yourself if you have the need. I won't mind."

Ignoring D'Angelo's disgusting suggestion, David grimaced at the bed, then noticed several metal folding chairs stacked against the wall behind him. As soon as he set one up for himself, D'Angelo started the video and turned off the light.

David could see clearly enough to know that D'Angelo was watching him rather than the film. He was determined not to show any reaction, no matter what he was about to see.

First quality, D'Angelo had said. First-quality filth, maybe. David knew films like this existed and was fully aware that there were people out there who took advantage of children every day in real life, but he had never had to look at it happening in living color on a big-screen. His stomach threatened to reject what little dinner might have been left in it as he watched the perverted scene unfold. He chose a spot on the edge of the picture to stare at to keep from looking directly at the little girl and what was being done to her. . . .

He could barely hide his relief when the series of horrors came to an end, and D'Angelo exchanged video cassettes. Fortunately, the slimeball didn't insist on conversation in between.

Watching two adults fornicate was easy after what he had just seen. Observing the act, even at close camera range, held little interest for David under any circumstances. He slid down in his chair, crossed his ankles, folded his arms over his stomach and had no problem looking utterly bored.

A man and woman were on a bed in a room that looked a lot like the one David was in. They were grunting and moaning along to the big finish, when a bodybuilder wearing nothing but jogging shorts burst into the room. His face was partially hidden beneath a phony-looking brown beard, but there was no doubt that it was D'Angelo's giant sidekick, Butch.

The new arrival lifted the man off the woman by his hair and threw him out the door. Shouting obscenities at the woman, which made it clear she was supposed to be his wife, he grabbed a belt and lashed her thighs, while she did her best to scoot away from the blows.

David had no trouble identifying Nikki Farris. Her face registered real pain, and some shock that she had actually been hit, before she got back into the role of terrified wife begging understanding and promising never to misbehave again. She put up a token resistance as the angry husband used a conveniently placed necktie to secure her wrists to the doorknob.

Her screams were undeniably authentic, though, as he proceeded to whip her back from shoulders to knees with the belt, raising welts the camera zoomed in on whenever possible. Nor did she have to fake her cries when he dropped his pants and held her hips in place for him to shove his unbelievably huge prick into her ass. When he was finished, her blood smeared them both, but he wasn't finished with her yet.

David clenched his fists beneath his armpits, gritted his teeth, and forced himself to keep his gaze on the screen as if he was unaffected by the violence.

The husband had untied his wife, but when she tried to get out the door, he proceeded to use his fists and feet to subdue her, systematically battering every inch of the woman's head and body. She was no longer able to defend herself, let alone escape, but he didn't stop the beating.

Suddenly David could hear another man's voice coming from off-camera. He had been so traumatized by what he was watching, he hadn't consciously picked up the intrusion at first. Someone was ordering the actor to leave her alone and arguing with the cameraman to stop filming.

But neither man heeded the commands. It was not until a blond-haired man tackled the actor from the sidelines that the enraged giant regained a semblance of his sanity. He spun around, smashed the blond's jaw with a bloodied fist, then jumped over him as he fell.

The camera panned from the back of the man fleeing out the door, past the blond struggling to get to his feet, to the body of the girl on the floor. The picture zoomed in to scan the damage close up. One arm and a leg were bent in such a way that bones had obviously been broken. Rivulets of blood trickled from her nose and gaping mouth. But the most damning evidence was the unnatural angle of her head and the open, sightless eyes.

Cinnamon had been absolutely right about how her friend had been killed.

The blond man staggered a little as he rose, rubbing his face. "For chrissakes . . ." His hand fell as he stared down at the dead girl and turned toward the cameraman. "Shut that fucking thing off. And burn that tape!"

David had thought that nothing could shock him more than what he had just seen, until he saw the face of the blond man as clearly as if he was standing in front of him.

It was Jerry Frampton.

David stretched his arms above and behind his head, located the bug, and tapped his fingernail against it three times. He had been told to try to keep D'Angelo and the tape in the same location as long as possible to give the feds a chance to close in and catch him red-handed.

D'Angelo turned on the light and removed the tape from the VCR. "Well?"

"How do you want your money?" David asked in what he hoped was a nonchalant voice.

D'Angelo's smile was almost as grotesque as his films. "I'll give you an account number at a bank in Nassau. When I'm sure the money's been deposited, we'll meet again, and you'll get the tapes."

David paused to give that some thought, and to give the police another few seconds. "I suppose that would be okay, as long as I can check the tapes again. I wouldn't want to *accidentally* take the buyer a copy of *Sleeping Beauty*."

"*Sleeping Beauty*," D'Angelo repeated with a chuckle. "Yeah, that's a good one. Don't worry. We'll work something out." He pulled a briefcase out from under the bed and packed all the videos in it.

David remained seated despite the hint that it was time to leave. "I can't say your movies are my usual fare, but I do recognize good camerawork when I see it. You do it yourself?"

D'Angelo clicked the case shut and picked it up. "Always. For the kind of product I handle, it's better to involve as few people as possible."

"Does Jerry Frampton get a piece of the million, or does he really think the tape was destroyed?"

D'Angelo narrowed his eyes threateningly, but when David showed no fear, he gave a nasty laugh. "I should have known you'd recognize him. But what the hell do I care? That son-a-bitch wants to forget who got him started, but I've been holding on to this tape just in case he ever needed his memory refreshed. I was getting ready to offer to sell it to him right before you came into the picture."

David snickered along with him. "What about—"

Pop! A sound that could have been a car backfiring outside was loud enough to penetrate the cushioned walls. In the next seconds, a hailstorm seemed to hit the metal garage door. Not hail, David realized instantly, *bullets!*

In a lightning quick move, D'Angelo reopened his case, extracted a gun, and pointed it at David. "You fucking bastard!"

Raising his hands, David stood up carefully and did his best to look bewildered . . . which was not entirely an act. There wasn't supposed to be any shooting. "What's the matter? What's going on?" In his own mind, he concluded that Butch, of the big body and small mind, had decided to shoot it out rather than surrender peacefully.

D'Angelo's wild-eyed gaze darted around the room as if he only now realized there was no backdoor. The sound of the garage door opening jarred him into action. With the briefcase in his left hand and the gun in his right, he moved in on David, then shoved him around so that he was facing the door and shielding most of D'Angelo's heavier body.

David felt the gun barrel jab the nape of his neck and tried again. "Look, I don't know—"

"Shut the fuck up! You think I'm too stupid to recognize a fucking trap when I'm standing in it?"

David figured panic would be appropriate about now, but he didn't have time to let it show before the door to the room was kicked open.

"Come out with your hands up," a man's voice demanded from outside. David was fairly sure it was Agent Quick.

"I'm coming out all right," D'Angelo said in a mocking tone. "Right behind your stooge. Either you back off and let me leave here safely, or I blow him away."

David couldn't hear anything for several seconds. While the feds were deciding how to play it, his sweat glands bounced into overdrive.

"We don't know who you have in there D'Angelo, but he's not one of ours. We're here because of an anonymous tip."

"Yeah, right," D'Angelo countered. "And I'm the tooth fairy. Now either you can all back clear across the parking lot so I can get to my car—it's the black Lincoln—or I can take you guys out one at a time as you come through this door. But Wells here is gonna get the first bullet."

Another pause had David frantically trying to recall an appropriate prayer, but his childhood hadn't included much religious education. *Now I lay me down to sleep . . .*

"We're moving away." Moments later the same voice called out from a distance. "Come on out.

You've got an open path to your car. Just let your hostage go free first."

D'Angelo grabbed a fistful of David's hair as he poked the gun into his neck again and cocked it. "Okay, asshole, the rules here are real simple. You behave, you live. You fuck up, you die. Now walk nice and steady out that door and turn when I tell you to so I can keep you in front of me while I back up to my car.

David saw Butch's bullet-ridden body as he stepped over the threshold. But he also glimpsed two agents pressed flat against the walls on each side of him.

"Shit!" was the last thought he had before all hell broke loose.

18

Holly awoke Saturday morning filled with a whole spectrum of emotions. She was satisfied with the way last night had gone. She and Philip had had a pleasant time chatting over a good dinner, laughing over a political satirist's jokes at The Improv, having a nightcap in her apartment, then saying good night without any excessive intimacy—all the way *friends* should. She had intentionally made an extra effort to put everything out of her mind except treating Philip nicely, and he had clearly done the same. The evening had almost gone the way their dates used to go—before the Ziegler hearing triggered the events that had turned her life inside out.

Initially, Philip had not wanted her to contact any of the Little Sisters, but he could see for himself how much Holly's last weekend with Dr. MacLeash had helped her. He actually encouraged her to return and spend more time with the woman. The guilt Holly had felt over telling that lie had practically vanished.

On the other end of the spectrum, she was tense over not hearing from David again, and anxious to find out what April thought about the murders.

Holly was over halfway to Newark, Delaware, when she heard the brief report on the radio. The names she heard caused her to come to a skidding, fishtailing halt at the side of the highway.

Mick D'Angelo and Butch Olkowski, killed in a shoot-out with the FBI in Miami late Thursday night. Two FBI agents and a police officer injured but in stable condition.

Publisher Jerry Frampton arrested hours ago.

Reporter David Wells critically wounded.

Wounded? Critically? What did that mean? Holly's mind whirled with questions.

Should she go back home, stay where David would know where to reach her, and hope to receive word, or go on to April's and make inquiries from there?

How had it happened? *Who* wounded him? The FBI? D'Angelo? Or the person who had killed Ziegler and O'Day? Was it her fault for sending him on the chase, or for not warning him about the Little Sister Society? *Dear Lord, don't let him die.*

Frustrated with the sketchiness of the radio news report, she pulled the car back onto the road and continued on to April's considerably faster than she normally drove.

The sedate beauty of the University of Delaware campus failed to quiet Holly's nerves as she followed the directions April had given her. The MacLeash home was a two-story white clapboard with bright-blue trim. A big picture window was framed in tied-back, ruffled curtains. The front yard showed evidence of meticulous care and the wooden swing hanging on the front porch was a perfect finishing touch. It fit Holly's impression of April exactly: pretty and neat, while still offering a warm welcome to passing strangers.

The only thing that seemed out of place was the number of automobiles parked in the double-wide driveway. Since she doubted that a childless couple would have use for four cars, she guessed that they already had visitors this morning, perhaps some of Professor MacLeash's students.

Holly was right about visitors, though not about their identity. Sitting in the living room, as April brought her into the house, were Rachel and Bobbi, looking hostile and timid respectively.

"I hope you don't mind the impromptu get-together, Holly," April said with an apologetic smile. "But after I spoke to you, they both called with concerns and I thought it would be best to air our feelings all together."

"That's fine," Holly said, thinking quite the opposite, but worry over David's welfare was uppermost in her mind. "On the way here I heard a news report on the radio about Jerry Frampton being arrested and David Wells being wounded, but there were no details. Do you know what happened?"

"Rachel will fill you in on what she was able to learn." April glanced at Holly's overnight bag. "Good. You decided to stay. Let me give you the fifty cent tour before we get started. Excuse us for a few minutes, ladies." Bobbi nodded and Rachel waved them away.

Holly would have preferred to forget the tour, but she didn't have it in her to be rude to April. From the living room they passed through the dining room into the kitchen. The decor was predominantly Early American, complementing the house and April perfectly.

In the kitchen, April knocked on a closed door. "Theodore, may I interrupt for a moment? There's someone here I'd like you to meet." She turned toward Holly and whispered conspiratorially, "He was probably taking a nap, but it makes him feel better if I pretend he's working. Ever since we converted the garage into a library, I think he does more sleeping in here than in our bed."

The door was opened by an elderly man who did indeed look like he'd been caught napping. April placed her hand on his elbow to urge him forward. Speaking a bit louder and slower than her normal tone, she said, "Theodore, this is a friend of mine, Holly Kaufman. Holly, this is my husband, Professor Theodore MacLeash."

Holly had to forcibly stop her jaw from falling open while she shook his hand. April's husband? He looked more like her father, or even her grandfather. The balding, bespectacled man whose shoulders were stooped with age had to be well over seventy years old.

"Holly went to school with me. She lives in Washington, D.C., now. We became reacquainted when I went there recently."

Theodore squinted at her over his trifocals, until he remembered. "Oh, yes. It's hard to keep track of all your goodwill missions these days." With a smiling glance at his wife, he told Holly, "April doesn't know how to let go of her patients. It doesn't matter where they've moved to, if they call her for help, off she goes, abandoning me to fend for myself."

April kissed his cheek. "I only go away so you'll appreciate me more when I get back."

Holly had the uneasy thought that she could be looking at herself and Philip. Though younger than Theodore, Philip was still a much older, doting man, providing the protection of a comfortable, secure relationship—no risks, no heartbreaks . . . no excitement. No wonder she and April got along so well. They had apparently chosen the same way to cope with their problems. It was just that Holly was no longer certain she wanted such an unemotional, *safe* life.

"Will Cheryl be joining you?" Theodore asked.

"I'm not sure," April replied with a frown. "Will *you* be having lunch with us?"

"No, no. You girls enjoy yourselves. Pretend I'm not even here. Say hello to Cheryl for me." He gave his wife a peck on the forehead and retreated back into his sanctuary.

"Were you talking about Cheryl Wallace?" Holly asked as April took her up the stairs from the kitchen.

"Yes. She's been staying with us since the hearing."

"Didn't you say she was married?"

April stopped on the second-story landing and turned toward Holly with a sad sigh. "Cheryl suffered a relapse. Her rather immature husband couldn't handle it, and we didn't want to put her in an institution where the media could make a big deal over it. This was the best place for her to recuperate."

"I'm not sure I understand," Holly admitted.

"Cheryl had a nervous breakdown after her attack in college —completely withdrew from everyone for about a year. Then she pulled herself back together and had seemed fine ever since. If I had thought for one minute that this might happen, I would never have agreed to her testifying."

Holly read the mixture of guilt and anguish on April's face. "I don't see how you could have known. And I gathered it was her choice. No one pushed her into it, did they?" She saw the uncertainty in April's eyes before she spoke.

"Perhaps *pushed* is the wrong word. But we did encourage her once she made the decision. At any rate, she's here so that I can care for her privately. She has an extreme fear of strangers right now, so I want to explain who you are and see if she'll agree to meet you. She's most at ease in our attic room, but I try to get her to come downstairs at least once a day. Just stay here for a minute while I go up and talk to her."

As April ascended the narrow flight of stairs, Holly couldn't help but think that there was something very eerie about a mentally disturbed woman living in the attic, even if she *was* an old friend and the owner of the house was a psychologist. Then again, this visit wasn't turning out anything like she had imagined. She liked April and had been looking forward to talking to her. It was the rest of the people she could have done without.

Rachel and Bobbi both intimidated her, though in different ways. Theodore made her contemplate how bleak her future with Philip could be. And Cheryl was a reminder of her past and the way she had withdrawn after her own horrible experience. It made her wonder if she was susceptible to another breakdown someday. She didn't want to believe she was that unstable, but apparently Cheryl hadn't thought of herself that way either.

The only character missing from this macabre play was the evil femme fatale, and she truly hoped Erica wasn't expected to show up. Holly didn't think she could tolerate observing her with Rachel and Bobbi after the things Bobbi had related the other night.

Her reflection ended as April came back down. "I'm sorry. She's just not up to it."

"I understand." Truthfully, she was relieved.

April showed her the room she'd be staying in. Without being asked, she explained, "I know the house seems large for just the two of us, but we usually have one or two needy students boarding with us. With everything else that's going on, I declined this term." After April pointed out the guest bath, she took Holly back downstairs through the kitchen.

In a voice she hoped sounded only mildly curious, Holly asked, "Will Erica be coming today also?"

"No. She's tied up with a business deal. Somewhere in Florida I think her secretary said."

That gave Holly an opening to return to her original question once they returned to the living room and sat down. "Speaking of Florida . . ."

April smiled and turned to Rachel. "We're all anxious to hear about what happened in Florida."

Rachel straightened in a way that made Holly think she was making a report to her superior officer. "It was a major fuckup if there ever was one. David Wells, the reporter Holly gave the Frampton information to, obviously managed to make contact with the pornographer, Mick D'Angelo, but got himself in over his head. The Miami feds let Wells play undercover cop, hoping to grab themselves a real prize, but somehow the setup went sour. D'Angelo and his bodyguard were killed, and the reporter was shot by D'Angelo.

"The word is they did manage to get hold of a briefcase full of pornographic videotapes, one of which was supposedly a genuine snuff film. There was a little custody battle over the evidence between our guys and the City of Miami boys in blue. It was finally decided that the feds would get everything except the snuff film, since the homicide actually fell under the jurisdiction of the city.

"In the evidence the feds got was a tape of the conversation Wells had with D'Angelo before the shooting started. On that tape, Wells verbally ID'd one of the players in the snuff film as Jerry Frampton and D'Angelo confirmed it."

"Good heavens," April murmured. "That's better than we ever could have expected."

"Don't break open the champagne. It goes downhill from here. The feds arrested Frampton early this morning on pornography charges before Miami could make their move on the accessory to homicide charge, but he was free again almost immediately. He's too prominent a citizen to be denied his rights, and no matter how high the judge set the bail, he could afford it."

"But won't he still have to be tried?" Holly asked.

"Normally, yes, but there's more. Somehow, between the time that the evidence was sorted and the snuff film was to be viewed in the state attorney's office, the tape was erased or exchanged for a blank one. Mind you, all it would take is a good strong magnet rubbed against the cassette. Either way, the evidence of the homicide is gone.

"To make matters worse, someone leaked the whole mess to the local media down there, so by now, every law enforcement agency in the country's laughing behind our backs. There was even a sarcastic editorial about it on Channel Five's morning news."

April sighed aloud. "I haven't had a chance to hear or read much news lately. Do you think Jerry Frampton was behind whatever happened?"

"More than likely his attorney handled the details, but unless someone involved has an attack of conscience, there's no proof. David Wells is now the only person left alive who saw that film. His testimony will be needed to back up the audiotape. Regardless of that testimony, though, Frampton's attorney is going to point out that any number of people could bear a resemblance to Frampton. Even D'Angelo's taped confirmation of Frampton's involvement can be gotten around, since he's no longer able to bear witness. I understand sounds were picked up from the movie, but the chances of Frampton's voice being identified beyond a doubt are probably slim to none."

Holly noticed how Bobbi's intent gaze followed the conversation, but she was in her meek personality that morning and not offering comments one way or another.

Fear tinged Holly's voice as she made herself ask, "Is David going to make it?"

Rachel raised an eyebrow at her. "What do you care?"

Holly was shocked by her callousness. "It's because of me that he went down there. I had no idea he'd be risking his life when I passed him the lead."

Rachel gave an indifferent shrug. "He took the risk to get a big story. Instead he got himself shot in the head. Sometimes the end justifies the means."

"Rachel, *please*. The news said he was critically wounded. I need to know how bad it is."

"It doesn't sound promising. He's in intensive care in Jackson Memorial Hospital in Miami—probably the best place in the South to be if you have to get yourself shot. The last report was he was still unconscious and under guard."

Holly stiffened. "Under guard? But—Oh my God. They think Frampton might try to make sure he never wakes up. Is that it?"

Rachel nodded and all four lapsed into a dejected silence.

April reached over and patted Holly's knee. "Remember what you just said to me about Cheryl. It was *his* decision to follow up on the lead you gave him. Nothing you did put him in jeopardy."

"I suppose you're right, but, I don't know, maybe if I had been more honest with him—"

"I told you so," Bobbi interrupted in her aggressive voice as she whipped off her glasses. "You're going to have to do something about her, April."

Holly glanced from one to the other, and her stomach released a bit more acid as she realized Bobbi was referring to her. "I have to go," she announced abruptly and stood up. Even Bobbi reacted with surprise. "I can't sit here, wondering, waiting for a third party to let me know how he is. I have to go down there."

April rose and took Holly's hands in hers. "This is more than just a guilty conscience, isn't it?"

Holly's resigned sigh was her answer.

"You truly care about him, don't you? You let down the walls and discovered you could feel again. Don't you see what a milestone that is?"

Holly lowered her gaze, but left her hands in April's. "I didn't want to ever be this vulnerable to a man again."

"Love isn't a weakness, Holly. Emotion—any emotion—is a strength. You just have to learn how to channel it. Let it work *for* you instead of against you. When you allow yourself to feel, you can be anything, do anything you wish. Tell me, just now, weren't you thinking that if you went to his side, somehow you could make him better?"

"I don't know what I was thinking. I just feel so helpless."

"Then go to him, give him your new strength,

bring him back to testify against the man who hurt you."

Holly blinked. She hadn't been thinking of her revenge at all, but apparently it hadn't left April's mind.

"However, before you go," April said, releasing Holly's hands, "let's have the talk you came up here for." She waited for Holly to be seated again. "I can understand how you must be concerned over what's happened. You didn't know any of us until a month ago, and realistically, you still don't know any of us well enough to trust us. But I'm going to ask for that trust anyway. None of us is a murderess, Holly. You must believe that."

Holly felt Bobbi's narrow-eyed stare before she saw it. The woman had slipped out of her mousy shell again and her thoughts were easy to read. *Except for Erica.*

Rachel drew Holly's attention. "Bobbi said you were with a friend the night O'Day was killed. Who was that?"

"David and I spent the weekend at a mountain lodge in Maryland."

Rachel smirked. "Of course, he's not in any condition to confirm or refute that alibi at the moment, is he?"

"What do you mean?"

"I mean, what happens to your alibi if he doesn't wake up?"

"I don't need an alibi," Holly protested. "I haven't done anything wrong."

"Hmmph," Rachel snorted. "Did anyone else see you that night? Desk clerk? Waitress? Bartender?"

Holly paused and made herself review the Saturday night in question. Rather than get dressed to go out, they had ordered room service, and when it was delivered, she had shyly retired to the bathroom. It wasn't much better than the night Ziegler was murdered, when she had been home alone. But surely Philip would be willing to say they were together. *Good Lord*. She was thinking of lying to defend herself from something she hadn't done to begin with.

When she didn't answer, Rachel went on. "It seems to me that *we're* the ones who should be concerned about *you*. In all the years the Little Sister Society has been operating, we've never had a single violent incident. The trouble didn't start until you came into the picture. I can account for every one of our member's whereabouts during both murders—except yours.

"April and Cheryl were here together. Not only can they vouch for each other, but Professor MacLeash will corroborate their story. Bobbi, Erica, and I were having a girls' night out when Ziegler was killed. There are a number of people who could easily be encouraged to verify they saw us. Last Saturday night, Erica was at home in California, and Bobbi and I were out together again."

Holly could not imagine Bobbi hanging out at bars, least of all with Erica, but she could hardly call Rachel's bluff when she couldn't prove her own story.

As usual, April tried to ease the tension. "Rachel's not accusing you of anything, Holly. She's just showing you that we can't afford to start being suspicious of each other. At any rate, didn't you say there were some suspects already, Rachel?"

"Actually, the computer has picked quite a few," Rachel replied with a nod. "The use of drugs to subdue the men implies the killer isn't big or strong enough to overcome them with force, which would mean a woman, or a weak man. Ziegler and O'Day opened their hotel room doors to the murderer, which suggests that he or she was either recognized or expected. If it was a stranger, it is more likely the men would have invited a woman into the room than a man. And third, the weapon used suggests a woman as well. The mutilation is sexual to begin with, as was the message, and it was done by two serrated blades sawing smoothly back and forth—in other words, the guess is it was an electric carving knife—something found in most modern kitchens."

Holly made a face at the picture Rachel created, then noticed that she was the only one bothered by it. She supposed Rachel was used to this sort of thing, but April and Bobbi looked as though they'd heard it all before. Had this entire "get-together" been staged for her benefit?

"Since both murders occurred in the same part of the country," Rachel continued, "the investigative team began searching for women in that region who have criminal histories of violence against men. Once we've narrowed down the field of possibles and start questioning the suspects, we'll know better whether we're on the right track.

"It's not known yet why Ziegler and O'Day were chosen as victims. If one of the female suspects saw the list of names Cheryl gave to the Senate committee, we haven't figured out how it got into her hands, but anything is possible.

"At the moment, we're trying to keep a lid on what the possible connection between Ziegler and O'Day could be, but agents may soon be assigned to guard the other eight men on the list until the killer is found. The problem with that is, once they all start talking, someone is liable to remember the names of other women besides Cheryl who were victimized."

"Well, then," April said, "let's hope this whole thing is solved in a few days and we can *all* stop worrying."

Holly wanted to be relieved of that worry desperately enough so that she told herself that she believed April and that none of the Little Sisters was a murderess. But she couldn't ignore the feeling that they weren't completely innocent either.

Her anxiety over David's condition took precedence over all else, however, and as soon as Rachel finished her update, Holly intended to leave.

Bobbi spoke before she could do so. "As long as we're together, I have some positive news. Adam Frankowicz is back in New York. It may take a little while to do any damage, but I've initiated action against him for tax evasion. I guarantee you he'll be a lot poorer by this time next year."

Finally, Holly simply excused herself to use the phone she had seen on the kitchen wall. A few minutes later she had reservations on a flight to Miami out of Washington, D.C.'s, National Airport that afternoon. She could make it if she hurried.

Retrieving her bag from the upstairs bedroom, she couldn't help but think about the woman secluding herself up in the attic. Part of Holly wanted to go up and try to talk to Cheryl, tell her she understood first hand how she felt. The more logical side of her brain argued that she couldn't spare the time, and besides, April was much more qualified than she. Her interference might do more harm than good.

Holly had been looking forward to spending more time with April, but now all she could think of was how fast she could get away.

She made the proper apologies and promised to come back another weekend, inching her way toward the front door with each word. Just as it looked like she would be free to depart, Rachel offered to "see her to her car."

"I just wanted to make sure you didn't get the wrong impression in there," Rachel said as Holly unlocked her car door and placed her bag in the backseat.

Holly assumed she was trying to apologize for suggesting *she* could be the killer. Her assumption was wrong.

"I didn't want to bring you into the society. And I don't trust you. Whether your joining us right before Ziegler was murdered is relevant or not, I think you're trouble. As long as you keep your mouth shut, I'll leave you alone, but if you say anything to anybody about us, I promise you, I'll turn this case around on you so fast you won't have time to take a piss. And just so you understand that I'm perfectly capable of proving you're the killer, no matter how innocent you are, I'm going to let you in on another secret."

Holly tucked her hands beneath her arms in a defensive manner that hid how badly she was trembling. She wanted to drive as far and fast as possible, but she also wanted to hear the secret.

Rachel moved close enough for Holly to smell alcohol on her breath. "April needs to believe that all of us have obeyed the rules she set down for going after the fifteen men, and we let her have that consolation. But the truth is, there have been times when one or two of us have had to bend the rules to break the man."

Holly sifted through the implied confession until she began to understand.

"Think about it," Rachel said and walked back to the house.

Holly thought about it all the way to Washington, but it only took the first few minutes to figure out what Rachel meant. If Rachel wanted to, she could fabricate proof of someone's guilt or destroy evidence of a person's innocence, in the same way the snuff film had been eliminated. Bobbi could do the same through the IRS. And surely, with the computer wizard's help, Erica could play havoc with a company's market value and create any number of difficulties for its owner.

That was the secret they were hoarding so carefully. She recalled Bobbi mentioning that she could lose her job. It would be a wonder if she didn't end up in jail if she had manipulated any of the men's tax returns.

Rachel could be planning to ensure that one of the women suspects was arrested, or she could just as easily make it look like Holly was the guilty party. Of course, there was the possibility that one of the suspects was the killer, but Holly wasn't at all certain. In her mind, Rachel was still the likeliest candidate. She had the motive, means, and personality, and if she didn't commit the crimes, she could very likely be protecting the real murderess—particularly if it was Erica.

Just because Rachel said Erica was in California when O'Day was killed didn't mean it was any more the truth than her claim that the two of them and Bobbi had been together when Ziegler was killed. But would Bobbi agree to a lie that would protect Erica?

Yes, Holly thought instantly, Bobbi would lie if it meant creating an alibi for herself at the same time. Hadn't *she* briefly considered lying to protect herself just a short time ago?

Bobbi's visit to her apartment replayed in Holly's memory. Wasn't it possible that she was pretending to hate Erica? She was certainly capable of projecting extremely different personalities in the blink of an eye. Couldn't Bobbi have been hiding her own guilt by pointing a finger at Erica?

As Holly contemplated one scenario after another, she realized all three were perfectly capable of performing the mutilation that had been done to the two men.

Then again, perhaps they could provide each other with an alibi for the night Ziegler was killed because they *were* together . . . in his hotel room.

So far, Bobbi and Rachel had both threatened her. Would Erica be next?

She should go to the police. Yet, what proof did she have? She had no doubt that Rachel would find a way for her story to backfire. It was doubtful that anyone at the lodge in Maryland would swear to seeing her the night O'Day was killed, so without David, she had no solid alibi for that time.

Even Philip had advised her to do nothing, and that was clearly the safest path to take. But suddenly she was sick to death of the safe path. She was tired of being afraid of everything, including her own feelings.

She had been a victim once, and she had allowed it to haunt her for fourteen years.

No one was going to force her to be a victim again!

Holly's foot pressed harder on the accelerator. She had to get to David. He had to regain consciousness.

He was the only one she could think of who could expose the whole ugly truth and find out who the killer was before she found herself hopelessly entrapped.

It occurred to her that she would have to confess to telling David a few lies in the past, but surely he would understand.

19

Holly felt as though she had been pushing her way through quicksand for the last six hours. Surely traffic to the Keys after the hurricane had moved faster than that heading for National Airport. And how had the plane stayed up in the air at the slow speed it flew? In spite of a non-English-speaking cabdriver who must have thought she'd enjoy the scenic route through Miami, Holly finally reached the hospital.

Her frustration reached a dangerous level when the nurse behind the desk in the intensive care unit told her she couldn't release any information on David Wells, and he wasn't permitted any visitors.

Desperation enabled Holly to improvise. "But I'm his sister. I've been traveling all day to get here."

The nurse's face lost some of its sternness. "Oh, that's different. What's your name?"

Holly frantically sifted through the stories David had told her. "Jill. Jill Wells."

The nurse ran her finger down a list on her desk. "Oh, yes. Here you are. I wasn't told to expect any of his family today. Mr. Wells has been moved to a private room. I'm sorry to say, he hasn't yet regained consciousness, but he *is* in stable condition."

Holly listened to the directions to get to David's room, but her mind was analyzing what the nurse had said. Most important was the fact that he was no longer in intensive care. That had to be a good sign. But why wasn't any family expected to visit? The way David described them, they were extremely close—not at all the types to stay home if their brother was seriously injured.

The uniformed police officer sitting in front of the closed door to David's room smiled broadly and rose as Holly approached. Hoping the same ploy would get her past another obstacle, she smiled back and said, "I'm Jill Wells, David's sister. Nurse Johnson said that it would be all right for me to see him."

The officer picked up a clipboard from behind the chair and scanned a sheet of paper similar to the one the nurse had checked. Giving her another smile, he knocked three times on the door.

"What now?"

Holly blinked at the strength of the irritated voice. It was David, but he didn't sound like someone who had been at death's door a few hours ago. And he was very definitely *not* unconscious.

The officer pushed open the door, but held up a hand to keep Holly from proceeding before he announced her. "There's a woman here to see you. Says she's your sister, Jill."

"*Jill?* No kidding. Let her in."

The officer stepped aside to let Holly enter. Her eyes widened in shock as she saw David striding toward her, looking extremely healthy except for a large white bandage on the left side of his head.

"Honey, I told you not to—" He halted the moment he saw her, and his welcoming grin turned to a sneer of contempt so quickly that Holly turned around to see if someone else had entered the room behind her.

"Thank you, Officer," he said, then waited until the door was closed again before speaking to Holly. "What the hell are you doing here?"

She had been worried sick, had run herself into the ground trying to get to him, and he barked at her as if she were his worst enemy. "I—I heard you were critically wounded in a shoot-out. David, I don't understand. I thought you might have been dying." She set her bag on the floor and crossed her arms over her stomach, as if that could stop it from churning.

"Oh? And I guess I'm supposed to believe you came flying to my side because you really cared one way or the other?"

Wrinkling her forehead in confusion, Holly wondered if his head injury had altered his mind in some way. "David, please, you're frightening me."

"You can cut the act, lady. I know exactly what you're here for. I realize it took me awhile, but then, you *are* one hell of a distraction."

He turned his back on her, walked to a chair behind a desk in the corner, and sat down. The computer system set up there with the power still on let Holly know he had been working when she'd arrived. If he had suffered brain damage, would he have been able to arrange for a private hospital room to be partially converted into an office so that he could keep writing while he recuperated? Something was very wrong here.

He glared back at her for a second before his fingers started pressing keys. "You may as well leave. You can find out whatever you want to know by reading my story . . . just like everybody else. And, by the way, a favor for old times' sake—please don't

spread around the fact that I'm alive and well just
yet."

As if walking on eggshells, she crossed the room
to him. "I didn't come this far to be sent away like
a naughty child. At least tell me why you're acting
like this."

He swiveled his chair toward her, but didn't get
up. "Fine. I'll spell it out. I received some very en-
lightening information a few hours ago. Let's see
how many clues you need to guess what I found
out. Dominion University."

Holly's chest rose with the sharp intake of her
breath.

David's voice was mocking as he praised her.
"Aah. Not bad. Only one clue. In case you're interested, some of the other clues were: thirteen, fourteen years ago, Cheryl Wallace, Erica Donner,
Rachel Greenley, Timothy Ziegler, Billy O'Day, and
last but not least, Jerry Frampton." He smirked at
her and pointed to a chair. "You'd better sit down
before you fall down. You look worse than I feel."

She did as he suggested rather than running out
the door as she was tempted to do. "I wanted to
explain before you left, but you—"

"Don't give me that shit," he snarled, slamming
his hand on the desk. Wincing, he placed his hand
over his injury as if the impact had run straight up
his arm to his head. "We were together the whole
fucking weekend before I left. How much more time
did you need?"

"David, *please*. When I heard about O'Day being
killed, I panicked. I know I should have told you
everything right then and there, but I wasn't thinking clearly. And then Bobbi was at my apartment,
waiting for me when you left, and—"

"Bobbi?"

"Yes, she—Oh, God, David, I wanted to call you, but you never gave me your number, nor did I have your address to go see you in person. I left two urgent messages at your office." She knew her eyes were filling with moisture and she looked away to keep him from seeing.

He was too angry to believe the desperate sincerity in her voice. When he'd called in to his editor that afternoon, he'd gotten his messages. One was from Valerie saying she had interesting news. Two *were* from Holly, but there was no urgency mentioned, so he had just assumed she wanted to talk—until he spoke to Valerie and realized that what Holly really wanted was an update.

"Forget the tears, lady. It's too easy for you to sit there and tell me how you were *going* to tell me everything, after I already figured part of it out on my own."

She gripped the arms of her chair to stop her hands from shaking. "You may not believe me, but I swear it's true. I'll admit to lying to you before, but everything changed between us since the beginning. If you had let me talk to you the night you called, instead of playing one of your games—"

"Nice move—put me on the defensive. It might have worked under different circumstances, but we're talking about murder here."

With a resigned sigh, Holly asked, "Have you said anything to the police?"

He met her frightened gaze and hated himself for wanting her even now. "No. I had this ridiculous notion that I should talk to you before I turn you over to them. Obviously, you weren't home when I called this afternoon. I was giving you until tonight to answer your phone, then I was going to dump what information I had right in the FBI's lap.

"But understand one thing. I hate liars more than I hate getting on airplanes. The only reason I waited was because my instincts told me that no matter what else you are, you couldn't knowingly be involved in murder."

Her relief was instantly evident, and he wondered why he had let her off the hook so easily. "It was the same instincts that told me there was a story behind the odd group of women that met with Erica Donner that day I first saw you in the hotel. And then my instincts were telling me you wanted me for something besides a playmate. You kept telling me you weren't interested, but I didn't listen, did I?"

"I wasn't . . . at first." She blushed in spite of herself. "All I was supposed to do was pass you the information on Frampton, but then you—"

"Seduced you? Maybe I did, or maybe you seduced me. Either way, I'll accept responsibility for that part of this mess, and I thank you for confirming that you were the one who got the lead on Frampton to me. I assume you were also the one who cut out the lines of the tabloid article that stated how he had been a star quarterback at Dominion."

Holly angled her head at him. "I don't understand. I thought you were angry because I gave you a lead that almost got you killed."

"I'm not angry about getting a hot lead. I'm pissed with you for lying to me! I was so furious when I first heard there was a connection between you and all those people, I could have wrung your neck." Actually, he had been fantasizing about locking her in a pitch black-room, where he could take advantage of her fear of the dark while simultaneously arousing her to mindlessness, then forcing the truth from her.

Holly knew it didn't matter, but she wanted to know which one had gotten to him before she did. "Who told you? Rachel?"

"If you're referring to FBI Agent Rachel Greenley, I've never spoken to her. No, a very talented researcher at *The Washington Times* came up with the facts I needed to put it all together.

"Remember how you told me you and Erica Donner went to school together? I knew then you were lying about the school being Georgetown. I already had a detailed bio on Donner and knew she'd graduated from Berkeley, after she'd transferred there from Dominion. I am also aware that she *and* Rachel Greenley were freshmen at Dominion the same year as Cheryl Wallace. However, my friend in Research couldn't place you there at that time. And I couldn't find out anything about the other two women. This morning I learned that, with regard to you, we just hadn't checked far enough. You *were* there, but it was the year before.

"Now those facts alone aren't very condemning, unless you know why I was in the Kessler Hotel lobby the day I first saw you." He paused to see if she'd squirm. She didn't, and he dropped the bomb he'd been holding. "Tim Ziegler had called me with an interesting story about Cheryl Wallace and Erica Donner systematically destroying the lives of a certain group of fraternity brothers."

David thought Holly looked adequately stunned, so he went on. "He was murdered before he could give me any more than a few hints, but I was sufficiently intrigued to check it out. After Cheryl Wallace waved her list of attackers' names in front of the senators, a lot of reporters tried to find out who Ziegler's fraternity brothers were, but either they didn't succeed or they were convinced to keep it quiet.

"I found out their names this morning. My researcher friend managed to get ahold of the Dominion yearbook from thirteen years ago. When I spoke to her, she read me the names listed under the picture of Ziegler's fraternity."

Holly had gotten over her initial shock and was reduced to staring at a spot on the floor, but David wanted her to hear every detail. "Imagine my surprise when I heard the names Billy O'Day and Jerry Frampton. That's when I remembered Wallace's comment about two of the men being star football players. Just to make sure I wasn't jumping to any false conclusions, I had my friend look up the football team and verify who the first-string quarterback was."

Holly waited for him to repeat the name, but he didn't bother. Quietly she said, "No one was supposed to be hurt."

"*Hurt*? Lady, they're *dead*! My instincts may be telling me you aren't a murderer, and I know for certain you were nowhere near O'Day when he was killed, but there's no way you're going to convince me that this is all a string of incredible coincidences!"

Holly shook her head. "No. I wanted to believe that's what Ziegler's murder was, but now . . ." She bent her head and covered her face with her hands. "Oh God, David, I'm so scared."

He had to force himself to remain seated while every muscle in his body strained to go to her. *She used you. She's a lying bitch who's probably putting on an act for you right now.* By the time she raised her head and let her big, misty, blue eyes plead with him for understanding, he had reinforced his guard against her. "I assume the meeting that day had something to do with Cheryl's gang rape. But if you weren't plotting murder, what *were* you discussing for so long?" When she didn't answer immediately, he pushed harder. "You said you wanted to explain. Let's hear it. Now."

By reminding herself that even if he hated her, he might be her only hope, she found the fortitude to tell him the whole story. "The day you saw me at the hotel was the first day I'd met those women, and I've only seen Cheryl Wallace on television." She related what she'd learned that day, the events that led to the creation of the Little Sister Society, including the names of the fraternity brothers involved, what had happened to Erica, Bobbi, Rachel, and April, and how they had successfully exacted retribution on eleven of the men.

Despite his anger with Holly, David found himself sickened by the abuse of the women and intrigued with their ingenuity, but his experience as an unbiased reporter helped him conceal those feelings. "None of that explains how you fit into this tale of revenge when you weren't even at Dominion that year."

"No, I wasn't. Jerry Frampton and Tim Ziegler used me for their entertainment the year before."

He remained silent while she described how they had tricked and raped her. Though her story was appalling, his resentment for what she'd done to him was too great to be erased simply because he now knew what made her tick. He could empathize with her fears without forgiving her deceitfulness, and he gave her points for knowing how to deliver a concise report. She answered every question that popped into his head before he could ask it.

When she paused, he pushed for one final explanation. "So you joined the society that day to go after Frampton, and I was the reporter you picked to do your leg work. Lucky me."

She shook her head in protest. "I tried to tell you before. I was only supposed to pass you the file and follow your progress. No one should have gotten hurt. No one ever had before." Although she didn't believe she was getting through to him, she went on to fill him in on everything that had occurred with the other women since that first day.

Even though he had told himself she'd been using him, his gut still twisted when he heard her admit it aloud. It was the final evidence he needed to put her back into the category of being "just like every other woman." When she finished, his tone remained emotionless as he agreed with her reasoning about coming to him before the police.

"You're going to have to tell the FBI everything you told me. Greenley might still try to turn it around on you, but you'll have the advantage of having opened up first." David massaged his temples as he organized his thoughts. "After the D'Angelo fiasco, I've got a little pull with the feds down here. They're the ones that put out the report that I was critically wounded and unconscious. The thinking was, if whoever destroyed the film wanted me out of the way, too, they might stay clear in hopes that my death would occur naturally. I was giving depositions for hours today, and there will be more tomorrow. Once that's done and my physical appearance in court is no longer vital, I'll have a miraculous recovery."

"But what if Frampton sends someone after you then?"

He gave her credit for looking genuinely concerned. "I get to have a baby-sitter until the case goes to court, whether I want one or not. In the meantime, this arrangement is a little reimbursement for my trouble. Plus, by keeping the bad guys away, they're also keeping other reporters off my back. It's giving me a chance to get my story done before granting interviews to anyone else."

"How badly *were* you hurt?"

He shrugged, again ignoring her worried expression. "The bullet grazed my scalp and gave me a slight concussion. I was unconscious part of yesterday, while all the red tape was getting fucked up. Today, I've got a hell of a hangover, made twice as bad by the damn depositions, to say nothing about your little contribution. They've offered painkillers, but the first one knocked me out for the night and left me groggy for hours this morning, so I turned them down today." He rubbed his temples a bit more. "The worst damage seems to be to my hair. It's going to look pretty strange until it grows back in where they shaved it."

Holly had been thinking the same thing, but to comment on it seemed too intimate under the circumstances.

David lifted a few sheets of paper until he found the card with Senior Agent Quick's home phone number on it. "From everything you told me, it sounds like Frampton or Frankowicz might be next on the killer's agenda, and it could happen any time. Frampton probably would have been better off staying in jail for a while."

Without waiting for a response from her, he called Quick and gave him just enough information to convince him to race to the hospital room with recording equipment. "He'll be here within the hour," David told Holly after he hung up, then turned his attention back to the computer monitor, effectively demonstrating that her presence was no longer a distraction.

"David?"

He kept his eyes on the monitor. "What?"

Recalling Rachel's heartless comment about David being shot, she asked, "Does the end justify the means?"

That caused him to look up and deepen his frown. "Am I supposed to understand that?"

"My conscience needs to know. Was risking your life and getting shot worth the story?"

"Absolutely," he answered without hesitation. "Although I may have felt differently had the bullet struck an inch to the right. What about you? Were your means justified?"

Holly thought of the sweet revenge and feelings of power she had expected to enjoy, and wondered where they were now. Instead, she had crippling fear, a guilty conscience, and a vacuum in her chest where her heart used to be. She replied to his question honestly. "No."

"Too bad. You worked hard enough for it."

Every snide comment he made was like another dash of salt on her fresh wound. She felt bruised and battered.

Like a victim.

What had happened to her resolution that she would never permit anyone to make her feel that way again? David had caught her off guard, with her heart exposed, but she could piece it back together, in time, as she had before.

As he put his mind back to work, she kept talking to herself, rebuilding her inner strength, reminding herself that she had never expected anything permanent to come of their relationship. It was only the frightening situation she found herself in that had blurred her reasoning. With each positive affirmation, she sat a little straighter in the chair and lifted her chin a bit higher.

She *had* set out to use him for her own purposes, but *he* was the one who had pursued her. Had it strictly been her sex appeal, or had there been more to his dogged determination? Now that she was calming down, she replayed some of the things he had thrown at her when she first walked in. Reality dawned.

He had been checking on *her*. Why? Because he had seen her go up to Erica Donner's suite while he was lying in wait in the hotel lobby.

"It was all for a story, wasn't it?" she accused, her self-control returning by the minute. She saw the acknowledgment in his eyes, though he said nothing. "You bastard. How dare you call me a liar and act so self-righteous? I may have intended to use you, but it was for your skills as a reporter, and I was certain you would be rewarded with a good story for your efforts."

As it all became clearer, her own anger mounted, until she could no longer remain seated. She saw him about to defend himself and cut him off. "Don't. There's no way you can justify what you did to me. I would have been satisfied if we had just become friendly acquaintances. But it wasn't enough for you to befriend me to get information on Erica Donner. No, you had to *possess* me, body and soul, until I couldn't withhold anything you demanded of me."

Her eyes glittered with new awareness. "Well, congratulations, Mr. Superstud. You got exactly what you set out for—my body, my soul, and a story to die for. The story was to be your reward from me. What was *my* reward supposed to be? A good fuck? Let me tell you something, *love*, no man is *that* good."

She lowered her lashes and took a deep breath. When she met his gaze again, her voice was level. "We both lied, David. And we both used each other, but what you did was so much uglier. Considering the fact that you got shot and I only got my feelings hurt, I'd say we're about even." Tightly reined fury and disgust sent her marching toward the door to escape before she fell apart in front of him.

"Holly! You can't leave."

She froze without turning around.

"Agent Quick will be here any minute. No matter how either of us feels right now, you have to talk to him."

How could she have forgotten? "I'll be back in fifteen minutes," she said. As she opened the door, she pasted on a smile for the police officer and offered to get him a cup of coffee. She'd be damned if she'd let the rest of the world see how David had hurt her.

By the time she returned, she was calm, cool, and collected . . . at least on the outside. Inside was going to take a lot longer, but she told herself the comfortable, emotionless void would return eventually.

Three very average-looking men greeted her as she re-entered David's room. The FBI had apparently arrived.

20

Jerry Frampton glowered at the typed message, as if by sheer willpower he could make more words appear. Something that would let him know if this was a hoax, police entrapment—or the real thing.

> I have a movie I'm sure you'd be interested in trading for something I want from you. No cash necessary. Go ALONE to the Clifton Hotel on Glades Road in Boca Raton. Register at the front desk. A room has already been reserved in your name. Wait for my call. If I am told you have not checked in by 4 AM, I will turn the video over to the FBI, who will not misplace it as easily as the Miami police did. Bring this note and the envelope with you. If you obey all of my instructions to the letter, no one will get hurt.

That fucking prick D'Angelo! He should have had that greaseball taken out months ago, when his attorney first suggested it, but he had hesitated out of a left-over sense of indebtedness. Just goes to show what loyalty was worth these days. He glanced at his watch again—one-thirty A.M. He had to make a decision soon, and he couldn't think of anything else to do but go.

The message had been delivered in a plain brown envelope by a private courier service at midnight. His personal signature had been required. Since there was no return address, he questioned its origin, but the courier could only tell him that he had picked it up at the front desk of the Clifton Hotel, as he had been instructed. Jerry then called the service's night manager and was informed that they received a telephone request for the pickup and special delivery. A sizable cash payment was left for the courier in a separate envelope to guarantee prompt, efficient attention, even if it meant tracking the recipient to a location other than his home.

The next call Jerry made was to his attorney. Afraid of a wiretap, he ordered the man to come to the estate immediately. The attorney assured him that the cop had been well paid to *erase*, not *exchange*, the tape, but it might not have been quite enough to overcome the temptation to extort a bit more, given such a golden opportunity.

They weighed the risks and alternatives and came to the conclusion that Frampton had little choice except to check it out. Before he left the privacy of his well-guarded estate, he reconsidered taking a gun. The attorney effectively discouraged him, however, by pointing out that if he was walking into a police trap instead of a meeting with a greedy cop, the attorney could always find a way to refute anything Frampton said to them. But if he was caught carrying a concealed weapon while he was out on bail, he'd be going back to jail and staying there this time.

He also gave a second thought to taking a guard with him. Though this business over D'Angelo and the tape was his primary concern, he hadn't forgotten about Ziegler's and O'Day's murders. But a guard could later turn into a witness, and he knew it was best to handle this matter alone.

Thus, alone, unarmed, and prepared to confront a dirty cop, Jerry Frampton drove his new red Ferrari to the Clifton Hotel.

21

Rachel gulped down the entire contents of her glass without taking a breath, then closed her eyes while the fiery amber liquid hit her stomach. When she reopened her eyes the tremors had calmed enough for her to dial the number.

"Hello?"

The rich, masculine voice confused Rachel. "Who's this?"

"Nat Russell. Who's this?"

"A friend of Erica's. Let me talk to her." Rachel's thoughts had been filled with bad news and warnings, but hearing the country western singer's voice knocked her mind off track. She knew Erica occasionally had a celebrity escort for special functions. Their pictures often appeared in magazines and tabloids. But what was the man doing in Erica's house before noon on a Sunday, answering the private line next to her bed?

"Rachel? I'm a little busy at the moment. I'll have to call you back."

Rachel almost agreed until she heard Erica whisper "*Stop that*" and let out a light giggle. Erica *never*

giggled. "No. This is urgent." She could tell Erica
was covering the mouthpiece and saying something
to Nat, and she ordered herself to give Erica a
chance to explain.

"Erica!"

"Gawd, Rachel. What's the problem?"

"What the hell is Nat Russell doing in your
bedroom?"

"You're the detective, darlin'. *You* figure it out."

Rachel hiccuped and swallowed the growing lump
in her throat. "How could you do this? I thought
that—"

"For chrissakes, Rachel, you've been drinking
again, haven't you?"

"So? I needed a drink after what just happened.
Erica, I need you. Here. *Now!*"

The sigh Rachel heard over the phone was one
of boredom, disgust, or both, and she had to push
the lump back down again. Her voice was reduced
to a whimper. "I thought you loved me."

"And I do, darlin', but I never promised not to
have other . . . friends. Now, why don't you go sleep
it off, and I'll call you later tonight?" Erica was extremely glad that because of the secrecy of her business, she had her phones regularly checked for taps.
The last thing she'd need is some snoop hearing
this conversation.

Rachel was about to hang up when she remembered her reason for calling. "*No!* This can't wait."
Her words picked up speed as her earlier panic renewed itself. "It's all coming apart. I wanted to warn
you so you'd be prepared when they come to question you. Bobbi and I have both been suspended
without pay pending further investigation. I can't
reach April at all. It had to be that simpering little
pussy, Holly, that squealed!"

"Rachel, please calm down. I don't understand anything you're saying."

Rachel made herself set aside her personal turmoil and behave like the trained professional she was so proud of being. Correction, *had been* so proud of being. "Where were you this weekend, Erica?"

"Didn't April tell you? I was in Florida. I just got back about an hour ago."

"*Where* in Florida? Did you take your private jet, or a commercial flight? Do you have any witnesses that can swear to your whereabouts between the hours of one and three this morning?"

Erica hesitated, clearly reinforcing her own professional armor before speaking. "What's this all about? What's happened?"

"Jerry Frampton was murdered in Boca Raton, Florida, sometime this morning. Same m.o. as the others. Bobbi and I have already been questioned, but they had nothing solid to charge us with. We can prove we were both in Washington this morning, and our other alibis should hold up. But they know *everything*, Erica. Holly must have spilled her guts. It's the only thing I can figure."

"What exactly do you mean by *everything*?"

Rachel gave a dry laugh. "Webster's definition. They asked me about certain cases Bobbi and I handled, and they knew about *our* relationship. They wanted me to tell them about your *unusual* marital history." She could visualize Erica on her knees, begging forgiveness for being unfaithful, doing *anything* to ensure her continued protection.

"I see. Then I suppose I should be expecting visitors soon."

"Not necessarily. I figured if you get your pilot to fly you here immediately, we can put our heads together to firm up your alibi for the hours in question. Everything will be just fine once we're together again, you'll see."

Erica cleared her throat, and murmured something Rachel couldn't hear. When she spoke again a few seconds later, her voice was hushed. "Listen to me, Rachel. I don't know what you *think* I was doing during those hours, but I don't need your help with an alibi. Nat and I were in Disney World, in Orlando, Friday and Saturday, and we were at one of the clubs dancing most of the night. Several hundred people saw us—he's rather recognizable, you know.

"We flew back here at dawn on my jet. Anyone can ask me anything they want. I'm innocent as a babe. The last thing I intend to do right now is go flying to someone who is bound to be a prime suspect in three murders. As far as I'm concerned, honey, as of this minute, it's every girl for herself."

Rachel tried to absorb the cold finality of Erica's words. "You can't push me out of your life this easily, Erica. I swear, if you don't come to me today, I'm going to give them some answers to their questions."

"You can't threaten me anymore, Rachel," Erica stated in a diamond-hard voice. "You just had your power stripped, and without it you're nothing but a big *lez* with a drinking problem. It's your word against mine, and I'll deny everything. Who do you think the authorities will believe? A civil servant who used her position for personal gain and put two innocent men in jail by creating crimes that didn't exist? Or a leader of industry with millions in taxable dollars behind her? Good luck, Rachel. And goodbye."

Rachel stared at the phone receiver, unable to

believe Erica had hung up on her and unwilling to accept the fact that Erica really didn't care. She dropped the phone and staggered to the kitchen.

Her power had been stripped. She would soon lose her badge, the first love in her life—she might even end up in prison—and the second love had just hung up on her.

Erica didn't love her. She had been with a man all weekend. Rachel's brain slowly analyzed what else that meant.

Erica didn't kill Frampton. Which meant she probably didn't kill Ziegler or O'Day either. Rachel had been certain it was Erica, since Ziegler was drugged, then cut and left to bleed to death, the same way Erica's second husband had died. Also, right after they had talked of coming up with a special punishment for O'Day, he was killed. She had been positive Erica had done it for her—a unique, very private gift. Then, when she heard about Frampton, she recalled April saying Erica was in Florida, and she had no doubts left at all. But she'd been wrong about everything.

Knowing all the facts, Rachel had initially deduced that it was one of two women. If the murderess wasn't Erica, it had to be the other.

She was about to pour herself another drink, but took a long swallow straight from the bottle instead.

Erica thought she didn't need her anymore, but she didn't know about the tape Rachel had hidden in her stereo cabinet. The night Erica became drunk enough to brag about how she'd gotten rid of her first two husbands, Rachel had had a tape recorder running under the bed.

It had been clear to Rachel that Erica was pulling away, and she planned to keep the tape as insurance that Erica would never abandon her. However, she also knew Erica would be furious if she found out, so she simply held on to it as a last-ditch measure. It had never been necessary to tell Erica about the tape.

The necessity had now arrived, and Rachel hadn't had the guts to use her insurance. The pitiful truth was that she couldn't blackmail Erica, because she loved her too much to hold her against her will. Nor could she turn her and the tape over to the police.

Carrying the half-empty bottle of bourbon with her, she went to the stereo cabinet and extracted the tape. For a moment she considered listening to it one last time, but when she remembered the sounds of lovemaking and erotic dialogue that flowed through the confession, she changed her mind. Her heart was hurting too badly for that.

She unwound the ribbon of tape from its plastic case, dropped it all in a steel saucepan, then lit a match. In seconds, her insurance against Erica's abandoning her was gone.

There was only one thing left to do, she thought, taking another swig from the bottle. The real perpetrator had to be protected. Rachel owed April too much to let her suffer for such worthwhile deeds.

She composed her thoughts as she found paper and pen to write out her confession. In perfect agency format, Rachel described how and why she had killed Ziegler and O'Day. She couldn't claim to be in Florida when Frampton was hit, but she knew who had been there besides Erica and the real murderess.

Holly Kaufman. Rachel laughed aloud as she realized there was a way she could save April and get revenge against Holly at the same time. How ingenious of April to convince Holly to go flying to her reporter's bedside! Unfortunately, Rachel didn't have specific details of how Frampton had been lured to his death, but she figured the rest of the confession would make the last part believable.

She claimed that the two of them had planned the murders together and that, with Holly's reporter friend getting shot, she had the perfect excuse for being in the vicinity. Rachel knew Wells was under guard and not permitted to have visitors, so Holly was undoubtedly asleep and alone in a motel room at the time of the murder. She'd have no alibi. It couldn't have worked out better if Rachel had planned it in advance.

She considered blaming Holly for all three, but if the reporter regained consciousness, he could swear to Holly's whereabouts during the O'Day murder. It was safer this way.

When she was finished with that chore, she went to her bathroom closet and removed several containers of the antidepressants April had prescribed for her. She had been saving them up for this moment—an event she had thought about often over the last thirteen years.

As previously planned and mentally rehearsed so many times, she prepared the stage. Her alarm clock, set to go off in three hours, was placed on the coffee table in the living room next to her final report. The front door of her apartment was unlocked and left open a fraction of an inch, with the pen lodged in the bottom to keep it from closing.

When the alarm continued to sound without being turned off, some neighbor would come to complain and, finding the door unlatched, should investigate further. Otherwise, it could be days before anyone might come to check on her.

Going over her arrangements one more time, she nodded approvingly.

She sat down on the couch, dumped all ten containers of pills on the table, then one handful at a time, washed them down with the rest of the bourbon. At one time she had thought about eating her gun, in the more traditional law enforcement manner, but that was such an unattractive way to go.

Settling back to wait for it to take effect, however, she thought of something that had never been in the plan before. She stumbled into her bedroom, pulled off the tailored, mannish clothes she was wearing, then slipped into the black lacy nightgown she had bought yesterday as a gift for Erica.

At least she would die feeling pretty.

"Holly Kaufman?"

She looked up at the man who had stepped in her path just as she was entering the lobby of her apartment building. As soon as she acknowledged her name, he flashed his badge and photo identification.

"Agent Thackery, FBI. Would you come with me, please?"

Holly's brows rose in surprise. "I beg your pardon?"

"I'd suggest you come along peaceably." His face was expressionless.

"May I see your identification again, please?" Holly asked just as politely. He held on to his badge case as she compared the picture with the man. "All right, but where is it you want to take me and why?"

He put his case away and said, "FBI headquarters. Senior Agent Quick from Miami asked me to bring you in for questioning."

"Agent Quick is here? In Washington?"

Agent Thackery nodded curtly. "He arrived a short while ago."

Holly thought he didn't sound too pleased about it. She couldn't imagine what other questions she could possibly answer, but she didn't seem to have any choice. She left her overnight bag with the doorman, Pete, then left with Agent Thackery.

Upon arrival at the FBI building, she was taken to a room furnished with a rectangular table and eight chairs. Recording equipment was set up at one end of the table. On impulse, she tested the door-knob after she was left alone.

Locked! Instantly, panic set in. What was this all about? Was she under arrest? Had Rachel already found out that she had talked and made good on her threat? Where was Agent Quick?

As if on cue, Quick entered the room with Agent Thackery and a woman who was just as colorless as her male counterparts.

Quick greeted her with a smile. "Miss Kaufman, this is Agent Varden, and you met Agent Thackery. Thank you for coming in. Please have a seat." Once she sat where he directed, the others took chairs around her. "I just need to ask you a few more questions," Quick said, still maintaining his friendly demeanor. "Perhaps the best place to start is for you to tell us everything you've done from the time you left Wells's hospital room at eleven-fifty last evening."

She reminded herself that this man was not her friend, despite his smile or tone of voice. He was an FBI agent, just like Rachel, and he would be more apt to believe his colleague than a stranger. She straightened in the chair with her hands folded on her lap and tried to remember every detail of the time that had passed.

"I took a cab—a Yellow one—to the Miami Inter-national Airport. The next flight back here was on

Delta at six-thirty this morning, so I took a room in the airport hotel. The plane had mechanical difficulties, and we never left Miami until about nine. Then there was a stop in Atlanta, and I think it was around one-thirty when we landed at Dulles. As it turned out, I could have taken a later, nonstop flight and gotten in sooner."

"And from there?" Quick prodded when she stopped her narrative.

"Um . . . since my car was at National Airport, I had to take a cab there. With everything that had happened, I really didn't feel like going home yet, so I decided to go by my office and catch up on some paperwork. Oh yes, I went through a McDonald's drive-through on the way and picked up lunch. By the time I got to my office, it was a little after three. The building security guard checked me in and out again about eight. I'm afraid I fell asleep in my office. It all just caught up with me at once, I guess. Then I went home and Agent Thackery was waiting for me."

Agent Varden spoke to Quick. "I should be able to verify the cabs, the hotel stay, the airlines, and the time spent at the office without any problem."

"Fine," Quick replied. "Then contact the rental car agencies out of the Miami airport. Other than a cab, that's about the fastest way she could have gotten up to Boca Raton and back in time to catch that flight."

"Boca Raton?" Holly asked. "Why would I have gone there?"

Agent Thackery looked skeptical. "Are you implying that you haven't heard any news today?"

"No, I haven't. I just told you what my day was like. Besides," she murmured, "every time I've listened to the news lately, it's been bad."

"It's all right, Miss Kaufman," Agent Quick said in a soothing voice. "Before I explain, I just want to clarify one thing. You checked into the hotel, went directly to your room, and stayed there until . . . When?"

Holly frowned. "Five-thirty, five-forty-five. But I didn't stay in the room the entire time."

"Oh?" Quick asked. Varden and Thackery inched closer expectantly.

Holly shook her head. "I couldn't sleep and thought I'd go buy a magazine or book to read. But the newsstand was closed."

"What time was that?" Varden asked.

"About two, I think."

"Did you see or talk to anyone at that time?"

The memory made Holly smile despite the circumstances. "Yes, as a matter of fact, I did. There was this very nice maintenance woman changing the trash bag in the can near the newsstand. She guessed what my problem was and offered me a book that someone had thrown away and she had salvaged. She was only going to leave it in the employees' lounge at the end of her shift, so I took it."

"Describe her," Quick said abruptly, and Holly did the best she could. "What happened to the book?"

"I have it right here," Holly replied, then realized where it was. "I mean, it's in my overnight bag. I left it with the doorman at my apartment building."

Quick glanced at Varden and gave her a sign to go. Turning back to Holly, he began the explanations she'd been waiting to hear.

"Jerry Frampton was murdered in a hotel room in Boca Raton around the time you say you were talking to the maintenance woman. If that checks out, you're in the clear."

Holly felt the blood rush from her head. "Why would you suspect me? I was the one that warned you that he might be next."

"That's true. Unfortunately, we never had a chance to warn *him*. Since I took your statement in Miami, I've been temporarily assigned to work with the task force investigating the murders. But to answer your question, you are a suspect because Rachel Greenley accused you of doing the Frampton murder."

"Dear God! She knew I was flying down there. All she had to do was follow me down on the next flight, kill him, and blame it on me."

"If she did follow you down there, she used a false name. We're in the process of showing her picture to all the airline employees on duty yesterday and this morning to see if anyone remembers her going out or coming back. It's a time-consuming job with a slim chance of success. The thing is, she would have known that that would be the first thing we'd do, and her size and red hair make her somewhat easy to spot. It's why she wouldn't have normally been assigned to field work. So if she flew to Florida and back, she probably wore a disguise. On the other hand, she could have felt safe accusing you because she really *didn't* do it."

Surprisingly, Holly followed his logic. "But even if she didn't kill Frampton herself, I have a feeling she knows who did. Can't you force the truth out of her?"

Quick shook his head. "Not anymore. Rachel Greenley committed suicide a few hours ago. Left a deathbed confession—which is usually considered strong evidence—that she killed Ziegler and O'Day, and you murdered Frampton."

Holly wrung her hands together and looked from

one man to another. "It's not true. I could never kill anyone. And even if I could, wouldn't it be stupid to let the authorities know what was going on right before I did it?"

Agent Thackery arched one eyebrow at her. "A very smart killer might do just that to throw us off."

Holly leaned toward Quick with a pleading expression. "Don't you see? She's done exactly what she threatened to do if I told anyone about the Little Sister Society."

"Personally, I think that's what it is. However, my opinion doesn't hold much weight in a court of law. We have to verify everything you said before you're off the hook. Of course, that automatically presents another problem. If Greenley lied about you killing Frampton, what else did she lie about? What if she didn't do it herself? Who did? Maybe she lied about taking out Ziegler and O'Day. There's a possibility that she's protecting a third person."

"Erica."

"That was my first thought after what you told me about them, but Erica Donner has a solid alibi . . . for this morning, at least. We're still checking on the other times, but my instincts are telling me we're on the wrong track entirely."

Holly remembered what David had said about trusting his instincts. "Bobbi Renquist?"

Again Quick shook his head. "Not for Frampton. She was working in her office on a special project with several others until after midnight last night. By the way, she and Rachel were both suspended yesterday pending an investigation of their files. If Renquist tampered with a few accounts, she'll pay for it."

"Is that why Rachel killed herself?"

"In a case like that, the reasons have often been

building up over many years, but there's always that one last straw. I guess for Greenley, getting caught was it."

"What about Bobbi's claim that Erica murdered her husbands?"

Quick shrugged. "The three cases will be reviewed, but it's unlikely that they'll be reopened based on an accusation from a jealous schizophrenic. Donner will be questioned—politely—but unless she confesses, there's no new evidence against her. As to April MacLeash and Cheryl Wallace, we dispatched an agent to question them this afternoon, but he hasn't checked in yet."

"Rachel mentioned some suspects that the computer came up with."

Thackery responded to her. "We're still working on those as well. So far that angle hasn't panned out, but we aren't eliminating the possibility that the perpetrator is an outsider with a more obscure motive. We're just going to have to expand the area of our search for possibles."

Quick stood up and Thackery followed his lead. "Under the circumstances, Miss Kaufman, I see no reason to officially detain you at this time. However, I'm going to ask you to stay here while Agent Varden completes her verifications. Then she'll take you home and stay with you."

"Stay with me? Like, under house arrest?"

Quick waved his hand in a negative gesture. "Just a precaution. We don't want anything to happen to you while we're trying to unravel this puzzle."

Holly didn't want to think about what his words implied. She knew when she decided to talk that there were risks involved. "Wait," she said as Quick was about to close the door on his way out. "Please.

Could you leave it open? I promise I won't go anywhere."

"Of course," he replied with an apologetic smile. "Can I get you a cup of coffee or a soda?"

"Coffee would be nice, light, no sugar. And I, uh, I need to—wash my hands."

"Oh, I'm sorry. I'll have Agent Varden escort you in just a minute."

The minute turned out to be twenty, but Quick did bring her a cup of coffee and several magazines to occupy herself in the meantime.

What she really wanted was a telephone, but she didn't have the nerve to ask. It wasn't that anyone was expecting her to call. She just wanted to hear a familiar voice tell her everything would be all right. She assumed her parents would be home from their trip by now and hoped it had been a pleasant weekend for them. But if it hadn't been, she certainly didn't want to burden them with her multitude of problems. Now that she thought about it, she hoped they hadn't been listening to the news either.

Philip would undoubtedly like to hear from her, but he could wait for an update until tomorrow. She frowned at the thought of how he would react to what she'd done. He'd been so firm about her not going to the authorities and endangering herself and her parents. And he would certainly not be happy to learn that she had flown to Florida to see David, but she was sure she could reassure him, once—

Her thoughts froze and hung in space for her to examine. Did she really want to reassure him again? Did she honestly look forward to reestablishing their relationship on the same old ground now that David had exited from her life? Could she truly be satisfied being with Philip because it was better than being alone? An image of April and Theodore flashed in her mind.

Although she had repeatedly turned down Philip's marriage proposals and told him numerous times that she didn't love him the way he loved her, hadn't she also allowed him to think that her feelings might change someday? In other words, hadn't she purposely kept him dangling at arm's length just so she wouldn't be all alone? Somehow, she had always justified it before, convincing herself that he was as pleased with their relationship as she was.

How cruel she had been!

What she had been doing all these years was not so different from what Ziegler and Frampton had done to her, or what David and she had done to each other. Using another human being without concern for their feelings was despicable, no matter how that use was softened or sugar-coated.

She had to put an end to the lies. Even if it hurt Philip terribly to hear the truth, eventually he would be better off than waiting forever for something that was never going to come. And if he chose to end their friendship, or even their professional relationship, she would manage . . . somehow.

With that decision made, and put off till tomorrow, she found she could think more clearly about her most immediate dilemma. Quick had told Varden to check car rentals from the Miami airport. To rent a car, one had to show a driver's license, a major credit card, and sign an agreement. Since she hadn't done any of that, there would be no doubt about her having remained in the airport while Frampton was being murdered.

Unless I hitched a ride, or stole a car, or forced someone at gunpoint to be my driver, then killed that person as well. Those alternatives were so ludicrous, they made her smile. But that was because she *knew* she could never do those things. What might an FBI agent think who didn't know her personally?

Her smile vanished. Regardless of what the law stated, they could think she was guilty until proof of her innocence was established.

Holly didn't remember seeing the desk clerk at the hotel when she had gone looking for something to read. That left only the maintenance woman. Surely they would find her, and she would remember giving the book to the lady in front of the newsstand. Wouldn't she?

Suddenly she realized how general her description of the woman had been: Caucasian or Hispanic, between thirty-five and fifty years old, shorter and plumper than she, wearing a green or blue uniform with a printed scarf covering her hair, and slightly accented speech, probably Spanish. Would that be enough? Would the woman have any better recollection of what Holly looked like? How hard would the agents in Miami work to find the woman?

Holly forced herself to leaf through the magazines Quick had given her, but with each passing minute, her fears mounted. If only she could talk to David. . . .

No! Thinking about him was worse than considering what would happen to her if they didn't find the maintenance woman, or if they found her, but she didn't remember Holly. David simply represented another part of her life to be boxed up and stored away behind a carefully locked door, to be ignored, if not completely forgotten. She reminded herself of what April had told her. David was practice, nothing more. And now, practice was over.

At one in the morning, Agent Varden took Holly

home. Outside of the office, the agent relaxed considerably.

"Please call me Diane. This situation is difficult enough without the formality."

"Thank you. I prefer Holly, also. Are you allowed to tell me what you learned?"

Diane asked for directions to Holly's apartment and got them on their way before filling her in on her progress. "So far, so good. Your schedule checks out the way you gave it. There's no record of your renting a car, no regular taxis took a passenger to and from Boca Raton during the hours in question, and no public transportation was available for the trip. That eliminates all the obvious methods, but not the more, shall we say, *inventive* modes of travel. You'll be in a much better position if we can find your book-rescuing cleaning lady. Which reminds me, I'll need to see the book before you unpack your bag."

Holly nodded, but the reminder that she was still very much under suspicion countered Diane's earlier attempt to put her at ease.

Diane was content to stretch out on the couch with a pillow and a light blanket. She seemed to fall asleep instantly, but Holly had the distinct impression that the slightest unusual sound would bring her to her feet with her gun cocked.

The nap Holly had taken in her office ruined her own chances of sleeping any more that night, but she remained in her room, trying to read until she thought it would be reasonable to get up and move around.

"It would be best if you remained here for the next few days," Diane told her as they ate breakfast together.

Holly hated the idea of being confined and yet

she also understood the reasoning behind the advice. She figured a cooperative attitude would aid her questionable status of being somewhere between a witness and a suspect. "All right, but could I have someone bring me some work from the office?"

"Certainly. We want to make this as comfortable for you as possible."

After they cleaned up the breakfast dishes, Holly called Philip and asked him to come by. In spite of her insistence that there was nothing to worry about, she could feel his tension vibrating right over the phone line.

"I'll explain everything when you get here," she promised.

As she waited for Philip's arrival, Holly told Diane a little about him and their long-term relationship. Diane wouldn't leave the apartment, but she did go into the spare room that Holly had set up like an office. Saying that she'd be making a few calls, she closed the door, but Holly knew she'd easily be able to hear anything that was said in the outer room if she wanted to.

Philip's reaction was as bad as she had expected. Pacing back and forth, he was too upset to keep his voice hushed. "How could you stick your neck out like this? We discussed the risks involved. I thought you agreed with me to let the professionals handle it."

"I did, but when Rachel threatened to make me look like the guilty party, I figured it was riskier to remain quiet."

His face was flushed as he stopped pacing and hovered over her. "But what in God's name possessed you to go to Florida like that? If you had stayed at your friend's like you said you were going to, no one would have been able to accuse you of anything."

Tipping back her head to face him, she tried to keep her voice level in hopes of calming him. "I told you, I felt responsible for David being shot. I couldn't stand not knowing if he would live or die because of what I'd done."

Philip sat down beside her and grasped her hands. "Is that the real reason, Holly?"

She had to fight the urge to squirm away from his intent gaze. "Yes. I felt guilty that I hadn't warned him about what he might be walking in on. As it turned out, Frampton *was* next on the killer's list."

"The hell with that reporter *and* Frampton. It's *you* I'm worried about. My God, Holly, there's an FBI agent camped in your apartment!"

"Diane is here for my protection. I have every confidence my innocence will be proven and the real killer will be found." She hoped he believed that more than she did. His distressed features slowly smoothed and he eased the tight hold he had on her hands.

"I'm sorry, honey. You don't need me adding to the weight already on your shoulders. What can I do to help?"

He sounded like the old Philip again, and she was able to relax. "Nothing, really. Just cover for me in the office for a few days, and I'll work on the project you brought me while I'm here."

Suddenly Philip moved his hands to her face and held her in place for a hard kiss. Holly was even more stunned by what he said next.

"Marry me, darling. Let me protect you and care for you like I've always wanted to. I just know everything would work out if you were truly mine in every sense." He glanced at the closed office door, and suddenly his eyes glowed with an idea. In a conspiratorial whisper, his words came out in a rush. "We could sneak out of here while the agent's in the other room. We could drive to West Virginia, get married tonight. Then we could go away, maybe a honeymoon in Australia. I've got more than enough money saved up. By the time we came back, this whole mess would be cleaned up and no one would punish you for leaving."

Philip's face was flushed again, only now it was obviously excitement, not anger, that was raising his blood pressure. "Philip, please. You aren't thinking clearly. Running away would only make me look guiltier. And what would happen to Earth Guard?"

He shook his head. "One call to Evelyn and she'd take care of putting matters on hold until we got back." He pulled her to her feet. "We could do it, Holly. It would solve everything. Let's just go. Now. While that agent thinks we're still sitting here talking."

Holly could barely believe it; he was completely serious. "Sit down, Philip," she said firmly, then sat back down herself. He perched on the edge of the sofa, ready to leap up again any moment. "What you're suggesting sounds very romantic . . . on the surface. But we would both regret it, if not tomorrow, next month or next year. I can't run away from this, and you can't protect me from life anymore. You've done a wonderful job of it up to now, but I'm finally ready to grow up and stop hiding behind you."

She cut off his protest before he could get it out. "You know it's true. I just never saw how I was hurting you in the process. This is very difficult for me, but I don't think it should be postponed any longer."

Taking a deep breath, she gathered her courage. "You are my dearest friend in the world. I care deeply about you. But I don't love you the way you want me to."

"Holly, we've been—"

"Please let me finish. I have finally realized how unfair our relationship has been. I've let you believe there could be a different kind of future for us one day, but that was a selfish lie to keep you from leaving me alone. We're *friends*, Philip, and that's all we're ever going to be. I'm hoping you can accept that truth, but I'll understand if you can't."

He studied her face for a moment, then looked away. "Is there someone else? The reporter?"

Holly ignored the instant tightening in her chest. There was no need to tell him what part David had played in her decision to be truthful about their relationship. It would only hurt Philip worse than he was hurting already. "No. There's no one."

Philip's held breath came out in a relieved sigh. He hadn't lost her yet. "You're under a lot of stress right now, honey, and I don't want to make it more difficult by arguing with you. I'll leave you alone for now, but I'll be standing by in case you need me. No matter what you've said, it doesn't change the way I feel about you or the fact that I'd still be happy to share any part of your life that you're able to, including friendship, if that's all you want from me."

After he left, Holly went over his final words. At first she'd thought he had accepted and understood what she'd tried to tell him, but the more she thought about it, the less certain she was. She had the awful feeling she'd just been given another pat on the head by a forgiving father.

22

Agent Varden spent the next several hours on the phone in Holly's spare room, but she left the door open once Philip left. Holly hoped Diane was accomplishing more than she was. Papers were spread over the kitchen table, but she couldn't keep her mind on any of it. She made lunch for them both, but that didn't even use up an hour. She was trying to come up with a distraction of some kind when her intercom buzzer sounded. Diane reached the speaker before Holly.

"Yes?" Diane asked.

"David Wells is here to see Miss Kaufman," Pete, the doorman, stated in a more formal voice than he normally used.

"It can't be," Holly whispered. "He's in a hospital in Miami."

Diane held up a finger and said, "Ask for identification."

Pete's response was indignant. "I just identified him with my own eyes. He's been here before. Of course, he didn't have half his head bandaged like he does now."

Holly narrowed her brows. "It must be him. What could he be doing here?"

"Okay. Send him up." She switched off the intercom and turned to Holly. "I heard the official version of your connection with Wells in your taped testimony. Is there anything else I should know?"

Holly felt her cheeks pinken and knew that answered the question as well as words would. "We . . . got involved . . . for a while. But it's over." A light knock spared her from further explanation.

Diane waved Holly away from the door as she opened it, checked the corridor, then let David come in.

He swayed a bit as he entered. Holly thought he looked like death warmed over. The last time she had seen him look this bad was—"Dear God, David. Don't you have any sense at all? You just flew in, didn't you! How stupid can you get? Wasn't your head hurting bad enough from being shot? You had to drink yourself into a stupor, too? Oh, sit down! I'll get the coffee and aspirins."

Diane glanced curiously at David as Holly headed for the kitchen.

With a lopsided grin, he said, "Sympathy isn't one of Holly's strong suits." He made his way over to the couch and groaned as he stretched out with his head propped up on the cushioned arm.

Holly reentered the room just as Diane was offering David the pillow she'd used last night. Setting the mug of black coffee and bottle of aspirins on the coffee table in front of him, she said, "Don't pamper him, Diane. He's not nearly as helpless as he appears."

David rolled to his side and took a sip of coffee. "So, the lady's still wearing her war paint." He rolled back onto the pillow with his eyes closed.

Holly was afraid he was about to go to sleep. "*David!* What are you doing here?"

"Had news for you," he mumbled without opening his eyes. "Made Quick promise to . . . let me . . . tell you personally."

Holly waited for more, but the soft snore emanating from his open mouth was all she got. He'd passed out! "Call Quick," she ordered Diane. "I want to know what he meant by that."

As Diane made the call from the spare room, Holly picked up the kitchen extension. Quick barely had a chance to say hello when Holly demanded, "What's happened? What kind of a promise did you make him?"

"Who is this?" he asked stiffly.

"This is Varden. That was Holly Kaufman. We have David Wells passed out here—"

"Passed out? What the hell happened?"

Holly answered, "He's terrified of flying, so he drinks too much, but that's not important. He said he had news."

"Yes, that's right. But he asked if he could deliver it personally. Said he owed you that much. I had no idea—"

"Just tell me what he was going to say!"

"The maintenance lady not only remembered you, she recalled the name of the book. You're in the clear."

Holly felt like crying. "Thank you. Thank everyone."

"Thank Wells," Quick countered.

"Excuse me?"

"When he heard what was going on up here, he checked himself out of the hospital and went searching for the maintenance woman on his own. Turns out she was off for the next couple of days.

It may have been awhile before our people could have tracked her down with everything else they had in the works."

"David did that? For me?" Holly's voice was filled with wonder.

"Like I said, he insisted he owed you a favor and made me agree to let him tell you. But under the circumstances—"

"Yes, thank you." Holly hung up and went back into the living room. She could hear Diane still talking in the other room as she sat down in a chair and stared at David. Why had he gone looking for the woman? For her? Or for a story? But if it was for a story, he could have let Quick tell her the results. And he certainly hadn't needed to get on a plane when it wasn't absolutely necessary. If he had wanted to tell her personally, he could have managed that over the phone.

Then she remembered his quirk about calling her. It made no sense, but he definitely had a thing about using the phone with her. She didn't count the one time he had called. A flutter crossed her stomach the moment she allowed herself to remember it. On the other hand, any hang-up he had about the telephone couldn't be as serious as his fear of flying.

She didn't want to jump to any conclusions. He could have a perfectly logical reason for what he'd done. His actions did not necessarily imply that he'd forgiven her or that he cared. Besides, she hadn't forgiven him and wasn't sure she ever could.

Simple human kindness had her make a fresh pot of coffee and keep it warm until he woke up on his own two hours later. But leftover resentment stopped her from checking on him when she heard his pain-filled groan. She remained at the kitchen table until he made an appearance.

"There's a bag of ice in the freezer," she told him as he began his sobering-up ritual with a handful of aspirins, washed down by a tall glass of orange juice. He poured himself a cup of coffee and, balancing the ice bag on his head, slouched onto a kitchen chair. She knew better than to ask him anything until he was on at least his third cup of caffeine.

Right on schedule his eyes recaptured a spark of life. He stretched and blinked at her as if he had just noticed her sitting there.

"I hope you realize, your recuperating time is going to get longer as you get older."

She sounded completely disgusted, but David focused on the fact that she had everything ready and waiting for him. If she really hated him, would she have made the coffee, or prepared the bag of ice, or removed the lid from the damn aspirin bottle so he wouldn't have to struggle with it?

"I spoke to Agent Quick," she informed him in the same tone of voice. "I understand I have you to thank for clearing me of a murder charge."

David shrugged. "No one really believed you did it. I just figured I could pitch in and move things along a bit faster."

"Well, I do appreciate your efforts. Thank you."

"You're welcome," he replied with equal formality.

"And now, would you please tell me why you risked your health to come and pass out on my sofa?"

He smirked at her. "I wasn't risking anything. The doctor told me he was going to release me in another day anyway."

"You did *not* have to get on a plane, though. You could have called."

"No. I—It wouldn't have been the same as talking to you, face to face. It wasn't just the maintenance woman that I wanted to tell you about. I thought a lot about what you said . . . about us being even. You were wrong. I was too angry when I found out you'd been lying and using me to see the truth of what I'd done to you." He paused and rubbed his forehead. "I had this great speech all worked out on the plane and now I can't remember any of it."

"I don't need any speeches, David. There's nothing left for either of us to say." She picked up his coffee cup and carried it to the sink.

"I suppose you're right," he said to her back. "I really don't know what I thought I was going to accomplish by showing up here like some damn gift horse. Maybe it was just an elaborate way of punishing myself for being an ass."

The intercom buzzed in the living room, but she knew Diane would take care of it. As she rinsed the cup and glass, she sensed David coming up behind her. For the briefest moment, she felt him touch her hair and her breath caught in anticipation.

"I never meant to hurt you," he whispered. "And I'm sorry if you really feel what I did to you was ugly, because, whether you believe me or not, you were the most beautiful thing that ever happened in my life."

It would have been so easy to turn to him then. If he had touched her, she would not have been able to resist. But he made no move and her moment of weakness passed.

"Excuse me," Diane said as she entered the kitchen. "Agent Quick is here to see you both."

"Great," David said, reaching around Holly for

the cup she had just washed. He poured himself the last of the coffee, then waited for Holly to dry her hands and lead them back to the living room.

"So what have you got?" David asked even before they all sat down.

Agent Varden frowned at David, then gave Quick a questioning look.

Quick nodded his understanding and said, "I know. It goes against my grain too to share information with a reporter, but we made an agreement. If he breaks it, I get to send him out on another assignment where the next bullet might do more damage than the last one."

David grinned at Varden without offering any further explanation.

Quick addressed Holly. "I was thinking if I told you what we'd discovered so far, something else might occur to you that you hadn't told us yet. Any little thing at all."

"I'll certainly try to help," she assured him.

"At the moment, it looks like Greenley's entire confession was a lie. She was probably half gone when she wrote the thing and may have actually forgotten what she had been doing at the time of the first two murders. At any rate, she, Renquist, and Donner were all seen together at Greenley's favorite haunt when Ziegler was hit, and she and Renquist were there again when O'Day got it. Donner was definitely on the West Coast for that one. As to Frampton, one of Greenley's neighbors is positive she saw her go out jogging at dawn Sunday.

"Also, the two women you did not meet, Samantha Kingsley and Paula Marconi, have been cleared as well. That brings us to the two you were positive could not be involved, April MacLeash and Cheryl Wallace."

"And I still feel the same way," Holly said. "April was the one who set down the rules for the women to follow. She felt very strongly about the punishment fitting the crime. And Cheryl hasn't been in any condition to do anything."

"Why do you say that?" David asked.

"I didn't mention it before because April didn't want it to get out, but Cheryl . . . isn't well."

"Explain," Diane said.

"Apparently, she had a nervous breakdown after the hearing and April's been taking care of her."

"Where?" Quick demanded.

"At her house in Newark, Delaware. I told you I was there Saturday morning."

"But you didn't mention Cheryl Wallace being with you."

"Well, that was because she wasn't actually *with* us. She—I know this sounds odd, but she's been staying in April's attic. According to April, Cheryl's completely withdrawn from everyone. She said Cheryl reacted the same way in college after she was attacked. I know how she feels. You see, I did the same thing for a while."

"Did you see Wallace while you were there?" Quick asked.

"No. April checked on her and said she wasn't up to joining us. I got the impression Cheryl doesn't like to leave the attic room at all."

Quick was on the edge of the sofa. "So, you only took MacLeash's word for it that Wallace was in the attic."

Holly immediately understood what Quick was getting at. "I have no reason to doubt April, but her husband, Theodore, mentioned Cheryl being there when I met him."

"Hmmm." Quick got up and paced a bit. "All

right. Here's what happened. The agent we sent up to Newark to question April MacLeash said no one answered the door and neither did any of the close neighbors, so he drove on up to Wallace's house in Connecticut.

"No one was there, either, but the next-door neighbor was very helpful. She was positive Mrs. Wallace hadn't been there since the hearing and Mr. Wallace left the house right after it ended and hadn't returned. He'd told her they were taking a trip to Europe. The neighbor's been collecting their mail for them ever since. Our agent stopped at the MacLeash home again on his way back and an elderly man answered the door."

"That would be Theodore."

"Yes. The agent said the man seemed rather disoriented, yet defensive at the same time. Insisted no one by the name of Cheryl Wallace lived there, and his wife was away on business for a few days."

Holly frowned. "He did seem to have a little trouble recalling something when April was speaking to him, so he may have a memory problem. But I also remember him mentioning that April goes away from time to time to visit patients who've moved away."

Quick raised an eyebrow. "How convenient. Let me give you a few more pieces of the puzzle. The possibility that Greenley was protecting someone looks a lot stronger today. We just found out she'd buried the lab findings on the fingerprints from the Ziegler murder. There was one set of prints not identified. That in itself wouldn't be so astounding, but combined with the deduction that there might have been a witness to the murder—"

"A *witness*?" David exclaimed.

Quick nodded. "Possibly. We haven't released this

information in hopes that the person would come forward without fear of the killer going after him or her. But it hasn't happened. Here's the scenario: We know the killer wore gloves during the murder, and yet someone wiped the doorknobs and took a quick swipe over a few surfaces throughout the suite. The haphazard way this was done suggests it was someone other than the methodical killer.

"The conclusion is that someone besides the murderer was in the hotel room after Ziegler was killed. That person either witnessed the murder or discovered the body afterward, panicked, wiped some areas she remembered touching, and took off. Note, I said she. That's because the unidentified prints were in the bathroom along with a, uh—" Quick cleared his throat.

Diane rescued him. "A used tampon was found in the trash can. It's logical to assume the woman who put it there was in the bathroom after the maid had cleaned, since the trash can would undoubtedly have been emptied, even if other things were skipped. Thus, we came to the conclusion that Ziegler had a woman in his room when he returned there in the early evening to get ready for his party. When the killer arrived, she may still have been in the bedroom."

"But why wouldn't she have, called the police?" Holly asked. "Or at least come forward afterward?"

"It's hard to say," Quick replied. "Panic can cause people to do strange things. Then again, what if the woman was there to do harm to Ziegler herself and someone beat her to it? She might be afraid of getting blamed for the deed. Or, there's the possibility that the woman recognized the killer, and is keeping quiet out of loyalty or for purposes of blackmail."

Quick let them consider that much, then added,

"Of all the women you told us were involved in the Little Sister Society, one has never had her finger-prints put on file anywhere—Cheryl Wallace. And now, I have a question for you, Holly. Describe April MacLeash."

Holly was reeling from the suggestion that Cheryl might have been in the room when Ziegler was killed, but she forced herself to answer Quick. "April is, um, petite, smaller than I am, very attractive."

"What about her hair?"

"Blond-on-blond frosting, a little lighter than mine. She wears it short." Holly used her hands to demonstrate as best she could. "Why?"

"After analyzing every hair and lint sample and particle of dust gathered at the three murder sites, the technicians have finally come up with a common denominator. Light-blond hairs, chemically treated, all between one and three inches long, were found in each batch of evidence. DNA testing has been ordered to confirm that the blond hairs came from the same person and whether that person is a female."

"Dear God," Holly muttered. "It has to be an incredible coincidence. I can't believe April would be capable of butchering a man."

Quick turned to Varden. "Call Thackery. Tell him to get that search warrant for the MacLeash house and a warrant to obtain a hair sample from April MacLeash."

"Maybe I can help," Holly injected. "Let me call April and ask if I can come talk to her." She noted the suspicious glance that passed between the two agents. "One thing about April that I'm absolutely certain of, she'd never turn her back on someone who needed help. If she's at her home, she'll take my call, and I'm sure she'll agree to meet me. If she's not there, Theodore might remember me and tell me where I can reach her. I'll use the kitchen phone. Diane can listen in on the extension in my office. If that's not enough, there's another phone next to my bed. All right?"

"It *could* save us some time tracking her down," Diane said to Quick.

"It could also spook her into taking off," Quick countered.

"But consider this," David said. "If April is the killer and Cheryl witnessed the first murder, isn't it possible that Cheryl's stay in the attic might not be by choice? In which case, wouldn't April also love to get her hands on Holly about now?"

Quick sighed. "You're suggesting I send her in as bait, aren't you?"

"I could go with her," David said. "The killer was trying to make a statement. Maybe she'd like to make it to a reporter. Between Holly and me, we might be able to get a confession out of her."

"We'd have to wire Holly," Varden noted. "But it could work."

Quick shook his head. "I can't afford to put another civilian on the line."

"I'm already on the line," Holly said. "Rachel and Bobbi had each threatened me before, then Rachel tried to get me convicted of murder. If April really is a killer, isn't it possible that she could try to get back at me for talking? My father always said the best defense is a good offense, and I'd rather make the first move—with you all right behind me of course—than sit on the sidelines and worry about when she might come after me. However, I want to go on record as saying the only reason I'm doing this is because I don't believe April is guilty. The woman I got to know would never commit such a violent act. She was extracting revenge by using her brain."

Quick massaged his jaw and paced a few more yards, but he knew when he was outnumbered. "Okay. Call her."

Holly smiled and went into the kitchen. As the phone rang at April's house, she heard both extensions being picked up. The enormity of what she had just committed herself to do was sinking in, and she concentrated on sounding desperate and depressed. It didn't take much effort.

Theodore answered, and after a gentle hint, he remembered Holly. A few seconds later, April came on the line. Her voice lacked the friendly welcome Holly was accustomed to hearing.

"Holly? Are you all right? I wasn't sure I would hear from you again."

"Oh, April, please don't hate me for talking. I was so scared and now so much has happened. Did you hear about Rachel?"

"That she was questioned? Yes, I—"

"No, no. She *killed* herself."

"What?" April exclaimed.

"In the letter she left, she confessed to the first two murders, but the third—April, she blamed *me*! I didn't do it, I swear. *Please*. Let me come talk to you. I always feel better after we visit."

For several seconds, April said nothing. When she spoke, her voice seemed almost too calm. "All right, Holly. I'll let Theodore know you're coming to visit. He's being very protective of me at the moment. By the way, how is your reporter friend?"

"Not nearly as bad as it sounded. In fact, he's here with me now. If you don't mind, I'd like to bring him with me. He sympathizes with what happened to us, and I thought, maybe, if it's all right with you, he could help."

Again April paused before speaking. "No, I don't mind at all. I'd like to meet him."

Before saying goodbye, Holly gushed her thanks and promised to be there as fast as she could.

Quick filled David in while Varden called Thackery to get him moving on the warrants in case they became necessary after all.

As soon as Diane hung up, she told Quick, "I have a recorder and remote in the trunk of my car. I'll set it up in Holly's backseat and ride up with them. I can stay out of sight, but if anything happens, I'll only be a few feet away."

"Fine. I'll wait here for Thackery to get the warrants and pick me up. Hopefully, we won't be too far behind you."

Holly wished she could work up half the excitement she could feel coming from the others. This was the sort of activity they both thrived on. She just wanted it to be over with. After letting Pete know that Quick was still in her apartment, they took the stairs from the lobby to the underground parking garage.

Diane transferred the equipment to the floor of Holly's car, tucked the remote into the waistband of Holly's jeans beneath her blouse, and tested it. "All set," she declared. "I hope you two won't mind if I stretch out in the backseat. I didn't get much sleep on Holly's couch last night."

Holly couldn't imagine taking a nap, no matter how little sleep she'd had, but as she backed the car out of her parking space, Diane slipped down onto the seat and closed her eyes with a comfortable sigh.

*   *   *

Philip was at the end of his patience.

When he left Holly, he'd gone out and sat in his car across the street. At first, he didn't leave because he couldn't decide where to go. Then he remained to keep an eye on anyone entering the building who might pose a danger to Holly. It was a relief to know that an FBI agent was in her apartment, but if he saw any of the women Holly had described going inside, he could provide backup protection. They all sounded very unstable to him and he feared any one of them might try to retaliate against Holly for revealing their secrets.

Then he saw David Wells get out of a cab and go inside the building, and he forgot all about the women. What was he doing back in Washington so soon? Philip thought of a number of reasons for Wells to want to speak to Holly—some of them legitimate, most of them not. He kept reminding himself that they weren't alone up there. The agent was with them.

But the agent had been there when Philip was asking Holly to run away with him also. What if Wells had the same thing in mind? What if he was telling her lies to convince her to leave with him?

As the length of time stretched into hours, he considered paying Holly another visit, just to make sure the reporter was sent on his way.

He was mentally preparing himself for a confrontation when he recognized Holly's car exiting the garage—with Wells in the passenger seat. Whatever that bastard was up to, Philip intended to put a stop to it. He turned the ignition on and took off after them. He didn't know how that no-good reporter got away from the woman agent, but he wouldn't shed Philip so easily.

Keeping his eyes on Holly's car and traffic in general, he reached over and opened the glove compartment. His fingers probed inside, beneath the tissue box and all the automobile papers, and pulled out the gun he kept there for protection.

If it was the last thing he did, he would make Wells regret the day he looked at Philip Sinkiewicz's woman.

23

Scared?" David asked in a quiet voice.

It was the first word spoken between them since they had left Holly's apartment, and they both knew the silence was not merely for Diane's sake. Holly glanced at David and nodded.

Slowly, he stretched out his hand to her, palm upward, and waited.

She knew better than to touch him, but to refuse his offer of comfort was beyond her ability. Placing her hand on his, she let him reassure her that she wasn't alone—at least for the moment.

Diane awakened shortly before they reached April's house and went over the ground rules one more time. "Try to relax and get her talking without sounding like you're interrogating her. As soon as possible, insist on seeing Cheryl. And David, play up the story you're going to do on all the women. If we're on target, she'll grab at the opportunity to tell her side of it."

She wedged herself down on the floor behind Holly as they pulled into the MacLeash driveway. "Okay. I'm ready whenever you are."

Holly took a deep breath, gave David a half-smile, and got out of the car. She didn't hesitate to let him hold her hand as they waited for someone to answer their knock.

David was about to knock again when Theodore opened the door a crack. "May I help you?" he asked, peering over his trifocals.

"It's all right, dear," April said from behind him. "I told you I was expecting them."

Theodore stepped back cautiously and opened the door wide enough for David and Holly to enter.

April came forward with a smile, but Holly thought it looked forced. The usually perfect hairdo was unkempt and purple smudges under the eyes marred April's usual prettiness.

"Theodore, you remember Holly. She was here Saturday morning with my other friends. And I believe this gentleman is David Wells."

After introductions and greetings were exchanged, Theodore excused himself to return to his study, and April suggested they make themselves comfortable.

Diane's advice turned out to be unnecessary, for as soon as they were seated, April began to talk. "I can't tell you how relieved I am that you asked to come, Holly. And you, too, Mr. Wells. I really haven't been sure where to turn." She ran her hand through her hair, mussing it more than it already was. "I thought I could hold it all together. I was only trying to help everyone, you see. I don't understand how everything went so wrong." April sighed and folded her hands on her lap. "Tell me about Rachel."

As Holly filled her in on what she knew, tears slipped down April's cheeks, but she still held herself rigidly in place until Holly had told her most of what Agent Quick had related about the murder investigations. She didn't need to tell her what conclusions the FBI was drawing; April guessed.

"In many ways, I *am* guilty," April said. "Guilty of playing God with everybody's lives. And look what a mess I've made. Three men murdered. Rachel's gone. Bobbi and Cheryl may never recover."

"April," Holly said gently, "where is Cheryl?"

April sniffled and looked up at the ceiling. "In the attic. I made a terrible mistake about that, too. And now I don't know how to fix any of it."

When it didn't appear that she would say more on her own, David stepped in. "I want to do an article on what happened to all of you in college and how it affected your lives. Naturally, I'll have to bring in the murders. If there's anything you'd like to tell me . . ."

April met his gaze and held it for several seconds. "There was an FBI agent here earlier, but Theodore told him I was away. I suppose I'll have to talk to one of them eventually. Maybe it will be easier if I tell you first."

Holly was afraid to breathe, lest a movement on her part would stop April from confiding in them. She had described April as petite, but at the moment she looked like a tiny child whose fragile body could no longer bear the weight of her own life. She was tempted to put her arms around her and tell her it wasn't necessary to say anything, but Holly knew she couldn't do that.

Combing her fingers through her hair again, April began. "The hearing was very difficult for Cheryl. It was as if it was all happening again, including the insinuation that she had been at fault. We really hadn't expected that attitude to prevail. But Cheryl wasn't completely beaten. She decided she wanted to confront Ziegler, alone, to remind him that regardless of the outcome, she would always know the truth. She saw it as a way to stand up to her enemy one last time, then dismiss him from her life.

"It was a good idea, in theory, and though I wasn't in complete agreement, I didn't stop her. Just before his victory party, she called him and he agreed to see her in his suite for a few minutes. I waited in the lobby for her.

"I started worrying when she hadn't returned in a half hour, and after another fifteen minutes or so, I decided to go up after her." She paused and massaged her temples. "Everything blurs a little after that. I'm still not sure how I managed it all."

"Take your time, April," David said softly. "Just tell us what you remember."

She met his gaze again and seemed reassured by what she saw there. "I got to Ziegler's suite just as the door was opening. Cheryl was coming out. There was ... blood ... on her hands and face, and some on her clothes. She was staring at me without seeing, and when I spoke to her, she didn't seem to hear anything. Then I looked past her, into the room ... and I saw him." April closed her eyes but it was clear from her expression that she could not block out the gruesome scene she had faced.

"All I could think of was protecting Cheryl. I pushed her back inside and closed the door. I used a washcloth to clean her up as fast as I could, but I couldn't do anything about the blood on her clothes. I put one of Tim's suit jackets on her and tied one of his handkerchiefs over her hair to disguise her as much as possible. Then I thought about fingerprints. I couldn't even remember what I'd touched, let alone guess what she had. I wiped a few things, stuffed the cloth in my purse and led her out of there.

"We took the stairs all the way down into the underground garage, and I got Cheryl into my car without attracting any attention. I had already told people I was leaving earlier in the day, so I kept to that story, only I said I took Cheryl with me right after the hearing ended and we came here. Rachel made sure it was official. I never told Rachel what had happened, but thought she'd figured it out. As it turns out, she had come to the wrong conclusion."

"So Cheryl killed Ziegler?" Holly asked, though she still didn't believe it.

"I don't know," April cried. "I mean, I thought she did, but now I'm not sure. I kept waiting for her consciousness to come back from wherever it was hiding and tell me what happened. But weeks passed and she wasn't making any attempt to communicate with me.

"Then I went to visit a patient in New York and stayed the night. When I returned, I found out O'Day had been killed the same way as Ziegler. Theodore had no idea if Cheryl had left the house or not. Rachel had told me how the men were cut and the next thing I knew, I was looking for our electric carving knife. Even though I didn't recall ever using it, I was sure we had one, but I couldn't find it.

"I was convinced that Cheryl had killed both men, but I couldn't turn her over to the authorities. I did the only thing I could think of. I locked her in the attic."

Holly glanced at David, but he was keeping all his attention glued to April.

"You said you were no longer sure," David prodded.

"No, I'm not. She definitely didn't leave the attic

this weekend, so someone else killed Frampton. Yet I understood the murder was done in the same way. Then I got to thinking about our knife and now I'm sure I gave it away years ago."

Holly tried to correlate everything April was saying with what facts Quick had given her. "Isn't it possible, then, that Cheryl wasn't the murderess, but a witness?"

April frowned. "I don't know what to think anymore."

"Would you bring Cheryl downstairs, please?" Holly asked. "Let us try to talk to her."

"I'll bring her down, but I'm afraid it won't do any good."

Diane was following the conversation going on inside so intently, she practically missed seeing the man pass by the car. Inching up a little, she watched him slowly approach the house. The way he was moving was highly suspicious.

She could hear David and Holly murmuring suppositions to each other. April had apparently left the room to get Cheryl. But the man outside now had Diane's complete attention. Suddenly she realized who he was—Holly's friend, Philip. She had only seen him for a moment that morning before leaving them alone to talk, but she was positive it was him.

Rather than walk up to the front door, he knelt down beneath the big front window and peered inside. Diane couldn't tell what he was up to, but she thought she'd better get rid of him before he disrupted the scenario.

Quietly, she slipped out of the car and started toward the front porch. She was almost there when Philip suddenly stood up, pointed a gun at the glass window and fired through it.

David had just turned Holly's face toward his when he saw the figure in the window and acted without thought. He shoved Holly to the floor and threw his body over hers, a split second before glass exploded into the room. Dizziness and nausea assailed him from the sudden movement, and he blacked out.

Holly looked up to see Philip about to fire at David again. *"No!"* she screamed at the same moment that another shot sounded.

"Drop the gun," Varden ordered from behind Philip, "or I'll hit something vital with my next bullet."

Philip glanced over his shoulder at her, but he kept the gun trained on David. "Get away from her, Wells," he shouted. "Holly's mine. She's always been mine, and she always will be."

Holly twisted out from beneath David's unconscious weight so that she was now partially shielding him. "Philip, please put the gun down. You don't want to do this."

"You're wrong, Holly. I want this more than you can imagine. Now move away from him so I can reclaim my prize."

Holly saw the gun waver in his hand and interpreted it as hesitation. "Your prize? What do you mean?" She thought if she could get him talking, the mad look in his eyes might go away.

Philip angled his head, and his expression softened slightly. "Why, *you're* the prize, my dear. And that womanizing bastard stole you from me after I'd worked so hard to win you. All I have to do is get rid of him, and then you'll be all mine again."

With a false show of calm, Holly said, "Please listen to me. You can't win me by hurting someone else. I'd never be able to forgive you." Very cautiously, she rose to her feet. "I explained to you that we could never be more than friends. It has nothing to do with David. It has to do with *me*, facing life without your protection, or anyone else's." She took a slow step forward, keeping her body between David and the gun. When Philip lowered the weapon a fraction of an inch, she took another small step.

Though she wanted to lash out at him, she kept her voice gentle. "I'm not a prize to be won or lost, Philip. I'm a woman, and neither you nor any other man will ever control my life again. Now, give Agent Varden your gun, and we'll forget all about—"

A bloodcurdling scream cut her off. Holly jerked around and saw Cheryl pointing at Philip with an expression of pure horror. April tried to drag her back out of the room, but she wouldn't budge. *"It's him,"* she shrieked. "The man I saw in the hotel room. He killed Tim Ziegler!"

Philip whipped the gun toward Cheryl and pulled the trigger, but his shot went high. Varden instantly fired three shots into his back before he could aim again. As he fell to the porch floor, Holly ran outside.

Shaken and bewildered, she dropped to her knees beside him. "Dear God, Philip! What have you done?"

"I punished the rapists," he whispered, his eyes glassy as he focused on her face. "I had to eliminate your attackers . . . so that you could finally love me . . . without them coming between us. But Wells—" He coughed and blood trickled from the corner of his mouth. "I should have eliminated him . . . when I first realized . . . you looked back."

Holly gaped in stunned silence as Philip's head lolled to the side and he exhaled his last breath.

*   *   *

Holly felt as though she should be doing something, but she had no idea what that might be. Three days had passed since her personal holocaust, but the shock remained.

Philip, the man she had thought of as her dearest friend and mentor, was dead. No matter that he had confessed or that his hair matched the samples found at the three murder scenes. Regardless that hidden in his bedroom closet had been a canvas tote bag containing latex gloves, a pill bottle with a few grains of Valium in it, and a battery-operated carving knife on which blood samples of the victims were found. Holly could not think of him as a vicious killer.

How was it that she never sensed he was so disturbed or harbored such violence inside?

The tote bag had held one other piece of evidence that offered a glimpse into Philip's tortured thoughts. On a blue, lined index card, he had printed:

Jerry Frampton————For the Little Sister Society
Adam Frankowicz————
William O'Day————For Stella
Timothy Ziegler————For Holly

As soon as Holly was told of the alphabetical listing of the four names, she knew for certain Philip had seen the sheet of paper bearing the fraternity brothers' names weeks ago in her apartment. The index card was the kind she kept in her briefcase. He had apparently copied the four names that hadn't been crossed out while she was out of the room, then after talking to her parents and getting their input, he had formed enough of the picture to begin his plans for retribution.

Holly knew that Stella was Philip's mother's name, though he'd only mentioned her once or twice. When she realized how much it bothered him to talk about her or the father he had never met, Holly never pushed him on it. However, she did recall his attending his mother's funeral some years back. After she was buried, he had become so despondent, he had tried psychiatric help for a while, at Evelyn's insistence.

When Agent Quick questioned the ever-efficient secretary, she was able to supply the doctor's name and number. Philip had only visited the psychiatrist a handful of times, but what he had revealed in those sessions was sufficient to explain the gnawing resentment that motivated him to commit murder.

Quick had come by Holly's apartment that morning to personally relate what he had learned from the psychiatrist. He told her of the abuse and neglect Philip had suffered because of his unwed mother's plight, and the cruel hatred he had quietly endured all his life because of his father's heartless actions.

The doctor had detected his silent rage and had tried to convince Philip to continue seeing him or another therapist in order to work out his feelings. He had warned his patient that one day he could lose control of all that pent-up anger if he allowed it to continue seething without neutralizing it.

His warning had gone unheeded and had been proven correct —with fatal results.

At least Cheryl seemed to be doing better. Seeing Philip framed in the window had recreated the image she had seen of him through the bedroom doorway, and it had all come back to her in a flash.

Right after she arrived in Ziegler's suite, he had gotten a call and said he had someone coming with an emergency. Rather than leave and miss her opportunity to say her piece, she had gone into the bedroom to wait her turn. She didn't want anyone to know she was there, so she stayed hidden in spite of how long it took. She couldn't make out what was being said, but when she heard a sound like a motor, curiosity made her peek out of the room.

The grotesque performance she witnessed literally terrified her into silence. After Philip had left, she had slipped in the blood on her way to the door of the suite, and that was how April had found her.

April had called last night, sounding more like her old self. She said Bobbi had been given a one-year sabbatical leave, based on her willingness to spend that time in a mental health clinic. Erica wasn't returning her calls, but April never worried much over Erica. She was like a cat—always landed on her feet.

Holly's parents also seemed to be on the mend. Their weekend honeymoon had been what they needed to begin putting all the misfortunes of the past permanently behind them and look to the future once again. Having lost a close friend in such a tragic way seemed to have helped Bernie accept the futility of revenge.

Evelyn handled closing up the office for two weeks until the curiosity over Philip's death quieted down.

There was nothing Holly needed to do, no loose ends left to tie up, and yet she felt . . . *incomplete*. She was vascillating between making dinner and going out when the phone rang, offering a temporary reprieve from having to make a decision.

"Hello?"

"Hi."

"David?" The sense of being incomplete faded, until she realized this was only the second time he had ever spoken to her over the telephone. "What's wrong? Why are you calling?"

"Nothing's wrong." He hesitated a moment, then reluctantly admitted, "I just wanted to hear your voice."